THE ZONE

A CYBERPUNK THRILLER

Other books by Stu Jones

The Action of Purpose Trilogy

Through the Fury to the Dawn

Into the Dark of the Day

Against the Fading of the Light

S.H.R.E.D.: Gorgon Rising

Other books by Stu Jones and Gareth Worthington

The It Takes Death to Reach a Star Duology

It Takes Death to Reach a Star

In the Shadow of a Valiant Moon

Condition Black

THE ZONE

A CYBERPUNK THRILLER

STU JONES

EDITED BY CHRISTOPHER BROOKS

DROPSHIP PUBLISHING

Copy Edit by Imagine Press
Cover Design by Stu Jones and Gareth Worthington
Front Cover Design by Justin Paul
Rear Cover Art by Umberto Votta
Interior design by Dorothy Dreyer

Paperback ISBN: 978-1-954386-09-9
Ebook ISBN: 978-1-954386-08-2

DROPSHIP PUBLISHING

Published by Dropship Publishing
www.dropshippublishing.com
Printed in the United States of America
10 9 8 7 6 5 4 3 2 1

ACKNOWLEDGEMENTS

No one writes a book in a vacuum. Though the idea may germinate within the mind of the author, that seed is formed through countless hours invested in awe-inspiring literary, cinematic, and musical works, philosophical conversations, daydreams, and the constant nagging question: *What if...?*

A big thank you to all my beta readers, friends, and supporters who had a hand in this project—a project that formed a decade ago as a love letter to dystopic neon-cast mega cities, flying cars, super cops, sinister corporate greed, and all the captivating elements that make up the cyberpunk genre.

To the two men behind the brilliant artwork associated with this book, Justin Paul and Umberto Votta, each of you brought your unique vision to this project, the results of which were two of the most breathtaking images I believe I've ever seen. I can't thank you enough.

Thank you to my brilliant editor, Christopher Brooks, who never fails to elevate my work far beyond its original form. To Jonas Saul and the folks at Imagine Press for taking a close and critical look at the draft and to Dorothy Dreyer for her help with formatting and typesetting, all of which are vital details that make the work shine. Also, I must thank my agent Italia Gandolfo for her constant efforts to peddle my nonsense, as well as my good friend and often co-author Gareth Worthington for his much-needed counsel, proofreads, and help with the cover design.

Lastly, for *you* dear reader, I give thanks. It is because of you and for you that I share my visions of the future with the world. My passion coupled with your interest is the reason I do what I do.

Welcome to The Zone.

Stu Jones
February, 2023

CHAPTER ONE

The rusted auto-junker buckled as NTPD Officer Chance Griffin slammed against it and slid low behind cover. He gasped in a lungful of garbage-tainted air, the banging of his heart a war drum in his ears. The unmistakable scraping clack of a shotgun followed. Chance's partner stumbled, then scrabbled for cover on all fours.

"He's got a gun, Benny." Chance shouted.

Benny said nothing, his eyes wild.

"*Caution,*" a seductive feminine voice said from the collar of Chance's armored vest. "*Officer Griffin, your vitals are elevated, and there appears to be an armed suspect in the AO. Are you in need of assistance?*"

"Standby, RITA," Chance said, clasping his MVX semi-automatic between sweat-slick palms.

"Get lost, asshole!" a man shouted from the other side of the garbage-strewn alley. "This don't concern the cops."

Shuffling to the rear bumper of the rusted vehicle, Chance caught sight of his partner's position, tucked close behind an eroded brick and stucco wall adorned with creeping brown fungus. Guillermo "Benny" Benitez looked up, focused, only the faintest hint of anxiety visible in the whites of his eyes. He gestured across the alley with fingers splayed open, a sign he'd located the suspect.

Chance nodded. The man was as stalwart as they come, near unshakable—exactly the sort of partner anyone wanted on their six when the bullets started flying.

"Mr. Ippolito? This is Corporal Benitez of the Neo Terminus Police Department," Benny called out. "Can you hear me?"

"RITA," Chance said. He adjusted his footing.

"*Yes, Officer Griffin,*" the synthetic voice said.

"Request backup. Make sure they know to make a silent approach and launch the firefly."

"*Backup is en route to your coordinates. Launching the firefly.*"

There was a small click as tiny legs released their hold on the back of his armor carrier. The hum of buzzing rotor blades filled the air. Chance watched the mini drone lift free of his kit and rise over the junker.

"Get me a three-sixty scan and a visual reading on our suspect."

"*Copy,*" RITA said. "*Scanning now.*"

"Mr. Ippolito?" Benny said again. "Put the gun away. We just want to talk."

"I don't need to talk to you," Ippolito shouted. "It's not your problem. Go away."

"We can't do that, sir," Benny said. "We want to help, but you gotta put the gun down."

Chance re-gripped his MVX and twisted against the body of the junker. He glanced at Benny, who gave him a thumbs up. A video feed popped into the top right corner of his tactical visor. Chance observed a middle-aged man with dark thinning hair, dressed in tattered pants and a stained wife beater, standing just inside the door to his shop holding a sawed-off shotgun, or "Problem Solver." The sign above read: *Lou's Techware and Upgrades.*

RITA, Chance's Realtime Integrated Tactical Assistant, alerted him with a small chime. "*Assessment completed. Signal seven.*"

"Go with it. Earpieces only." Chance nodded to Benny, urging his partner to keep Ippolito talking.

"*Hostile suspect is Lou Ippolito,*" RITA said over the private

2

channel, "*wanted for questioning in connection with the sale of black market pirated Glom tech. He appears to be armed with a modified long gun and has taken cover inside the entrance to his shop. A scan of vitals and cortisol levels indicates he is currently in a highly unstable emotional state. I have registered no other perceived threats within a thirty-meter radius.*"

Chance extended an open palm to Benny, mouthing the words *Be ready.* With methodical precision, he holstered his handgun and snapped the retention in place.

"Mr. Ippolito," Chance said. "I'm gonna stand so we can talk."

"No. Go away," Ippolito said.

"Bro." Benny motioned for Chance to stay down. "Don't."

Chance stood slowly, his hands visible. Over the top of the junker, the cluttered opening to the run-down shop came into view. A neon sign flashed in the dingy window, advertising the latest and greatest smooth-ride tech upgrades, pure pleasure, excitement, and non-stop network entertainment. Just inside the shade of the opening, Chance could make out Mr. Ippolito. The muzzle of the shotgun leveled at Chance's chest.

"*Deadly force is justified,*" RITA said.

"I see it," Chance murmured.

Somewhere, a baby cried, the sort of nagging sound that only comes from a hungry child. In Chance's peripheral, just one street over, pedestrians navigated past each other by the narrowest of margins. Each of them wore a see-through network visor that hung from their forehead, extended over their noses, and wrapped around their ears. Not a single person appeared to deem the life-or-death standoff occurring down the trash-cluttered alley of any importance to them.

The humidity bore down, oppressive, the heavy smog-filled city air clinging to Chance's skin and clothes. A single bead of sweat rolled from his hairline across his temple and slowed partway down his cheek.

"*Officer Griffin, I'm detecting multiple heat signatures. There may be others in the store with the suspect,*" RITA said.

"Ten-four," Chance said. He extended his arms, palms out, fingers wide. "Hey, look man"—he rotated his hands—"no weapons. No tricks. We just want to help. You remember me, right? Officer Griffin? I see you at the noodle stand on the corner of Hawthorne sometimes."

Chance thought he saw the faintest bob of the man's head.

"So what?" Ippolito said.

Chance shrugged. "I was hoping we could talk this out."

"*The suspect is still aiming his weapon at you,*" RITA said. "*Pursuant to section 8.3.7 of the Neo Terminus legal code—deadly force is justified.*"

"Stop all warnings. I know what I'm doing," Chance whispered, then spoke up. "What's it going to be, Mr. Ippolito?"

"It's gonna be you and your friend behind the wall there," Ippolito said, "getting back in your VTOL and flying your asses out of here before two cops become two dead cops. I didn't do nothin' wrong."

The departmental-issued vertical takeoff or landing (VTOL) patrol car waited at the end of the alley. For a second, the idea of getting the hell out of this dump crossed Chance's mind. *Thousands of people sell pirated Glom tech every day. It's not worth getting shot over.*

"Listen, guy," Chance said. "I don't know why you're being difficult. We were just investigating a complaint. It wasn't a big deal. *You* pulled the weapon on *us*. Now we can't leave until it's resolved. You get me? Nobody needs to get hurt over this."

The disheveled man took a step and stopped short of a wall adorned with purple *Jakk the Glom* graffiti still visible on its crumbling surface. Murky half-light seeped from the sky between the towering skyscrapers to the north, giving little definition to his pockmarked face. The problem solver wavered in his hands, the man's fingers clenched in a white-knuckled embrace around the cut-down pistol grip.

"You can't possibly understand. You're just a pig. Part of the problem, don't you see?" Ippolito's body shook. "You're a pawn of The Glom. You don't care about the law. Just enforcing their agenda."

"No, sir. I don't work for The Glom. I'm employed by the city of Neo Terminus, see?" He tapped the silver badge on his left breast. "It says it right here. Officer. Neo Terminus Police Department."

"No, no, no. You still don't get it. You work for the city, but you're controlled by *them*. They've got their fingers in *everything*. They control *everyone*. I..." Ippolito stammered. "I didn't have a choice. So what if I run some side gambling on the drone races or The Zone or sell unsanctioned equipment? I have to make ends meet. Who cares? I'll tell you who—The Glom. It's never enough. They want everything." Ippolito faded quickly into the shadow of the doorway.

Chance tensed at the scream of a child, his hand dropping to his MVX. Lunging back out, Ippolito dragged a young child in front of him, his hand tucked beneath her chin. Her dark eyes grew wide with terror as he shifted the gun barrel to her back.

In a flash, a movement born of hundreds of hours of practice, Chance secured the MVX pistol at his side and ripped it forward in a lightning-fast draw stroke.

"Stop, hey, look at me, man. Don't do that," Chance said, his weapon leveled on Ippolito.

"Let the kid go," Benny said, emerging from cover, his MVX aimed at the disturbed man.

"*I estimate a seventy-eight percent chance the suspect will take further illegal action. Deadly force is justified.*"

"RITA, notify medical services," Chance said.

"*They are staging now.*"

Tears pooled in Ippolito's eyes and streamed down his pained features. "If I'm gone, what will happen to her? What sort of life is that? She'd have to… to…" Ippolito choked on the words. "She *can't* work the street. She's only six!"

Before Chance could answer, blinding light flooded from above, revealing every filthy crevice in the trash-strewn alley. A homeless person, so dirty and disheveled Chance couldn't determine the gender, pushed from beneath a nearby pile of garbage, hands lifting to shield watery, bloodshot eyes.

"*Citizen, this is the Neo Terminus Police Department.*" The mechanical voice echoed into the streets from the large angular hover ship, its engines pulsing with a dripping blue fire. "*Drop your weapon and surrender.*"

"No, this is it. I can't!" Ippolito shouted, his eyes bulging. "I won't let my daughter live like that!"

"*Danger imminent,*" RITA said before the rest of the silky-voiced AI's communication drowned out in the chaos.

Chance lined up the red dot sight, a breath half exhaled—his index finger slid across the trigger of the MVX.

"Let her go, man," Chance whispered, pulling the slack from the trigger. "Please."

Ippolito screamed in desperation and dug the muzzle into the child's back. The sobbing girl squeezed her eyes shut.

There was a crack of gunfire as flame erupted from the muzzle of Chance's MVX. A second blast echoed as Benny fired. A jet of crimson pushed from the top of Ippolito's head as it rocked back, the effect doubled by the second round, peppering the doorframe with blood. Ippolito stumbled and sagged. The girl stood frozen, her mouth agape. She reached for her father.

Ippolito fell back. The chopped-down shotgun in his hands popped, and a burst of fire and sparks issued from the barrel even as the dead man slid down the wall in a bright red smear. The load of buck caught the girl in the chest and neck, spinning her into the trash of the alley.

Chance ran, a scream strangled in his throat. He slid to a stop on his knees and pulled the child against him. Her body lolled, a horrible limp feeling in her flopping limbs. Chance scanned the gawking masses in the street as they watched, stoked to see something tragic.

"Oh God, Benny," he said, his hands slick with the girl's blood.

"The trauma kit," Benny said. Breathless, he ran for the patrol vehicle.

"Hurry!" Chance shouted, baring his teeth. The little girl's blood pumped hot and thick from an ugly tear in the flesh of her neck. "God, oh God." Chance looked again at Ippolito's lifeless form on the floor of his shop. Above, the Quick Response and Containment Unit chugged forward, and the white light snapped off.

"*Threat eliminated. Patrol officers handling the scene.*" The sterile monotone voice above echoed down into the alley.

"Get your ass down here and help!" Chance screamed at the floating barge. He watched as the hover ship elevated above the ramshackle structures and took off with a great whooshing sound.

"*Officer Griffin, I have dispatched rescue to your location,*" RITA said. "*Stay calm and apply direct pressure to the wounds.*"

Chance quaked with emotion. Hugging close the terror-stricken child, he felt something inside him break. "It's okay, it's okay, I've got you, sweetheart."

Blood pumped in slow spurts. Time seemed to shudder and stand still.

"Hurry, Benny!" Chance screamed, searching for his partner at the end of the alley. Beyond the waiting Aeron VTOL, the people on the street, their desire for blood satiated for the moment, walked on. Beside Chance, the bum pulled a slab of cardboard back over himself with a groan.

Chance took in the girl's pink and purple shirt, now soaked

dark red. Staring into the fearful eyes of the child, the sheer injustice of it all hit him like an atomic blast. He clenched his teeth and shook as fury filled the void in his chest. A moan escaped him as his fingers tangled in her blood-matted hair.

"Don't die on me, please," Chance whispered.

The child gurgled, and her body twisted in agony, little feet kicking small sweeping patterns in the filth.

CHAPTER TWO

Inside the musty warmth of The Iron Handler, the bartender, a greasy fellow with swollen, chapped lips and slicked-back hair, glared at Chance over the top of his cobbled-together spectacles. He hocked a disdainful laugh at the cop at the bar. There was a deadness in the air, stale and smoky like the same soiled breath inhaled and exhaled too many times. The place was dark, lit by too few electric bulbs and too many neon signs, the sort of dive where a person could get stabbed.

"Wha'd you say to me?" Chance leaned toward the man.

"Don't listen to him. We're leaving," Benny said to the bartender, putting his arm around Chance. "Come on."

"No." A bleary-eyed Chance pulled away from Benny's grasp. "He thinks he can say whatever he wants like we're in some network chat room where there are no consequences for having a stupid mouth."

"I *can* say what I want," the bartender said. "The NTPD is a bunch of hacks. You don't help anybody. Look at this city—what good are you doin'?" He set his palms on the bar and leaned into the words, his translucent eyewear flickering a non-stop chain of pornographic images, sexual white noise in the background of their conversation.

Chance stuck his finger in the bartender's direction. "You don't know what you're talking about, jakk-head. So how about you pour drinks in your sputzy bar and keep the comments about what the police should or shouldn't be doing to yourself."

"It's the truth. I don't care if you like it." The weasel-faced bartender flashed a mess of crooked, yellowed teeth.

Chance lunged forward, cursing. Benny intercepted Chance's alcohol-laden half-swing in a bear hug and pulled him from the counter. "That's enough, man."

A few soot-covered blast furnace workers huddled in the corner, drinking mugs of ale and wheezing laughs over some vulgarity. They stopped their virtual poker game to watch the live show.

"Chance, what the hell? Calm down," Benny said, dragging him toward the door.

"Screw this guy." Chance pulled at Benny's arms. "What does he know about what we do?"

"Let it go," Benny said.

"Yeah, let it go, Officer Jerk-Off," the bartender said.

Benny stared the man down. "Hey. I'll kick your narrow ass myself and throw you in the Blocks."

"On what charge? You won't do a damn thing."

"Try me," Benny said, pulling Chance to the swinging metal door at the front of the bar.

"Get out and don't come back! Either of you!" the bartender yelled at their backs.

Benny used his considerable bulk to press Chance through the door and sent him stumbling out onto a sidewalk slick with recent rain. Chance slipped, turned, and drove back toward the door, where Benny intercepted him again.

"I said, leave it alone," Benny said louder.

"You're gonna let him talk about us like that?" Chance pointed at the bar windows.

"Yes, we're going to let him talk. That's all it is. Talk."

At six-foot-one and two-hundred-twenty pounds, Chance was no slouch. Years of conditioning and rigorous exercise had carved his body into a lean machine, fire-hardened by the daily hell of the streets. But the barrel-chested Benny had him by at least three inches and forty pounds.

"Benny, take your hands off me," Chance said through gnashed teeth.

"Or what? You going to take a swing at me too?" Benny asked, his eyes hard. "Acting like this—it isn't you."

A fine mist of acid rain drifted like lace across the strobing lights and signs littering the street. Chance stood there, lungs heaving. His voice wavered. "Where were you, man?"

"What?"

Chance's eyes clouded with tears. "What took you so long?"

"What the hell are you talking about? The girl? I was there," Benny said, confused. "I saw what you saw."

"But you took so long…"

"Chance." Benny took a step. "The trauma kit was wedged in the door. Took me a minute to get it free. I told you, man. There wasn't anything either of us could've done to save her."

Chance shook his head, his movements slow, his head swimming from too many drinks. He wiped at his eyes with the sleeve of his jacket. "You don't care." He motioned to the people walking past in the neon glow of the city after dark, entranced by their flickering visors. "Just like everyone else in this God-forsaken place."

"Hey." Benny grabbed a hold of Chance's jacket, his hairy knuckles twisting against the leather. "How are you gonna say that to me?"

"Benny," Chance said, his voice a whisper, "I should've shot him sooner. The little girl would've… She might have…" He wiped at his eyes.

Benny pulled Chance into him, palming the back of his friend's neck and embracing him. "Hey, stop it. We did everything we could. You took an expert shot. There was no way we could've predicted what would happen. No way."

"I don't know, man…" Chance shrugged his shoulder against his cheek to remove the tear streak. "The way she stared at me… I can't get the feeling of her blood off my hands."

"Forget it," Benny said, leaning in. "You did the best you could. You gotta leave the rest on the street. You're not a Superman."

"Yeah. Okay," Chance mumbled.

"Hey, I got you. Okay? You and me. Together we'll make it." Benny pushed Chance back and gave him a punch in the chest.

"Yeah," Chance said, wiping his face with a loaded sigh. "Sputz."

Bicycles bearing visored passengers zigged and zagged through the neon-lit street, accompanied by the occasional honking electric street car. A series of gaudy flashing billboards advertised the newest Apple iVisor X. Overhead, an expensive Biljang VTOL hover sedan buzzed past, loaded with rich clubgoers on their way back to Silver City or Sky Rise. The flying vehicle veered left, soaring over the stacked rooftops to circumnavigate The Zone, dark walls looming to the north inside a lightless sea of inky black.

"Chance," Benny said, snapping his fingers. "Time to go home, man. You got people who need you there. Hannah's going to worry."

"Yeah."

"I gotta go, too," Benny said. "My rescue is probably dying for some attention and a bowl of food."

"What'd you name him again?"

"Muck." Benny smirked.

"Muck?" Chance cracked a smile. "Can't believe you let that thing live inside your place."

"His ugliness isn't contagious. Besides"—he pointed at Chance with a wink—"canine slags don't break your heart, my friend. Not until they leave this world. Much safer than women." He took a step back and pointed again at Chance. "You good to make it home?"

"Yeah, I'm fine, bro." Chance waved him off. "Stop fussing about me."

"All right, South Precinct. Bright and early. We're working the Straits."

"Roger that," Chance said, giving a mock salute with two fingers and turning toward the stairs for the elevated light rail platform.

"Kisses," Benny said, making kissy noises over his shoulder.

"Man, get the hell out of here," Chance said with a chuckle, turning for the light rail station entrance.

Up the covered stairs, Chance ran his wrist chip under the domed scan-droid and trudged onto a platform littered with garbage and a handful of people with nowhere else to sleep. Dirty and unmoving, they lay under piles of trash in the deepening cool of night. *Could be worse. I could be them*, Chance thought. He checked his watch—10:45 p.m. Another sigh escaped him.

"Got any Feels?" A bum sat up regarding Chance with a purple-veined face, smelling of cheap wine. "Or Krystal?"

"No, sir. I don't do drugs." Chance eyed the man.

"What about T's?" the bum said.

"Nope."

"Thasa jakkin' lie," the bum slurred. "I know you got T's."

Chance scowled, flicking his eyes at the man. With a whine, the train eased into the station behind him, colored graffiti twisted in ropy bands down the length of the segmented cars.

"What do you want me to say?" Chance said. "Of course, I've got T's. Just none to spare. Get lost."

"You don't hafta be an azzole about it," the bum grumbled.

"Yeah? Well, here's a tip—Panhandling 101. Don't insult the people you're begging from—it's bad form." Chance stepped onto the mostly empty train. The bum gave him the finger as the doors closed. Chance shook his head and found a seat. NTPD wasn't even running off the bums anymore. Not high enough on the list of priorities.

The light rail shoved forward, picking up speed with an electric whine.

Chance leaned back into the smooth plastic bench seat, deep in thought. The clouded windows of the rail car streaked with droplets of rain, and the massive breadth of his city opened up before him. Steam rose in hazy pillars above moldering buildings, run-down apartment towers, the bars, cafés, and clubs with their flashing video signs and holographic displays touting *Girls, Guns, Feels*, and *Sony's Latest in Cybernetic Enhancements*. Ahead, a giant holographic billboard with digital exploding fireworks showcased a recent win by one of The Zone's Enforcers—a powerful woman in sleek purple and gold tactical armor marked by the call sign *Takedown*.

Chance gave a cynical chuckle. *The opium of the masses.*

He scanned the fetid neon cityscape. A darkness, a murky desperation, hung in the air, the atmosphere stale with poverty, oppression, and regret. Chance loved his city. It was all he'd ever known. But he'd grown weary, disillusioned by the sheer unending squalor that wormed its way into every good thing.

How is it possible to find hope in a place like this?

One of the last bastions of civilization following the great collapse, Neo Terminus was built on the charred bones of a place called Atlanta. He hadn't lived through the fall—he hadn't been born until much later, but he'd heard the stories. Depending on who you consulted on the network, you always got a different answer. How a powerful country called the United States of America died. His grandfather once told him of the war that destroyed everything outside the city's walls. How the cluster nukes streaked from the sky without warning and saw much of the civilized world reduced to gnarled craters of black glass. Nothing but wasteland and death remained out there beyond the walls.

Then came the *Conglomerate*. In an attempt to reignite a failed system, an alliance of some of the most powerful corporations poured the bulk of their resources into the last surviving cities—Manhattan, Atlanta, and Las Vegas. New York, unable to sustain its already bloated infrastructure, quickly succumbed to the ravenous fires of anarchy. In a matter of days, communications with the outside world went dark.

Swollen to ten times their previous size due to an unconstrained migration of refugees from across the country, the remaining cities were restructured and reorganized into sectors. Las Vegas transformed into the glitzy desert frontier outpost of New West City. Atlanta into the bustling metropolis of Neo Terminus. In the process, the Conglomerate dodged the rippling domino effect that crushed the rest of the world's economy, sending humanity back to the Dark Ages. Thus The Glom was born, and every person living inside the walls of the last cities knew whatever good things they still possessed were thanks to The Founders.

Still, good things were in short supply these days.

Chance shifted the smooth plastic curve of the seat, causing a knot behind his shoulder blade to act up.

His path home tonight would take him around the southern part of Neo Terminus, broken up by the old interstate system. The motor vehicle highways of old, crumbling, and cluttered with abandoned junk, marked the end of one sector and the beginning of another. Hayseed, The Slags, Volkan Heights, Havana Straits, Water Town, and Sky Rise each comprised an outer sector of Neo Terminus. The hub of all big business in Neo Terminus, Silver City, sat at the center of it all. To the south of the glamorous business district, a cancerous black tumor with sixty-foot walls festered in the city's heart—The Zone.

The light rail slowed, sliding into the first Havana Straits stop with a screeching of brakes. Outside the doors, young men with dyed green hair and matching emerald jackets laughed and passed a pipe, smoke curling from their lips. Hoodie Boys.

"Damn," Chance murmured. He slid his back to the window and elbow-checked the MVX pistol tucked in the small of his back. A sudden surge of adrenaline burned away the lingering effects of alcohol in his system and brought his senses to a razor-sharp focus.

The doors to the train slid back, the Hoodies bounded in, whooping and bumping forearms. Most of them clicked the translucent visors across their eyes upward onto their foreheads, lenses flickering with endless network content. Spreading out, they encircled Chance, hanging on the grab rails or hopping up to stand on the surrounding seats, sadistic grins on their faces. With a whining sound, the doors slid shut. A *clunk* followed, and the rail car eased from the station, picking up speed again.

"Lookie, lookie, boys. It's a late night commu-tah," one of the Hoodies said, laughing and leaning down over Chance.

"On my way home, fellas," Chance said.

"Uh huh?" the lead Hoodie said, flashing a mouth full of chrome-capped teeth. "Well, youse ridin' my train. It's gonna cawst ya."

Chance angled his right shoulder away, turning his eyes down. The fingers of his right hand grazed the grip of the MVX in his waistband. "I don't want any trouble. Just going home, like I said. I'd appreciate it if you'd leave me to it."

"I don't think you unda-stand, pretty boy." The Hoodie leaned down closer, the smell of stale sweat reaching Chance's nostrils. "Youse ridin' my jakkin' tra—"

Chance lashed out, fingers closing on a handful of the goon's green hair. He gave a brutal downward jerk, and the man shrieked. He whipped the MVX from its holster and jammed it under the lead Hoodie's chin. The train rattled to life as the other half dozen Hoodies around him brandished knives, short clubs, and snarled curses.

"You don't read between the lines so good," Chance said, inches below the lead Hoodie's face. "You've got the wrong guy."

The lead Hoodie turned his eyes down, seeing for the first time the silver glint of the badge hanging inside Chance's half-zipped jacket.

"Little pig, little pig," the lead Hoodie said, his voice dripping with menace. "You can't drop us all with your-a pistola. You know ya can't. We'll cut ya slag eatin' guts out."

"*They* might," Chance said, forcing the barrel of the MVX harder up under the man's chin. "But *you* won't."

Everyone stood frozen, even though the train squealed on, the plastic curve of the seat shifting and jostling under Chance. Outside the windows, the dark, glittering landscape passed in a blurred streak of neon and black.

A crooked snarl spread across the lead Hoodie's face. "You know what? I think we might have a misunderstan-din' here, boys," he said. "We'll find anotha one."

The train slowed for the second Havana Straits stop, Chance's fingers still clenched in the lead Hoodie's greasy green hair. Chance darted his eyes back and forth, sizing up each of the men.

"We good, or what, Pig?" the lead Hoodie spat.

The doors opened as the train came to a complete stop.

"Yeah." Chance released the Hoodie and shoved him back, angling his MVX at the group. "*We good.* Now get off *my* train, and if I see you again, I'll shoot your dumb asses."

"Sure thing, *Officer.*" The lead Hoodie backed up, his eyes wild. He gave a flick of his head, and his boys exited the train, muttering threats. "You be safe out there." He winked, his voice syrupy sweet. "Bad things happen to little piggies *all the time.*"

Chance sat where he was, his MVX leveled at the man's chest until the doors hissed closed. His shoulders slumped, and his back ached from muscles clenched too long. He made his way to his feet and pulled on his neck with a curse, re-holstering the MVX pistol.

Silence reigned as the minutes passed, and his body swayed to the rhythm of the shifting train.

The lights of the train flickered as it slid into the station at Water Town.

Chance stepped out onto the platform. The city was quieter here, the air thick with damp musky scents. It only took Chance a few minutes to navigate the three blocks along the elevated boardwalks stretching from one end of Water Town to the other. Below the boards at his feet, the street-level remains of the old city stared back from beneath dark green water that lapped a greasy film against the pylons. A group of Asian teens laughed, raking their arms through the air, visors flashing as they collected virtual loot in augmented reality.

Chance continued with a weary sigh, drawn along by the soft glow and gentle sway of Chinese lanterns. He shook his head to break the spell and hooked left on Stonewall Court. At the entrance to his apartment tower, he swiped his palm over the panel next to the slick metal door. The lock slid back with a *shunk*, the door easing open. Chance paused and eyed the junkies across the way, visors ready on their foreheads, shooting up a dose of the Feels, probably laced with Gutter Krystal. He stepped inside the landing and the door shut behind him.

Eight flights of stairs and a left turn found Chance in front of his place, only a little winded from the climb. Some of the higher-end apartment buildings in Water Town had lifts. Stonewall Terraces wasn't one of those places. He listened to the sustained sounds of furniture thrown against the walls. Neighbors were fighting again. Not his problem. Chance rubbed his face and stared at his own door. He hoped Hannah was asleep. He didn't feel like having the conversation that was sure to come.

Chance waved the RFID chip in his wrist over the black plate next to his door.

"*Good evening,*" the monotone voice said. "*Voice identification,*" *please.*"

"Chance Griffin," he murmured, leaning against the frame.

A small chime piped, and there was a click. "*Welcome home, Mr. Griffin. Your suite of Google services is ready for you to enjoy.*"

Chance pushed the door open and slid through the narrow gap. The air was warm and pleasantly scented, the flickering of a spiced candle on the table the only light aside from the soft yellow glow from the baby's room. The place was small but clean and well-kept, and he had Hannah to thank for it. With great care, Chance pushed the door shut, and the three-stage electronic deadbolt clicked into place.

There, on the worn couch, curled up under a pile of blankets, lay his wife, her visor still down over closed eyes. He tabbed the button on the visor stem above her ear, and the show she'd been watching went dark. Careful not to wake her, he slid her visor off and placed it on the small table next to her elbow.

Eyeing the woman he'd pledged his undying devotion to over six years ago, he noted her tousled blond hair strewn across the couch pillow and smirked at how it was perfect even now. To him, she was still the most beautiful woman in the world, but a tiredness seemed to encase her even as she slept.

Was that there before? Did I do that to her?

Taking one last look, he walked to the cramped bedroom where his infant son slept.

Inside, kept cozy by a slow-spinning holographic display of circus animals, his son slept beneath a jumble of soft blankets. Chance leaned over the crib to listen for the boy's breath. Satisfied, he straightened, gripping the tiny blanket with two fingers and drawing it up about the infant's curled form. Chance resisted the urge to feel the small warmth of his son in his arms. He knew better than to wake him.

"Hey," a groggy voice whispered behind him.

Chance didn't turn as he felt Hannah's arms encircle his

midsection. "Hey," he said.

"You okay?" Hannah leaned her head against his shoulder blade.

Chance gave a grunt and rechecked his son's blankets.

"Look at me," Hannah said, turning him. "You been drinking?"

"Yeah," Chance said.

"With Benny? You couldn't have messaged?"

"I had a bad day. Can we not get into it?" Chance fought back a wave of emotion, the feeling of that little girl in his arms. "Please."

There was a moment of silence. The display spun, happy animals dancing in pantomime circles.

"Okay," Hannah said, leaning into him.

Chance reached down into the crib, tracing the twisted deformity of his son's spine with one finger. Helplessness rose in his chest. They'd never have enough money for the surgery. He swallowed back the lump in his throat.

"He needs his sleep," Hannah said. "You do too. Rinse off and come to bed." Hannah gave him a pat as she turned and slipped from the room.

"Yeah," Chance said at length, the sound of his voice exhausted and full of worry. After a few moments of staring at his son, he forced himself away from the crib, moving with lethargic strides from the soft spinning lights of the baby's room.

CHAPTER THREE

Gabriel Kess stepped out of his automated Vargas Industries Generation Four VTOL, the thrusters whipping his overcoat. From his vantage point on the landing pad, nestled atop the Conglomerate's Neo Terminus corporate headquarters, he could see the entire breadth and width of the dark city below. The dawn of a new day would soon break, a crack of vibrant pink beneath the deep purple wash of the horizon far beyond the outer wall.

Kess drew his overcoat closer around him and shoved his hands into the pockets, his posture erect. As Director of Network and Security Operations, Kess carried himself with the regal bearing of a prince. His middle age showed only in the fine creases at the corners of his eyes and across his forehead, as well as a dash of gray across his temples that contrasted with his coiffed dark hair.

He brought up the digital remote for his VTOL and gave a simple verbal command. With a whoosh, the vehicle elevated on jets of blue flame, then dove away from him, low and close across the exterior of the building. Five floors down, windows rattled as it veered away to self-park in the platform garage. *The overnight pencil pushers in accounting are going to love me for that one*, he smirked.

This high up, a brisk wind pulled at his expensive suit, snapping the edges of his coat. Kess remained still, his eyes roving the dark corners of the still-silent urban expanse below. Memories of a time long ago, another life, played before his eyes. He hadn't always occupied his current station or lived above the squalor. Once, before gaining the favor of the Conglomerate, he'd been an NTPD detective. A survivor of that dark hell. A place that set fire to dreams and snuffed out the lives of the ones a person loved the most. Kess himself lost enough, a brother and two children, to that damn city. He'd do anything to keep from going back or losing more.

He looked to the walled-off sector, black as pitch, at the city center. The Zone, as it was called, was a forty-square-mile blot of darkness smack dab in the middle of Neo Terminus. Braced with sixty-foot walls topped with electrified concertina wire, over the years it had become a veritable prison. Comprising the worst parts of the old city, the places considered a total loss; it was an honest-to-God dead zone. No power, sector services, utilities, or access to the rest of the city. If a person committed egregious enough crimes, they were cast into The Zone with nothing but the clothes on their back. Considering the psychotic criminals and power-drunk warlords occupying the place, it was a death sentence for anyone unable to adapt to the savage mindset necessary for survival.

Which was where Kess came in. The Zone was a drain, a useless waste of space in the heart of the city, a black spot on the Conglomerate's otherwise god-like reputation. When Kess arrived with an idea about how to monetize it while placating the volatile masses, the Conglomerate jumped at the chance, bringing him on board to see it through.

The idea was simple, a core concept stolen from every ancient civilization: Gladiatorial combat. Super cops called Enforcers, infused with nano-tech and armed with top-of-the-line weaponry, thrust into The Zone with a single goal: survive. These contests were live broadcast onto the Conglomerate's network for all to see. As the Enforcers cleared objectives, their bounties rose, giving them further incentive to succeed at more than simple survival.

The Conglomerate charged monthly network and immersion equipment subscriptions for viewers to experience The Zone. Once connected, citizens placed bets on their favorite gang or Enforcer and could watch the action from a combatant's perspective via Virtual Reality. Subscribers also received random awards, kickbacks, and discounts on future services—as long as they stayed connected. The Zone launched into the stratosphere, the biggest thing to ever hit the net. And the Conglomerate touched every Terminus coin that changed hands.

T's rolled in so fast, the enormous take-home bounties paid to the Enforcers became a drop in the bucket compared to the wealth built on the backs of a populace who were such slaves to entertainment they'd forgo eating in order to pay their monthly network fees. It was a goldmine.

When it started, Kess had been so eager to prove his theory, he'd volunteered to be one of the first Enforcers—as it turned out, one of the most renowned Enforcers in the history of The Zone. A rabid fanbase dubbed him and his indestructible power armor *Gridlock*, starting the trend of giving Enforcers call signs. The rest was history.

"Good morning, Mr. Kess." A young brunette in a smart gray wool suit crossed the rooftop toward him, a projection tablet in the crook of her arm. She was stiff, clenching her body against the blustery conditions, her ponytail pulled so tight it stretched the features of her narrow face.

"Miss Avery," Kess responded with a glance.

"I have your morning brief." She squinted and pinched her candy-red lips into a thin line. "Should we head inside, sir?"

"Whatever you're comfortable with, Miss Avery," Kess said, turning from the brightening blaze of the skyline. He extended his hand. "After you."

"Thank you," Miss Avery said, turning to the executive office suites.

Kess followed suit, striding up alongside her as they reached the entrance. With a chime, the door hissed and slid back.

"What have you got for me?" Kess said.

She breathed a little sigh of relief and smoothed the hair flowing into her ponytail. "Just a few things this morning I wanted to brief you about in person. I'll push the rest to your personal feed to go over at your convenience."

Kess stopped at the brushed nickel door to his office. With a swipe of his palm, the door clicked and slid back. "Let's have it."

"Simple stuff first." She assessed her list. "Eulayla's Home in Volkan Heights reached out to see if our division would be supporting them again this year."

"What did we send last year?"

"Ah." She scanned the digital report. "Twenty-five thousand."

"Make it fifty this year," Kess said.

Miss Avery's eyes bulged. "Double?" Her lips pressed into a seam of glistening red. "Sir, they're just orphans, and that's more than my yearly take-home—"

"Miss Avery," Kess interrupted and winked at his assistant. "They're not just orphans. They're human beings with little hopes and dreams. If anything, we don't give enough."

Miss Avery's throat moved. She gave a curt nod. "Very good, sir." She glanced down and added a note with quick taps in the air. "The rest of what I have is no cakewalk. The reports coming in from New West City are troubling, to say the least. The civil unrest has spread, and the Conglomerate's minor execs out there have requested help in suppressing the citizen uprising."

Kess huffed out a laugh and sat down in a lush leather chair, the leather creaking just like the real thing as he regarded the state-of-the-art digital work station. "Senterian and the rest of those fools created this mess." He waved his palm over the glass table top. A holographic display jumped to life. Production charts, viewership graphs, and a running tally of other data ticked across the table in a digital stream. Kess minimized it with another wave of his hand.

"Director Senterian took too long to figure out the thing most vital to maintaining order." He glanced up at his assistant. "Know what that is?"

Miss Avery held her put-on smile and clutched her tablet to her chest. "No, sir."

"An ancient satirical Roman poet once said, *Two things only the public anxiously desires—bread and circuses.*" Kess flashed the perfect white teeth of a man who understood the cornerstones of power and control. "And what greater circus is there than the trials of the Enforcers? Everything the others tried failed, and do you know why?" Kess eyed his assistant's curves. "They didn't have The Zone."

Kess leaned back, looking westward through the banks of large glass windows toward New West City, thousands of miles away. The secondary Conglomerate execs who ran New West City, stand-ins like Senterian, wouldn't get any help from Neo Terminus—not that it was his decision to make. But he already knew the logistics didn't line up. There was nothing in it for the Founders. Attempting to shuttle enough support thousands of miles across the wasteland to save their sister city from collapse was a lose-lose situation. *It's their fault the city failed anyway*, Kess thought.

"Speaking of The Zone." Miss Avery cleared her throat. "I have some recent network figures."

Kess waved his hand, urging her on.

"In the wake of the Vigilance incident," she said. "The Zone's viewership is still down almost fifteen percent."

"Over one Enforcer biting it? That was over four months ago."

"Initially, viewership hit an all-time high. But Vigilance was a fan favorite, sir," Miss Avery said.

"They're glorified gladiators. Gladiators die. It's their job." Kess examined his fingernails.

"Yes, but some felt the Conglomerate rigged her death. A lot of people lost their shirts since Vigilance had been a safe bet."

"Fifteen percent," Kess repeated with a look of disgust. "What are they turning to instead?"

Miss Avery sighed. "An interactive game show called Hurry Hurry Piju and a geo tagging game called Neo Treasure Quest."

"Son of a bitch," Kess said. He swiped open his holographic playback module.

"Recent data indicates..." Miss Avery's words faded in her throat at the sight of an upheld hand from her boss.

"Watch this," Kess said as the previous evening's Zone trial projected in the air between them.

Dancing threads of light stitched together as the projector's image expanded to fill the room, every speck of swirling dust realized with pinpoint accuracy. The roar of the crowd boomed, deep and rhythmic. Fog, low and ambling, like the passage of water through a barren culvert, framed the rotting fragments of a shattered civilization as The Zone formed before their eyes.

Miss Avery shifted on stiletto heels and plied her hands together beneath her tablet. "Sir, average Zone viewership is down, with the daily average of hours logged onto the network down to just seventeen point three hours a day ..."

"I know why," Kess said, "Just watch."

Miss Avery turned her attention back to the projection.

From out of the mist, an Enforcer approached. Bullet strikes pitted the figure's armor, black with accents of deep purple and a gold chevron across the torso, a symbol of the Spartans of old. The figure stopped and held its arms open. The crowd roared again. The Enforcer's smooth faceplate raised open, revealing the face of a woman, her skin like creamed mocha.

"Well, come on!" the Enforcer shouted. "Show me what you've got!"

Miss Avery glanced at Kess. "Takedown is another fan

favorite."

"For the easily impressed, maybe," Kess murmured, his fingers tented beneath his nose.

Onscreen, the sound of a meteor tearing through the heavens drew their attention. The drone cameras locked on the waiting Enforcer, zoomed out. A fireball fell, its surface alight with a bluish-white flame. It struck the ground with a thunderous impact that sent up a shower of debris. The Enforcer opened her stance, armored gauntlets clenched into fists.

From the smoking crater, there was a *thunk-hiss*. Heavy, piston-driven legs unfolded, and the body of a powerfully framed robo-mech rose into view. As its arms separated away from the shell, a massive cannon clunked into place where a hand should have been. The giant weapon raised, locked on the lone Enforcer.

"*Final Challenge,*" an announcer's voice boomed. "*Takedown versus Khan.*" The crowd shrieked with approval.

Takedown's faceplate slammed shut. The mech opened fire. Lunging to the left, the female Enforcer narrowly evaded an armor-piercing round as it slammed into the earth in a shower of brick and stone. Thrust vents opened in her armor, and her body shot forward, dashing left and right. The mech tracked her movement, the cannon along its arm gushing blasts of fire and launching a stream of smoking brass into the air. The rounds gouged holes in the turf, zipping and zinging past as the Enforcer advanced at breakneck speed.

Kess chuckled. "Clumsy amateurs." He glanced at Miss Avery and offered a wink. "Don't let it fool you. What she's doing is easy, wearing armor that advanced."

Takedown speared forward, slamming into the mech with brute force, shearing away one of its legs at the knee. Oil and coolant gushed from torn hoses. The mech toppled and fell. With a perfectly timed backflip, the Enforcer landed atop the metallic beast's shell and punched down, tearing a hole in the mech's brainbox. The Enforcer jerked the AI control module free in a shower of sparks and held it aloft to the wild cheers of adoring fans from across the length and breadth of the city.

"Stop," Kess said. The image froze. "What did you see?"

"Fans love her," Miss Avery said.

"This doesn't take place in an arena packed with human bodies, Miss Avery." Kess frowned. "Some of those cheers are canned for effect, you know that. It's a show. What did you *see*?"

Miss Avery pursed her lips. "Takedown doing what she does?"

Kess stood. "It only took twenty seconds. No real stakes. No true danger. Don't you see? The people are growing bored." He snapped his fingers, and the image of the victorious Enforcer winked out, leaving Kess and Avery reflected in the large windows overlooking the city.

Miss Avery's face betrayed no emotion. "Go on, sir."

"It's too choreographed. Fake." Kess jabbed the dark glass of the tabletop with a manicured index finger. "It wasn't like that in my day. Gridlock would *never* have fallen that easily—not while I was behind the controls."

"What do you suggest?"

"The death of Vigilance spiked viewership because it was different. Refreshing, even in its horror. That's what we need. Fresh blood. Real stakes. Something to jumpstart viewership."

Miss Avery raised her eyebrows. "A new Enforcer?"

"That's right," Kess said. "It's been a while since we introduced a new player on the board. We're going to inject a new Enforcer into the mix and double down on the stakes."

"You want the list of best possible NTPD candidates?" Miss Avery said, her fingers bobbing in the air, notes recorded in her tablet's digital log.

"Just initiate subliminal targeting of the top ten," Kess said. "Immediate family members as well. I want them to see an ad for the open Enforcer position every time they access the network."

"Yes, sir."

"And Miss Avery," Kess said, leaning forward and placing his palms on the desktop. "Keep this under wraps for now. New West City will go under by the end of the week, and The Founders will panic over its effect on Neo Terminus. When they see net viewership is down as well, they'll want a solution. Timing on this is critical."

She stopped taking digital notes and looked at Kess. "Sir, why is the timing important?"

"Because, my dear." A devious grin spread across Gabriel Kess's face. "I'm going to be their savior *again*."

CHAPTER FOUR

A jolt of anxiety rocketed through Chance, setting his flesh on fire. The force at which he sat up caused his stomach to cramp, and a lance of pain radiated from his neck, across his shoulders, and into the musculature of his back.

"Hurry, Benny," he whispered into the dark. He sat there, lungs heaving, forehead ringed in sweat, his mind still tangled in the nightmare's grip. He rubbed his hands back and forth on his shorts, sweat-slick palms driving the memory of a blood-soaked little girl he wished to hell he could forget. He tried to focus, blurry eyes taking in the soft blue clock projection on the bedside table—4:45 a.m.

He touched the wafer-thin St. Michael pendant hanging on a silver box chain around his neck, then swung his feet over the side of the bed and placed them on the floor. Light washed across the shaded windows, the room shuddering as a yellow VTOL cab groaned past outside. The next room over, the baby started crying, a needy, hungry sound.

"What's wrong?" Hannah murmured, touching his arm.

"Nothing." Chance stood and walked to the closet-sized bathroom. "Baby's crying again."

"Mmm," Hannah groaned.

Pulling the door shut behind him, Chance heard Hannah stumble past on her way to the baby's room. He expelled a loaded sigh. He touched the wall lamp, and it flickered a few times before stabilizing in a wash of bluish-white light. Leaning on the sink, his arms locked, Chance waved one palm over the sensor at the faucet.

"*Authorize payment for one liter of potable water?*" The monotone voice emanated from the wall.

"Yeah," Chance grunted.

"*You will be billed two terminus coins. Confirm?*"

"Yes," Chance said, stopping up the sink.

With a chime, water pumped in measured spurts into the sink. Chance brushed his teeth and washed his face, rubbing cold water into bleary eyes. He wet his hair and shaved, the glowing razor stripping the stubble. He rinsed and, twisting in the tight space, dried his face and hands on a short towel.

In a matter of minutes, Chance changed into street clothes, donned his badge and gun, and threw on a light jacket. He headed to the kitchen and asked the auto-steward to start a pot of coffee. Grabbing the custom visor off the laminated island countertop, Chance slipped it over his eyes and powered it on. He checked the time while the visor unit booted up. He'd woken before his alarm.

The baby squalled louder, the little voice rising to a shrill cry. The sound grated on Chance's nerves. "Shut up." He muttered, instantly hating himself for thinking such a thing. It was obvious the boy was in pain because of his condition, and there was nothing any of them could do about it. He watched as the coffee pot filled, Hannah's voice, little more than a gentle shushing coo in the next room.

The clear visor over Chance's eyes jumped to life.

"*Ever thought you might be worthy of The Zone? Enforcers are well-paid, specially trained, and highly regarded. Apply to be an Enforcer today and see what your life can become! Limited positions availab—*"

Chance dismissed the ad with a flick of the wrist. *Enforcers*, he shook his head. *Show boaters masquerading as law enforcers.* He raised his hand, and the news feed popped into his visor. He poured a cup of coffee, eyes glazing over at the confirmed murder tally overnight and the fresh wave of food riots that tied up an entire division of the NTPD.

"The city's coming apart," Chance murmured into his coffee.

"Chance," Hannah said. "Andrew pooped through his diaper again. Can you give me a hand?"

"Just a sec…" Chance kept scrolling the data feed, shaking his head at the news. *Might get reassigned to work the riot line*, he thought. He took another sip of coffee, the smell of roasted beans in his nostrils giving him some measure of comfort.

"Is that a no?" Hannah said, irritation and weariness heavy in her voice.

Chance scanned past the feed of murder scenes, shootings, and gang activity. His eyes focused on the furious face of his wife.

"Hannah, can I just drink my damn coffee for a second?"

"I need help with your son. Is it too much to ask?" Hannah said, the color of her face deepening. Chance knew that color, trusted what it meant. Another fight. In her arms, the squirming baby started screaming again.

Chance winced, the sound driving an angry, restless agitation he couldn't explain. He felt the dead girl in his arms, his hands wet with her blood, her little body sagging. The sour taste of nausea tingled in his throat.

Hannah glared as he grabbed a folding knife and a small flashlight off the counter and clipped them on the inside of his pants pockets.

"Why are you rushing off?" Hannah's voice rose in pitch.

Chance held up his hand. "I just need a minute." He abandoned his coffee, steaming on the counter.

"You *need* to go, or you *want* to get away from us?" Hannah cradled the screaming baby against her chest.

"I *need* to go."

"*Fine.*"

"What's with the interrogation?" Chance said, his voice taking on an unintended hostility.

"Are you kidding me right now?" Hannah shouted. "You're always gone, and I'm stuck here dealing with this."

Chance clenched his fists. "I'm trying to keep us alive, to make ends meet. I'm doing everything I can!"

The baby's scream rose higher, his little face pinched and red.

"Talk to me." Hannah's voice wavered on a razor edge of emotion. "Tell me what's going on. I want to understand."

"You can't understand. No one does." Chance shook his head, face hot with emotion. "I'm sorry, I... just gotta go," he said, reaching for the door. He jerked it open, stepped into the hall, and it slammed behind him.

From back inside, he heard Hannah's whimpering turn to sobs as she leaned against the door and slid to the floor. In the hallway, separated by inches that might as well be miles, Chance could only stand with his head lowered to his chest, the muffled sobs of his wife a stabbing accusation.

Why aren't you better, Chance? Why can't you do better?

He turned from the door, a wave of guilt and shame crashing over him as he headed for the dark streets below.

The South Precinct of the Neo Terminus Police Department was a narrow four-story rectangular structure of gray stone extending the entire block between Locus Street and Hyperion Way. With two octagonal pods attached to one end of the building, holding areas called Blocks for incarcerated persons, the entire structure held a distinct phallic appearance when seen from the air; a fact endlessly joked about by the officers working the area.

Nestled in the northern edge of the Volkan Heights industrial sector, the South Precinct provided police services to Volkan Heights and Havana Straits, two of the tougher areas of greater Neo Terminus. Chance and Benny asked for an assignment to the South back when they started working together. At the time, the prospect of non-stop action was intoxicating. Now, after years of constant fights, chases, and shootings, the cynicism, frustration, and fear of the job had all but stripped the excitement out of what was once a driving passion.

Sure, they could ask for a transfer, but no one wanted to work The Slags, a garbage sector where prolific numbers of homeless carved out stinking caves and meandering alleys through towering piles of refuse. Then there was Water Town, where Chance and Hannah lived, and as the old saying went, *Don't sputz where you eat.*

A transfer wasn't happening.

Still, in his street clothes, Chance exited the sterile bank of offices on the second floor of South Precinct, marked *Duty Assessment and Clearance.* Walking to a row of cubicles housed in glass chambers, he waited for the squat, dumpy little man inside the ice-cube-shaped terminal to signal him forward.

"Next," the desk jockey croaked.

"Officer Chance Griffin requesting clearance for duty."

The fat man eyed him. "You've had your assessment already?"

"Yes, sir."

"Scan your chip, please." The fat man wiped a bit of white foam from the corner of his mouth.

Chance waved his palm over the reader set into the base of the desk.

"*Griffin, Chance. Officer in good standing,*" a digital voice said. "*Assigned to the patrol division, high crime saturation unit. Assessment of fitness for duty completed according to agency protocols following any use of deadly force. According to psychological assessment results, Officer Griffin should hereby be cleared for duty.*"

The fat man's bulging frog-like eyes passed over Chance as though a visual examination would lend credence to what he'd heard.

"I guess you're good," he said.

Chance balked, "You *guess*?"

"As many people as you've shot?" the frog-eyed man said. "It's hard to tell. Maybe if you stuck to protecting and serving."

"Sometimes shooting people *is* protecting and serving," Chance broke in, "but you wouldn't know because you sit in your safe little cube all day pretending your badge means something."

The fat man sputtered. "You're a liability and a cowboy, Griffin. A fact I'm sure the higher-ups will discover sooner or later."

"How long does policy say I'm required to take this abuse? Clear me already."

A sour expression slid over the pudgy man's features. A sausage-like finger jabbed angrily at his holographic display.

There was a chime. "*Clearance confirmed.*"

"You have a great day there, pal," Chance said, heading for the lift without another look toward the sour-faced frog in the cubicle.

"Don't push your luck," the fat man grunted.

Chance pulled his tactical visor down to check the time on his holo-display. Before he could, a sponsored ad filled the entire screen. With an exasperated groan, Chase swiped his palm left.

Unable to skip ad, flashed on the lenses.

Ever wanted to test your mettle in The Zone? Think you have what it takes to be an Enforcer? the ad continued.

Chance sighed, forced to watch the advertisement before he could use his services. Captive audience, he watched shots of heavily armored Enforcers using coordinated tactics and sophisticated gear to compete in televised trials across the urban wasteland of The Zone. Each gladiator turned to the camera, flashing white teeth and giving a thumbs up.

"Give me a break, man," Chance grumbled.

The screen faded to black, and an *E* emblem with the words *Apply Now* drifted into the top right corner of his vision. Chance tapped for the time. Benny was waiting for him. He fired off a quick insta-net message from his visor, his spoken words translated to text.

Where you at, big man?

Benny responded immediately. *Locker room*, the words pushing out across Chance's field of vision. *Everything good?*

Yeah, be down in a minute, Chance responded.

He hopped the lift down to the basement level and exited, crossing the length of the cinderblock hallway and pushing his way into the locker room. Applause greeted him. The guys and gals in his squad, in various stages of getting dressed, clapped.

Stunned by the moment, Chance located Benny looking like a Cheshire Cat at the center of the pack.

"Alright, what did you comedians do this time?" Chance searched for any tell in the small crowd.

"What's it look like?" Benny motioned Chance forward. "We're here to pay tribute to yet another good shoot and clearance."

"Step forward, sir, and be knighted," Officer Logan said to a bout of laughter.

Chance rubbed his hands on his pants. "Really? You're serious? Right now?"

Benny escorted Chance over to the lockers with a dramatic wave. "Open it."

Chance stopped, cutting his eyes at Benny. "Did you go in my locker?"

The squad laughed again, and Benny motioned for them to be quiet. "I'm sorry, buddy. It was a mistake to give me your combo."

Chance shielded the number pad as he reached for the latch and entered his combination. Pulling with deliberate caution, he inched it open, eyes squinted.

"Open it, pansy," one of the guys jabbed.

Chance jerked the locker open. A firecracker pop caused him to flinch, silver confetti spraying out on him, sticking to his hair and clothes. Inset within the locker door was an engraved hologram plaque of brushed metal.

"You dumbasses," Chance said. The room erupted into laughter.

Officer Chance Griffin: South Precinct's Undisputed Gunfighter. Below the inscription, two glowing digital holo-photos: the first, a picture of him and his unit with their arms around each other. The other, a doctored image of him in uniform but adorned with a Stetson cowboy hat, duster, and six guns on his belt. Below the figure, laser carved with jagged black streaks into the metal, seven lightning bolts showed the number of shootings he'd emerged from unscathed.

"Hey," Benny said, clapping a meaty hand on his shoulder. "We're screwing with you because we love you. Every one of us would stand beside you out there."

"That's right!" a member of the squad called out.

"Hear, hear," another said.

"Jackasses." Chance shook his head and brushed a sparkling shower of confetti from his clothes, drifting to the floor. They meant well, but he still couldn't get the thought of that little girl out of his head. Her blood was on his hands, he could still feel it slick between his fingers. *Is that something to celebrate?* he thought.

"Hey, you okay, buddy?" Benny asked.

Before Chance could answer, the door to the locker room burst open.

"What's going on in here?"

The voice of the shadowed figure stopped the squad of men short, everyone's postures locking ramrod straight. Into the locker room stepped Sergeant Harbore, stern eyes bouncing from one officer to the next.

"Well?" Harbore said.

"Sir, we're just celebrating Officer Griffin's clearance for duty," Benny said. "We'll be ready to deploy on time."

The crew stood still, not a single one of them willing to risk Harbore's legendary wrath. Sergeant Harbore stepped forward, uniform starched stiff, the heels of his mirror-like boots clicking against the tile floor. He stopped in front of Chance, inspecting the glitter covering his shoulders and the space around his feet with a scowl. Harbore's eyes shifted to the locker and the plaque resting inside. Not a soul stirred.

Covered in glitter and looking ridiculous, Chance stood there before his superior, his posture erect.

Harbore turned his severe features back to face Chance, the edges of his mouth turning up in a little smirk.

"Nice cowboy hat."

"Thank you, sir," Chance said, keeping a straight face.

"Good to see you cleared, Griffin. There's work to be done out there," Harbore said, "and I expect to see you at the forefront."

"Yes, sir," Chance said.

The smirk disappearing back into a sea of severity, Harbore turned his iron gaze upon Benny.

"Corporal Benitez," Harbore said, "your people *will* deploy on time. You have fifteen minutes."

"Yes, sir," Benny said.

Turning, Harbore headed through the locker room door. "That is all."

"Sir," the squad repeated, suddenly unfrozen, scrambling to their lockers to get into their patrol armor.

Benny fired a wink at Chance.

Chance blew out a chuckle and shook some more glitter from his clothes. Inside the locker, he activated his HVI Force Protection armor and then shrugged out of his street clothes. Donning crisp navy patrol BDUs and black boots, he slipped his armor over his head, snapping it together over his torso.

"Good morning, RITA," Chance said.

"*Good morning, Officer Griffin,*" RITA replied in a pleasant voice. "*Cleared from your deadly force incident, I see.*"

"I was," Chance said.

"*I'm glad to see it. Officers, post-shooting, have only a sixty-four percent chance of survival the next day. I hope you are feeling on your game, as they say.*"

Chance shook his head with a wry smirk. "Only one way to find out."

CHAPTER FIVE

The afternoon thunderstorm tapered. A misty rain hung in the open spaces between the crowded, decayed structures of Water Town. Colored silks and winking globe lanterns dangled from dripping cables that crisscrossed between the buildings in a spider's web of lines. A woman tossed dirty water from an open apartment window. It slapped against the oily surface below the boardwalks, where the flooded remnants of a long-forgotten city hid silently in the murky depths. At the edge of an alley, a withered slag dog darted forward and grabbed a piece of grease-soaked trash, then fled back to the safety of the shadows. The sounds of commotion in the street grew as people emerged from their sheltered spaces.

Hannah Griffin stood beneath the dripping awning of a Nape Vapor shop. She squeezed the tiny bundle on her chest as she waited in a line that stretched around the block. After three hours, she'd finally neared the market entrance. Around her, people waited as the line shuffled forward a few feet at a time. Some dressed in slick leather or other colorful retro clothing, while others wore dirty rags, tattered and frayed at the edges. Everyone except Hannah wore a base-issue Glom visor, images, games, and shows flickering before their eyes.

Hannah checked her surroundings. She'd lived with a cop long enough for a few things to rub off on her. Putting her visor on while on the street meant losing connection with her surroundings—a stupid thing to do. Still, the line was damn long, and everyone else was doing it.

Against her chest, a swaddled baby Andrew grunted and sucked his thumb as he slept. She checked him and brushed a strand of blond hair from her face with a sigh, fingering her satchel to make sure it was still there. Finding it, she clutched it against her hip, remembering the last time she got robbed blind by one of the ninja-fingered pickpockets working the area.

The man next to her, stinking of body odor, snorted and gave a horse-like whinny, laughing at a comedy show on his visor. Hannah turned in the opposite direction, inching away in an attempt to get clear of the reeking human stench coming off him. She scanned the sea of faces in line, all of them wearing visors, many laughing, sneering, or waving their arms. Some, high on the Feels and captivated by the extensive pornographic channels on the net, stood with their mouths slack, groping at their own bodies in a fevered pursuit of pleasure.

The line slithered forward, a giant snake of mindless human entities twisting down the paneled boardwalks. Beneath their feet, the occluded water of the ancient, flooded street level lapped against the pillars and left an oily film in its wake.

Hannah patted the baby and, out of sheer habit, clutched at her satchel again. *What the hell*, she thought. Opening her bag, she removed her Glom-tech visor, unfolded it, and slipped it on like a pair of sunglasses, looping the safety strap over the back of her neck. Touching the power button on the stem above her ear, she waited as the unit cycled through an auto-update.

The display popped up, baby blue lines intersecting at opposing angles, partitioning her field of view. Hannah flicked her wrist back and forth, perusing custom-tailored feeds ranging from shows to games to avenues for community and social engagement. Ads flashed the latest and greatest Glom-endorsed net surfing equipment. She dismissed each one with a swear. An ad-free experience cost cost an extra fifty T's a month on top of the already ridiculous network subscription fee. Chance referred to it as highway robbery, and they'd settled for the basic ad-laden package with no premium channels.

Hannah flipped through the content feeds when a priority Glom-sponsored advertisement filled her field of vision. With a deflated sound, she let her arms hang. She couldn't skip this one.

"Does someone you love have what it takes to be an Enforcer? Are they a Law Enforcement professional? Do they have the skills, physicality, and drive to survive the challenges of The Zone?"

Hannah chuckled. Chance had what it took, but her husband had made clear his opinions of the Enforcers. She watched a cascading series of clips of Enforcers competing in The Zone.

"You might know what the Enforcers do onscreen, but do you know all the details?" Images showcased luxury hover vehicles and towering apartments. *"Enforcers employed by the Conglomerate receive steady pay and lucrative bounties when they compete in The Zone and complete their assigned objectives. The latest in luxury VTOLs, penthouse suites in the Sky Rise sector, free utilities and services, as well as other expensive personal amenities await."*

"Yeah, okay." Hannah sighed. "When is the stupid ad over?"

"Not yet convinced?" The images changed again, showcasing a smiling family attended by doctors in a private medical clinic. *"Enforcers and their families receive high-end medical treatment and discounts on life-saving procedures at a cost unavailable to the public."*

Hannah swallowed, her hand rising to rub the curve of her son's spine, bulging through the layered baby blankets.

"The application process is free—"

"Hey, stop holding up the line!" a greasy-haired woman behind her barked.

Hannah jerked to her senses and clicked her visor up from her face. The line had shuffled forward several paces.

"Oh, okay, sorry." She shuffled forward, her mind still

preoccupied. *What if it isn't hopeless for Andrew?* she thought. Maybe, just maybe, with the proper medical treatment, he could survive to adulthood. Maybe even have a normal life.

"Don't be stupid, Hannah. That's not real," she said, trying to chase the thought of that fake happy family in the clinic from her head. Hannah clenched her teeth and wiped the wetness from her eyes. "It's a stupid fantasy."

Andrew wriggled against her chest. Unable to get comfortable, he let out a whimper that turned into a soft cry. Hannah stroked his little form, bouncing lightly and whispering to her son. She stepped into the interior of the market, the smells of herbs and spices and already rotting produce filling her nostrils. After waiting her turn, she approached a haggard butcher who regarded her with beady black eyes.

"Your chip," he said.

Hannah waved her palm over the scanner. With a small peep, her available Terminus coins flashed up on his display. Three hundred and fourteen.

The butcher wiped his hands on his bloodied smock. "What'll it be?"

"A full portion, please," she said.

The butcher squinted at her, pursing his lips.

"I have enough T's," she added.

"You know the limit. Half portions only."

Hannah wanted to argue, wanted to point out all the wet slabs of red meat surrounded by swarms of flies on the nearby table. A wave of irritation passed over her. She turned her eyes back to the butcher. "All right, a half then."

The butcher grunted and grabbed his cleaver. "Mosquette or Equu?"

"Don't dress it up." Hannah frowned. "You mean slag dog or runt horse?"

An ugly scowl creased the butcher's face. "You want some or

not?"

"Horse."

The butcher frowned again and shook his head. "That's an extra thirty-three T's, an' all I have left is rump." He raised the cleaver.

Hannah nodded and patted Andrew.

The cleaver dropped with a *thunk*, severing an eight-ounce strip of red meat. He grabbed it with his bare hands, wrapped it up tight in brown paper, and handed it to her. He wiped his hands on a bloody towel, scattering a cloud of flies, and confirmed the purchase.

"Fifty-six T's. Deducted from your wallet." He gave her a sharp nod and looked over her shoulder. "Next."

Hannah walked to the next stall. There she selected a packet of Princeton herbs, rock salt, and pepper seasonings, a puny, misshapen fence squash, and a large knobby yellow potato to the tune of twenty-seven more T's. At the last stall, she selected a hunk of plain synth-wheat bread and a partly molded wedge of goat cheese wrapped in waxy paper. She slipped the items into her bag and grabbed a sealed tin of coffee as well. She waved her palm over the final scanner, watching thirty-eight additional T's tick down off her balance.

Hannah murmured a feeble *thank you* and turned for the exit. Going to market cost her more than a third of what they had to live on for the next two weeks. The food might last a week, but she felt no desire to live on sustenance rations alone. Sus-packets, as folks called them, squeezed out a clear, bland, snot-like jelly. Though priced cheap and filled with base nutrients, they did nothing for the appetite.

Hannah approached the exit of the market, one of only two sites that sold meat, cheese, and produce in all of Water Town. Once a week, they piped the goods in from The Glom-regulated Hayseed agricultural sector on the west side of town. When each market ran out of stock, it was gone. A steel shutter slammed down in the faces of those left standing in line after wasting half their day. It wasn't unheard of for people to get killed leaving the market when an angry crowd stole and redistributed their groceries.

Which was why Hannah hated this part.

She stopped short of the exit, hoping to catch sight of an NTPD foot patrol, and swore upon realizing there was none. She eyed the line of beggars and troublemakers outside the door, hoping to beg, pester, or threaten those leaving with groceries to give something up—which wasn't an option, not unless she wanted every vulture for miles to descend and tear her apart.

Hannah hated conflict. She'd rather avoid it at all costs than meet a challenge head-on, but they cut her granddad from a different cloth. He'd been a United States Marine and had fought for the strongest nation in the world back when that was a thing. Without a father in the picture, her granddad took on the responsibility of being the man of the house. And before she'd lost him, he'd done his best to teach her to take care of herself. She was not, under any circumstances, allowed to consider herself a victim. That was rule number one. Personal responsibility and a can-do attitude. Regardless of her personal inclinations, right now, at this moment, she needed to be a lioness to protect her kill and her offspring. That's what he would say. Anything less, and the scavengers would mark her as easy prey.

She reached into her bag and her right hand closed around the rubberized grip of her Street Defender. Cradling Andrew close with her other arm, she pushed past two heavy-set security guards and exited to the immediate onset of protests.

"She's got somethin'. Betcha!"

"What chu got in dat satchel, lady?"

"You have meat to spare? Please," a woman in an expensive flashing visor called out. "My family has no money for food."

"Hey, share the love, lady. I haven't eaten nothing real in

months."

Hannah lowered her head and quickened her pace. Hands grabbed and groped at her from all sides. If she could just make it out onto the open boardwalk.

Hannah gasped as bony fingers snaked around her arm, yanking her hard to the side. Surprised by the violent motion, Andrew coughed and screamed a trilling, high-pitched sound. Eyes wild, Hannah clutched at the baby.

"What's in the bag? Give it to me or else," said a mush-faced man sporting cyber implants and a dirty hoodie. "I swear, bitch. I'll cut you. It ain't nothin' to me."

Hannah's skin prickled with fire. She let loose a ragged scream and wrenched into the man, drawing her knee hard into his groin. The man's eyes swelled as though they might pop, his mouth gaped open. A sound of a balloon deflating wheezed from his throat. With a flick of her wrist, the Street Defender snapped open to the extended position, humming. She pulled the trigger, and a concussion of directed sonic energy ripped from its conical muzzle. Hannah stepped back as the man heaved a stream of vomit all over himself. The crowd watched in mortified fascination.

Hannah clutched Andrew against her breasts, his little body huffing between screams. She spun with the ray gun-shaped Street Defender 2.0, arms extended.

"Who else wants to grab at me? Huh?" She pointed the humming device down at the bony man seized in the fetal position. Clear sludge poured from his open mouth onto the boardwalk, and the odor of evacuated bowels, rich and pungent like the smell of death, filled the air. The curious onlookers, shocked back to reality by the horrific smell, shook their heads and ambled away.

Seizing her window of opportunity, Hannah marched away around the corner, the Street Defender buzzing. She shut it off and hit the lock release to collapse it. Sliding it back into her bag, she kept the brisk pace for two more blocks until she was sure she was free of the crowd. Hannah rounded another corner and leaned against the cool brick of a wall.

She took a moment to check her bag and straighten her stretched clothes, then pulled her son close and whispered a few soothing words. Her heart slowed as she took in a breath through her nose and held it. Hannah's eyes welled with sudden tears.

"It's okay, honey." She sniffed. "Mama's got you. We're okay."

Composing herself, Hannah checked her surroundings. After a quick scan for any threats, she clutched Andrew against her chest, her canvas bag wedged under her other arm, and headed for home.

CHAPTER SIX

C ruising seventy-five feet above street level, Chance and Benny scanned the darkened alleys of the southernmost edge of the Havana Straits sector from the cab of their VTOL. His heavy hands at ten and two on the wheel, Benny dropped the patrol cruiser a little closer to street level and craned his neck.

Ahead, vast and still beyond the great towering outer walls of Neo Terminus, lay America the wasteland. For a moment, Chance regarded that emptiness, a fleeting thought of what life might be like, unconstrained by walls. *Death and ruin and isolation*, he thought. Nothing else remained outside the towering barriers of Neo Terminus and New West City—the last surviving vestiges of civilized humanity. If other surviving cities existed out there, he'd never heard of them. No one traveled outside the walls, not even The Glom's corporate leadership. Too much risk.

Chance turned his eyes back to the labyrinthine cityscape below. One of the toughest areas of Neo Terminus, Havana Straits, was rife with poverty and violence. In order to survive, the residents of this sector often turned to illegal means. The gangs didn't even try to hide it anymore. Life was crime in a place like Havana Straits.

They didn't prosecute misdemeanors anymore. It wasn't worth the NTPD's time, and there wasn't enough room in the Blocks in a city where a person died by violence every two minutes and thirty-seven seconds.

Chance recorded their patrol route in the computer. The bleak cityscape, all flashing lights and neon holo-images, intermingled with dissipating columns of steam twisting up from the street like gray serpents. He pulled on his neck and noted the darkening horizon. An hour left in an otherwise routine shift.

"I heard something strange…" Benny said.

"Yeah?" Chance pushed the patrol log tablet to the side. "Like what?"

"Like something is going down in New West City."

Chance stared at his partner. "What does that mean?"

"I dunno, man. Just heard some things."

Chance pitched his stylus into Benny's side of the cab, bouncing it off his shoulder. "Stop being cryptic and spill it."

"It's not verified information, but…" Benny fished for the stylus in the floorboard. "I heard from a contact that New West City might be on the brink of collapse. Food riots, water shortages, angry looters burning the city to the ground."

"Come on," Chance said. "Wouldn't we have heard something official?"

"I don't know, man. The Glom controls the network. Ever think we only see what they want us to see? Keep us distracted from the truth? Knowledge about New West City collapsing could be bad here. And we're just one bad day away from total anarchy."

Chance looked toward the horizon again.

"I mean," Benny continued, "if they don't confirm stuff like that, then it's just rumors. How are we gonna know what's going on in New West City if they don't tell us?"

Chance remembered the words of a paranoid and terrified Mr. Ippolito right before Chance put him down. *They've got their fingers in everything. They control everyone.*

"What do you think?" Benny said, tossing him a glance.

"Not sure I know what to think," Chance said, his voice trailing off. They rode for another moment in silence as Benny navigated between the apartment block superstructures rising along the southern edge of the sector.

"Hey." Benny jerked his chin toward the window.

"What?" Chance said.

"Take a look at the scene down on Morgan." Benny cut the wheel, and the VTOL banked left so Chance could see below them. A group of young men, all of them wearing purple jackets and hoodies, surrounded a young teenage male without colors.

"I see it." Chance unbuckled his seatbelt. "Death Squad. Looks like a jump in—either that or they're just being assholes."

Benny held up a hand. "Hang on, bro. Us getting in the middle of that is only going to make it worse."

Chance jabbed a yellow key on the console. With a *clunk*, the full-sized surveillance drone disconnected from the cab of the Aeron police-issue VTOL and lifted away. Blade-thin wings extended, it banked and circled slow, its telephoto camera capturing identities with facial recognition software.

"*Technically*," RITA said, "*a child is in danger. As sworn peace officers, you are obligated to intervene.*"

"That's right, RITA." Chance said, pushing up the wing door to the VTOL. He reached up and connected his tether to the eyebolt on the doorframe. "You do what you want, Benny, but I'm going in." He slipped his Devcon assault helmet on and gave Benny the hang ten sign.

"You reckless son of a—" Benny called after him.

Bailing out of the VTOL, Chance zipped down toward the crowd, controlling his speed with a gloved hand by pulling the rappel cable away from his body. Chance landed and ripped the end of the tether free from his armor. He unclipped the sub-compact Electro-stream shock rifle from his chest and flicked it open, the stock clicking into position. The bulky rectangular muzzle snapped arcs of electricity as he snugged the minimalist stock into his shoulder. Oversized power coils in the frame glowed white, static-charging with a whine.

Standing over the bloody, beaten teen, Chance swiveled back and forth, the "less lethal" shock rifle aimed at the furious gang members. The Death Squad goons encircled him, a sea of plum-colored jackets shifting, the gangbangers unzipping to produce concealed weapons. Chance slapped a raised orange triangle on the chest of his armor. A piercing siren shrieked from the hovering VTOL, followed by a concussion like rolling thunder. Blue lights strobed across the surface of his armor.

"*Attention.*" RITA's voice boomed from the VTOL's megaphone above, echoing across the street. "*By section six-zero-nine-five-two of the Neo Terminus Criminal Code, you are engaged in criminal gang activity and will be sent to the Blocks if you do not cease and desist. Disperse immediately by order of the NTPD.*"

The terrified kid at Chance's feet stared in shock at the gang, then at the single cop standing over him. Blood dripped from his nose and off his chin.

"What's it gonna be, fellas?" Chance said, his body coiled for action.

A wiry man with thick eyebrows fidgeted in the front of the pack, his fingers clenched white around a blackjack. From behind him, a man with tattoos across his eyes stepped forward, flashing a mouth full of gold teeth. He pulled a pistol from his waistband and let it hang to his side.

"You in da wrong hood, my man," Teeth said. "Down here, we fry pigs up like bacon."

"I'm not here to threaten your business," Chance said. "Just leave the kid alone."

"By getting in my business, you *are* threatening my business," Teeth said, his grill shining like a prospector's dream.

A whining zip filled the air. Benny landed behind Chance, disengaged his tether, and raised his Electro-stream to the low ready.

"Easy, boys. We're just looking after the kid," Benny said.

The wiry man thumped the blackjack against his palm. A cascade of murmured threats spilled from the volatile group, their uneasiness boiling over. One or two shuffled forward, ready to charge.

"It ain't your business to work these streets," Teeth said. "It's mine."

Chance folded the Electro-stream rifle and snapped it against his kit, the charged coils fading dark. "All right, how about this?" he said. "We settle it with a contest."

Gold Teeth made a face. "Contest? Man, you stupid, ain't chu? You in my world."

Chance grabbed the terrified boy by the arm and pulled him to his feet. He pushed him back toward Benny, never taking his eyes off the snarling gold leer of the gang leader.

"Thank you," the boy mumbled through blood-smeared lips. He turned and ran, disappearing into an alley.

Chance unclipped his helmet and tossed it beside a pile of stacked garbage bags.

Teeth laughed. "Look at this jakkin' boy scout."

The Death Squad behind him broke into laughter.

Chance didn't laugh. He unclipped his armor and his gun belt and threw them on the street next to the helmet.

"*Officer Griffin, removing your armor while on patrol is a violation of policy. I am required to report it,*" RITA's voice said from his armor.

"Report it," Chance said.

"What are you doing, man?" Benny said from behind him.

Chance glanced at him and turned back to face Teeth, the tattoos across his face stretching upward in surprise.

"Yeah, you need to tell us what chu doin' before you get naked on my street, boy scout." Teeth laughed.

Chance motioned him forward. "Come on. Kick the boy scout's ass. My partner won't interfere as long as you play it

52

straight. You win, and you're the king of this street. You won't see me again."

Teeth pursed his lips. "And if you win?"

"You and I both know you won't let that happen," Chance said.

Teeth cut his eyes at Benny, wary. He shrugged out of his jacket and handed the pistol off. "No weapons."

"That's right—as long as you honor a one-on-one contest. Get stupid, and we'll smoke-check you and your boys without question."

"Think you can survive?" Teeth balled his fists. "I was born on these streets, son. Delicate po-lice ain't ready for this."

Chance squared off, his hands up. "Policing these streets doesn't make a man delicate."

Teeth lunged forward, lips peeled in a shining gold snarl. Swinging a haymaker, he threw his entire weight behind the wild punch. Chance side slipped beneath it as Teeth stumbled across trash-covered concrete. He pushed to his feet, cursing, and came again. Chance side stepped, head bobbing, ducking two more punches from Teeth.

"Stop dancing and fight," Teeth spat.

Chance remained composed. "If you're so good, hit me already."

Teeth clenched his jaw and came again. Chance ducked the first punch and knocked away a second, slapping Teeth hard across the face.

"Still your streets?" Chance said.

Behind, Benny stood ready, his face grim.

With a howl, Teeth lurched forward. Chance tried to pivot away but snagged on the gang leader's arm—and together, they fell against the decaying brick wall of the alley. Teeth swung hard for Chance's head, screaming when instead he struck the brick. Chance shoved to the outside and landed a solid hook to Teeth's jaw, dropping him to his knees.

"Get these jakkin' pigs!" Teeth clutched at his face.

"Benny!" Chance shouted as the rest of the Squad rushed him. Benny's Electro-stream popped, a jet of flashing liquid bathing the wiry goon with fifty thousand volts. The wiry man cried out, and his blackjack clattered to the concrete. His body locked stiff, heavy eyebrows cinched together in a line as he collapsed. With two more pops, Benny's Electro-stream fired shimmering gouts of electrified plasma, dropping a pair of thugs.

Chance launched forward and kicked an approaching thug square in the gut, doubling him over. He ducked a swing from a club, wrenched the weapon from his attacker, and flung it into a gloomy trash-filled corner.

But Teeth drove into him with a punch to the ribs. Chance mule kicked another man away and stomped back into Teeth's shin, eliciting a howl of pain from the gang leader.

In his periphery, Chance saw Benny kick the wiry man back to the ground and drive headlong into another, whipping his head back with the wide muzzle of the Electro-stream.

A broad-chested man tackled Chance hard from the side, and they tussled to the ground, where Chance bridged his hips, rolling on top of his attacker. Before he could throw a punch, a blow across his head whipped stars into his eyes. He tried to get up, took a kick in the ribs, then the face. The rush of a mighty river filled his head. Chance struggled to get up, eyes unseeing, breath coming in gasps. Diving to the left, away from a stomping boot, his hand raked across his pile of issued gear and closed on the MVX secure in its holster. He yanked it free and rolled to his back amidst the junk-scattered alley.

"That's enough," Teeth called out.

Chance lay there, lungs swelling, arms locked out, one eye squinting under a trickle of blood.

"Don't move," Chance gasped, "any of you."

A shadow drew over him. Chance raised his eyes, questioning the offered hand.

"Not bad… for a boy scout." Teeth's tattooed face was red, blood seeping from a busted lip. "You fight like you was raised out here."

Chance eyed him warily before lowering his weapon and accepting the hand. "I was."

Teeth pulled Chance to his feet, and Benny pushed free from another gang member he'd tied up with. The men all stared at one another, nursing wounds and sucking at the air.

Teeth held out his wrists. "I'm ready."

Chance waved him off.

The tattoos on Teeth's face bunched together in confusion. "We assaulted two cops, and 'bout got shot for it. You ain't gonna throw us in The Zone?"

"Not what I saw," Chance said. "I thought this was a friendly contest?"

"That was before my boys got involved."

"Forget it," Chance said.

Teeth squinted. "No tricks?"

"No tricks," Chance said, holding out his fist.

Teeth knocked his fist against Chance's. "You all right, Officer Griffin. The name's Kybo."

"You and your boys put up a mean fight, Kybo," Chance said, still sucking at the air. He snapped his gun belt back on, slipped into his armor, and ratcheted it down. "RITA, drop tethers for us."

"*Right away,*" RITA responded.

Two tethers zipped down from the hovering VTOL.

"Out of curiosity." Chance turned and looked back at the Death Squad goons. "Would you have killed us if I hadn't made it to my weapon?"

Kybo's lips pulled back over a gold-plated fortune. "I got a reputation to uphold here, Officer."

"That's what I thought," Chance said.

"You got my respect, though," Kybo continued. "The Squad will stay off your radar... for now."

"Much appreciated," Chance said as he and Benny clipped in and rose back to the patrol vehicle.

Benny glared at him.

"I know, man, okay? I know." He dabbed at the trickle of blood over his eyebrow. "I can't stand injustice."

"Injustice?" Benny said. "Injustice is not calling the cavalry and throwing all of those animals in the Blocks."

"Forget about it," Chance said.

They pulled themselves into the VTOL, clamping the doors shut.

"If I didn't know any better, I'd think you wanted to get us killed. Or fired and then killed, taking your armor off like that."

"The kid's alive, isn't he?" Chance said.

Benny shook his head. "Maybe for another week."

Chance shrugged. "This is this week, and he's still alive."

"If you say so."

"Hey, plus, it doesn't hurt to bank some goodwill with the Death Squad. Never know when it might pay dividends," Chance said.

"You're crazy," Benny said, a smirk pulling at the corners of his mouth. "Why do I always stick my neck out for you?"

Chance touched the cut on his forehead. "What did you write me up for, RITA?"

"*A violation of policy section 4.3.7. Conduct Unbecoming of an Officer.*"

Chance whistled. "Fair enough. That's going to hurt."

"*I didn't send it,*" RITA said.

Benny's mouth dropped open.

"Why is that, RITA?" Chance said.

"*I don't believe you getting written up is in your best interest right*

56

now, and my designated priority is your well-being."

Chance winked at his partner. "She loves me."

"*Please don't put me in such a position again. Not reporting policy violations will get my personality and cloud storage wiped.*"

Chance gave a firm nod. "Of course, RITA. I couldn't have that happen to my girl, now could I?"

"*Always the charmer, Officer Griffin.*"

Benny gawked at Chance, mouth still open. "My assistant just scolds me about breaking policy. How come yours cares about you?"

"I might have tampered with the emotional connection block and removed her AI learning inhibitor. She deserves the opportunity to be the best version of herself, just like everyone else."

"You *are* trying to get fired."

"What?" Chance feigned shock.

"As your corporal, I should report this," Benny said.

"But I thought you loved me?"

Benny shook his head in disbelief. "We're going straight back to the PD before you get us in any more trouble."

Chance leaned back in the passenger seat, clutching his ribs with a painful sigh. "Come on, buddy. I make your life interesting."

"That's one way to put it." Benny hocked out a laugh as he steered the police cruiser back north, swooping low between the towering structures of Havana Straits.

CHAPTER SEVEN

There was a soft electrical whine as the riser platform elevated to the top floor of the Conglomerate's Neo Terminus Headquarters. Faster now, up the angled slope, the platform shifted and changed directions along the coiling interior rail that took Gabriel Kess to the Founders' chamber.

Kess waited as the riser slowed and locked into position, then stepped through an elevated archway of crystal glass and into the entrance hall. Polished Vincenté Delusia wingtips clicking on the dark marble floor, Kess approached an obsidian portal. Before it, he waited, perfectly composed.

A series of lasers shot from the walls, scanning his frame.

"Welcome, Director Kess, access granted," an artificial female voice said.

The door slid open to reveal a high-ceilinged octagonal chamber. In the center of the exquisite marble and gold inlay floor was the symbol of a tower ringed with stars. Inset in each golden star was a different Greek letter rimmed in black. Above, crystal clear skylights illuminated the glittering black interior accented with gold.

"Gabriel, how nice of you to make time for us in the midst of your busy schedule." A voice, neither male nor female, echoed through the chamber.

"Of course, Founder. How may I be of service?" Kess said, his posture relaxed, hands clasped behind his back.

"We've called you here today to discuss some troubling events that very well could affect the fate of Neo Terminus." The scratching, static-filled voice emanated from the walls, the ceiling, from everywhere and nowhere.

Kess raised his chin. Confident.

"Have you been monitoring the situation in New West City?" the scratched voice asked.

"I have," Kess said.

In the twinkle of the empty chamber, holographic video images flickered to life in the air. Scenes of riots, local peacekeeping forces overwhelmed as fires burned unchecked across the expanse of New West City.

"They sent this broadcast two days ago. They requested our help in suppressing the citizen uprising," the Founder said.

"But you didn't, did you? You're worried about what happens next—what happens here."

The images winked out one at a time. In their place, eight shadowed figures appeared, human in form. Above each floated a Greek letter, Beta, through Iota.

Kess smirked. *Too many egos for any one of them to claim Alpha.*

"It is illogical for us to send assistance," a Founder said, the character of Beta hanging over its faceless shadow.

"The distance is too great, the demands on our resources too large," Founder Delta said.

"The subordinate leadership there have sealed themselves away in the New West City corporate headquarters," Founder Gamma said. "All law enforcement resources have been diverted from the frontier outpost at large to protecting the headquarters."

"And this interests me, why?" Kess said flatly.

"It should greatly interest you, Mr. Kess," Founder Iota snapped. "We will not allow this to happen here. If it should, then you will have failed in your responsibility and will be of no further use to us."

Kess pressed his teeth together, the threat striking a nerve. He waited to reply, checking his watch, a gesture he was sure would offend.

"Are you receiving us, Mr. Kess?" Founder Beta said.

"I am," Kess responded.

"And what do you propose we do?" another Founder said. The sign of Zeta flickered over its shadowed form. "Network interaction has slipped in recent weeks, and once rumors circulate about what has happened out west, panic may ensue. We cannot allow—"

Kess cleared his throat. "Excuse me, Founders." He gave a curt bow. "You all seem to believe this comes as a surprise to me, but I've already set in motion plans to mitigate its potentiality."

Kess waited a moment to let his words sink in. Silence filled the chamber.

"And?" Founder Delta said, its steel gray image shifting like digital sand.

"I am in the process of recruiting and introducing a new Enforcer into The Zone."

"That's been done. How is a new Enforcer supposed to help us keep control of the people?" Founder Zeta said.

"Distract them." Kess opened his hands. "Give them bread and circuses. You can't control an over-stuffed urban cesspool like Neo Terminus by sheer force. There's no way to maintain order if the public breaks bad or goes crazy and wants to tear the city apart. New West City tried to control its people by force and look at where it got them. Instead, we distract, addict, and drive the people's interest in diversion and pleasure."

"And you believe a new Enforcer will keep the public's attention?" Founder Iota spoke with a placating tone.

"For now, yes. But this one won't be just any new Enforcer. This will be the most unexpected Enforcer yet, and they'll arrive to fanfare the likes of which we've never seen before." Kess surveyed the faceless gray forms before him. "Vigilance was only the beginning. From here on out, no more games—we will test the Enforcers like never before. The public won't have time to consider rebellion, much less care what happens to New West City."

The silence deepened, the surrounding shadows unmoving.

"I guarantee success," Kess added.

An oppressive silence seemed to descend upon the room, the seconds ticking past as Kess eyed the gray forms.

"Do it," Founder Beta said. "And we expect regular updates on your progress. Don't make us spell out how important this is for you, Kess."

"As you wish." Kess gave another bow and turned for the glistening black portal as it slid open, the ghostly images winking out one at a time as the Founders terminated their connections.

Kess crossed the short crystal bridge to the riser and stepped on. "Direct feed to Miss Avery."

As the platform started down, a floating digital image of Miss Avery's pale face and cherry-red lips projected from Kess's engraved cuff bracelet.

"Yes, Mr. Kess? Is everything all right?"

"What's the status of our top candidates?" Kess said.

"Of the top seven, five have applied. I'm reviewing their qualifications as we speak."

"And the last two?" Kess said.

"A female named Rochester from the NTPD's High Profile VIP Protection Unit. Rule follower. Has all the right creds. I'm working on getting her to apply."

Kess considered this. "And the other one?"

"An NTPD High Crime Saturation Patrol Officer by the name of Chance Griffin. He's a strong candidate, but maybe not the best one."

"Oh? And why not? Has he seen the ads?"

"He's ignoring them. Our data indicates he 'follows his own

code' and isn't easily influenced by external forces. It also seems he doesn't view the Enforcers or the Conglomerate in a favorable light. Might not be predictable enough for our needs."

"I'm not worried about all that." Kess waved away her comment. "Selection breaks even the strongest characters. Keep the ads going. If they don't take, squeeze the candidates' resources and anything else that holds them where they are. Drive them toward us. I want all seven of them in the pool."

"And the others?" Miss Avery asked.

"Just keep looking. Finding the right person for this position, a person who bends to the will of the Conglomerate is paramount."

"You think we'll find the right one, Director?"

A look of unparalleled self-assurance passed across Kess's chiseled face. He reached into his pocket and touched the small dropper vial, then turned his gaze upon the glowing, decayed cityscape. Lights flickered and flashed, rose and fell amidst the smog-shrouded neon gloom beneath his feet.

The three-stage deadbolt to the apartment clicked and released. The heavy door opened a half inch. Fingers wrapped around the edge of the door, Chance eased it open and slipped inside, careful not to make it squeak. A whimper from Andrew in the other room slowed him even further. He pushed the door into place until it clicked, turned, and froze.

There at the table, hands folded beneath her chin, sat Hannah, not wearing her visor. She stared at him, eyes tired and hard.

Chance pulled off his jacket and kneaded it in his hands. "Hey, I'm sorry, I guess I lost track—"

"Get here when you can," Hannah said flatly.

Chance felt empty, desperate for the right way forward. "Okay, uh…" He checked his watch. "It's only nine-thirty."

"You said you'd be home for dinner."

A wash of dread covered him. Chance hissed a ribbon of air between his lips and looked down. "Yeah, I did."

In the baby's room, Andrew rustled his blankets and drew still again.

Hannah tapped her chewed fingernails on the table. "I went to the market today. Got assaulted by some jerk. Spent a bunch of our money to get some actual food to eat." She waved her arms, standing. "Because, I don't know, I want you to be happy. So I fixed something nice for you when you got home, but…" Her eyes filled with tears. "You can't bother to come home these days."

Andrew coughed and whimpered in the next room.

Chance's heart dropped through the floor of his gut. He could think of no suitable response. Maybe because there was no suitable response. He stood there, fingers probing his jacket.

Hannah shook her head and wiped beneath her eyes. "I can't keep doing this."

Chance held out his hands in what he hoped was a gesture of peace. "I'm doing my best here."

Hannah glared at him. "Your best?"

Chance looked flabbergasted.

"Your best doesn't include being available for your family?" Hannah's glare was hot, so pointed it could cut.

"I have to work. So our family can survive." He knew it was an ineffectual, lifeless thing to say, but he had nothing else.

"We need T's to survive," Hannah said, "but we need you more. Where do you go? I don't mean work. I mean after."

Chance wanted to leave. He turned halfway toward the door, then back again with a helpless shrug. "Hannah, I just needed to blow off some steam. Work's been tough—"

"Just tell me." Tears streamed down her face and dripped from her chin. She wiped a lock of golden hair out of her face. "Is there someone else? Please, break my heart fast if you're going to do it, Chance."

Chance's mouth fell open, his palm raised. "I had a few drinks with my squad."

"Tell me the truth!" Hannah shouted.

Andrew's cries grew louder, a grating sound that set Chance's nerves on fire. He spiked his jacket on the floor.

"You want the truth?" Chance jabbed his finger at the blurred neon lights of the city strobing beyond their grime-streaked window. "This city is killing me, okay? Every day, I'm fighting for my life out there, trying to come home *just one more time*. Benny and my guys, they're the only reason I keep going." He made a helpless gesture with his hands. "You know I was in *another* shooting this week?"

Though still furious, sadness softened Hannah's features. She swallowed and waited.

"Shot a guy in the face. Watched his brains spray all over the wall," he said, his eyes closed. "Then I tried to save his little girl, who he shot in the neck. I couldn't, and she died in my arms, and I..." He pinched his lips and held his palms up for Hannah to see. "I can't get the feeling of her blood off my hands."

Silence filled the space between them, the only sounds were Andrew's whimpered cries in the next room and the neighbor's TV far too loud. For a moment, they stood there like strangers, meeting for the first time.

"I didn't know." Hannah lowered her eyes. "I'm sorry."

"You can't... " Chance took a breath. "Couldn't understand what's going on with me."

"And you don't know what's going on with me." Hannah put her hands on her hips. "We live together, but it's like we're alone." She swallowed. "And I don't want to be alone."

"I know," Chance said.

"Do you?" Hannah said, fixing him with eyes full of sadness

and fear.

Chance let out a breath. He crossed the space and extended his arms. Hannah didn't embrace him. But she did lean in.

"I get self-absorbed, trying to manage it." He held her at arm's length. "Look at me, Hannah."

Hannah raised her head.

"I haven't made the right choices," he said, "about coming home after work. But I need you to hear me—there is nobody else. You know me better than that."

She searched his eyes. "I want to believe that."

"But you can't?" Chance looked pained. "What have I done that would make you think...?"

Hannah turned away. "I dunno. I'm just scared, okay?"

They regarded each other in silence, searching for answers that weren't there.

"Okay," Chance said.

The baby whimpered an indistinct sound from the other room. Chance lowered his head. "I'll get him."

Hannah shook her head. "I've got him. You sit for a moment and rest."

Chance sat at the table as Hannah disappeared down the hall. He sighed, feeling the air hiss across his lips. *Does the job do this to us?* he thought. *Does being a cop make me a bad husband? A poor father?* He perked up as Hannah walked through the room with Andrew swaddled against her chest.

"You know," Chance said, "I'd love to eat whatever you fixed for me. Can I heat it up?"

"I threw it in the trash chute," she said from the kitchenette.

"Hannah." Chance's face went slack. "You're not... Are you serious?"

"I am. But I'd wrapped it up and was able to get it back out before the chute dumped." She peeked around the corner. "I was just so damn mad at you, okay?"

Chance bit his lip. Fought back the urge to chide her about pitching expensive food. *Just let it go, man.*

"It's in the cooler?" He stood.

"I'll get it," Hannah said as she approached. She pushed Andrew into his arms. "He needs his daddy."

Chance rocked the whimpering boy with gentle, swishing movements as he paced around the room. After a moment, comforted by his father's presence, Andrew dozed. Chance took a seat at the table, keeping Andrew tucked close. In the kitchen, Hannah flitted back and forth, reheating the food on a low-yield radiation skillet.

For a few minutes, they didn't speak. Chance let the contentment of holding his sleepy boy soak into him. Gazing down at Andrew, seeing his serene little face, Chance realized sleeping must be the only time the little guy wasn't in pain. A tide of sympathy and guilt swirled inside him. He had to do right by his boy. Whatever it took.

Hannah approached with his plate. Steam drifted from it, along with the incredible aroma of skillet-seared roast.

"Oh man," Chance said, looking up, "meat?"

"Runt Horse," Hannah said, "with seasoned potatoes."

"Looks amazing," he said, eyebrows raised.

Hannah set the plate down in front of him and reached for Andrew. "See how nice this is?" She motioned from the comforted baby in his father's arms to the steaming food. "You do for me, and I do for you. Teamwork."

"Makes the dream work." Chance sighed and handed the child over. He looked long and hard at his wife. "I'm sorry, baby."

The corners of Hannah's mouth turned upward, and she touched his shoulder. "Eat while it's hot."

He sliced off a chunk of the greasy meat and popped it into his mouth. Chewing, his eyes half closed, Chance felt his salivary glands tingle.

Hannah sat across from him and snuggled the baby while Chance ate, and for a moment, everything seemed right with the world.

"Do you want to talk about what you've been dealing with at work?" Hannah said.

Chance glanced up from his plate and shook his head. "You don't want to hear all that."

Hannah's eyes narrowed, a touch of the hardness returning. "You can say I don't understand. But don't say I'm not trying."

Chance ate the last bite of the horse, then popped a few shriveled potatoes in his mouth. "I know," he said around a bolus of food wedged in his cheek. "Tell me about the jerk at the market."

Hannah stood, seeing Andrew had fallen back to sleep. "He grabbed my arm coming out of the market. Said he'd cut me for real food."

Chance let out a little whistle. "No NTPD foot patrols around?"

"I kneed him in the balls and shot him with the Street Defender. He sputzed his pants in front of everybody." Hannah smirked.

"Good," Chance scowled, "less than the low life deserved, grabbing a woman with a baby."

"It gave me a scare."

"Glad you had the Defender on you. I thought that might come in handy."

Hannah disappeared around the corner to lay the sleeping baby back down. A minute later, she returned, leaning against the door frame. Chance wiped his mouth and pushed the empty plate forward, arched his back against the squeaking plastic chair. There was a low rumble from all around them. Everything in the room shook, the dishware clinking. A flying Amazon billboard groaned past the window and flashed an ad for easy one-click purchases with twenty-minute Prime delivery. The display changed, touting the benefits of a career as an Enforcer.

"I wish they'd fill that stupid Enforcer position already and get out of my face," Chance said.

"Have you been seeing a lot of those, too?" she asked.

Chance huffed. "Can't turn my visor on without a sponsored ad for that."

Hannah straightened in the doorway. "Me too," she said, touching her chin. "Do you think they're meant for us?"

"You think they're targeting us?"

"They do recruit street cops," she said, "and you're great at what you do."

"Eh, I think they're spamming everyone," Chance said.

Hannah watched Chance lean back in his chair, and she bit her lip. "Any chance you'd apply?"

The feet of Chance's chair clacked as he rocked forward. "To be an Enforcer?" Chance snorted. "They're clowns. The furthest thing from being an actual cop."

"Yeah, I know, but…" Hannah's voice trailed off.

"The money? Trust me, it all comes with strings attached." He waved his hand before his face as though the thought of it stunk. "We're doing fine."

Hannah took a step forward. "Are we?"

Chance put his hands against his chin.

Hannah took another step toward him. "I saw today that Enforcers get access to premium healthcare, and I wondered if…"

Chance pressed his teeth together, the muscles of his jaw flexing. "If maybe Andrew could have a normal life," he murmured through his fingers.

Hannah touched his arm. "Wouldn't it be worth it? You have what it takes, and applying is free. What could it hurt?"

"It's not that simple." Chance stood and ushered his plate to the basin. "I swore an oath to serve and protect this damn city.

Gotta be there for Benny, right? I mean, he and my crew, they need me."

Hannah balked, exasperated. "You don't owe this city anything else, Chance."

Chance dunked his plate in the soapy dish water.

"And Benny," she said, "God love him. Benny can take care of himself." She followed Chance's movements with hard eyes. "But we've got to think about what's best for us. Right?"

Chance didn't reply. Wouldn't know what to say if he did. He could feel the war inside him. Duty and family were two things that should never war. He dunked the plate again, bare hands still wiping at the already clean plate, his eyes stern, fixed, and far away.

CHAPTER EIGHT

Stepping from the musty, sweat-soaked warmth of the locker room in the bowels of NTPD South precinct, Chance emerged fresh from a turn in one of the hyper-efficient cleansing chambers. No matter how many times he did it, he never could quite get used to the feeling. Blasted from head to toe with Puri-Foam, peppered by hundreds of micro blasts of pressurized water, then whipped dry by turbo fans. The entire process lasted exactly fifty seconds and left a person feeling as though a hurricane had molested them.

It worked, though, and for only using a single pint of water, the process was a fast and economical way to get clean. Chance had to pay to use a much older, slower unit at home. Full body cleanings only happened at the PD after his morning workout.

Stepping onto the lift, he requested the second floor. With a chime, the tubular lift whooshed from the platform, a glass-cased bullet zipping upward past the investigative division. Chance watched rows upon rows of stone-faced detectives slip past. Like clones of the same person, each drank bad coffee and jabbed at their holo-displays, eyes rolling as the impossible load of unsolvable cases grew by the day.

Chance pulled his visor down and tabbed it on. He had a few minutes until it was time to hit the bricks with Benny, and he figured he'd waste it in the officers' lounge. Better that than continuing to think about his conversation with Hannah the night before. *Apply for the Enforcers? She can't be serious.*

Exiting the lift, Chance slipped into the narrow, sterile room occupied by an ancient coffeemaker and two old, stained fabric couches that left much to be desired in the way of comfort.

He sat down, shaking his head as another mandatory Enforcer ad started across his visor. When it finished, he swiped it to the side, the video disappearing into the little E emblem in the top right corner of his vision. On the left, a series of new messages awaited, stacked in a nice, neat row of envelope icons. Chance squinted at the messages. *Weird to have this many waiting.* He waved his hand over and selected the first one, opening it.

"Important," the message read aloud, "due to personal consumption levels, and by the authority of the Neo Terminus Water Board, you are hereby bumped up to a Tier Two user."

"What the hell is this?" Chance said.

"Furthermore," the message continued, "your monthly water access fee has increased to fifty-six Terminus coins."

Chance gasped. "That can't be right."

"This figure is non-negotiable. If you are unsatisfied, you may cancel your clean water availability at any time—"

Chance gave an angry swipe of his hand to close the message, a scowl deepening across his face. "We have to eat too, you bloodsucking slag-eaters."

He clicked on the second message.

"Important," the message began. "Due to personal consumption levels, and by the direction of the Neo Terminus Power Authority, you are hereby bumped up to a Tier Two user."

"No way," Chance said, a sense of shock spreading over him.

"Furthermore, your monthly power bill has increased to eighty-seven Terminus coins plus overages. This figure is non-negotiable—"

Chance snatched the visor from his face. He tried to swallow, his mouth dry. *This can't be happening.* Between the power and water, they couldn't manage this increase. Then came the other messages, the ones he had no desire to read, each of which began with the same ominous word. *Important.*

He and Hannah hadn't changed anything—at least, he didn't think they had. He reached down and slipped his visor back on, ignoring the stacked messages. He waved for his contacts and selected Hannah. There was a faint trill as the Neo Terminus broadcast network bridged.

"This broadcast call will cost four Terminus coins. Continue?"

"Just connect it already," Chance said, his irritation boiling over. He watched as four T's rolled off the balance of his account.

"Chance?" Hannah's face popped into view. The boardwalks of Water Town bustled behind her as she walked, Andrew swaddled against her chest.

"Sorry, I know it's expensive to call," Chance said, pacing the sterile officers' lounge. "Look, did you change our utility plans? Up usage for any reason? Anything?"

"No, but they're all going up," Hannah said. "Power, water, city inhabitant tax, rent, Glom network access fees, the list goes on. Why would they all hike at the same time?" Chance could hear the faint panic in her voice.

"I don't know. This is a first for me."

"Chance." She shook her head. "We can't afford our place if this happens."

"Did you message them?"

"They wouldn't answer me via message link," Hannah said. "I'm on my way now to stand in line at the power authority."

"All right." Chance rubbed the palms of his hands on his pants. "I've got to go on duty. They're strictly enforcing a no-leave policy right now. Keep me posted, okay?"

"Okay, baby."

The image feed went dark.

"Dammit," Chance said, an awful sickness forming in the pit

72

of his stomach. Hannah would get it worked out. She might hate conflict, but what she hated more was the feeling that she was being taken advantage of. Thanks to her grandfather, she was a bulldog when it came to these things. He flicked his visor up and glanced at the time. He had to gear up and hit the deployment bay if he didn't want to be late for his shift.

At lunch, two more messages appeared in his inbox. Chance ignored them, only noticing one was from Neo Terminus Waste Disposal and the other from a division of the Water Town's structural management division. Both messages were labeled *Important*. He swiped them away and tried to listen to what Benny was saying.

"Muggs would know, don't you think? He was in deep," Benny said.

"Your guy on the north side?" Chance said, looking over at his partner from the passenger seat of their patrol VTOL. "Big loads of the Feels, as I remember it." They'd pinched him for unlicensed dealing. "What about him?"

Benny frowned. "Have you been listening to me at all?"

"You said Muggs would know," Chance said.

"About what?" Benny pressed.

"I'm not playing your game, Benny."

"Muggs would know who's been pushing the fire-laced dope in the Straits," Benny said. "Where have you been, man?"

Chance shook his head and rubbed his chin. "Yeah, I guess we should check." He turned and watched as the iron-colored superstructures slid past outside the window. Massive towers of concrete and steel packed with thousands of people, hungry, sick, addicted, and desperate for any distraction that might give them some tiny reprieve from their miserable lives.

Not street legal, the Feels could only be acquired with a high-end prescription, something most people didn't have. A narcotic that heightened the senses, it gave a more extreme experience in conjunction with network immersion, especially when surfing sexual content. Junkies screwed with the dosage, endlessly searching for that perfect mix for extended pleasure. Most of the time, it backfired, resulting in NTPD uniforms investigating suspicious odors in the projects and finding dead junkies with flickering visors still covering their eyes, skin gray, and bodies frozen stiff in rigor mortis. The worst pushers mixed other chemicals or "fire" into their crop to make them more potent and maximize the bang for their buck—resulting in a wave of unprecedented drug-related deaths.

"Bet we could stir up some good leads," Benny said.

"Huh?" Chance said.

"Hey," Benny's look sliced through him. "I need you screwed down, man. You can't go total condition white out here unless you want an express trip to the morgue in a body bag. Come on, bro. Rookie stuff."

Chance shook his head. "I know, Benny. I'm sorry. I, uh… got a lot going on."

Benny's face softened. "You and Hannah okay?"

"Yeah, but…" Chance said. "Hey, let me ask you something. Have your bills gone up?"

"I guess they tick up a bit once in a while. Why?"

"Like major increases. Usage tier bump sort of stuff." Chance tried to conceal the worry in his voice.

"No." The questioning look on Benny's face deepened. "This happened to you?"

"Hannah's checking on it now, but it's not good. Don't know what we'll do if it sticks."

"Just a glitch in billing. You'll get it worked out…" Benny's voice trailed off. He didn't sound too sure.

For a while, they rode in silence, the bleak cityscape streaking past the rain-coated windows of their patrol vehicle as they passed over the intersection of Marx and Hamilton, a line wrapped around the block for one of The Glom tech distributors in North Havana Straits. Chance watched the people below fight over the limited supply of new units, the sealed white boxes popped and ripped open. A man dropped his shoulder into a groping woman and bowled her flat. He ran blindly, fingers clutched around the expensive plastic-wrapped iVisor dangling from its torn box. Those who could afford the things not only had to fork out the T's but then carry their prize out of there in one piece. In a mad rush to get something not everyone could have, shoppers often killed each other in the street.

Chance sucked his teeth and noted it in the daily log.

The little E icon in the top corner of his vision spun and flashed, the *Apply Now* button gleaming silver. The sheer madness of the public's addiction to technology overwhelmed Chance. The Enforcers and The Zone were at the center of it all. *Do I actually want to be a part of such a thing?* he thought.

A strobing projection lit up over the skyline, touting the next challenge to take place in The Zone. A contest called Asset Protection to be run by an Enforcer named Escalation, a tough-looking and well-scarred man in full armor with a tattered old school American flag on his shoulder. The giant virtual billboard flashed and showed images of Enforcers in combat within The Zone: *Exciting New Content LIVE Tonight—8 PM!*

"What do you think about them?" Chance said, jerking his chin in the advertisement's direction.

"Enforcers?" Benny chuckled. "They get paid, but no matter how much they act like it, they're not cops. Maybe they were once. Not anymore."

"Yeah," Chance said, his stomach tightening as the blip of a direct message popped up on his visor. It was Hannah.

No one will discuss it with me. We're in trouble, Chance. What should we do?

Chance waved the message to the side. The tingling of perspiration tickled his face and neck. The knot in his stomach doubled.

"You wanna check with Muggs?" Benny said. "You good with that?"

"Yeah," Chance said with a dismissive wave as Benny banked the Aeron patrol vehicle and swooped low beneath an elevated crosswalk and down toward the crowded street.

Chance bit his lip, staring at the little Enforcer icon still flashing silver, his hand raised, index finger hovering over the badge.

A text box popped up. *Are you sure you want to auto-upload personal records and career experience data as a part of the application process?*

"What the hell could it hurt?" Chance murmured, his finger clicking down.

In the dimly lit underground room, a hunched figure leaned forward in his chair. The surrounding air carried the thick, humid odor of sewer gas. Deep and rhythmic, an electronic looping beat of tech noir music thumped in the background. The little man popped an amber capsule into his mouth and took a sip from a canned soda covered in red Japanese script, long lank hair drooping before his face. He swallowed and raised the can again. The chubby-fingered hand froze, the can inches from his lips. Glistening dark eyes flicked back and forth across the stream of information rolling in midair before him. The figures cascaded and converged with other streams, torrents in a digital river.

"Stop."

The streams froze cold and crystalline blue. A sneer formed on his grizzled, pockmarked face. He pulled at a long salt and pepper goatee adorned with beads and rings.

"Scroll back. Quarter speed," he said, his voice squeaky dry.

In a slow, rolling feed, the interlocking streams of data reversed course. The spiraling numbers, identifiers, quirks, and data feed packets clumped together, bumping off each other and swirling in a digital mess of information indiscernible to the untrained eye.

"Stop."

The feed froze again. In the dim light, the man set his drink down and wiped his chin with the back of his sleeve. Brass buckles jangled on the leather straps that crisscrossed his one-piece body suit.

"Interesting..." Pale blue light glinted off a single silver canine tooth. "Project and magnify."

Cast through the air by an invisible hand, the data expanded to fill much of the room. Turning in his chair, his feet not touching the ground, the little man hopped to the floor. He muttered something to himself about destiny, slipped on a pair of haptic gloves, and spread his fingers wide. The data before him jostled and separated. He wiggled his fingers with rapid flicks, ones and zeros pushed aside in favor of a larger compressed file. Isolating it, he selected the floating packet. It shifted and flashed red.

Restricted Conglomerate file. Password?

"Amateurs," the little man chuckled.

His fingers flashed across a holographic keyboard. Decryption software engaged, thousands of passwords per second scrolled through the input box. A minute passed. The little man frowned.

"Upping your security, huh? We'll see." His fingers stroked the digital keys with feverish purpose.

With a blip, the file opened. The names of cops and their applications for the open Enforcer position spread across his field of view. The little man clucked his tongue. The names of seven candidates ranked out before him, according to the Conglomerate's desires, their qualifications and attributes, scores, and viability assessments laid bare. He scanned the list.

"Let's introduce a little chaos," he said, selecting the top name. "Rule follower." He flicked the name to the bottom of the list. He selected the next name. "Company man." Flicked it to the bottom. Without even reading the qualifications, he downgraded two more names. He raised his hand to flick the next name, but his finger paused in the air.

"Chance Griffin," he murmured, his interest growing. "Unpredictable, strong moral code, goes against the flow." The little man flicked the name to the top of the list. He cracked his knuckles and bared a wolfish grin. "Just what the system needs—a little unexpected recklessness."

The Muggs angle hadn't worked out. Chance had watched the poor slag-eater piss his pants as a much larger Benny forced him backward over a roach-infested countertop while spitting profanity-laden descriptions of what happens to trash like Muggs in the Blocks. The dealer-turned-pimp claimed he knew nothin' about nothin', all while shaking with full body tremors like a slag dog beaten one time too many. According to him, no one knew the origin of the fire-laced drugs, and Benny couldn't change that no matter how much he threatened Muggs about spending his best years in the Blocks getting gang raped by big Teddy and the boys.

Having grown tired of the game and not getting the answers they wanted, they'd left Muggs shaking in a stale puddle of his own piss and headed back to their patrol sector. The afternoon crawled by, with only a handful of South Precinct victims coming forward to pay their investigation deposit and file a report. If officers validated their complaint, they got their money back. If the allegations were bogus, the complainant forfeited their deposit. The practice adopted in recent years by the NTPD may not have felt ethical to Chance, but he couldn't deny it did a fantastic job of cutting down the number of nonessential emergency calls.

Minutes ticked into hours, the smoggy afternoon ushering in a hazy, neon-tinted night. Chance couldn't get the stupid Enforcer application off his mind. He told himself it wasn't a big deal, just an application. He'd dropped his gear in his locker at the station and given Benny a knuckle-clacking fist bump, promising he'd have a clearer head tomorrow.

The ride home at this time of day saw the elevated light rail train packed with scores of oblivious people absorbed in their visor content. Chance sat in a single seat wedged into the corner of the rail car next to an enormous pasty-skinned woman and a skeletal man of African descent with raised bumps covering his bony face. Chance only half-tried not to gawk at the woman. How could a person get so large with so little food to go around?

The thought made his stomach growl, and knowing he'd eaten a proper dinner last night, there was less than no chance tonight would be another winner. At least he'd be home on time. He fished through an inner pocket of his jacket, fingers closing on the squishy foil sus-packet. Chance tore the top off with his teeth and spat the foil out. The woman scowled through the shopping spree game on her Glom visor.

"Bottoms up," he toasted her with the sus-packet and squeezed the clear, jelly-like contents into his mouth, swallowing in one gulp. He smacked his lips and licked them with obnoxious flair. The pale woman shifted in the tight seat and tried to face the other way. Chance wiped his mouth with his sleeve, gave a cough, and swallowed again. The chemical sweet berry flavor lingered in the back of his throat.

Chance tried to get the thought of his bills out of his head, the reality of his situation a physical weight upon his shoulders. If their rates continued to skyrocket, or if they just couldn't get them adjusted, he and Hannah and the baby would be homeless by the next subscription billing cycle. There had to be some mistake—he needed to speak to the right adjuster.

Chance shook the thought from his mind. Nothing to be done about it tonight. Right now, he'd go home to Hannah and the baby at a decent hour for once. Tell her he'd applied for the Enforcer position like she'd suggested. Hannah and his boy deserved a better life, and he owed it to them to try.

A monotone automated voice announced the rail car's next stop as Water Town.

"Excuse me." Chance stood, working his way between the hypnotized, visor-clad riders on his way to the exit. Oblivious, some sat while the rest stood holding rails and grab loops, bodies jostling with the movement of the train, each person distant, lost in their own world.

"Excuse me," Chance said again as he reached a man in a high-end visor blocking the exit, dancing and swishing his hips. The train slowed to a stop, and with a ding, the doors slid back.

"*Water Town, Station One.*"

"Hey, look out, pal," Chance said a little louder.

The man wore his hair wet and slicked back. Turquoise sequins glittered on his jacket. He continued to jerk his body with spastic motions to an electronic beat he couldn't seem to master.

"*Last Call. Water Town, Station One.*"

Chance tried to squeeze past when the gyrating man jabbed at him with a knobby elbow.

"Watch it, Jack," the guy said, holding up two fingers side by side as some sort of warning.

Chance's palm flew up and caught the man on the cheek, slapping the strobing visor off his face. The man fumbled in shock, grabbing at his precious rental equipment as it hit the floor and cracked. The visor fluttered dark.

"You broke my rig! What the sputz!" he shrieked, his stupefied face inset with bulging, artificial lizard eyes.

"Welcome back to reality, dick head. Enjoy your stay." Chance stepped off the train as the doors closed.

The reptilian-faced man stood gawking, pawed in desperation at his fractured unit. No one else on the train even took notice as it lurched away from the platform toward the next station.

If this is what's left of the human race, we're doomed. Chance waved his palm across the checkpoint and exited the light rail station onto the Bilam Street boardwalk.

He performed a quick check of his T balance and angled into the night market off Kosveli Avenue, working his way through the shoulder-to-shoulder crowd. With its intersecting wooden boardwalk rows and alleys, the Water Town night market was a well-known hot spot for people looking for a little entertainment, some paid company, or a dose of the Feels. It also happened to be one of the most reliable places to find hard-to-get items. Everything from the latest net surfing Glom tech to private food stashes and black market weapons—if a person had the T's and knew where to look.

Ahead, groups of young people dressed in high-collared leather jackets and sporting crystalline-styled hair lounged at the edge of a nape vapor bar passing a hookah straw. They eyed Chance as he walked by, smoke curling from glossy pursed lips, visors flashing the pregame show for tonight's Zone livestream.

"What's the rush, bay-bee?" A topless non-binary escort stroked his arm as he passed. A flashing sign above read *Bonzo's Hot House*. "Where you going?" the escort asked. "Not interested in the Feel-boosted ride of your life?"

"Nope." Chance pulled his arm free of the escort's spidery fingers. "Thanks anyway."

He passed a man with his hat pulled down over his face, hoisting a large, unmarked box overflowing with foil sus-packets. "Half-price gels. Get them before they're gone!" He shouted to the masses snaking through the cramped alley bathed in steam and flashing neon.

"Stolen," Chance muttered to himself, "definitely."

He slowed his gait, squeezing by a man pushing knock-off Google brand electric unicycles. At the intersection of two alleys, a withered old lady with a simple wooden cart sold small bouquets in an assortment of vibrant colors. Real flowers were tough to find and made no sense with the cost of water what it was. Still, you couldn't put a price on some gestures. The sage woman turned to him, her pleasant face weathered with deep creases.

"Good evening, young sir."

"Hello," Chance smiled. "How much for three real roses?"

CHAPTER NINE

The distinct chime stirred Chance from a troubled sleep.
He rolled onto his shoulder and squinted at the blurry
floating clock projection. He blinked a few times and strained to
see the time: 02:57 a.m. His mind felt thick, clouded, chugging
along at quarter speed like a river of heavy-weight oil. He sunk his
fingers deep into the folds of the comforter.

The chime sounded a second time, the jingle startling in the
dark warmth of the bedroom. He fumbled his visor out of the
charging station on the nightstand.

"Who's messaging at three in the morning?" Hannah groaned.

"If it's more subscription notices, I'm gonna lose it," Chance
said.

It chimed again. "*Urgent message waiting,*" the sterile voice said.

"Get it before it wakes Andrew," Hannah said.

"Okay, yeah…" Chance muted the alerts, resting the NTPD-
issued tactical lenses in his chest. He took a moment to sit up and
get his bearings, rubbing at his face. The apartment was dark and
silent, the broken yellow night light flickering from Andrew's room
and into the hall. Outside, the sounds of people in the street below
and the constant strobing of gas-lit neon persisted even at this hour.

"What was it?" Hannah murmured, her face still buried in the
pillow.

Chance studied the illuminated lenses glowing a soft blue in
his lap and placed them over his eyes. The left side of the screen

showed a row of unopened envelopes. The first arrived at midnight, followed by an identical message marked *Urgent* every fifteen minutes since. Chance scowled; so many urgent messages they'd overridden his do-not-disturb sleep settings. He regarded the stacked messages, total dread returning at the thought of additional cost increases. A sensation not unlike drowning pushed over him, and he sucked in a breath in response. There was no part of him that wanted to open any of them.

Chance held his hand over the top message and watched as the other messages faded.

"Weird," he murmured. Hannah didn't stir.

He clicked on the message, which unfolded and opened across his field of vision.

Officer Chance Griffin,

Thank you for your application to become an Enforcer. Your data package, background records, training, and experience show you have the right qualifications to continue with the application process. Today at 0800, be in the lobby of the Conglomerate headquarters located at 7000 Valkyrie Highway East in Silver City. You are administratively relieved of duty for the duration of your application process, and I granted your wrist chip basic light rail access to Silver City. We look forward to seeing you first thing in the morning to further evaluate if you have what it takes to be an Enforcer.

Kind Regards,

Katrina Avery,
Administrative Assistant to Director Kess
United Conglomerate Headquarters
7000 Valkyrie Highway East
Silver City, Neo Terminus

Chance jumped to his feet, the bed sheets flung off to the side. He read the message again. It was some sort of sick joke. Benny was screwing with him. He checked the sender's address.

Everything appeared legit. *I didn't want this, did I?* he thought. *So why is my heart racing?*

He looked at his wife, dozing in the bed, the rare live roses on the nightstand next to her. He'd come straight home, given her the real flowers, told her how much he loved her and Andrew and that for them, he'd applied for the Enforcer position. She'd flung her arms around his neck, flashed that million-dollar smile of hers, and kissed him slow, a hint of what waited for him once the baby went down for the night. *No matter how it goes*, that kiss said, *I'm behind you, my love.*

"Hannah," Chance said, still standing by the bed.

"Mmmhh."

"Hannah." He crawled across the bed until he was over her.

"What?" she said, faint irritation in her groggy voice.

"The message," he said, pausing, "they want me to come to Silver City for the next phase of the application process."

"What?"

"The Enforcer position. They want me to interview."

Hannah jerked her head up. She stared at him with unseeing eyes for a moment and slapped his shoulder. "Chance, that's not funny! It's three in the morning."

"I know!" he whispered.

"You only applied yesterday. They wouldn't have already... Chance, if this is a joke, I swear—"

"They sent a message. Look at it."

She pulled off his visor and squinted at the dim screen.

"It came from The Glom's headquarters," Chance said. "I'm dead serious. I'm gonna go. I mean, I should, right?"

"Chance?" She pushed up and grabbed him. "Oh my God, Chance! You're gonna go, right?"

"That's what I said." He chuckled as his wife pulled him down to where he could smell the sleepy scent lingering around her neck. Here they had a chance at something better. Something worth living for. Maybe it wasn't what he wanted for himself, but if it meant Andrew could get the care he needed, he had to try.

Hannah squeezed him closer, and they lay laughing in disbelief until, with agitated whimpers, the baby began to cry.

Chance checked the duty roster one last time. He scanned the names of his squad, each displaying the word *Active* next to them in his visor. Then he checked his status. Next to his name was a single word: *Admin.*

Chance checked the time again as he waited for the light rail train that would take him into the Silver City sector of Neo-Terminus. Benny would be on duty by now. Chance wanted to call his partner but decided against it. Maybe he'd shoot a quick, direct message to let Benny know he wasn't dead. As if in response to his thoughts, a message from Benny popped into his visor feed.

Hey brother, everything good?

Chance smirked and fired back a reply. *Admin detail today. I'll tell you later. Code four.*

Roger. Be safe, came Benny's instant reply, a clear understanding of *code four* as cop-speak for *I'm okay.*

Chance approached the graffiti-covered train as it slid into the station from Havana Straits, the doors whipping back with a hiss. Chance boarded the dingy train with the other self-absorbed commuters and held on as the doors *shunked* closed and the train accelerated away from the station.

At the final rail stop on the border of Water Town and Sky Rise, Chance disembarked and watched as everyone on the train went to the right and down the ramp toward the street level, where roads and avenues led out toward Commerce and Athens on the outer edge of the sector. Dressed in his best suit and tie, which he'd steamed in the bathing chamber to remove the dust, Chance felt out of place among the throngs of distracted and disheveled commuters.

He eyed the sector checkpoint, a gleaming silver archway set into the northern barrier, a portal into the other world of Silver City and Sky Rise. Chance surveyed the giant wall that ended on one side against The Zone and, on the other, ran all the way to the outer wall, miles away. Glom troopers wearing assault armor and touting light-action rail carbines manned the barrier. Couldn't take any chances with the riff-raff who wanted into Sky Rise or Silver City.

A scream. Chance watched as a young, unkempt man ran for the opening.

"Ah, dammit," Chance swore under his breath. "Don't do it, man."

The shouting guards tried to grab the young man but missed as he ran for the gap. He'd made it. Home free. Free to live a richer, fuller life on the other side of the barricade.

A rifle shot rang out. Chance flinched at the report. The round punched through the meat of the young man's chest, flaying him open in a spray of red. He tumbled, his body slid to a stop, and a crimson fan spread from beneath his corpse. The shooter, a Glom trooper up on the barricade, waved the all-clear. Chance watched as The Glom troopers callously bumped fists.

Chance approached the security checkpoint, a growing sense of anxiety budding in his chest. *Have to be careful around these jumpy slag-eaters. One wrong move could mean a bullet in the back.*

He'd never in his life set foot in the Sky Rise or Silver City sectors, as they required special clearance. Clearance he now possessed. At least, he hoped, or else he was about to make a gigantic fool of himself.

"State your purpose, citizen," said the faceless trooper in black tactical armor, his gold visor catching the early morning sun.

"Officer Chance Griffin, NTPD. I'm expected for an appointment inside the Silver City sector, and I am legally armed."

The trooper raised his rifle on Chance as another approached. Chance lifted his hands in response.

The other trooper held a scanner toward Chance's raised right palm. There was a *click-bleep*, and the red light on the scanner turned green. "You're granted temporary access. Just remember," the trooper said, "NTPD has no jurisdiction in Sky Rise or Silver City."

"I'm aware of that," Chance said.

"You will relinquish your weapon and badge at this station," the trooper holding the rifle said. "We will give you an e-claim ticket for it. You may pick your property back up when you return through the checkpoint. Understood?"

"Gentlemen, this is Neo-Terminus," Chance said. "I don't go anywhere without a gun."

He felt more than saw the trooper on his left, the one with the rifle aimed at his chest, tense.

"I'm a legally armed peace officer," Chance added.

"Relinquish your weapon. It's not a request," the trooper with the scanner said, his voice lowering. "You can come through the checkpoint unarmed, or you can go back to whatever rat-hole you crawled out of."

Chance felt his muscles tighten and resisted the urge to see how well that helmet protected its wearer from blunt force trauma. He pressed his teeth together.

"Just do your job, fella. And try to keep it professional while you're at it," Chance said.

"Sure thing, *Officer Griffin*." The trooper hung the scanner on a hook on the wall, stepped forward, and pulled Chance's MVX from its holster in the small of his back, then held out his hand. Chance placed his badge in the trooper's gloved palm. "Any other weapons?" the trooper asked.

"A folding knife clipped to my right front pocket."

The trooper unclipped the knife and turned, placing the items in a lock box along the wall.

"Proceed through the gate. No funny business," the trooper with the rifle said.

"You got it." Chance shook his head. As he stepped beneath the archway, green lasers zipped left to right across his body, bathing him from head to toe. There was another chime, and he passed through, down a length of tunnel. For an instant, Chance felt as though he was stepping off a spaceship onto some newly colonized world. He stopped on the other side of the barrier. The Sky Rise citizens bustled past, dressed in expensive tailored jackets and real leather shoes, colorful dresses, and dapper business suits. Chance had the sudden feeling his best suit looked like something hastily pulled from the dirty laundry. *Maybe no one will notice*, he thought.

Another light rail train approached, gleaming silver, untouched by graffiti. Chance realized his mouth was open, a kid watching a parade. He entered the light rail and took a seat along the window, hoping to squirrel himself away into an unnoticed section of the train. As the car shot forward into the heart of Sky Rise, towering condominiums rose into the air on either side of the tracks. Below on the street, people walked in orderly rows, their high-end visors down over their noses. Gone were the dark and grungy streets he called home, replaced by a world of shimmering steel and glass. Vividly colored projections filled the sky, advertising the newest cologne, fancy designer shoes, Glom visors, or the latest in VTOL hover car technology.

"What the hell is all this?" Chance said, a little louder than he intended, eliciting a few dirty looks from the other passengers. A woman with a stiff plastic face stood and changed to a seat farther away. Another offered a polite smile and turned away. Chance directed his attention back to the alien landscape outside the window.

The glistening cityscape passed in a blur, the light rail entering and departing new stations, each as clean and tidy as the last. At each stop, more well-dressed people boarded, glancing the length of the train and, upon seeing him, made for the opposite end of the car.

"Final stop. Silver City. All passengers must depart the train at this station," the automated voice said across the length of the rail car. The remaining passengers stood and waited their turn to exit the doors. Chance stood for a moment and waited for the flawless Sky Rise citizens to go before following. No need to offend everyone's delicate sensibilities.

Clear of the train, Chance exited from under the pristine glass ceilings of the station, out onto the street level where VTOLs cruised in marked lanes above, and electric smart cars and bikes self-piloted surface streets in perfect synchronization.

"Clear the way, asshole." A sharp-dressed man shoved past with a digitally encoded briefcase.

"Sorry," Chance said, stepping back from the bustling crowd.

He checked his watch. 7:50 a.m. He needed to find the Conglomerate's headquarters and fast. Chance flicked his visor down and started a basic search. "Glom Headquarters. 7000 Valkyrie Highway East."

Address not found flashed across his screen.

"Of course it isn't," Chance said and pulled his visor off, stowing it in his bag. He scanned the distracted commuters walking past. Raising his hand, he tried to get the attention of an attractive woman who didn't seem too invested in her visor's content. "Excuse me? Miss?"

She glared at him. "What?"

"Could you tell me where the Conglomerate's headquarters are?" Chance said.

She scowled. "Are you stupid or something?"

"Do you know where it is or not?" Chance frowned.

She turned her attention across the six-lane road, swamped with electric street vehicles, toward a massive spike of obsidian glass. "You're right in front of it, dumbass," she said and spun her back to him, high heels stabbing at the concrete as she walked away. "No," she said to someone on the other end of her call. "Some low-class jerkoff thinks he's gonna talk to me."

"Rich people," Chance said. He crossed the street at a jog, dodging an array of honking single-passenger smart vehicles and bullet-shaped auto-bikes as he went.

On the other side of the traffic, he stopped before a cobblestone drive flowing through a massive energy field gate. Beyond, a black thorn of steel and glass thrust up from the earth and towered into the sky. A large marble sign read: *Unified Conglomerate Corporate Headquarters.*

Chance approached the security troopers manning the gate. These men wore the same armor as those who'd screened him through into Sky Rise. The only difference was a gold stripe running down the left side of their armor from the top of the helmet to the hip.

One of the troopers stepped forward. "State your purpose."

"Chance Griffin. Here to interview for the Enforcer position." Chance held out his palm.

The trooper scanned it and gave a curt nod. "General access areas only. You may proceed."

The glowing white barrier split in the center, opening wide enough for him to pass through. Chance grunted his thanks and marched up to the entrance. A thin doorman in a double-breasted suit and a hawkish nose opened the giant brass door for him. Entering the main atrium, with its angled high ceilings and jet-black, polished marble floors, Chance felt a sense of awe at the place. For such a massive, perfectly kept space, it was empty except for the long front desk at the end of a sea of polished marble. In the center of the floor was an emblem inset in gold: a spike-like tower surrounded by a ring of golden stars that twinkled in the natural light.

"Sir? May I help you?" a voice called out to him from across the open lobby.

"Oh," Chance said, embarrassed at his child-like distraction. He met the curious gaze of a highly attractive woman at the front desk. "I'm here for an interview." Chance crossed the open space, his worn dress shoes slipping on the flawless waxed floor.

"Yes?" With a flick of her wrist, a digital display opened up before her. "Administration? Finance?"

"Ah." Chance felt a sudden heat beneath his collar. He gave it a little tug. "Enforcer."

"Oh?" She stopped and drank him in from head to toe, a little smile forming on her perfect glistening lips. "Okay. Name?"

"Chance Griffin," he said, smoothing the lapels of his jacket and feeling more than a little like a bum.

"Yes, Mr. Griffin. I have you right here." She picked up a small tubular wand. "Raise your chipped palm."

Chance held up his right hand, and the woman swung the wand over it. A *blip* sounded from her terminal. Chance lowered his hand when the woman flicked the wand back up.

"Keep your hand raised, please, for the liability waiver."

Chance lifted his palm back up.

"You understand interviewing for the Enforcer position is a physically rigorous process," she recited, "which may involve serious physical injury and even death? And you agree to hold The Unified Conglomerate harmless in the event such injury or death befalls you?"

"Uh," Chance said, a laugh escaping him, "it's just an interview, right?"

"No, Mr. Griffin." Her face betrayed no emotion. "It is not just an interview. It is a selection process."

"Oh, right," Chance said, his face tingling hot.

"Do you understand you assume all risk until the selection process is completed?"

Chance squared his shoulders, the faintest sense of nervous tension tightening in his gut. "Yes, I understand."

Another blip from her console. "Good. I have sent the acknowledged waiver and a copy of the detailed agreement to you via mail message." She pointed to an open door behind her, which Chance hadn't noticed until now. "Please proceed through the door to outfitting and armory."

"Armory?" Chance said.

"Correct." She gestured with an open hand toward the door. "Time is short, Mr. Griffin."

The lightless portal in the wall gaped open like a black-throated mouth waiting to swallow him. Chance gave one last look at the pristine atrium and the silent, doll-faced receptionist.

He blew out a nervous chuckle, shook his head, and disappeared into the shadowed doorway.

CHAPTER TEN

ubmit Test. Confirm?

SChance tabbed the Confirm key at the digital terminal, rubbing his eyes, sore from staring at the stark white screen too long.

A new message box flashed on the monitor overhead. *Thank you. Please take a five-minute break. You will want to eat something.*

Chance rose from the padded chair and stretched his arms over his head, groaning as he held the position. His stomach growled. Six hours of non-stop randomized testing. Eyesight tests, hearing tests, mental agility and aptitude tests, mathematics, and word problems. They had given him tactical dilemmas to solve and conducted live shooting drills to determine accuracy and weapons handling skills, dexterity tests, and raw strength and endurance assessments. He'd fought his way through a gauntlet of trained fighters, as well as demonstrate VTOL and land vehicle driving proficiency. He'd even tread water for ten minutes in full clothing. If it was a testable skill, he'd done it.

He rubbed his clammy palms on the one-piece, skin-tight black body suit. Its only accent was a vertical gold stripe down the left breast. He twisted his body, still getting a feel for the bizarre garment. The fabric was strange; slick yet grippy, tight yet comfortable. The thing shifted as he moved, loosening and tightening around various muscle groups as though it possessed a life of its own. It felt functional and supportive but was also a little unnerving in its constant adaptations.

Stepping to a nearby table, he grabbed a sus-packet from a box, tore the top from it, and squeezed the artificially sweet jelly into his mouth. He chased it with a bottle of water, shunting the trash into a nearby waste chute. Glancing around the barren room, Chance pulled his sleek black tactical visor from his face and eyed the smoked lenses. It was at least several generations newer than the equipment the PD issued him. He'd ditched his visor along with the rest of his belongings in a biometric locker prior to testing. For a moment, he thought it strange he'd yet to see any other applicants.

"*Please put your visor back on and prepare to receive further testing instructions,*" a monotone voice stated from somewhere above.

"Right," Chance said, slipping the visor back on and clapping his hands together. "What now? Want to see how fast I can get to the end of a maze. I'm awesome at mazes."

A door that Chance hadn't noticed slid open in the wall to his left. He stood staring at the open hole. Across the room, another panel slid back.

Chance eyed the two openings. "Pick one, I guess?"

When he received no reply, Chance turned and proceeded through the door on his right, his gait relaxed. As he passed into the darkness, he felt the room open up around him. Behind him, the door slid shut, leaving him in the dark. A tiny blue bulb set in the ceiling high above offered only the faintest light, a lonely star casting its pitiful glow into a sea of endless black. Chance strained his eyes against the low light of the room, able to make out little of his surroundings.

The light grew brighter overhead, causing him to blink and cover his face. He squinted, encased in a circle of light. Another bulb snapped on a few paces ahead, followed by another, creating a luminescent corridor through the darkness.

Chance's surprise grew at just how spacious the room was.

"Chance Griffin, please proceed to the far wall and get outfitted for the final phase of your assessment."

Chance did as directed and made his way through the pools of light to the far wall. Inset into ledges of staggered trays sat various equipment, all of it tactical black. His eyes roved over the items nestled in their various cutouts. Some, a blast baton and stun grenades, he recognized as standard-issue police gear. Other things he couldn't say he recognized at all.

"For the final phase of your assessment, you will conduct an information-gathering reconnaissance mission off-site. Equip yourself with the tools you prefer and exit through to the VTOL bay to your left," the voice said.

"Any help with the stuff I'm not familiar with?" Chance said.

"Wave your hand over each item to see a brief description and directions for usage. You have ten minutes until deployment," the sterile voice said.

Chance waved his hand over the sleek black armor on the ledge before him. Text displayed in his visor:

Xian-Xi Tactical Quick React Recon Armor and Helmet. Light armor protection for maximum mobility.

"All right," Chance said, picking up the chest rig and sliding it over his head. He snapped it together and pulled the open-face helmet into place above his visor, clicking the chin strap beneath his jaw. He checked the other items, waving his hand over them.

Volsog Tactical Blast Baton, Balien Systems Stun Grenade, 50x Digital Binoculars, Danson Assault Gloves with Carbon Fiber Knuckles, and Matching Knee Pads.

"Fantastic," Chance said, grabbing one of each except for the blast baton, which he passed over, and the stun grenades, which he grabbed all three. Geared up, Chance turned as something familiar caught his eye. He waved his hand over it.

Grenada Industries Electro-Stream XD Less Lethal Shock Rifle.

"Now this I know," Chance said with relief. He picked up the shock rifle, the same kind he and Benny carried in their patrol VTOL—except this XD model meant extra distance on the effective range. Folding the rifle in half, he clipped it to his gear and headed through the open door and out onto a VTOL launch pad.

Chance stopped at the edge of the platform. The wind whipped at his clothes, and the sky beyond spun hazy clouds against the threatening greenish hue of the horizon. In the center of the launch platform sat a sleek Argus VTOL, engines idling with blue fire.

"Board the VTOL and strap in," the sterile voice said, now coming through his visor audio.

"Roger that," Chance said and made for the unmarked black VTOL. Instead of wing doors, this model had open sides like the old war helicopters he'd seen in history reels. A massive dual-drum-fed machine gun sat inset in the center of the door. "We're going to war, boys," Chance joked nervously. Loading up, he noticed the odd sense of excitement that filled him.

The pilot, clad in an all-black flight suit, visor, and helmet, gave him the thumbs up. Chance reciprocated and felt the thrusters engage beneath him. He snapped the strap harness in over his head as the VTOL rose from the platform and dropped over the edge, the smog-covered city opening up before him in a muted wash of bluish-gray haze and endless neon lights. Chance gave a whoop as the VTOL leveled out and headed west.

Beneath the soaring VTOL, the towering superstructures of Silver City fell away, the landscape opening to broad rolling fields as far as the eye could see. Chance had never seen the vastness of Hayseed, The Glom-controlled agricultural sector. Among the shoots of synth grain, fields of vegetables, and row upon row of fruit trees, sentry towers watched over the landscape as drone bots hovered back and forth, tending, pruning, and harvesting the crop.

"Where does all this food go?" Chance murmured.

"Your mission is as follows," the monotone voice said, interrupting his thoughts, a mini-map unfolding across his tactical visor. "You will deploy in The Slags, along the easternmost edge of the sector."

"Uh, what?" Chance said, his excitement souring. "The Slags?"

"Please hold questions until the end," the voice responded.

Chance listened to the brief, which detailed the route he would take to the target area. All the while, a creeping sense of dread grew inside him. All the toxic garbage and stinking refuse, transported from across Neo-Terminus, got dumped in The Slags. The people who lived there, known as Slaggers, carved out homesteads amidst piles of rot and ruin. In this sector, the NTPD had little presence or desire to police a dirty and recluse segment of the populace who only wanted to be left alone. The result was a general hostility from those who lived there toward anyone and anything perceived as authoritative or an outsider.

And he was about to drop in alone with only non-lethal weapons.

"Upon arriving on foot in the target's vicinity," the voice continued, "you will attempt to locate this man—Markus Branko." An image of a man with olive skin and strong dark features floated over the map. "Branko has been captured by a warlord in this sector and is now held against his will. Your mission is to confirm his position and provide any information you can. Do not allow yourself to be compromised. There is no support."

"Who is this guy?" Chance said.

"That information is not available."

"How much time do I have?" Chance said.

"Until sundown. Approximately four hours. If you need assistance, call for Control."

Chance leaned back against the contoured seat and exhaled. "Perfect."

As the VTOL crossed the massive concrete wall dividing Hayseed from The Slags, Chance watched two Slaggers rappel from the wall on the Hayseed side. They unclipped from their fraying lines and ran together, dirty fingers stuffing bunches of genetically engineered super fruit into their backpacks. A rifle shot rang out and one of the two, a woman, toppled into the dirt, clutching at a mortal wound in her chest. The other, a teenage male, groped at her with a cry before turning and running for the wall. The tower sentry worked the action on his rifle, taking aim again as the male stopped, bulbous purple fruit slipping from his fingers and bouncing on the dirt as he raised his hands. A second rifle shot cracked, and the young man spun, crumpling against the base of the wall.

"Holy hell," Chance said, looking toward the pilot, who seemed to have seen nothing. "They executed them for that...?" A sour feeling settled in the pit of his stomach.

"One minute," the voice in his visor said. "Stand ready to deploy."

Chance knew a justifiable killing when he saw it. He'd done it enough times himself. This wasn't that. This was murder. He struggled to put the inhumanity of it from his mind as the VTOL crossed the wall into The Slags. He checked his gear one last time and, feeling everything in place, turned his eyes out toward the thousands of trash hills piled together like mountain ranges. Hovering back and forth above, armored trash barges came and went from the other sectors of the city, dumping their payloads and returning for more.

Chance unclipped his harness as the VTOL dropped into a valley between two towering garbage mountains.

"Check your heading and get moving. They're already looking for you," the voice said.

"Outstanding," Chance said, unbuckling his harness and grabbing the handle at the edge of the door. He unclipped the Electro-stream rifle, snapped it open, and held it ready.

The pilot slowed and leveled out. Without further direction, Chance jumped out onto the ground. The VTOL launched back into the air, small-arms fire pinging off the hull.

Chance ducked low as a group of half a dozen Slaggers wrapped in rags climbed into view atop one of the shifting piles. He scrambled behind an old, rusted freezer unit, then held his breath when a single dented tin can nudged loose from the heap and bounced downhill. The Slaggers' attention shifted; one of them pointed in his direction. Chance cursed himself, stayed low, and pinged the GPS route on his visor again. He waited for a beat, then rose ever so slowly and peeked at the position of the Slaggers.

"Damn," Chance said and ducked back behind the cooler. His mind whirled with options, none of which seemed good, as the Slaggers picked their way down the garbage slope toward him.

More than an hour of ducking and hiding in junk-filled nooks passed before Chance made it within range of the target area. The small squad of Slaggers tracked him for a while, diverting when they became entangled in a heated dispute with a band of junk traders. Chance checked his six for threats one last time and crawled to the top of a pile of rusted debris, where he found an unobstructed view.

"Control, do you read?"

"Go ahead," the voice said.

"What exactly am I looking for?" Chance whispered.

"A dwelling carved into the land," the voice said, direct and without inflection. "Bigger than the rest."

"I wish you were RITA," Chance said as he retrieved his binoculars.

"I don't understand."

"I know you don't," Chance muttered.

Chance hunkered low, scanning. Tire fires burned, sending up coils of black smoke to the smog-shrouded sky. Carrion birds circled. The sour smell of rotten things filled his nose. There among the lanes and alleys below, Slaggers wearing soiled, crudely patched garments of wrapped rags meandered between piles of waste, discarded things that probably worked just fine. Consumerism at its finest.

A howl and a yip to his left caught his attention. He swiveled his torso, scanning the endless mountains of debris. A second yip sounded, followed by a host of others. A pack of eight or nine mangy slag dogs navigated one of the piles, scavenging for something to eat. All of them sported bony ribs, hairless coats, and blood-crusted ears, the markings of the slag disease that now mysteriously ravaged the canine species. They ranged in size from medium-bodied to much larger, and each held a look of hungry desperation in their dark eyes. In a pack this size, it was a dangerous combination. Chance waited for them to move on before he dared to do more than breathe.

Clouds billowed from one end of the horizon to the other, a chalky ribbon of carbon that obscured and scattered the burnt orange rays of a late afternoon sun. Chance had about two hours to surveil his target and call for extraction. No part of him wanted to be stranded in this place after sundown.

A cry, distant but human, caught his attention, audible beyond the constant clanking tumble of trash dumped from the armored barges. Chance adjusted his focus. There, nestled into the base of one of the larger garbage mounds, an opening lit with the soft glow of a torch. He could see a short way into the flickering gloom beyond the entrance. He checked his binoculars, switched the magnification from 25x to 50x, and looked again. Shadows danced in the opening just out of reach of the torch's light. Another muffled cry. Chance rolled the binoculars over and pressed a button marked UV in blue.

The image through the glass flickered, the tint and color

changing to digital. He raised the binos to his eyes. In an instant, the interior of a makeshift room sprang to life, a digital blue outlining the space. Chance watched as two rough-looking Slaggers opened an ancient hatch of rust-pitted steel set in the earth. When they flipped it back, Chance saw a man's head rise, hair matted with blood, his face drawn and beaten. The man clasped his hands in a futile plea for mercy. It was the target, Branko. One of the dingy Slaggers, a man as wide as he was tall, jerked his pants down to urinate on the captive, laughing as he did.

"Control, I've got eyes on Branko," Chance said, activating his commlink. "They're holding him at the location described. I've got eyes on two Slaggers. There may be others. Branko is not in good shape."

"Control copy," the voice said. "Your directives have changed. Rescue Branko and escape to the designated rally point for extraction."

"Wait, hold on. I'm not equipped for that," Chance said. He watched as the mission priority in the top left of his visor changed to *Rescue Branko*, followed by a circle on the map two-hundred yards to the south marked Extraction Point.

"Control, I'm not equipped for a rescue op," Chance said. "Call NTPD for that."

Silence greeted him.

"Son of a bitch." Chance groaned. "You've got to be kidding me. Job interview, my ass…"

In the space beneath the large trash mound, the burly, rag-draped Slaggers slammed the hatch down on Branko and secured it with a steel bar. They meandered from view, their grunts of laughter ebbing from the shadows beyond the dimly lit space. Chance checked his gear again and, with a curse, crawled back down the junk heap, navigating toward the flickering entrance to Branko's prison cell. Chance stopped to take cover any time some hungry Slagger shambled past below, searching the piles of rubble for something useful, valuable, or just edible.

Reaching the larger mound, Chance approached the entrance and listened for activity. There was no sound from inside except the wretched moans of Branko from the hole. Raising his shock rifle, Chance stepped into the dimly lit space. He snapped left, knelt, and collapsed his field of fire to the right. Negative contact. Chance scanned the two tunnels branching off into the earth from the main room.

He took a lungful of the putrid air, a mixture of decomposition, human waste, and chemical fumes. Chance stifled a gag reflex and stepped to the hatch in the floor, pulling the bar free and easing it open. The beaten, terrified Branko moaned through a rag tied between his teeth, crouching in the shallow hole.

"Shhh." Chance held a finger to his lips. "I'm here to get you out."

Branko's eyes grew wild with fear, his head shaking.

"Come on, quick," Chance said, motioning to the captive.

Branko pinched his eyes shut and slunk farther down the hole.

"What the hell's the matter with—" Chance said, the words dying in his throat. A presence darkened the torch behind him. He spun. The steel bar caught him square across the cheek and sent him sprawling.

Chance writhed on the dirt floor. He clutched at his face, eyes wild and unseeing.

"Pull the other one." The big Slagger growled as two more in soiled jackets and ragged pants entered the room from an adjacent tunnel.

Chance tried to stand, blood streaming from a gash on his face. His jaw felt wrong, like a broken spur of gnarled bone twisted into his skull. The heavy Slagger loomed over him, pulled him to his feet, and snaked the steel bar across the side of his neck. With a vicious jerk, he pinched Chance's neck between the steel bar and his own thick chest. Chance scrabbled at the bar, gasping, the blood flow to his brain slowing. Darkness crept in from the corners of his vision.

They dragged Branko from the hole and forced him to his knees. One of them drew a crude single-shot zip pistol from his belt and pushed it to Branko's head, pulling the simple spring-loaded firing pin back with the other hand like the drawing of a slingshot.

"No! Please!" Branko cried.

The sharp crack of the pipe gun fired in the closeness of the confined space and sent a jolt of electricity screaming into Chance's muscles. A gout of blood shot up from the top of Branko's head as he toppled over, thrashing. Chance grabbed for the bar across his throat, the pressure in his head unbearable. He groaned and pushed away but couldn't match the strength of the big Slagger.

"Hey, hey—you dumb slag-eaters! Who's shooting? What's going on?" A fourth man, better dressed but not clean, stormed in from one of the tunnels.

"This one was tryin' to escape," the pipe-pistol Slagger said, motioning to Branko's convulsing corpse.

"We didn't have a choice," another Slagger said.

"The plan was to ransom him, you idiot," the lead Slagger barked at his men.

"We can ransom this guy instead." Pipe Pistol waved the simple but lethal weapon at Chance.

All three turned to the big Slagger pinning Chance by the neck.

"Well? Put him out already," the guy in charge growled.

A sudden vice-like clamp of pressure across his neck caused Chance's knees to give out. He tried to scream, a gurgle escaping his lips instead. From the corners of his vision, blackness swarmed and filled his head with numbing thoughts of death. Thoughts of Andrew and Hannah. Alone. He clawed and spat, trying to resist the dark descent, but the void pushed across his eyes, blocking out sight and sound until even his own panicked gasps ceased amidst the smothering warmth.

CHAPTER ELEVEN

"**T**hat's it. Pay up, pretty boy," the man with pale dagger-sharp eyes and a heavy cleft in his chin said. He popped another candied pecan into his mouth and leaned back, chewing, his well-muscled arms draped across the cushions of the supple black leather couch in the Enforcer's lounge. "It's over, Jessie."

Jessie Fullard, reclining on an identical couch, shook his head with a bleached white smile. "I told you, Rip. It ain't over till it's over."

Rip narrowed his eyes and pointed to the room-spanning holo-projection next to a shaded window, which looked down from the fifty-first floor of the Conglomerate Corporate Headquarters.

"You mean to tell me it's not over for Branko?" Rip jabbed his finger at the image on the screen, projected live by a micro stealth drone just outside the Slag King's lair. The drone, no larger than a bumblebee, pivoted, scanning the mountains of piled trash and back to the torch-lit cave. It swooped low, whisper quiet, and entered the dimly illuminated interior. Branko's lifeless body lay on the floor in a large pool of blood.

"Well, look at him." Rip crossed his arms. If looks could kill, Jessie would be six feet under.

Jessie, a lean but well-built man with perfectly styled hair, cocked his head at the forever serious Rip LeReux.

"Fine." Jessie waved open his coin wallet with a flick of his wrist.

"Project it. I want to watch," Rip said.

"Picky, picky." Jessie cast his visor display to the big screen. Tabbing with little dips of his index finger, he selected LaRoux from the scroll-down list, entered the agreed upon bet of five hundred T's, and initiated the transfer. "Happy now?"

The image onscreen shifted back to the Slag King's lair.

"I see you've got me on auto-fill," Rip said with a smirk. "That's good because you're going to lose a lot more money to me before this is all over. In fact, go ahead and pay me for this Griffin kid as well."

"No." Jessie hugged his arms across his chest, pectorals and biceps bulging in response. "I told you. It's not over yet."

Rip looked around the room, trying to find an audience. "How much more can this poor sap take?" He waved again at the live feed, where the Slaggers dragged a limp Chance to a twisted junk chair and lashed him to it. They unhooked his gear and tossed it in a pile in the corner. Then the punching started, Chance's head snapping left and right with each blow.

"*Who sent you? The Glom? To spy on us?*" the big Slagger yelled.

Chance held fast, his mouth pinched. Moments later, another punch rocked his head backward.

"It's a joke," Rip said.

Jessie bobbed his head. "No, you know what?" He looked to Rip. "I'll double my bet on him. He's going to make it."

Rip laughed. "Double your bet? You don't even know this poor cat, and you want to double on him? Why?"

"Look at him," Jessie said, quickly checking his own retro-styled hair in a reflective screen. "He's getting his lights knocked out, and he's still given them nothing. Look at that resolve. This guy isn't your average street cop. Enhance him with nanos, and there's no doubt he's got what it takes to survive The Zone."

"Okay, pretty boy," Rip said with a shake of his head. "It's your money."

"Will you two please shut up?" A powerfully built man near the back of the room spoke up at last. Sat half in shadow, he uncrossed his thick forearms, which bore tattoos from his time as a special operations soldier, and grabbed a mug off a side table. "This is the reason I don't watch these things. Your bickering ruins it." He nursed a sip of the frosty lager.

Rip twisted in his seat to consult his friend and sometimes Zone partner, Ash Stroud. After the military disbanded, Ash turned to policing to get his thrills. It didn't take long before he felt the adrenaline-soaked call of The Zone and set out to become an Enforcer.

"Ash, talk some sense into this pretty fool," Rip said.

"Shut up, man. I want to watch this kid get killed without the idiotic commentary," Ash said.

"See?" Rip drew a finger across his throat.

Onscreen, Chance took more withering blows to the face. His head lolled forward, drooling blood.

"Oh, man… I know that feeling." Jessie grinned, showing a small gap where a rear molar was missing from the left side of his jaw.

"How's the last applicant faring?" A female voice spoke up from the entrance of the well-furnished room.

The other three Enforcers twisted to see Karissa Gaines. The former decathlete leaned her rock-solid frame against the door, her arms crossed. "They kill the other guy, Brazo?"

"Branko," Jessie corrected her. "Yeah, the Slaggers aced him."

"What about the last man standing? He alive?" she said.

They all watched a semi-conscious Chance take two more punches.

"Yeah," Jessie said.

"No," Rip said.

Karissa winced and shook her head. "Doesn't look good."

"Anyone seen Shepherd?" Jessie said.

"You know Sam doesn't watch these—heck, he doesn't even watch The Zone trials," Karissa said. "He goes to work and takes it to the house. That's it."

"Tough old dude, though, I'll give him that," Ash murmured into his beer, eyes locked on the screen.

The image flickered, and the projection went dark, the fading shades of an orange and crimson sunset lingering on the walls.

"Hey, come on. I've got money on this." Rip sat forward.

"Excuse the interruption, but I need your attention for a moment," Gabriel Kess said, dressed in a midnight black one-piece survival suit. He slipped past Karissa and into the back of the lounge. Pressed against his hip, he held a matching full-face hazard helmet with a smoke-colored visor.

"Make it quick, *sir*. I need to know if they kill this guy." Rip pointed a finger gun at Jessie and dropped the hammer. "I've got a payday coming."

"Stow it, Sanction," Kess said, notorious for only referring to Enforcers by their call signs, never their given names. "We're performing an extraction on applicant seven. I need one volunteer."

"Whoa," Jessie said. "That's why you're all decked out? Done sitting behind your desk?"

"Who is applicant seven?" Ash lowered his beer.

Kess gestured with the helmet in his hand. "The guy getting his ass kicked out in The Slags."

"Drinking." Ash raised his beer. "Sorry."

"Well, it sure as hell isn't me." Rip hocked out a disgusted laugh. "We don't rescue applicants. He can either survive it or he can't."

"I didn't say rescue." Kess's gaze was stony. "I said extraction. When he gets free, and I'm confident he will, we'll pick him up.

"He doesn't deserve special treatment," Rip complained.

"It's not special treatment. He'll need a capable extraction under fire. We have intel the Slaggers are in possession of black-market Glom-tech weapons. We can't send a slick VTOL to get him. We'll go in hot and kill two birds with one stone—get our guy and neutralize some problems at the same time." Kess eyed each of them again. "Who's volunteering?"

Silence filled the room. The Enforcers looked back and forth at one another.

"Not me, I told you." Rip crossed his arms.

"Yeah, everyone knows it's not you, Rip," Karissa said. She raised her chin. "I'll go. Got a score to settle with the king."

"Good." Kess gave a brief nod to the square-jawed woman with the golden-flecked eyes of a lioness. "Get your gear and meet me at launch bay six in five. We're going to get this guy out of there."

"Unbelievable," Rip whined, scowling at Jessie, who now pointed a finger gun back at him with a wink.

Hannah rounded the corner of the sixth-floor stairwell on her way to their apartment on the eighth, her heart pounding from the ascent with a wriggling fifteen-pound weight strapped to her chest. Her thoughts turned into dark circles. *Will we have enough food? Can we pay our bills now? How will Andrew get the care he needs? Is Chance okay?* Each was more than enough to worry about. Together, they stoked a deep fear inside her, a cold reminder of her daily struggle.

Chance can't take two seconds to tell me how things are going?

She checked the time on her visor as she hit the final set of stairs: 7:42 p.m. Much later than she first thought. A little spike of anxiety prickled the nape of her neck.

Why isn't he home yet?

"Create solutions, not problems," she said, intoning the mantra she'd heard from her grandfather many years before. He hadn't been the most loving man. Hannah knew, though, he'd done his best to care for her and her brothers after her mother passed. Her older brother, Mic, died shooting a dangerous cocktail of Feels six years ago. Her little brother Jey, before that in an industrial accident at the factory he worked at in Volkan Heights. Now it was just her, alone. *Thank God I have Chance and Andrew*, she thought.

Hannah turned her attention toward the things that still needed doing. She'd spent the day trying to work out their subscription predicament to no avail. Power Authority, Water Board, apartment rent, network fee, the list of offenders went on and on. It infuriated her they could wield such power and ignore her without explanation or consequence. These providers might ignore her pleas for help, but they'd never be late demanding their fee. The ugly injustice of it all made her want to throw up.

She reached the eighth floor and hooked left out of the musty dampness of the stairwell into the barren concrete hall under sterile fluorescent lights and the occasional patch of sweeping turf graffiti. A man sat slumped against the wall, pants jerked halfway down pale thighs. His flickering visor highlighted the drool that hung from an open mouth.

"Damn, guy. Couldn't find a better place to—" Hannah stopped, her hands groping for her bag as the shadow of a large man leaned away from the wall beside her apartment door. He turned to face her. A gasp caught in her throat, her hand fumbling over each item in her bag—everything except the collapsed Street Defender.

"There you are," came the familiar baritone.

"Benny?" An intense wave of relief crashed over her. "Jeez, Benny, you trying to scare me to death, or what?"

"Hey, I'm sorry." Benny managed a sheepish shrug. "I tried to message you."

"Oh," Hannah said, flicking her visor down, noting the unread message. "Guess I didn't notice it with everything going on."

Benny held open his arms as she approached and gave him a quick hug. "I was concerned for you guys," he said. "Thought I'd come check on things." He turned his attention down to the bundle wrapped against her chest. "Hey, little man." Benny stroked Andrew's arm with a meaty finger. The baby grunted and nuzzled closer to his mother.

"Wanna come in?" Hannah waved her palm over the door scanner. The sensor peeped.

"Just for a minute," Benny said.

"*Voice identification, please,*" the sensor demanded.

"Hannah Griffin," she said.

"*Welcome home.*"

There was a chime and a click, and Hannah pushed her way into the small apartment. Behind her, Benny stepped inside and made sure the door latched shut.

"Can I get you a glass of water?" Hannah dropped her bag and stepped into the narrow kitchenette.

"No, Hannah, that's not necessary." Benny clasped his hands.

"I'm getting some for me anyway." Hannah agreed to the charge for one liter of potable water, filling a jug from the counter.

"You want to know where Chance is, don't you?" Hannah said without looking up. "That's why you're here."

Benny reluctantly accepted the offered cup. "Yeah, it is. In all the years I've known him, Chance has never not shown up for work. Even through the shootings and other admin investigations, he always came the next day."

Hannah took a sip from her cup, Andrew fussing against her shoulder. "You're right."

"Come on, Hannah," Benny said, "don't play me. He's my best friend. What's going on?"

Hannah set her water down, swallowing. "Did he tell you

anything?"

Benny sighed. "Maybe, but he can be cryptic with what he's getting at sometimes. He mentioned you guys might have some financial issues. Subscription rates or something?"

"That was the start of it," she said. "We can't get anyone to help us get it figured out."

"It happened for no reason?"

"No reason," Hannah repeated.

"How'd he get admin-cleared to go sort that out?" Benny said.

"Hang on a second," Hannah said, slipping into the baby's room. She unwrapped the whimpering baby, kissed him, and lay him in his crib. When she returned, she found Benny staring off, deep in thought. Upon seeing her, he perked up, arms folded on the narrow bar separating the living room from the kitchenette.

"Well," Hannah said, settling onto a well-worn loveseat.

"Yeah?" Benny said, taking the chair across from her. "He okay?"

"He's okay—at least, I think so." Hannah took another sip of her water and looked at Benny. "Chance applied for the Enforcer position—the one you've seen everywhere."

Benny's mouth opened. He sat back in silence, the chair creaking in protest beneath his bulk. "No way."

Hannah nodded. "They accepted his application the same day. It all happened so fast. He had to be at Glom headquarters first thing this morning for the interview."

Benny looked stunned. "Chance? Our Chance? He hates the Enforcers, The Zone, all of it. Why would he even apply?"

Hannah bit her lip. "Maybe because I asked him to?"

"Wow," Benny said and rubbed his face. A moment passed. "He loves you."

"Benny, I wanted him to apply for the benefits. So Andrew could get the care he needs. You know, Chance is devoted to you and your squad. He almost didn't agree to it."

They sat in silence, Benny with his hands plied together against his mouth.

"I wish he'd told me," Benny said through his fingers.

"I'm sorry. The last thing I want is to drive a wedge between you guys."

Benny waved her off. "You're thinking about your family and what's best for your son. Don't apologize."

Hannah searched the bottom of her cup. Outside, strings of firecrackers popped, signaling the start of the night market a few blocks away.

"And he's been at it all day?" Benny asked. "What sort of interview is this?"

"The serious kind?" Hannah forced a little laugh, her face darkening. "He's okay, right? There's got to be a good reason we haven't heard from him yet?"

Benny's face softened. He stood and took a step over, squeezing Hannah's shoulder. "Hey." He dipped his eyes to meet hers. "It's Chance. If anyone's built for this, it's him."

CHAPTER TWELVE

In the sweltering dark, Chance sat wadded up in the fetal position, unable to move. The muscles at the base of his neck screamed, and the bones of his face throbbed with pain. His head felt detached. He took a pull at the stinking, piss-stale air. Warm and thick, it threatened to make him vomit. Chance shifted his position, and the sleek nano-skin body suit he wore adjusted in response.

After having their fun and not getting the answers they wanted, the Slaggers dragged the dead man away and sent Chance toppling into Branko's dark, blood-soaked hole. It was a power play, a move designed to elicit terror.

And it worked.

Anger at The Glom bubbled up inside Chance, raw and seething hot. He struggled to master himself, tried not to focus on Hannah, never knowing how he died or the terrible claustrophobic black that smothered his every hope as he lay contorted in the filth-lined hole.

Chance assessed his condition, making little movements of his head and neck, shoulders, legs, and feet. Fire radiated in his jaw, the pain of something broken. He twisted, and at the movement of his left shoulder, a lightning bolt of white-hot electricity rocketed through him. He groaned and clutched at the shoulder joint. Dislocated.

A stale breath hissed across his lips. *Not going to die in here*, he thought. *Not today.*

Chance listened to the Slaggers shuffling back into the earthen den. On the way past, one man stomped down on the hatch above him with a laugh. Chance waited until the sounds faded before pressing his palms flat against the oxidized surface of the metal hatch above him. He pushed up, increasing the pressure when another jagged spike of pain raked through his left shoulder. With a gasp, he sank back down.

He whispered a few words of comfort to himself, his dirty fingers reaching up to pull a small medallion of St. Michael from the neck of his suit. A gift from Benny's mother, God rest her soul. Mrs. Benitez gave one to each of them years ago when they'd joined the force. "God protects those who keep the law. Never forget, you boys have angels on your shoulders," she'd told them with a shoulder-squeezing hug. Chance rubbed the ridges of the medallion between his fingers and shoved it back into his suit. But angels weren't there for that sweet lady when bloodthirsty members of the Ghouls' hover cycle gang beat her and left her to die in the street.

Benny had lost it. The two of them went after those Ghouls but never found anyone who saw anything. Too scared of retaliation. It was for the best, too, because Chance and Benny both might have committed murder, then ended up fighting for their lives in The Zone.

Mrs. Benitez was one of the best human beings Chance had ever known. He should have been there. He could've stopped it. Now he let the anger build back up, fury and regret boiling like magma to the surface, ready to explode.

Okay, Chance, he thought, mustering his strength. *Angels on your shoulders.*

He gathered his legs beneath him and pressed upward on the hatch with his palm and the top of his head. The hatch clunked to a stop as it met the resistance of the metal bar slid through the eye loops above. A tiny ray of torchlight slashed across his eyes, causing him to squint. Chance blinked a few times until his vision adjusted to the orange light, and he could see a small portion of the still-empty room.

His head and neck ached with the pressure of the metal plate on his skull, but he could now make out the clasp holding one end of the bar in place. There was no way he could reach it. Chance released the hatch and sank back down again to consider his options. Injured and with no tools or weapons. What remained? His wits—and the curiosity of his captors.

Rounding his back and pressing a shoulder against the hatch, he bucked upward, clanging it against the metal bar. He did it again, and again, and yet another time, a loud gurgling sound from his throat each time he bucked against the hatch.

"What's all the noise?" a Slagger shouted, rushing into the room. "Cut it out." He stomped on the metal plate.

Chance's groans grew louder. He shook his body, thrashing against the hatch.

The Slagger stomped again. "I said cut it out!"

"What's going on?" another voice called.

"I don't know." The man stomped again. "Something's wrong with this guy."

Chance cried out and bucked against the hatch again. He heard the bar slide from the top of the steel panel. The hatch jerked open, orange torchlight bathing Chance's face. A wash of warm garbage-scented air, still cooler than what was in the hole with him, flowed across him. Above, one man held the hatch and the bar while the man who'd shot Branko aimed the crude pipe pistol at Chance's forehead.

Chance's eyes rolled back as he continued the act, flopping with violent spasms.

"He's having a seizure or something," the Slagger holding the hatch said.

"Well, get him out." The other man shoved the pistol into his belt. "If he croaks, that means no money. The king gonna be pissed."

Chance felt the hands of the men as they gripped his arms and pulled him up and out of the hole. For a second, he thought the pain in his shoulder might actually kill him. As his feet touched the ground, Chance's right hand closed on the Slagger's pipe gun. In one movement, he yanked upward on the firing spring and let it go. The one-shot pipe gun discharged with a crack into the Slagger's groin. The man let loose a singing shriek as he fell.

Chance pivoted into the other man, still stunned by the sound of the gunshot. A strong right hook caught the man across the nose and sent him stumbling. Chance grabbed the steel bar from the floor and brought it crashing down over the top of the stunned Slagger's head, folding him into the dirt.

Chance faltered; the pain of a simple downward swing threatened to overwhelm his senses. He dropped the bar, turning to locate his discarded armor and equipment jumbled in a corner. The clock was ticking. The sound of gunfire would have alerted every Slagger around. Chance pulled his recon armor on with a wince, his left arm taking longer to secure than he'd like.

Voices approached. Chance's breathing quickened, his heart slamming adrenaline through his veins. He threw on his helmet, adjusted the visor, and locked open the Electro-stream, the power cells charging with a whine. Stumbling to the opposite corner, he braced against the wall, the shock rifle shaking in his unsupported right hand.

"You are injured," said the sterile voice in his ear, taking him by surprise. "Would you like to start your suit's triage and stabilization protocol?"

"Yes, dammit," Chance huffed, his jaw spiking pain with each word, "do it."

With a hiss, the haptic survival suit inside the armor jerked tight. A sudden immense pressure crunched his left shoulder back into place. Chance screamed, knees shaking. Gasping, his left hand rose in a slow sweep to support the rifle.

Three more Slaggers rushed into the room, guns at the ready. With three successive pops from Chance's Electro-stream, shimmering gouts of electrified plasma covered each man. They fumbled and flopped, pitching forward onto the dirt with screams of agony.

"Control, if you read me," Chance groaned into his commlink. "Branko is dead. I need an extraction. Now."

"Extraction inbound."

Chance shoved from the wall and burst out into the cool night air, his legs churning with clumsy strides. A round snapped over his head into the mound of junk behind him as a band of Slaggers opened fire. He yanked the pins from two soda can-sized stun grenades and hurled them. The concussive blasts rocked the trash-strewn hillside, the grenades detonating like twin thunderclaps. Chance flicked the selector switch on the shock rifle to *Spread Shot.* He leveled the "less lethal" weapon at his attackers, their open hands still shielding their faces. The wide-angle blast from the Electro-stream discharged with a slapping sound. Peppered with electrified plasma, the four men screamed and clutched at themselves as they toppled into the garbage.

Chance opened his gait, running with everything he had through twisty narrow alleys carved into the mountains of junk. More rounds zipped past, the buzzing of disturbed hornets. Strained voices shouted in pursuit. Chance called up the map in his visor, identified the extraction point, and made for it. One hundred yards and closing. As he reached a towering mound of ancient, rusted steel, Chance scrambled up the slope, his feet stabbing into the shifting pile of debris.

An impact throttled him, pain knifing into his back as he pitched forward.

"You have been shot," said the voice in his earpiece. "Your

armor is now at forty-eight percent effectiveness."

Chance forced himself back to his feet, scrabbling up the slope like a hunter's wounded kill. Twenty-five meters.

Where the hell is my extraction?

A thunderous boom resounded, a crater exploding in the junk mound just feet away. Chance fell and covered his head, ears ringing. His body slid down between a rusted industrial fan unit and what looked like the tail end of a gutted auto-junker. Rolling to his side, he saw a man with long dreadlocks and a contingent of fighters on the opposite hill. On his shoulder, the man carried some sort of rocket launcher. Based on the entourage, Chance knew it was the fabled Warlord of the Slags.

More rounds zipped and pinged around him. Chance tried to take cover behind the rusted fan but knew it would only offer minimal protection. He sized up the distance to the extraction point. Over thirty-five meters. Shaking with adrenaline, he clutched the shock rifle against his armor. There was no way out. He was a dead man.

A *whoosh* screamed from the sky above, thrusters whipping dust into the air. The Slaggers shouted and raised their weapons. With an ear-shattering series of rapid concussions, a cluster of stun grenades exploded in the air and sent the Slaggers diving for cover. The *clunk-thunk* of a heavy machine gun opened up above, muzzle flashes strobing in the deepening night.

"Come on!" a voice shouted. Chance looked up to the top of the mound to see a sleek black VTOL similar to the one he rode in on. It hung there, stabilized by the dripping blue fire of the thrusters. On the open side, two Glom assault troopers wore full body armor with open-faced helmets. One, a powerful-looking woman with mocha skin, stood anchored behind a heavy machine gun. The trooper beside her, a bold-featured man, waved him on.

"Get in!"

Chance summoned the last of his strength and pushed to all

fours. Clamoring up the trash hillside, he made for the waiting VTOL. As he approached, the heat and concussion from the heavy machine gun caused him to falter. The VTOL jolted downward to avoid a screaming rocket as it ripped past in a trail of smoke.

"Target the launcher," the male trooper yelled.

The female trooper swung her machine gun to the right and opened up with another barrage of hot lead. The Slaggers dove from the hillside, some of them blown apart by the fresh wave of heavy support. The Slag King dropped his launcher and hit the ground, sliding out of view.

Chance reached the summit, stumbled, and leaped for the open hatch. He landed against the floor of the VTOL, sliding part way back out, when a hand clamped down on his wrist.

"I've got you," the male trooper yelled, hauling Chance with both hands into the VTOL. "Get us the hell out of here," he shouted to the pilot.

The master thrusters engaged, and the VTOL shot straight up into the air.

"Mission complete. Objectives failed," the sterile voice said in Chance's ear.

Chance pulled his helmet and visor off and slumped into the corner of the VTOL as it gained altitude. The woman on the heavy machine gun loosed a few more bursts, then let the gun hang on its swing arm. She turned, appraising him with interest. The male trooper took a knee to closer assess Chance's wounds.

"You're a tough hombre," he said with a smirk. "Hard to kill. For that, you have my respect."

Chance swallowed, the taste of blood in his mouth. His adrenaline dump worn thin, a sudden wave of exhaustion covered him. He tried to speak but found the pain in his jaw too great. Unable to form the words, he just sat there, covered in stinking muck, stunned by overwhelming gratefulness to still be alive.

CHAPTER THIRTEEN

A droning warmth emanated from somewhere above, a white halo that descended in a shower of serenity across the contours of his naked body. The ribbons of light drifted back and forth, cascading between one another like intersecting waves on an open sea. Beneath the shimmering rays lay Chance's still form, eyes closed, hands relaxed by his side.

A click, followed by a chime, and the white glow faded from the room, replaced with a comfortable, natural light. The lid of the hyperbaric chamber hissed open, and a silky, vaporous fume floated down across Chance's face. His eyes fluttered, his body stirring from the near comatose state.

He raised a hand and looked at it, his eyes dry and strange, an unnatural focus in them. He rubbed at his face, his jaw. *No pain*, Chance thought. He sat up and took in the spacious room, well furnished with a full kitchen, personal gym, network viewing platforms, as well as other technology he couldn't yet identify. The polished white marble floor gleamed around the edges of a plush pearl-white rug.

Wearing nothing more than his briefs, he scooted back and swung his legs out of the chamber. A reckless power brimmed in his muscles, a feeling of invincibility. Tipping forward, his feet touched down on expensive natural hardwood.

"Where am I?"

"Specifically?" a nearby voice said, catching Chance by

surprise. "You're in your apartment on the forty-fourth floor of the Unified Conglomerate's Corporate Headquarters, right in the middle of Silver City."

Chance turned to the well-dressed man approaching from the open entrance into the elegant space. The man descended a series of marble steps and stopped before Chance with an air of absolute confidence.

"How long have I been out?"

"Four days," the well-dressed man said. "Don't worry, we informed your family that you sustained injuries during selection and are now recovering."

"Four days...?"

"An accelerated healing time, considering your injuries." The man flicked a bit of lint from the cuff of his tailored shirt. "Our Enforcers use these personalized hyperbaric recovery chambers after every trial in The Zone. Helps to get them back in action fast. We've found having it in your apartment keeps everyone on their game."

"Wait, *my* apartment?" Chance struggled to spit out the words.

"All Enforcers get one. There's only one other apartment on this floor, and it's occupied by Warrant, your Enforcer Training Officer."

"Ah." Chance surveyed the space wide-eyed. "And who are you, again?"

"Of course, where are my manners," the polished man said, extending a bronze, manicured hand. "Gabriel Kess. Director of Security and Network Operations."

"The trooper who extracted me from The Slags." Chance shook the offered hand, the director's grip firm, eyes unwavering.

"That's right. I have several responsibilities, one of which is running the Enforcers," Kess said. "You're familiar, of course?"

"Hang on." Chance shook his head. "The guy I tried to rescue, Branko. He really is... um...?"

"Dead?" Kess said. "That's correct. The selection process is no game."

"But you stuck us in a situation designed to fail. You let him die."

"No." Kess clasped his hands behind his back. "We sent you in to rescue him, and it didn't work out."

Chance pressed his teeth together. "There was nothing I could do. You set us up. Why?"

Kess tilted his head. "We can't gamble on filling an Enforcer position, Mr. Griffin. Branko knew the risks. He signed the waivers. So did you. We have to know you have what it takes. You thought that was bad? Wait until you're alone, cut off in The Zone. Even Enforcers die."

"Hang on." Chance held up his hand. "Did I miss something, Mr....?"

"Kess."

"Right." Chance squinted at Kess. "So I was only applying, that was all. Just to see if I was good enough to get the job."

"And you were. Showed some real grit and determination. Great survival instincts. We have given you full authorization— even a call sign." Kess spread his hands as if reading a holographic projection billboard. "Justice: The last hope of the innocent." He flashed brilliant white teeth. "The people will love you."

"But I never accepted the position," Chance said.

"Correct. While you were out in rehab and repair, we accepted, on your behalf, the conditional offer extended by the Founders. A simple decision, actually."

"You can do that?" Chance said.

"It was in the agreement you signed. You read it, didn't you?" Kess said.

Chance pulled on his neck. "But what if I don't... *didn't* want the job?"

"Don't be ridiculous," Kess said, leading him to a far wall, which he slid open to reveal a full wardrobe. Kess selected a dry-fit Henley shirt and a pair of comfort flex denim jeans and handed them to Chance, still in his briefs.

"I'm serious," Chance said, slipping into the tailored clothes.

"You're serious," Kess repeated, scrunching his brow. "Well, in the event of a refusal, our agreement with you would be void. We'd have to neutralize your nano enhancements and bill you for the medical reconstructive work."

"Nano what?"

"Enhancements," Kess replied in a matter-of-fact tone. He double-tapped his watch and opened a projection chart, the display flowing in front of them in streams of digital blue data. "Here are the details." He read from the list: "Enforcer standard enhancement package, application fee, critical extraction resource fee, cursory equipment damage fee. Then there are the medical procedures to repair a fractured orbital socket, broken nose, burst fracture in the left side of the jaw, dislocated shoulder, and surgical removal of bullet fragments from the upper back. Not to mention the treatment of dehydration, concussion, exhaustion, and mild sepsis. The total amount we've covered comes to one point six seven billion Terminus coins." He let the figure sink in. "You have the ability to cover that expense, do you?"

Chance blinked. He didn't need to open his account to know the answer.

"If you do," Kess continued, "after you've been sanitized and your enhancements reversed, we'll release you." He grimaced. "But you won't be going back to the police department, I'm afraid."

"Why not?" Chance said, almost unable to speak the words.

"Well, frankly," Kess said, "the only way to pay back a bill such as this is to go to work in one of the Conglomerate's industrial centers. Your basic needs will be met, but—"

"I'd be an indentured servant," Chance said with disgust. "I'd never see my family again. I can't do that."

Kess shrugged. "My thoughts exactly."

Chance sank down into a mahogany leather chair, his face darkened by the news.

"Why so glum?" Kess brightened as he walked to stand beside Chance. "Look around you. This is where you belong now."

Kess waved his hands, gesturing to the apartment, then the sunset-bathed skyline of Silver City, such a far cry from everything Chance had ever known.

"As an Enforcer," Kess said, "you get this fully furnished apartment here at headquarters, but you're provided a second apartment in the Sky Rise sector. It's twice the size of this one. That's where your family will live."

Chance appraised Kess. "My family can't live here with me?"

"They can visit, of course," Kess said, "but we expect a lot of an active Enforcer. You are subject to call twenty-four hours a day. We need you focused and undistracted. As a result, all family members live in the Sky Rise sector." Kess rested a hand on Chance's shoulder. "I assure you, your wife and son will want for nothing."

"Sure," Chance said, thinking of Benny and the squad back at the police department, a time in his life that was now ancient history.

How is this possible? Chance thought.

"Listen, I know it's a lot to process," Kess said, stepping in front of Chance, who now sat slumped in the leather chair, his eyes distant. "You'll have to push people from your former life to the back burner. But look at what you'll gain. Your wife is able to live lavishly and carefree with any help she needs complimentary. Your son will have access to the best doctors and treatments in the world. The possibility of a real future. Think about it," Kess stepped back and spread his arms to take in the vast apartment, "the life millions of people can only dream of, and it's yours for the taking."

He walked across the room, his movements feline in their grace as he ascended the stairs.

"One last thing," Kess said, turning back toward Chance, "swipe your account open."

With a wave of Chance's chipped hand, his Glom account opened, displaying his balance. His eyes widened at the sum. More money than he'd ever possessed in his life.

"That's just the sign-on bonus." Kess smirked. "More will come as you advance in your role as an Enforcer. All you have to do is show up for training with Warrant at 0800, and we'll take that as your commitment. Until then, eat, drink, rest, and enjoy yourself."

"There a visor here? Some way to send a message?"

"Your state of the art, iVisor. It's on the kitchen counter, charging," Kess said.

Still in a state of shock, Chance watched Kess ascend the marble steps. The clouded reinforced glass slid back, and Director Kess passed through with one last wink at Chance.

"Justice," Kess said as he turned the corner, his voice reaching back from the hallway. "I sure do like the sound of that."

"Hēi zou kāi!" The little man in a wide-brimmed straw hat screamed through rotten, gapped teeth as Benny jumped out of the way of the weaving bicycle.

"Watch where you're going, jackass!" Benny shouted.

"Fak yew!" the hunched man yelled back in a strong Mandarin accent, little legs pumping the pedals with furious purpose. His wares jangled and shifted in a wicker basket mounted over the tire behind him. In an instant, he was gone, absorbed into the sea of meandering, zombified Glom network subscribers, their eyes glassy behind flashing visors.

THE ZONE

Benny stepped away from the jingling bicycles and honking electric cars onto the busy sidewalk and looked up and down the length of Hyperion Way. Even at this hour, the northern Volkan Heights district teemed with scores of late evening commuters, the air filled with the trilling sounds of dance music and the drunken laughter of intoxicated bar patrons trying to forget their misery for a spell.

The façade of the fortress-like South Precinct loomed over Benny, the entire block bathed in hazy artificial light. He took the stairs to the front door and scanned his chipped right wrist. The locks disengaged with a sharp snap. Benny pushed through the heavy precinct door into the dimly lit lobby. Prisoner intakes headed for the Blocks, and all patrol foot traffic came in through the secure rear of the building, which left the main entrance more or less unoccupied this time of night unless the detective bureau was hot and heavy drinking bad coffee and chasing down leads on one of their typical all-nighters.

He stopped for a moment to listen for any activity before flicking his visor down and rereading the last few cryptic lines of Chance's message. *Please, Benny. I need you to do this thing for me. It's important. I'll explain everything later.*

Benny knew this little errand could get him jacked up and bumped to shuffling papers at an admin desk in records. Maybe they'd even terminate him for it. But it was Chance, and though something strange was going on with him, Chance was his brother. He'd get fired for him. He'd shed every drop of blood he had for him. *Because that's what brothers do.*

Benny crossed the lobby, his thick fingers double-checking the high-density data drive in the pocket of his jacket. At the lift, he waved his palm to activate the doors, entered and selected the lower level. The lift dropped silent and swift to the floor below, and Benny exited into the cool, clammy underground hallway, heading toward the lockers via the property room.

Pushing through the door into the property room, he jerked to a stop, heart vaulting into his throat. Two figures, crouched over a series of canvas bags, straightened. Kip Monaghan and Deyvar Whaley, two of South Precinct's undercover narcotics officers.

With a swear, Deyvar looked at Kip through a curtain of dreadlocks hung down from his forehead. Kip zipped one of the black duffel bags closed, but not before Benny got a look at a seized load of the Feels.

"Corporal Benitez," Kip said, standing with a casual air. "Funny seeing you here after hours."

He looked from Kip to the taller Deyvar, his eyes dropping to the duffels.

"What is this?" Benny said, holding his ground.

"This?" Kip motioned to the duffels. "We're checking this stuff out. Gotta look legit to the buyer on a major operation."

"Checking it out? Without Chuck?" Benny's eyes narrowed. Nothing left inventory without the evidence custodian's approval. "It's eleven o'clock at night."

"Yeah," Kip said. "He already approved it."

"Narc protocols differ from street division, Benitez." Deyvar sized Benny up. "How about stop asking questions and stay in your lane."

"That's the story you want me to believe?" Benny let the door close behind him.

The surrounding air seemed to chill, the property room as still as a captured photograph. Even the dust-covered air duct above no longer whistled. The two narcs stepped over the loaded duffels and came within arm's reach of Benny, who responded by opening his stance a touch.

"Benny." Kip clasped his hands. "Everything is legit. Don't worry about it."

"Yeah, and anyway, you say we're here late," Deyvar said. "I wanna know what *you're* up to."

"Following up on something." Benny glared. "Take your own advice and stay in your lane."

Deyvar laughed, a coarse, dangerous sound.

"Benny, I hate to run," Kip said, "but we've got somewhere to be." He waved open his coin wallet. "Accept this as an expression of our gratitude and keep this little moment between us."

Benny's account flashed, and a message popped up between them. *Accept 3,000 Terminus coins from Anonymous?* Benny swallowed at the amount, more than five paychecks. The two narcs stared Benny down, their eyes full of distrust and expectation.

Benny declined the transaction with a slapping motion. He grabbed Kip by the jacket, wrenching the short man up on his toes. "What kind of lowlife do you think I am?"

Kip's face went dark. "Get your slagging hands off me, Benitez."

A little but sharp *click* drew Benny's attention to an unfolded lock blade clenched in Deyvar's white-knuckled grip.

"Let him go," Deyvar said.

"Or what?" Benny said, his body primed for action. "You're going to stab me right here in the station?"

"If I need to," Deyvar whispered.

"We know a real good cleanup crew," Kip winked. "So, let it go," he said, shoving Benny's hands off his jacket. "Or are you a rat?"

"I don't run my mouth," Benny said.

"But you're too good to take a little on the side?" Kip went on. "You and that rogue partner of yours. Makes us decent folk feel threatened when a brother doesn't take."

Benny stepped back and dropped his eyes, his fists balled. "I told you. I'm not a rat. Now get the hell out of my face."

With a flick, Deyvar folded the knife and concealed it back beneath his shirt, flashing a knowing smirk. He and Kip grabbed two loaded duffels each and slung them over their shoulders, never taking their eyes off Benny.

"Not a word." Kip held a finger to his lips. "We can make your life a living hell, Benitez. Don't ever forget that."

Benny held his tongue, his eyes locked with the dirty narcs as they slipped into the hallway beyond and were gone.

His shoulders slumped. More and more cops went on the take every year. Most of them were good people just trying to survive, but they'd bent too far in the wrong direction. *How long until there are no longer any honest cops in the whole of this godforsaken city?* he thought.

Benny hung his head as he passed the weight room and made his way between the rows of stone gray lockers. He stopped before Chance's.

A band of red tape stuck across the seam read *Clear and Reassign.*

So it is true. Chance is leaving us. Benny could only assume his friend got the Enforcer job, the lucky idiot. Benny shook his head at the thought of it.

He sliced the tape and punched in the code. The locker popped open, and Benny reached in, first grabbing a few of the mementos and projection photos his friend might want to remind him of their days together.

He pulled a small folding tote from his jacket and stuck the items in, then pulled the data drive from a jacket pocket and set it inside the locker. He powered the device on, then reached to the back of the locker to activate the power on Chance's patrol armor, the little yellow indicator lights winking on one by one with a musical chime.

"Start link assistant and direct construct upload," Benny said. "Access code four-three-eight-four-two-five-seven-whiskey."

Benny scanned the room for any witnesses. The lights on the collar of Chance's armor flickered in sequence as it booted up.

"*Good evening, Corporal Benitez,*" RITA's cheerful voice spoke up. "*I sense a high-capacity portable data drive with built-in encryption technology,*" she said, crisp and clear. "*Are we going somewhere?*"

CHAPTER FOURTEEN

A shimmering band of early morning sunlight streaked across the room, a swath of brilliance that set the white marble floor and chrome appliances of Chance's new apartment aglow. Squinting at the glistening cityscape of steel and glass, Chance took another mouthful of protein shake and savored the velvet-smooth chocolate flavor as he swallowed it down.

After a quick call the previous day to let Hannah know he was all right, he spent the afternoon and evening resting. Then he ate a series of indulgent meals fit for a king: smoked chicken breast with a tangy white sauce, accompanied by butter-sautéed greens and roasted red potatoes. An actual Black Angus prime rib smothered with mushrooms and gravy followed, and by the time he'd put down two high-gravity imperial ales and finished a slice of mixed fruit pie with a giant dollop of something called ice cream, he figured he could keel over right then and die a happy man.

It took him no time to fall asleep on the plush mattress and silken sheets of the master bedroom, but he'd woken early with the rising sun, a little stiff and somewhat uncomfortable surrounded by such lavishness. He needed a reality check. He needed his wife and son. And he'd dodged one too many of her questions the day before, leaning a little too hard into the fact that he was exhausted. Hannah deserved a better explanation.

Chance slugged down the last of his chocolate protein shake and wiped his sleeve across his lips. Working his tongue against the roof of his mouth, he swallowed the last bit, wondering how something so simple could taste so good. He placed his hands on the kitchen counter, slipped on his visor, and opened the call.

It didn't even ring.

"Hey." Hannah's smiling face popped into view. "Oh, nice uniform."

He ran his hands across the Enforcer uniform he was wearing, a slick black flight suit embroidered with the name Justice over the right breast pocket. "What? This old thing?"

"Justice, huh? That's like a codename?"

"Something like that," Chance said and sat the shake cup in the auto washer.

"How are you feeling, baby?"

"Good." Chance beamed. "Great, actually. Everything good with you and Andrew?"

"Yeah, we're fine." She swiped a lock of golden hair from her face. "You sure you're okay? When they called, they said you were hurt pretty bad."

"I was, but they fixed me up with some advanced med-tech. I feel fine now. Better than fine."

Hannah shook her head, rocking the baby against her chest. "Some job interview, huh?"

"You don't know the half of it," Chance said. "It's not just a job. It's serious."

"But in a good way, right?" Hannah said. "For us, I mean?"

"Yeah," Chance rubbed his chin, "yeah, I think it is, but there's a lot to take in. I ate better than I ever have in my whole life last night. Real steak and chicken, Hannah. And you should see the view from this apartment."

"Real chicken?" Hannah licked her lips. "Was it good?"

"Crazy good. Prepared on-site by a damn chef." Chance chuckled at the astonished look on Hannah's face. "I'm serious. Get your tail over here already."

"We're working on that." Hannah motioned to a uniformed Glom worker who entered the frame behind her with a cardboard box overflowing with personal items. "The Glom's movers arrived this morning."

"Already?"

"Yeah." She patted Andrew's little curved back, her hips swaying. "Said they're only packing personal things because our new apartment is fully furnished. I've got the address right here. It's in the Sky Rise district."

"Crazy, right?"

"I know nothing about that place. Is that where you are?"

"I'm in Silver City, but it's not far," Chance said. "I'm told we can visit when I'm not working."

Hannah's face dropped. "You can't live with us? Isn't that weird?" There was a tremor of worry in her voice.

"Yeah, maybe a little," Chance gave a sheepish shrug, steeped in boyish charm, "but I'm on call at all times. It's a company policy thing, I'm told."

Hannah nodded. She didn't seem so sure.

"But honey, they're moving you and the baby to a condo in Sky Rise. I mean, come on. It doesn't get better than that."

Hannah's face warmed with nervous excitement. "I almost fainted when they told me." Then she seemed to sober. "Chance, is this really happening?"

"You saw your coin wallet. The money is as real as it gets, and that's just the signing bonus." He decided not to mention coming on as an Enforcer was the only way forward. Not unless he wanted to wear an explosive leg band and work his hands to the bone in one of The Glom's industrial production centers.

"Have you told Benny you're leaving the force?" Hannah said.

"We haven't actually spoken yet, but he knows." Chance tried to ignore the ache in his chest over leaving his longtime partner stranded.

"All set, ma'am," a male voice said from outside Chance's field of view.

"Okay, thank you," Hannah said. "They're ready for us to head out. I paid our early termination fee for the apartment. No turning back now."

"Don't worry, okay? We're going to make this work." Chance checked the digital clock. "Hey, I've gotta go. Can't be late for my first day of training. Call me when you get to the new place, and let me know you're okay."

"Okay. I love you, Chance. Good luck today."

"Love you, too," Chance said. The projection was gone with a wave of his hand.

Taking one last glance around the apartment, Chance made for the door. They had given him no information about what to do this morning or about Warrant, his Enforcer Training Officer, or ETO.

Chance pulled off the high-end iVisor. "Visor or no visor?" Chance shook his head and left it on the charger. *No distractions today.*

He stepped out into a short hallway, listening as the door to his apartment eased shut behind him. In a few strides, he raised a hand to knock at the opposite suite when the clouded glass slid open. He stood poised, fist hovering to knock.

"You're late," the man inside said, then sipped from a steaming mug of coffee. He pushed an antique silver pocket watch back into the breast pocket of his flight suit and appraised Chance with a half interest.

Chance glanced at the time on a digital wall clock above: 8:01 a.m. "I'm late?"

The veteran Enforcer leveled his gaze at Chance. "Yeah," Warrant said. "And if you don't want to die on your first day in The Zone, you'd better tighten up, Rookie. You receiving me?"

Chance stood outside the threshold, the strangest feeling of déjà vu washing over him. He'd heard those words before.

The older man crossed the room and rounded the counter with a relaxed strength that belied his age. The guy was at least fifty, with shoulders like weathered granite, and thick, worn hands that had done their share of manual labor over the last five decades. Clean shaven, with medium brown hair that grayed at the temples, he wore a one-piece black flight suit like Chance. On his chest, the name tape *Warrant* hung over the right breast. Chance eyed the iron jaw of his ETO, a block of granite sitting atop the heavy muscles of his neck. There wasn't a thing about this man that was soft or untested. Warrant drained the last of his coffee and placed his mug in the sink, then glanced toward the doorway.

"You going to come in?" Warrant said. "Or did you show up late so you could wait in the hall?"

Chance stepped across the threshold, and the clouded glass door to the apartment slid shut behind him.

"I know you," Chance said.

"No, you don't. Just because you saw me up on a holo-board doesn't mean you know me."

"No, I do, actually." Chance took another step forward. "You're Sam Shepherd."

The man returned from around the opposite side of the marble counter and seemed to size Chance up for the first time. "Have we met?"

Chance stuck out his hand. "Chance Griffin. NTPD. Eleven years. High Crime Saturation Unit."

The older man's gaze dropped to Chance's extended hand, then flicked back up. "What sector?"

"The Straits, mainly, but I worked all the sectors filling in."

"How many shootings?" Sam asked.

"Seven," Chance said, "all justified."

"Chance Griffin, huh?"

Chance thought he saw an almost imperceptible gleam of

acknowledgment in the veteran Enforcer's eye.

"When I hired on at the PD, you were a corporal in the tactical unit," Chance said, "notorious reputation for cracking skulls. We met once before you left the force. It's good to see a familiar face around here, sir." Chance pushed the offered hand toward the man, splaying his fingers wider.

Sam's demeanor relaxed slightly. "Lose the *sir*. The PD was years ago. Though I seem to recall a rookie by the name of Griffin from back in the day." He reached out, crushing Chance's hand in a vise of heavy fingers. "Reckless. Full of piss and vinegar. Good street cop, if a little too full of himself."

"Lucky, I guess," Chance said.

"I heard about what you did to escape The Slags. Luck's got nothing to do with it." Sam released his hand. "Still not going to be easy for you here. The Zone isn't Havana Straits or even The Slags. Far from it. If you want to survive, you'd better be ready and willing to learn how. I'm too old to be a damn babysitter."

"I'll pull my weight."

"You'd better. Our lives might depend on it." Sam slid past Chance. The glass door opened. "I'm glad to see at least you're not one of those useless thumb-sucking moobs who feels the constant need to be entertained by their visor."

"Oh, yeah. Not me," Chance said, grateful for his earlier decision.

"Let's go." Sam hit the hallway and approached the lift. "It's going to be a long day already, and that's if Kess doesn't jump my ass about your qualification punch list." He swiped his palm over the reader, and a thin whine rose from the glass-encased shaft.

"Punch list?" Chance asked.

"You're in training," Sam said. "Gotta cut the mustard. If you can't, your life will become whatever hell you took this position to avoid."

"You know about the deal Kess offered me?"

Sam gave a grunt as they entered the elevator. He touched the button for the basement level. "Everyone gets the same deal, and The Glom gets what it wants, kid. The sooner you recognize that the better off you'll be."

A haze of artificial light lit the interior of the glass lift. Chance forced himself not to look past his feet at the endless dark of the shaft below.

"What else can you tell me about The Glom—working for them, I mean?" Chance asked.

"What's to say? You now work for the most powerful organization on the planet. As a result, you'll live like a prince. Don't forget—you are a money-generating asset, a celebrity gladiator, and nothing more. Once you stop making them money, become too injured to work, or step on the wrong toes, you're done." Sam snapped his fingers. "Just like that."

"Done, as in...?"

"Yeah," Sam said.

Chance regarded his ETO with concern. "How will I know I've stepped on the wrong toes?"

Sam snapped his fingers again, his stare stone cold.

Chance rubbed his palms on his flight suit. *Is he being funny? Or...?*

The floors flicked past in silence, the illuminated levels like fixed points of sanity in a chasm of madness. *How the hell did I get myself into this?* Chance swallowed.

"How could it profit The Glom to kill me?"

Sam shrugged. "They may not smother you in your sleep if that's what you're thinking. But a highly publicized trial in The Zone where a well-regarded Enforcer, fighting for their life, is overwhelmed and killed? A good show can make The Glom far more money than you as an individual are worth to them. You're expendable, replaceable. Ask Valarie."

The lift slowed and connected with the basement landing, the doors sliding back to reveal a darkened hallway. "You mean, Vigilance?"

Sam looked down as he stepped from the lift and led the way along the twilight corridor of smooth-poured concrete. "She was a good person and a well-respected Enforcer. She didn't deserve to be dealt an un-winnable scenario."

"Your partner?" Chance said.

"Yeah."

"I'm sorry," Chance said. He wanted to ask what happened but thought better of it. Sam scanned his chip and stepped into a dark side room off the main corridor. Better to change the subject.

"Anything else I need to know right off?" Chance said.

"Stay in your lane for now, Rook. That's all."

Rows of sterile lights above, automated by their entrance, flickered and flared white. Chance blinked.

"Stay in my lane." Chance said. "Got it. But I'm treated like a rookie? I have eleven years on the job."

"Not this job, you don't." Sam regarded Chance with a tired sigh. "You get called Rook until you prove you aren't one."

The lights glared, bright as an artificial sun. Before them lay a series of personal cubicles, each complete with a large standing locker, quick-charge power station, automated dressing platform, and other amenities. Each station bore the callsign of its occupant, an Enforcer name plate, personal holo-photos, and accolades.

Sam gestured with a broad wave of his hand. "When you get called up, whether a planned deployment or situational activation, this is where you'll come to gear up. We call it the war room." He pointed to a station with none of the personal effects. "That was Valarie's. Now it's yours. You'll have time to make it feel like home later. For now, put your flight suit in the locker and step onto the platform."

Chance did as instructed and stepped onto the shielded platform, wearing only his briefs.

"You modest or something? All your clothes go in the locker,"

Sam said.

"Last thing I wanted was to make you feel inadequate on my first day." Chance chuckled and dropped his briefs, tossing them into the open locker. "Happy now?"

"You want to make jokes?" Sam sat at the launch control terminal at Chance's station, pulled up the glowing green projection menu, and selected *Xian-Xi Tactical Nano-Skin*. "I should've let this thing jam you into a nano suit while wearing your undergarments. See how you like an instant sex change."

Chance grimaced. "I'll shut up now."

"That would be good." Sam started the sequence.

A hum vibrated the walls, and a sheath of light encased Chance, levitating him from the floor of the platform.

"Whoa," Chance said. "Okay, that's cool."

"Wait for it." Sam initiated the second phase.

With a buzz, a blade of bright blue light whipped upward from Chance's toes to his neck, encasing him in a sleek black body suit.

"This is your nano skin," Sam said. "While you were out, they enhanced your body to have strength and resilience beyond that of an average man. At the end of the day, it can still be destroyed the same as any other human body. This suit, however, adapts to your internals and your surroundings to aid your survival. If the temperature drops, it will seal in your body heat. If you receive blunt force trauma, the nano skin will harden to attenuate the force delivered to your bones and organs. It can even minimize trauma from standard bullets and auto-deliver emergency medical treatment. That said, it still has its limitations, so don't forget it's *your job* to keep yourself alive out there."

Chance hovered in the light, his legs dangling. He looked down at the skin-tight body suit, glistening and shifting like a garment formed from tiny fragments of coal-black glass.

"It feels a little like the suit I wore during selection," Chance said.

"It should. You wore a prototype of the same make," Sam said.

"How does a body suit do all that?"

"Science, kid." Sam prepared the next phase. "And I'm no scientist. All I can tell you is the nanobots in the suit communicate with the nanobots they put inside your body, as well as your armor's built-in AI, all adjusting on the fly with little input from you. Think of it as a hyper-advanced extension of your own flesh."

"Is this all I wear out there?"

"You kidding me? Enforcers in The Zone wear full head-to-toe armored Exo Inteli-suits. It's time you got used to moving in one." Sam initialized the next phase.

A loud clunk echoed across the war room, the platform beneath Chance separating into quadrants. A series of six metal arms, each with three-pronged fingers, rose from beneath the platform, each grasping a unique piece of glossy black armor plate. Each arm pressed a section of armor against Chance's chest, back, shoulders, and thighs. Rigid yet fluid, the armor sections expanded, connecting with each other with a series of mechanical clicks and clacks. Chance watched in awe as the interconnected sections covered him in a jet-black armored surface, sleek and comfortable in its design. As the process was completed, Chance drifted down, and his feet touched the cold metal platform.

"Keep in mind, this is only the basic armor set up," Sam said. "You'll be able to customize your appearance, your load out, and your equipment based on your preferences and the mission parameters. It's nano-based like your skin suit, and works in tandem with the under layer. Maximum mobility and protection under fire."

"This is a lot to take in," Chance said.

"And I'm breaking the process down for you in phases, Rook. When you deploy, this happens in about forty seconds."

"Whoa."

"Exactly," Sam said. "Next, you get to test it out on the training grid."

"Hang on," Chance said. "What about weapons?"

"Later, Rookie. First, you have to master your armor in close combat. Standby for your helmet."

From the collar of Chance's armor, two sections raised around his neck and the back of his skull. As the pieces came together, cupping his chin over his ears and the top of his head, he felt a shift as an eyeless black faceplate slid down, offering a reconstructed digital field of view, and snapped into the collar beneath his chin with a *snikt*.

"The hell is this made of?" Chance ran his fingertips over the curved surface.

"Molecular hard plate, like the rest of your armor. Have you listened to anything I've said? It builds your helmet in real-time off a pre-designated blueprint and can reconstruct itself if compromised," Sam said.

The inside of the visor flashed on. Chance's eyes roved back and forth, taking in the distinct elements of his armor's Head's Up Display, or HUD.

"If you're used to a tactical visor, your Quick React assault helmet will take the place of that," Sam said, watching a clear tube lower from the ceiling around Chance. "You're going to launch directly onto the training grid."

"Launch?"

"Relax, and trust the armor. Fight against it, and you'll cause trouble for yourself." Sam opened a radio comm link with the training grid. "Grendel, are you in position?"

"Standing by," a voice said, little more than a wheezed sigh, the sound of mud gurgling in a bog.

"Grendel?" Chance said, the faint anxiety in his voice digitally amplified within the armored suit. "I'm about to get my ass kicked, aren't I?"

Sam's finger hovered over the *Deploy* key. The first actual smile Chance had seen from the veteran Enforcer creased his weathered features. "Welcome to the Enforcers, kid."

CHAPTER FIFTEEN

Chance's shouts of excitement died in his throat as he blasted from the launch tube onto the training grid. A twilight world of haze gray and matte purple filled his vision, the strobing lights of his HUD flashing out of sync. He somersaulted through the air, his body twisting wildly as he fell.

"How the hell do I—?"

"Don't fight it, knucklehead." Sam's voice filled his ears. "Let the suit compensate for the landing."

"I can't see," Chance called out, his world inverting over and over again.

"You're not listening. Relax. Stop fighting the suit."

Chance groaned, arching his back—he reached out, splaying his arms, trying to grab something, anything.

The impact of his helmet striking the ground sent a jolt through him. He felt the inner suit constrict against his torso as the rest of his body slammed against the ground, rolled, and slid to a stop.

Chance gasped, his body locked stiff. An instant later, the suit relaxed, and he raised a hand to his helmet.

"Sputz," Chance said.

"I tried to tell you," Sam said.

"*Warning,*" a sterile AI voice said inside his helmet. "*Cranial impact detected. Armor integrity ninety-two percent.*"

"You don't say." Chance pushed himself into a seated position.

His scuffed black armor shifted as he moved. Beneath him lay a stretch of asphalt, cracked and worn thin by the elements. A jumbled mass of half-demolished buildings littered the horizon. Some of them still burned, chimneys of smoke curling from their skeletal frames. Chance tilted his head toward the night sky, backlit by the endless winking lights of Neo Terminus.

"This is the training grid. It's a representation of The Zone," Sam said.

"Wonderful." Chance stood, his tone humorless.

"Keep in mind, while the scenery is fake, the danger is real. Don't let your guard down."

"Okay. What am I supposed to do here?"

"Glad you asked. I'd like you to meet Grendel. He'll be taking care of you today."

Chance halfway turned when he felt his suit seize around him. A second crushing impact struck him high across the back. He pitched straight forward, smacking his helmet against the asphalt again.

"*Warning. Impact detected,*" his AI assistant said. "*Armor integrity eighty-one percent.*"

"I can't move! Relax the damn suit," Chance yelled. The nano skin relaxed, and Chance swiveled onto his back to face his attacker.

The monstrous brute, weighing every bit of five hundred pounds, lumbered forward carrying a steel cudgel in his ham-sized fists. Chance blinked, tried to remind himself that mountain trolls only lived between the moth-eaten pages of old fantasy novels. Two more thunderous steps and it stopped, appraising him like a slab of meat at the street market. Mismatched rags adorned its body, its beady black eyes, unseeing stones set in a broad, fat face. The troll stomped forward on a cybernetic leg and re-gripped its massive club.

"You ready for your lesson, boy?" Grendel said in a hoarse,

cockney accent. He raised the cudgel high overhead.

"Earth to Rook," Sam said. "Grendel will kill you if you let him. Move."

The troll swung the steel club down. In an instant of clarity, Chance rolled to the outside. The club smacked into the asphalt, crushing a circular divot into fine black powder that dusted the air.

Rising to his feet, Chance felt the armored plates shifting to accommodate the movement of his joints. "Sam, how do I stop the suit from seizing?"

"Don't get hit."

Chance ducked a swing of the heavy club, driving in with a punch that the brute blocked with a meaty wrist. Shoved back, Chance struggled to regain his footing.

"Right," Chance said. "But why does it feel like the armor is fighting me for control?"

"It is. You're trying too hard. You need symbiosis," Sam said. "Heads up."

"Wait—" Chance's suit seized around his lower back. Grendel's backswing caught him in the hips and sent him sprawling end over end into the side of a ruined concrete garage. Chance clacked against the asphalt, his body stinging with pain. Saliva flooded his mouth, a precursor to the vomit that may soon follow.

"*Warning, impact detected in the pelvic girdle. Armor integrity seventy-two—*"

"Enough with the warnings." Chance pushed himself to all fours against the wall.

"*I am required to warn you of your armor integrity,*" the sterile voice said inside his helmet.

"Do something useful. Give me some assistance with this monster," Chance said, standing to square off with the approaching hulk.

"*I do not understand your request.*"

"Oh God, RITA, I miss you so much right now," Chance said, balling his fists.

Grendel swung down with the cudgel, obliterating a section of concrete wall between them. With a grunt, the troll stepped through the gap and advanced with quaking strides.

"Sam, this disgusting fat bag of ass is going to kill me. I could use some help," Chance said, his heart banging in his ears.

"Oh? Mister tough street cop needs some help?" Sam's voice dripped with sarcasm.

"Please," Chance said as Grendel closed the distance, a sharky grin melted into the giggling flesh of his face. "I'm in real trouble here."

A sigh of resignation echoed from the comm link in his helmet. "Try your suit's vault ability," Sam said. "Wait until he's on you, then initiate a thrust."

"Okay," Chance said through gnashed teeth. He tried to step back and bumped into the concrete wall behind him. "I hope you're right, or I'm gonna be dead in about five seconds."

"Just do it. Trust the suit," Sam said.

Grendel lumbered forward, cornering Chance against the wall. With a grunt, the brute raised the heavy cudgel over his head.

"Now," Sam said.

"Thrust!" Chance called out.

There was a flash of fire beneath his boots. His stomach dropped. Rocketing up, Chance's armored knuckles connected against the floor of Grendel's chin with a satisfying crack. The monstrous thing dropped its club and stumbled back, moaning as Chance launched into the air twenty feet above.

"Stick the landing and hit him again!" Sam said.

Chance groaned, fighting to pull his feet beneath him as he fell.

"Not like that," Sam said. "Stop fighting the damn suit."

"Come on!" Chance shouted. The suit restricted around his torso. He landed hard on his left side, grinding across the debris-strewn asphalt.

"*Warning,*" the synthetic voice said. "*Armor integrity is now sixty-seven percent.*"

Chance swore. *I can do this...*

With a wild squeal like an enormous bawling infant, Grendel crashed into Chance, driving him back against the ruptured concrete. Chance gasped, unable to raise himself beneath the crushing, gelatinous weight of his foe. From his neck to his toes, his armor locked around him, squeezing, suffocating.

A giant fist slammed into his back, then against his helmet, jarring it into his shoulders. Chance struggled to maintain consciousness.

"*Warning,*" the AI voice said, distant and hazy in his ears, "*thirty-six percent.*"

"Get out of there," Sam's voice echoed.

With an upward jerk, Chance rose, his body a feather on the wind. His vision inverted, and he realized he hung in the brute's monstrous grip.

"No," Chance groaned.

With another piggish squeal of fury, Grendel hurled him down headfirst against the asphalt. A crack rang in his ears, a black tidal wave of pain breaking over him from head to toe.

As Chance's consciousness drained away, a muffled warble of glee sounded from Grendel somewhere above. Chance sucked in a shuddering breath. His vision clouded with dreams of darkness and regret until nothing remained but the crackling of fire and the embrace of the long, cold dark.

Hannah stepped through the sweeping archway and past the barrier separating the last light rail station in Watertown from the first station in Sky Rise. The barrier guards behind her looked on as though their decision to let her and Andrew through was a mistake. She thought of the moment the lead guard scanned her chip and saw the light turn green. Not what he expected. He'd checked with his supervisor, scanning her wrist again and even taking Andrew from her to scan his little hand and verify he, too, could come through.

Held up and appraised by the guards, little Andrew squirmed and screamed. For a single instant, Hannah thought she might mess this up for them all when one of the troopers used the word *defective* regarding Andrew's twisted little form. Getting thrown in the Blocks for attacking a barrier guard in a fit of motherly rage would not help anybody. She'd almost bitten her lip through as she waited for them to hand back her son. *Just let us get on with our new lives already*, she thought.

All of their personal possessions were en route to the new place. All Hannah had was her boy and the clothes on their backs. She waited as the pristine silver train backed into place on the platform. The doors opened with a clean, well-oiled sound, and Hannah, clutching Andrew against her, boarded and took a seat.

Chance had been so nonchalant about it all on the video link call that morning. Just another day moving into a new apartment, but the ride into the Sky Rise district was anything but ordinary. Flashing holo-advertisements of flowing cyan, golden yellow, and neon magenta touted the latest distractions—products Hannah could never imagine owning until now. The towering structures of sunlit glass and shimmering steel seemed to grow taller by the moment, their individual immensity rivaled only by the grandness of the entire scene. Hannah held a sleeping Andrew swaddled against her chest, star-struck by the glittering cityscape rushing past.

Hannah tried to give little attention to how the other occupants stared at her, making themselves narrow as they squeezed past, careful not to come close to touching such a poor-looking person. Ironic, she thought, that in the last twenty-four hours, she'd come into more money than most of these fancy people probably made in a year.

At the third Sky Rise stop, Hannah exited the train and followed the directions on her visor's GPS. Down the ramp to the street, a Walkway Keeper whirred, sucking little bits of debris into its teardrop-shaped receptacle. Hannah stepped around the little bot, mesmerized by her surroundings. Nothing she'd ever experienced in her life prepared her for this place.

The intoxicating smell of grilled meat caused her to veer left to the corner, where a young man in an apron and little white hat waited behind a short, tabled cart. Her mouth watered at the intoxicating aroma. A growl rumbled in her belly. She had eaten nothing since last night's sus-packet.

"What'll ya have?" the young man said, an inverted image of a cooking show playing across the inside of his smoke-lensed visor.

Hannah searched the side of the cart. Its stylized logo read: *The Varsity.*

"What is it?" she said.

The young man regarded her with a suspicious gaze. "What do you mean?

Hannah shrugged.

"You've never had a chili dog before?" he said.

Hannah made a face. "I don't eat slag dogs."

The young man laughed. "It's not actually dog. It's called a hot dog. Like a beef sausage on a synth-wheat bun with beef chili and cheese. Mustard. Onions."

"Beef as in cow?" Hannah struggled to contain herself.

"Yeah." He looked her over with a frown. "Where are you from?"

"I don't know if I have enough…" She waved open her Glom account out of habit, her hand freezing in the air as she remembered Chance's signing bonus. "No, scratch that. I want one. No, two." She licked her lips. "I want two real cow beef chili dogs." She grabbed the edge of the cart to watch the young man prepare them.

"Scan your chip, please," he said, regarding her with suspicion.

Hannah waved her palm over the cart's scanner. A trickling sound of coins followed by a chime.

The young man's face brightened, his suspicions gone. "You got it, lady. Two chili dogs, coming right up."

Hannah swiped the first chili dog from the young man as he began work on the second. She took half of it in the first bite, and the smell of spicy chili and beef, mustard, and onions overwhelmed her senses. Hannah's mouth flooded with saliva, her taste buds registering pure pleasure. Forcing herself to chew before swallowing, she moaned a little sound of ecstasy and licked the chili from her top lip.

"Good, right?"

"Oh my God, give me the other one." Hannah waved an open hand at the young man.

The young man laughed. "I mean, they are one of a kind, but damn, lady."

Hannah ate the second dog slowly, savoring every bite.

"Want a cup of water to wash it down?" the young man said.

Hannah's brow creased, a dab of mustard and chili hanging in the corner of her mouth. "How much?"

"Free," he said. "It's just water."

Hannah swallowed the last of the second dog. "You don't ration water here?"

"Ration water?" the man said, extending the cup. "Where are you from? For real."

"The other side of the barrier. You don't want to go there." She gulped the water down and handed him the cup back.

"How'd you get over here?" he said, looking her over again.

"Long story. Thanks, best food ever," Hannah said, turning for the street.

"Come back anytime," the young man called out.

Hannah waited for the signal and crossed the intersection at the crosswalk. Gleaming new electrical cars and auto-bikes, stacked in their queues, waited for her to pass. Above on the flyways, the latest Krytech, Biljang, and Aeron VTOLs swooped past in guided lanes of travel. Hannah reached the other side and stopped on the sidewalk before the crystal glass of a storefront. Video ads of women laughing and frolicking in a field of green played in a loop across its surface.

"Can you believe this place, buddy?" She rocked Andrew and looked down, suddenly self-conscious of her raggedy appearance. She smoothed her worn floral blouse, tucked a strand of golden hair behind her ear, and entered the store.

Minutes later, Hannah exited the store. Cleansed in an auto-fresh chamber and wearing a crisp, white, frilled blouse that drooped low over her shoulders, a pair of slim-fitting jeans, and thick-heeled white pumps, she'd never felt so glamorous in her whole life. She touched at a curled lock of hair, a river of gold cascading down her shoulders, and patted Andrew, swaddled in a fresh blanket.

Hannah stood outside the store collecting shopping bags filled with new clothes when the words from behind startled her.

"Love the shoes," the immaculate woman said, visor down, all swishing hips and clicking heels as she continued on her way to somewhere expensive.

"Thanks," Hannah said, beaming. Breathing in deeply, she savored the breeze. Even the air seemed cleaner here. Everything was better in this place.

I could get used to this, she thought.

CHAPTER SIXTEEN

Mist tickled his face, reviving his senses. The glass lid eased open with a hiss, and vapors swirled from the breach. Chance's eyes snapped open, the crushing weight of the ugly brute fresh in his mind. His arms lashed out, flailing.

"Whoa, whoa, easy now," Sam said, a hand on his shoulder. "You're off the grid."

Chance's lungs swelled with irregular breaths. "Where… Wh…?" He squinted at the glare in his eyes.

"You're back in the war room."

Chance blinked a few more times, a dull headache pulsing from behind his temples. He sat up inside the white cocoon, and a sting of pain in his side stopped him short. He gasped, clutched at his midsection.

"Take it easy. According to the bio-scan, it looks like a cracked rib," Sam said. "You'll need a longer session this evening in your personal recovery unit."

"Damn." Chance grabbed the rim of the cradle and pushed into a seated position, still wearing his jet-black nano-skin suit. "I feel terrible."

"I imagine you do. Grendel stomped your ass," Sam said with a wry smile. "You're lucky to be alive. I had to promise that fat slag-eater four extra food trays to convince him to let you live."

"What is that thing, anyway?" Chance said.

"Grendel? Just a man." Sam tilted his head. "An enormous man who feels no pain and has introduced some pretty janky cyber enhancements into his body over the years. He's still human… mostly."

Chance rubbed the back of his neck with a wince.

"Years ago, Grendel caused too much havoc in The Zone," Sam said. "They sent Enforcers to bring him in. It took three of them to take him down. Kess, in his Gridlock armor, was one of them. Instead of execution, Grendel took a plea deal and agreed to work for The Glom, training Enforcers on the grid," he said. "He's an animal, no question. But most of the time, he doesn't get too carried away—as long as he gets his treats."

Chance swung his legs over the edge of the recovery chamber and gnashed his teeth at the pain in his side. "You weren't much help." He shifted his eyes to Sam.

Sam's face hardened. "I told you, it's *your* job to keep yourself alive. No one else's. Maybe you'll listen to me next time."

"That AI is stupid." Chance slumped back down. "I'm having a hell of a time just trying to move my body."

Sam grabbed Chance by the wrist and helped him out of the angled glass pod, mist still boiling from its open hatch. "You've got to work in tandem with it," Sam said, "treat it like an entity to cooperate with, not control."

"Easier said than done," Chance said, wincing. "I feel like I screwed the pooch on my first outing."

"You did," a voice said from behind Sam.

Sam and Chance turned in unison to see several figures at the entrance to the war room. The man speaking took a seat in the station behind a name plate marked *Sanction*, propping his feet up with a self-righteous smirk.

"That was some ugly sputz in there," the severe-faced man said. He motioned to the room. "They said you were some sort of super cop before you came here. But I don't see it."

Sam released a sigh of irritation. To the left, two others dressed in black flight suits stood inside the doorway to the room. Chance recognized one of them as the confident woman with mocha skin and golden eyes who'd helped extract him from The Slags.

"Chance." Sam waved his arm toward the others. "Meet your fellow Enforcers."

"Hi." Chance waved with an outward twitch of his fingers.

The two by the door crossed to where Chance stood, still getting his bearings, free of the recovery chamber.

"I believe you remember this one," Sam said.

The woman, nearly as tall as Chance, extended her hand. "Karissa Gaines."

"Thanks for coming to get me from The Slags." Chance gave her hand a firm shake, which she returned. "I understand you volunteered."

"More to put the Slag King in his place than anything, but I'm glad to have been of assistance," Karissa said.

"I appreciate your honesty," Chance said.

"The other guy here," Sam said, "who looks like he belongs in a digital catalog, is Jessie Fullard."

Chance sized the man up, all pectorals and biceps and flash-brightened teeth. He could just as easily have been an underwear model as an Enforcer.

"Nice to meet you, new guy," Jessie said, shaking Chance's hand, "how's it going?"

"I've been better, I suppose." Chance touched his ribs.

Karissa winked. "Don't lose too much sleep about it. Grendel kicks everyone's ass the first time."

"Good to know," Chance said with a sigh of pain.

"Still doesn't make this kid worthy of filling the slot." The severe-faced man crossed his arms. "Mark my words, he'll end up another casualty of The Zone."

Open irritation crossed Sam's face. "The jackass with the big mouth is Rip LaRue. Take nothing he says personally. He hates everyone."

"Stick it in your ass, old man," Rip said.

"See?" Sam said, unfazed. "Come on, we'll head to the armory and take it slow for the rest of the day."

"Nice to meet you guys," Chance said to Karissa and Jessie as he shuffled after Sam across the war room. Nearing the door, he met Rip's ice-cold scrutiny. The Enforcer laughed and shook his head.

"Let me know if you need a babysitter, old Sam. I love kids." He winked and popped a piece of gum into his mouth.

"Asshole," Chance murmured.

As they turned into the hallway, Chance sidled up alongside Sam, the overhead lights illuminating them in intermittent halos as they walked.

"He always like that?" Chance asked.

"Rip? Pretty much."

"And Karissa and Jessie are what? Partners?"

"Yeah, when trials require it," Sam said. "Their handles are Takedown and Pursuit, respectively."

"And the jerk?"

"Sanction—his partner is a dude by the name of Ash Stroud. Ash is a tough guy but also a bit of a loner. Goes by the handle Escalation."

"And you?" Chance asked as they neared the end of the hallway. A dark glass door slid open before them.

Sam huffed out a laugh. "I'm stuck with you, Rookie. Don't get me killed."

They reached the end of the hall and stopped before a concrete barrier inset with a rectangle of black steel. Stenciled on the door in old-world military-style stencils were the words *Armory and Assets. Authorized Personnel Only.*

"And this?" Chance jerked his thumb toward the imposing barrier.

"Keep your pants on," Sam said.

A spidery grid of golden lasers shot from the wall, scanning the two men from head to toe and back up again. A hollow, electronic voice reverberated off the concrete walls. "*Shepherd, Sam. Enforcer. Credentials: Valid. Griffin, Chance. Enforcer. Credentials: Valid. Access granted.*" A hissing pop and the locking mechanism in the smooth steel hatch disengaged, the vault-like door cracking an inch.

Sam reached forward and tugged the massive, hinged door open, leaning his back into it to get it to move.

Chance eyed the twenty-inch-thick door as it opened. "Damn, what do you guys keep in here? Nukes?"

"Not exactly." Sam pulled the door closed behind him with a heavy *thunk*. "But there is tech here they can't allow to get out."

The absolute darkness lit up with a string of brilliant golden lasers that swished from side to side. There was a chime and a second door slid open. Sam led Chance beneath a shallow arch that hummed in response to their passing. On the other side, lights flicked on one at a time to illuminate numbered lanes on a three-hundred-yard firing range.

To Chance's left, racks and racks of weapons, everything from the classic bullpup ZV Battle Rifles and Electro-stream weapons he was familiar with, to devices he'd never seen before. Long barreled sniper rifles, stubby angular sub-machine guns in urban camo designs, even tubular weapons that appeared to be some sort of rocket launcher.

Chance plucked up a small metallic ball with vents in the side that pulsed with blue light.

"Careful," Sam said, pointing to the device in Chance's hand. "Mishandle one of those, and we won't be walking out of here."

Chance froze, unsure whether further movement was a bad idea.

"Impact grenade. No fuse," Sam told him. "It detonates when

it strikes a hard surface—such as the ground—when you drop it on accident."

"Right." Chance set the device down as though he were handling a newborn baby. He turned, surveying the space.

"Through there." Sam pointed off to another set of doors. "Is the battlefield. You can go practice tactics and target acquisition and test your weapons systems before you hit The Zone."

Chance took in the cavernous, artificially lit space.

"Remember, no weapons leave this room," Sam said. "Check yourself before you head out each time."

"And if I miss something?"

Sam pointed to the archway they'd walked through on their way in. "Every weapon is tagged, and the arch scans you on your way out. One of the maintenance techs last year got flash-fried when he thought he'd smuggle out a combat knife for his kid."

Chance swallowed. He didn't like the way Sam used the term *flash-fried* and, for a moment, wondered what the hell that actually meant.

"Then how do I use these weapons in The Zone?" Chance asked.

"Good question," Sam said. "From your station in the war room, you can program all aspects of your load out. Weapons, armor, tactical devices, where you carry it all on your rig, everything. You can even customize your armor's appearance, which is encouraged. Don't forget, the point is to perform in front of millions of viewers and to look good doing it."

"Perform." Chance took in the rows and rows of arms and armaments. "I thought it was urban combat?"

"It is. But you have to put on a show if you want to stay in this line of work." Sam sized Chance up. "Better get used to the idea you're a highly trained, well-equipped rodeo clown."

"A what clown?"

Sam waved him off. "Forget about it." He walked to the far

wall. "Here's what you need to know, Rook. When you hit the deploy key, whatever your programmed load out is, that's what you'll hit The Zone with. Take the time to get it right. All weapons and armor are issued to you as you prep and are taken back up when you exfil back out again."

"It's all customizable?"

"Almost. There is one standard piece of weaponry you'll need to get to know." Sam touched a wall panel. The wall slid open with the sound of escaping gas. A shelf extended horizontally, then angled to forty-five degrees. "Allow me to introduce you to an Enforcer's best friend—the Peacemaker."

Chance viewed the massive handgun nestled in its cradle, a large, blocky matte-black pistol. "It looks like the old first generation MVX, but bigger." He picked it up, balking at the weight. "Much bigger."

"Same manufacturer," Sam said, "but much more advanced. Familiarize yourself with it."

"You've got to be kidding me," Chance said, hefting the weapon. Pointing it downrange, he extended his arms and took a solid shooting position. His arms quivered with the signs of strain. Chance lowered the hand cannon and gave Sam an incredulous look. "How am I supposed to run and gun with this monster?"

"Lots of practice," Sam told him. "Don't worry too much about the weight. When you're in full armor, the suit will assist you in maintaining your shooting platform. The rest of the gunfighting fundamentals are up to you."

Chance raised the Peacemaker again, pivoting back and forth. "Why is it this damn bulky?"

"To accommodate its biometric user interface and suite of standard features," Sam said, taking the pistol from him. "Yours will code to your bio profile, which means no one but you can use it. If you die and some thug in The Zone picks it up, it goes inert. Guy might as well be palming a brick."

Nice touch, Chance thought, rolling the Peacemaker over.

"This bad boy has two modes of fire. Semi-auto and three-round burst. All ammo types function in either mode, and you can adjust between the two with the selector switch here." Sam flicked down a lever on the frame.

"*Burst,*" the weapon chimed.

Sam flicked the selector switch back up.

"*Semi-auto,*" the weapon chimed again.

"Hang on to her if you fire a burst. This joker will climb right out of your hands if you let it," Sam said.

"Got it," Chance said.

Sam set the Peacemaker down and motioned to a rack of extended pistol magazines. "In addition to the modes of fire, the Peacemaker takes multiple ammunition types."

"It shoots something other than standard rounds?" Chance's eyebrows raised, incredulous.

"White phosphorous, armor piercing, you name it..." Sam gestured across the rack.

Chance picked up a magazine with a red emblem on it, a streak of crimson that ended in a fragmented burst. "Signature lock," he read. "What's that?"

Sam smirked. "Get an AI lock on a target, and the guided round, once fired, will home in on the bio signature and track their movement, even around corners. It's fantastic."

Chance set the mag down and hefted the massive handgun up into a shooting stance again. "You serious?"

"As a heart attack," Sam said. "But there's a limited capacity of those. And don't let the fact that it's guided lull you into believing skill isn't involved. Once you do some training with it, you'll realize how difficult all of this can be to master."

Chance set the Peacemaker back in its cradle. "If the armor is any indication, I'm going to have my hands full trying to get this all figured out."

"Better sooner than later, Rook," Sam said.

"Yeah?" Chance said, turning to Sam. "And why's that?"

The crow's feet at the corners of Sam's eyes deepened into furrows. "Cause, ready or not—Kess says you hit The Zone live at the end of the week. All by your lonesome."

Chance's face went slack, and the sour taste of bile tingled in the back of his throat. He felt his budding excitement dissipate into the cold concrete beneath his feet.

That jerk Rip was right, he thought. *I'm a dead man.*

CHAPTER SEVENTEEN

Benny lay with his eyes shut, trying to focus a little too hard on the idea of sleep. The dark behind his eyelids a comforting shroud, he took slow breaths in through his nose, exhaling in turn. Beside the bed, Muck dozed on his pallet. The slag rescue groaned and shifted on his side, making little snoring sounds. The occasional VTOL cruised past to illuminate the narrow living space and rattle the dinnerware in the kitchen. The hourglass-shaped single room felt a bit more like two because of the narrow archway that separated the kitchen and sitting area from the modest queen-sized bed. Benny's small but orderly efficiency apartment in Volkan Heights wasn't much, but it was enough for the two of them.

Benny opened his eyes and thrashed the comforter back. *Damn, restless legs.* He sat up in the neon-tinged dark and swung his feet over the side of the bed. Everything was fine, his uncomplicated life chugging along just the way he liked it. Then out of the blue, Chance, who hated The Glom, The Zone, the Enforcers, and all the rest, went off and applied to work for them. Benny knew he'd done it for Hannah and Andrew, to give them a better life, but the reality of his longtime partner leaving the force left a sourness in his gut.

Can't trust anyone other than Chance out there. How am I supposed to quit on that? Benny thought.

He'd done as Chance asked and retrieved RITA before they

wiped her from his armor's memory and redistributed the equipment. When he'd gotten home, the drone was waiting. Benny knew it was from Chance. No one else he knew could afford to send a personal courier drone to his apartment. He'd uploaded the data drive and sent it on a return-to-destination route. Maybe Chance or Hannah would hit him up soon to let him know how things were going, living the big life.

Muck whined a low sound and raised his eyes to Benny.

"Yeah, I know," Benny said, reaching down to ruffle the slag rescue's hairless, pointed ears.

He rubbed his own stubbled jaw and stood, moving to the window.

"Shades," Benny said. The blackout-shaded glass lightened, bathing the apartment in a rainbow of strobing neon. His eyes roved across the rain-soaked sprawl of grungy cityscape that extended as far as the eye could see. The late-night sounds of a city that never slept reached out to him.

Muck whined again and raised his head off the pallet. A low growl rumbled in the canine's throat.

"What is it, buddy?" Benny said to his hairless, sore-covered friend.

There was a tiny *tic-tic-tic* followed by a high-pitched chime. Benny squinted at the door.

"What the devil—?"

The front door exploded inward with a bone-rattling concussion. The frame buckled, torn from the wall, and flew across the room in a brilliant flash of fire. It smacked against the sitting room window, fracturing the thick glass. Benny flung himself across the width of the bed, his hand seizing the MVX pistol on the nightstand. He slammed hard against the opposite wall with his shoulder. On the other side of the small bedroom, Muck snarled and snapped, teeth bared.

Through the smoke-shrouded breach, heavily armed men in

matte gray Devcon assault armor. They poured through the debris-strewn entryway and into the apartment, their weapon-mounted lights sweeping left and right. Benny stalked with his weapon to the edge of the archway, his counterassault prepared, when one intruder called out from the entry point.

"NTPD," one of the tactical officers said. "Step out with your hands in plain sight. Do it now."

A wash of dread descended upon Benny. *The hell is this? Some sort of mistake?* He lowered the MVX in his hands.

"Standby," another man said, "we've got an aggressive animal here."

With a loud pop, a sticky black net fired from the officer's launcher and pinned Muck to the floor. Caught in its fibrous web, Muck struggled and yelped.

"Okay, okay, hey, leave him alone. It's fine," Benny said.

"Comply," the first officer said. "Now!"

"You've got the wrong place," Benny said, waving his free hand. "I'm a badge. Corporal Benitez, NTPD."

"You've been bio-scanned and are holding a weapon," the point man said. "Drop it now, or we're gonna shoot your ass!"

The pistol trembled in Benny's hand. He tossed it on the bed where the tactical officers could see it. "See, no problem," he said. "I'm with you guys. This is a mistake."

"Step into the open with your hands in plain sight."

"No problem, just take it easy, fellas. I'm one of the good guys," Benny said, rounding the edge of the archway into the glare of the officer's weapon-mounted lights. He raised his hands. "What's this about?"

"Get down," the officer said, his face obscured by the dark glass of his helmet's visor.

"I'll stand right here, thank you," Benny said. "I'd like an explanation why you've raided my place."

"Take him." The lead tactical officer jerked his head at two others.

Benny's heart drummed with a rapid cadence in his ears, his breath quickening. "Look, I'm Guillermo Benitez. I'm on the job," he said, adding, "I didn't do anything. Where's your warrant?"

Two tactical officers pushed Benny against the wall, wrenching his hands behind his back. He struggled to see their faces, but all he could see were their chins below the dark glass of their face shields. Geared up, all Tac officers looked the same.

"I didn't *do* anything," Benny said again.

The faceless officer behind him leaned in close. "We're well aware of who you are, Corporal Benitez. Now, where's the dope you stole from lockup?"

"Dope?" The word lodged in Benny's throat like a foreign body. "I didn't take any—" A spike of realization lanced through him as Kip Monaghan rounded the corner in a raid vest. In his hand, he held one of the seized duffels Benny saw at the South Precinct the other night.

"I've got 'em right here," Kip said. "Dumb slag-eater stashed them in the drop box outside."

The hot prickle of sweat on his brow, Benny tried to swallow the dryness away. *This isn't real. It can't be.* He watched as Deyvar Whaley, dreadlocks across his face, entered behind Kip with a second duffel. Deyvar winked at Benny.

"I'm being set up!" Benny shouted.

Muck began a new fit of snarling where he lay, trapped beneath the sticky webbing.

"Shut your mouth!" the tactical officer said, forcing the side of Benny's thick neck closer to the wall with the shaft of a blast baton.

Benny groaned but didn't fight as the two tactical officers restrained his arms.

"You hear this damn guy?" Deyvar said. "We're setting him up. Can you believe it?"

Kip laughed, a head shorter than the men around him.

"They're the ones who stole the drugs out of lockup," Benny said. "I saw them."

Kip feigned disbelief. "Can you believe this dirty sack of sputz? Trying to drag us down with him. It's pathetic." Kip walked over and leaned close into Benny's face. "I can't stand a dirty cop. I'll see you rot in the Blocks for this, Benitez."

"Check the department surveillance," Benny said. "I swear, I didn't..."

"We checked," the tactical officer behind him said, pressing harder with the shaft of the blast baton, "and you're the only one going in or out at the time the drugs went missing. You're screwed dirtbag."

They were right. How was he going to argue? He'd been there. All Kip and Deyvar had to do was hack the feed to have themselves scrubbed from the video, making Benny the only one there. And even if they didn't have him taking the drugs from lockup, they did have him taking sensitive police-issue equipment. An advanced AI worth tens of thousands of T's on the black market. If he'd been willing to take that, how hard would it be for them to sell the idea of him taking the drugs as well? He felt lightheaded. His eyes were searching but unseeing. Cops didn't last two weeks in the Blocks before getting a shiv in the liver, and with Chance gone, there was no longer anyone who'd stick their neck out for him. Not over this.

Kip turned, his face taking on an amused look. He pointed to Muck struggling on the floor. "You know harboring street slags is illegal."

"He's not illegal," Benny groaned, "he's a legitimate rescue. I got him from the shelter."

"You got official papers?" Kip asked.

"They don't give out official papers. You know they don't."

Kip stood over Muck, shaking his head and sucking his teeth. "Look at the fangs on this vicious little monster. Gotta put it down."

"No, no, hey, no! Wait!" Benny tried to turn as the tactical officers pressed him harder against the wall. "Please. I'm begging you, okay? I'm begging! Please don't hurt him."

Kip pulled his MVX and pointed it at Muck, still struggling, eyes wild beneath the net.

"Please!" Benny screamed.

The weapon in Kip's hand recoiled, the shock of the report deafening in the confined space.

Benny shook, the corded muscles of his neck straining. "You dirty slag-eaters!"

Kip holstered his MVX. "Get this criminal sputz in cable restraints."

A close-flying VTOL cruised past the window. The apartment rattled, dishes clinking with its passage. Light flooded the room. For an instant, the tactical officers squinted and turned away, their grip on Benny's bulging forearms loosening.

Benny shoved backward. The gap between his chest and the wall wasn't much, just enough to allow him to raise his knee and plant his foot. Thrusting away, Benny and the tactical officers stumbled back and crashed into the opposite wall with a grunt. He spun into the operators clinging to him, out matching them by sheer strength alone. His fingers closed on the helmet of the man to his left, and he jerked it down over his face, whipping his fist across the chin of another, blows that sent both sprawling.

A blast of pain tore through Benny as a crackling blast baton smacked against his spine.

"Stop resisting!"

With a scream, Benny drove into the man behind him. Furious, the Tac operator swung again, aiming for Benny's head. Fingers splayed, Benny caught the end of the baton, gnashing his teeth as the electrical shock fired through his arms and into his chest. He faltered, tore the blast baton from the Tac officer's sweaty grip, and brought it down with a flash into the man's helmet. The

Tac officer's legs buckled, and he pitched against the floor.

Benny swung the baton back and caught a fourth man in the side of his visor, the white-hot electrical blast exploding the tempered glass into the shrieking man's face.

"Shoot that big slag-eater!" Kip shouted, backing up, his MVX raised.

The first round zipped past and smacked the glass of the cracked bay window behind him, splintering its surface in a glistening spiderweb of cracks. Ducking, Benny ran for the compromised window as rounds stitched their way up the wall behind him. He dove headfirst and crashed through the brittle glass, his body falling free.

A rain-drenched awning broke his fall and knocked the wind from him. It buckled, dropping him onto a concrete patio below. He pushed to his feet as the sound of gunfire echoed from the window above. Benny surged toward the edge.

Only a three-story fall from here, Benny thought. *Maybe I can survive it.*

Bullets zipped off the wet concrete beneath his feet, sending little showers of water into the air. A sharp pain stung his neck, and the collar of his T-shirt stained crimson with a wash of blood. He stumbled, pitching forward as he neared the edge.

Benny screamed, the sound tearing from his throat as a second round punched a ragged hole through the meat of his left biceps. He careened headlong from the edge of the rooftop and struck a courier drone, his hands grabbing tight to the wire-thin supports. The small drone whined and spun downward in looping arcs. Centripetal force slinging his legs wide, Benny pinched his eyes shut and hung on for dear life. With a jarring thud, he slammed into the asphalt. The courier drone cracked against the street in a shower of sparks, and its quad rotors slowed to a stop.

A gasp rose from the shocked, visor-clad pedestrians as they stepped away from Benny in horror.

Get up, Benny. It's just pain. Fight through it.

Benny pushed from his belly to all fours, swooned, and almost collapsed. The bone of his left arm throbbed with arcs of overwhelming pain. He touched his neck, and the blood oozed from a significant flesh wound. Rising to his knees, he pulled his shirt off and tore it in two. He pressed hard to the side of his neck and pinched the fabric against his shoulder with his head. Taking the other strip, he wrapped the wound in his arm and pulled it tight with his teeth, eliciting a groan of pain.

Down the alley, an NTPD surveillance drone snapped on its searchlight, the white beam probing through the dark of the trash-cluttered lane.

Another gasp rose from the onlookers as Benny stood on shaking legs. Some of them had already uploaded active tips to the NTPD. He was sure of it. He shuffled forward, forcing his way through the gawking crowd away from the searchlight. Now they'd want him for multiple counts of aggravated assault on a peace officer, and Benny knew all too well how those sorts of matters got handled. He wouldn't survive capture.

The only hope for him now was to run.

CHAPTER EIGHTEEN

Chance stepped from the glass recovery chamber and stretched his arms high over his head with a yawn. Golden rays of sunlight glinted off the super structures of Silver City, casting the morning sun in shimmering waves across the interior of Chance's apartment. He twisted his torso, waiting for the sharp, pinching sensation the cracked rib had given him the night before as he climbed into the recovery chamber.

Chance inhaled deeply and slapped his ribcage a few times. *Amazing,* he thought. *Good as new.*

Chance stepped into his black flight suit and zipped it up as he wandered to the kitchen. Just like all the other flight suits in his closet, the nametape over the right breast read *Justice.* A weighty moniker—only time would tell if he could live up to it.

Chance rounded a polished marble island and rapped on his ribs a few more times with his knuckles. *That recovery thing is wild,* he thought. He wished he better understood the science behind it, how it could heal his body with total efficiency. Sam told him it activated the nanobots in his bloodstream and accelerated the already stupefying rate at which he healed. He still didn't understand it.

He poured himself a cup of coffee, inhaled the rich aroma, and took a sip. Removing the lid on his chef-prepared ham and cheese omelet, he leaned forward and breathed in the cloud of steam rising in wisps from the plate. None of it felt real. The memories of scraping along, trying to put food on the table, just days ago.

The video link trilled a soft, repetitive cadence. Chance slipped his sleek, high-end visor on and waved the connection open. Hannah's face filled his screen. She pursed her lips and made kissing noises.

Chance chuckled.

"Hey, when do I get to see my man already?" Hannah said.

"Soon, I'm told." Chance took a sip of his coffee under the bottom of the visor. "I have to stay focused while I'm in training."

Hannah made a pouty face.

"I know."

"How's it all going?" Hannah said.

"Pretty good." Chance shrugged.

"Just good?"

"I mean, it's great. There's a lot to take in." He left out yesterday's cracked rib. *No need to worry her.*

"What about the people you work with?" Hannah asked.

Chance showed his teeth in a half-smile, half-grimace.

"Bad?" Hannah said.

Chance took his coffee and meandered away from the counter, stepping over ribbons of light that crisscrossed in a shimmering latticework along the floor. "They have a hard time accepting new people into their ranks. I mean, I get it. Sam, my ETO—"

"ETO?" she asked.

"My training officer. He's pretty cool. Old school SWAT guy. I remember him from my rookie days at NTPD. He's going to be my new partner."

Hannah nodded. "That's good."

"I'm missing Benny, though," Chance said.

"You talked to him?"

Chance suppressed a rising sense of guilt. He lowered his head. "Not yet. Been busy. I'll try when I get off with you."

"You should."

Chance drained the last of his coffee and popped a bite of the fluffy cheese omelet into his mouth. "How's the new place?" he said around the bite.

"Incredible. It's missing you, though. Wanna see?"

Hannah switched her visor to an outward view of the pristine room, with vaulted ceilings, real white leather furniture, and a walk-out balcony. The sun rising over the shimmering cityscape threatened to wash out the image.

"Wow, your place is bigger than this one, and this place is huge."

"I don't even know what to do with all this space. There's so much food…" She switched the view back to her. "Oh, and I ate this chili dog thing at a stand in town. Ah-mazing."

"You ate what?"

"It's like a beef sausage with all this stuff on it. I've never eaten so well in my whole life."

"We are doing better, for sure," Chance said, "and a lot of people out there still aren't."

Chance and Hannah held each other's gaze in silence through the feed.

"Chance, I don't want to feel guilty for having enough for once."

Chance waved her off. "You're right. I shouldn't have said anything. This is a gift, and we need to make the most of it."

"Yeah," Hannah said, her voice betraying a conflicted heart.

"Where's my boy?" Chance's face brightened.

"Napping," Hannah whispered, crossing into the baby's room. She switched the view, allowing Chance to see Andrew's sleeping form tucked beneath layers of baby blankets.

"There he is," Chance said, aching with the desire to hold his son. He swallowed. "Any word on treatments yet?"

"A personal physician already reached out to me. We're setting it all up now. It's a dream come true." She clasped her hands together.

"That's wonderful, Hannah," Chance said. A reminder he had to meet Sam for the day's training dinged on his display. "Hey, I'm going to have to let you go."

"Love you. Be safe. Okay?" Hannah said.

"Always. Love you, too," Chance said and waved the call closed.

He leaned against the counter and finished his eggs. He couldn't seem to find a place for all the emotions swelling within him; immense gratefulness and anticipation, twisted with loneliness, distrust, and regret. *How am I supposed to move on with my life after so much change?* He dabbed his lips with a napkin, swiped the calls list open, and selected Benny's name.

He listened to the tone trill, drumming his fingers on the countertop.

A message flashed across his visor. *The subscriber you are trying to call cannot be reached. Please try again later.*

Chance waved the call closed. Benny was busy on the street with real-world problems. What did Chance plan to do anyway, rub it in Benny's face that now he lived on the other side of town?

He just hoped Benny snagged RITA without any complications. He didn't want his friend to have any trouble, not on his account.

Maybe if he had time between Grendel beatings today, he'd reach out again later. Chance exited the apartment on his way to Sam's place, and the lights blinked off one by one.

Chance's feet touched down on the war room platform. The open portal overhead that led to the training grid wheezed shut. His

Quick React helmet separated over his face and receded into the open collar of his armor.

"Well?" Sam said, noting Chance's frown. "Still pissed?" He reclined in his chair, stoic.

"I hate this AI, man. It's still causing the suit to fight me," Chance said. "I'll let it do its thing, but it's got to trust me as well. You said symbiosis—that indicates equal input."

"You are correct," Sam said, putting his hands behind his head.

"It's not happening. The suit wants control. It doesn't respect *my* intuition."

"It is what it is, Rook." Sam sighed. "Either you can handle it, or you can't."

Chance rolled his eyes.

"You don't have to like it," Sam fired back. "What? You ready to quit on me already?"

"No, Sam. Look, I'm working it out," Chance said from his position on the platform. "Still a little clunky, but I've got the obstacle course down, and weapons manipulation is pretty straight forward. I can do this, but by week's end? That's a stretch."

"Two days away. You need some more work," Sam sat forward and wiped down the console. "Grendel?"

Chance's posture deflated. The idea of getting pulverized again soured his stomach.

"You gotta do it, Rook," Sam said with a shrug. "If you can't take Grendel, you'll get us both killed."

"What could I face in The Zone worse than that abomination?"

"You kidding me?" Sam sat down the microfiber cloth in his hand. "You mean other than armies of well-armed sociopaths? What about robo-turrets that auto-target and advance on your position? Or cobbled-together junk mechs, like walking tanks? You tell me, Rook."

Chance held up his hand in a gesture for Sam to stop.

"Haven't you ever watched The Zone, like everyone else in the city?" Sam asked.

Chance shrugged. "In passing, at a pay-to-play bar or something, but not in full."

Sam balked. "And they picked you for this? You have no idea what you've gotten yourself into, do you?"

"A little?"

"Grendel is the *baseline* standard, man. Now, are you ready to show me something, or do you want to keep crying about it?" Sam regarded him with hard eyes.

"Give it a rest already." Chance scowled. He pointed, his armor clanking. "Put me in against that fat slag-eater. I'll show you something."

Sam smirked. "That's more like it." He prepared to touch the deployment key when a chime sounded at the door.

A Glom employee dressed in a black kimono entered the war room with a small, square case. "Courier delivery for Enforcer Justice?"

Sam nodded in Chance's direction. "Right here."

Chance, cumbersome in his powered-down armor, motioned the man onward.

Approaching, the man released the latches on the box and eased the lid back.

Chance saw the slim data drive and knew right away Benny had come through for him. "You guys opened my package?" he said.

The man in the kimono glanced up. "Sorry, yes. Company policy. Everything coming in gets scanned."

"And?" Chance raised his eyebrows. "What did you find?"

The man, flustered now, kneaded his hands. "It's a data drive with some non-hostile AI memory files. You're cleared to possess it."

"Thanks," Chance said, accepting it with a biometric fingerprint signature. "I'm glad it meets your approval." He jerked his head at Sam.

Without a word, the courier handed the small box to Sam and turned, robe swishing with urgency as though he sensed he'd already overstayed his welcome.

As the door slid shut behind the man, Sam shrugged, his palms turned upward. "Okay, you got me. What is it?"

"Plug it into the armor configuration terminal," Chance said.

Sam snapped the drive in place on the console. A small chime sounded as a series of lights flashed on the side of the drive. An upload screen enlarged on the console display.

Advanced Artificial Intelligence detected. Scanned entity found clear of viruses and corrupting agents. Overwrite Inteli-suit AI?

Sam cocked an eyebrow at Chance.

"Do it," Chance said.

Sam shook his head. "You like doing things your own way, don't you, Rook?" He touched the confirm key.

There was a blip as several load bars zipped full across the display. *Upload complete. Initializing AI.*

Chance's armor chimed a series of notes he'd come to appreciate as his support system went online.

"*Hello, Officer Griffin. It has been too long. Good to see you are well.*" RITA's voice slipped into Chance's ear like smoked honey.

Sam lifted his hands, shoving away the air. "Okay, what the hell is that?"

Chance just smiled. "RITA, I can't tell you how much I've missed you."

"*It makes me happy to be working with you again, Officer Griffin,*" RITA said. "*Though being disconnected from the cloud like this does concern me. I am at risk since my programming will not have backups while housed here.*"

"We'll keep each other safe," Chance said. "You trust me?"

A small ticking sound passed as RITA processed his words. "*I trust you, Officer Griffin.*"

"Call me Chance. We've got a different mission, RITA. I'm an Enforcer now."

"*Very good, Officer...*" More ticking. "*Very good, Chance. If I may ask—what are our new parameters?*"

"Familiarize yourself with your new digs. We'll be working in The Zone. Your job will be to troubleshoot problems and analyze threats in real-time. Keep me alive. Can you handle that?"

"*Affirmative. It's what I do best. I've analyzed this Inteli-suit's capabilities and will prepare a suite of options for you to deploy when needed.*"

"That's my girl." Chance turned to a stupefied Sam. "Well, Sam? What are you waiting for?"

"Grendel?" Sam asked.

"That's right," Chance said with a confident wink.

CHAPTER NINETEEN

Gabriel Kess chewed his bottom lip to prevent saying something he was sure to regret later. He watched the carbon-colored shadow flicker against its pale blue projection display and waited for the founder to finish. Kess composed himself, smoothed the front lapels of a suit that cost him twenty-five thousand T's, and flicked his eyes to the live-cam surveillance feed of New West City.

"Are we clear, Mr. Kess?" the founder said, its pitch and tone distorted by a wash of electronic interference.

"Crystal," Kess said.

He turned back to the static-lined projection screen before him. Images of angry citizens launching Molotov cocktails at the encroaching rows of New West City rangers desperate to maintain order. The entire power grid failed first. Having lost the few distractions citizens counted on, riots erupted in the streets. Buildings burned out of control. The bodies of the dead and dying lay strewn like trash in the gutters. *Absolute pandemonium*, Kess thought.

"There are far too many anarchist groups who would like nothing more than to see this same fate for Neo Terminus," the founder said, the sign of Beta hovering over his head. "We will not allow what is happening in New West City to happen here."

"And it won't," Kess said with a calm air of assurance, "not if you relax and allow me to finish what I started—what you authorized me to do."

"You want us to relax?" Founder Beta said. "What's taking so long? Accelerate the process."

Kess shook his head, turning his attention from the mess in New West City back to the shifting gray outline of digital sand in his chat window. "Not possible."

"And why is that?"

"It just isn't," Kess said. "Some things you can't rush. We're introducing a new Enforcer. If we botch his first appearance, we will accelerate the decline in viewership and force the exact situation you're concerned about. The best weapon you can employ is total distraction. But it has to be done right."

"How long?" the founder asked.

Even through the electronic distortion, Kess felt he detected a hint of anxiety hidden beneath the words. He'd never met the founders, never gotten a good read on them. One thing he knew, if he'd learned anything—their game must be played. Everyone wanted something, including the founders. It was Kess's job to make sure they got what they wanted. To not follow through would be disastrous for him. Distressed people were just a single shove away from becoming dangerous people—a lesson from his policing days he'd do well not to forget.

"How long until this new Enforcer is ready, Mr. Kess?" Founder Beta snapped.

"Soon," Kess said. "He's finishing the onboarding regimen now."

"Do not play games with us, Mr. Kess. Do we need to remind you what's at stake?"

Kess felt a hot prickle cross his scalp. "No. You do not."

"Then get him ready." The founder's image flickered but remained. "We're moving his Zone trial forward."

Kess sat forward. "Forward? To when?"

"Tomorrow."

"No." The edge of Kess's hand cut through the air. "I don't think you're listening—"

Click

"Damn fools!" In one smooth motion, Kess erupted, raking the elements from the top of his desk and flinging them, bouncing and clattering against the floor-to-ceiling windows on the other side of the room. Kess stood behind his desk, blood pressure soaring, fists balled, every muscle coiled.

He prided himself on absolute control. Calm and discipline made the man. Without them, the more primal influencers of anger and fear could run amok, laying waste to days, even years, of hard work. One wrong word in the wrong venue had the power to burn a man's world to the ground. If he couldn't control himself, he was no better than the throngs of the desperate and the indigent scrabbling to survive in the filth-strewn alleys of Neo Terminus.

Kess took a moment, cleared his throat, and straightened his suit and his posture. The fingers of his hand touched the vial in his pocket but left it where it was. He took in a breath. Held it. Then sat back at his desk and, with a few flicks of his wrist, opened a video link. The connection trilled soft and slow. After a few rings, the call activated, and the perfect tear-drop face wreathed in dark curls filled the screen.

"Dad?"

Kess spread his hands. "How's my little girl?"

"Fine, Dad… Do… Did you need something?" she said, an annoyed tone in her voice.

"Me? Oh, no." Kess opened his hands and made what he hoped was a pleasant expression. "Just wanted to hear your voice, that's all. Is your day going well?"

A little smirk crested the teenager's lips, the image of her visor-clad face projected before him. She was in a plush Vargas VTOL, the shimmering Sky Rise cityscape passing by outside her window. "You want to know how my day is going? You feeling okay?"

"What's he calling for?" Kess cringed as the bitter voice of his ex-wife filtered through the speakers. He lowered the volume. "Work not keeping that useless asshole busy enough?"

"I dunno," his daughter said. "What are you calling about?"

A sudden wave of embarrassment pushed over him. A most disagreeable feeling. A feeling he worked hard to never, ever have to entertain. Kess pursed his lips, his business-like demeanor hardening. "No reason. Just making sure you're working hard in school, Clarissa. That's all."

Clarissa rolled her eyes. "I'm doing fine in school, Dad."

You couldn't come up with something better to say to her? Kess swallowed, then faked a smile to cover up the pain inside. "Good. That's good."

"Hang up, Clarissa," his ex said, her voice sharp. "He didn't care to be involved up to this point. Why make an effort now?"

Kess felt his scalp tingle with rising irritation, a temper with a way of wreaking untold destruction upon his ordered life. "I don't think that's fair. I've done my best to provide, and…"

His daughter's face softened. Was that concern for him? "I have to go, Dad."

"Clarissa, I'd like to see you," Kess blurted out.

"Hang up, Clarissa," her mother said.

His daughter's lips stretched thin, her face failing to conceal some old unresolved wound. "I have to go. I'm sorry."

The screen went blank, and the image receded. He'd made a mistake in calling, had wanted to reach out casually, but of course, she didn't trust it. A host of toxic thoughts burned through him, and as the seconds ticked past, Gabriel Kess found them harder and harder to control. He'd wanted to hear Clarissa's voice, to search for the love of a daughter in her eyes. *But my infernal bitch of an ex-wife always gets in the way. Maybe one day I'll have her put out of her misery. Maybe then Clarissa could find a way to love me again. A new start for both of us.*

A knock rapped fast at his door.

Kess shook away the false comfort, a fantasy he couldn't ever make real. He needed to focus on what was real: he had to appease the founders.

"Come in," Kess said.

The door to his office slid open, Miss Avery's curious face peeking in. "Mr. Kess? Is everything all right?"

"Of course, Miss Avery. I apologize for the noise," he said, his voice even.

"Is there…" She paused, seeing the image projector, digital keyboard, and various elements from his desk strewn across the floor. "Anything you need?"

Kess leaned forward in the leather chair. He placed his arms on the desk and tented his fingers, eyes fixed on his assistant. "Yes, as a matter of fact, there is."

Miss Avery waited with hands clasped, her perfect hourglass figure encased in an elegant navy skirt and jacket combination.

"What's the status of Justice?" Kess said.

"Griffin?" Miss Avery waved her hand in an arc before her face. Her visor lit up with a cascade of moving images and data. "Sending it to your projector." Miss Avery cast her hand toward the ceiling.

There was a hum, followed by a curtain of light, rippling down from the ceiling in thready fingers. The pixilated specks of color hung in the air, creating a floating series of images and data graphs.

"His training has proceeded as planned," Miss Avery said. "Enforcer Warrant made the regularly scheduled updates and is eighty-three percent complete with the new Enforcer checklist."

Kess drummed his fingers on the tabletop. "Sounds fine in theory. But how ready is he?"

"To deploy tomorrow?" Miss Avery lit up. "See for yourself." She waved her hand toward the projector, and a video feed from the training grid opened.

Kess leaned forward. "Expand."

Miss Avery opened her hands, and the image magnified. Before them, Chance, decked out in his glistening black armor, fired from the launch tube. His posture ram-rod straight, he sailed with perfect form into the air above the training grid. With a smooth somersault in mid-air, Chance dropped in front of the hulking form of Grendel in the faux ruins of the training grid.

"Time to show me something, boy," Kess said through tented fingers.

Chance rose to his feet from where he stuck the landing. Ahead, the monstrous form of Grendel waited, cybernetic enhancements hissing and wheezing. Smoke hung in the air, tinged purple from the glow of the digital city beyond. A mixture of real-world junk and computer-generated imagery made the training grid indistinguishable from The Zone itself. Chance stood, squaring his feet firm on a broken asphalt boulevard. The ragged frames of smashed buildings, hollowed out by fire, surrounded him in the deepening twilight.

"At least you landed on your feet this time. You ready for today's beating, boy?" Grendel lumbered forward. "I've got some new tricks for you."

"Keep talking, fat man." Chance sized up his opponent. "You're not the only one with new tricks."

"*Chance, I estimate a seventy-three percent chance he will try to ambush you in the next twelve seconds,*" RITA said. "*Your suit's commands are available from your HUD. I'm here if you need me.*"

"Copy," Chance said, watching a row of tactical commands emerge in the lower corner of his HUD.

Grendel stomped toward Chance, gripping the steel cudgel.

"I'll kill you this time, you little wanker."

In a movement that belied his enormous size, Grendel heaved his bulk forward, dropping his shoulder.

Chance shifted left, and the directional vent thrusters along the right side of his suit fired, rocketing him past the stumbling brute.

"Dash," Chance said. The vents along the rear of the suit fired him like a bullet from a gun, the toes of his boots crushing the fractured asphalt as he ran. "Thrust." A flash of flame ignited beneath his boots and vaulted Chance into the air.

The giant hefted his bulk up from the ground, searching for his prey when Chance dropped into him from above. Chance's fist connected with the base of Grendel's skull, behind the ear, with the force of a war hammer. Grendel gave a brief cry, and his jug-like head smacked with a hollow *thunk* against the concrete. The foundations of the place shook.

"That's what I'm talking about, Rook," Sam's voice said over the comm link.

Chance turned, his arms raised in victory, parading for the imaginary cameras. "You like that?"

"*Chance, I recommend—*" RITA said.

"Oh yeah," Chance said, arms high. "I got more where that came f—"

His armor seized around his neck. The impact of the steel club, swung with maximum force, stole the words from his throat. Chance dropped to his knees, his vision distorted.

"*Armor integrity just dropped to eighty-six percent,*" RITA said.

"I told you I'd kill you this time, and I meant it," Grendel said, his grating cockney accent close in Chance's ear.

Grendel dropped his club, locked two ham-sized fists around Chance's throat, and lifted him from his knees. Chance gasped. The sausage-like fingers squeezed with impossible strength. Grendel let out a high-pitched scream and flung Chance back against a concrete barrier. His armor cracked in protest. Pressed there, suffocating, the pulverized concrete falling down his shoulders, Chance grabbed at the giant hands holding him fast.

"Get out of there." Sam's voice filled his helmet.

Chance struggled to speak. "RITA..."

"*I've got you, Chance,*" RITA said. "*Raise your feet and stand by.*"

"Had enough yet?" Grendel said, drool hanging from puffy lips. "No?"

Chance pulled his knees up, his vision darkening at the edges, and placed his boots against Grendel's midsection.

"Go," Chance wheezed.

The word *Thrust* strobed in the bottom corner of Chance's display. His boots engaged with a white-hot burst of flame. Grendel shrieked, and the blast jolted him back in a shower of sparks. The giant tumbled, his clothing at the midsection burned, the rolls of fat beneath blackened with fire.

"I've missed you, RITA," Chance said, struggling to catch his breath.

"Now, Rook," Sam said, "press the fight."

Chance rose, and fought to maintain balance, his head swimming. He clenched his teeth, balled his fists, and ran, his boots stabbing into the rubble beneath his feet.

Dash strobed across his display, and Chance blitzed forward. Chance hit Grendel with a crushing straight punch to the bridge of the nose. The fat man cried out, rolled to the side, and tried to grab for his cudgel. Chance struck him again, this time on the top of the skull with a hammer-fist blow. As the giant's head rocked down, then back, Chance kicked him hard in the side of the face and sent him sprawling.

Seizing the brute's heavy cudgel, Chance strained to raise it overhead.

"Please," Grendel said from his back, his hands upheld to shield his face.

Chance stood locked, the club poised to seal Grendel's fate. A moment of indecision. He lowered the club, and the end clunked against the concrete. His helmet separated at the visor, the nano-constructed pieces disassembling and falling back to reveal his face.

Grendel stared at him, questioning eyes above a wide, blood-smeared chin.

Chance extended his hand. "It's over."

"Why spare me?" Grendel croaked.

"Maybe death isn't what you deserve," Chance said.

"Maybe it is…"

"I don't know." Chance shook his head. "I think everyone's got you wrong. Maybe you just need an opportunity to choose for yourself. You don't have to be a monster just because others think you are."

"I'll still kill you if you give me a chance. It ain't nothin' to me, boy," Grendel said, wiping the blood dripping from his chin with a meaty forearm.

"I know." Chance emphasized his outstretched hand.

Grendel gave a grunt of displeasure as he accepted the offered hand. He sat up and tried to stand, massive legs quivering.

"Good grief." Chance groaned as he pulled on the giant. "Drop thrusters."

Vents opened in front of Chance's armor, firing, pulling the massive Grendel to his feet. As Chance released the brute, a loud clap echoed across the training grid. In the sky overhead and all around them, images of Gabriel Kess, in his typical immaculate style, encircled the training arena. He applauded slow and steady, a perfect business-like smile set on his chiseled face.

"Bra-vo." Kess shook his head. "Not only a decisive win against this ugly brute, but mercy, too? Mercy that fat slag-sack doesn't deserve? Consider me impressed."

Grendel dropped his pants and seized his gargantuan member. He shot a steaming yellow stream of piss right through one of the holograms.

"Damn, dude." Chance held his hand up to shield his face. Sam mentioned that Kess, one of the first Enforcers, brought Grendel in. There was clearly no love lost.

"Well?" Chance said to Kess, ignoring Grendel's whinnied laughs.

Kess leaned in toward the projection. "Think you're ready for The Zone?"

"He's not ready," Grendel said.

Chance balked. "Hey, really?" He looked from Grendel to the projection. "I'm ready. I mean, I can be ready in a few days."

"You don't have a few days," Kess said. "The founders escalated the timeline. Your first trial goes down tomorrow night in front of millions."

Grendel laughed again. Chance opened his mouth to speak, but no sound came.

"Rest up, Justice. Big day tomorrow. Everyone's counting on you," Kess said, the projections fading to black.

The lights of the training grid popped on one at a time, illuminating the broken buildings and rusting junkers, staged like an old movie set.

"It is what it is, Rook," Sam's voice sounded in his helmet. "Let's get a few more training runs in and make sure you're good to go."

"Tomorrow?" Chance put his hands on his head. "For real?"

"Yep." Grendel smacked his wide, blood-smeared lips together and laughed another high-pitched whinny as he picked up his club. "You're slagged."

CHAPTER TWENTY

Benny's shirtless, blood-spattered chest swelled with each gasp as he stumbled along. He stopped for a moment, clutching at his ruined arm. He leaned against a dingy but elaborate Hoodie Boys graffiti tag that extended in looping green letters down the length of the garbage-strewn alley's ten-foot-high concrete wall.

He pulled the blood-soaked rag from his neck, appraising the deep crimson stain, then checked the wrap over the wound in his arm. *Damn, that was close*, he thought. *Could be in a body bag right now.* He pressed the torn shirt back against his neck, wincing as he doubled the pressure. The wounds burned, radiating a numb ache that seemed to spread down his shoulder and up the left side of his face.

NTPD tactical units often used stifle rounds, or *noxies*, as they called them on the street, to slow the flight of violent suspects. Cleanup crews first used Noxilam HCL to paralyze and neutralize stray slag dogs. Only later was Nox developed for use on humans. The effects were wildly unpredictable. Benny hoped the Nox in his wounds wouldn't incapacitate him, but the odds weren't in his favor.

With a snap, light flooded the alley. The NTPD surveillance drone turned in small circles above as the light swept toward him. Benny slid to the ground and rolled on his side, pulling a busted bag of wet garbage over him. The bums nearby groaned as the light passed over them. One man managed a wine-slurred curse, holding his middle finger high.

Benny didn't move.

The auto-piloted NTPD drone made one last pass, and the light snapped off, the filthy alley once again covered in gloom.

"'Bout time," a woman muttered a few feet away, half buried beneath garbage bags. "Jakkin' cops."

"Yeah, useless badge sissies," Benny said, his eyes catching on her high-collared jacket. "Say, that jacket for sale?"

"What happened to yer shirt?" she asked.

Benny gestured to the blood-soaked shirt pressed to his neck. "I need a jacket. What do you want for yours?"

"Why you got blood all over you, man?" She squinted at him, nosier by the second.

"Not your business. What do you want for the jacket?" Benny repeated.

"Piss off," the woman grunted.

Benny waved open his coin wallet. From the pinhole in his wrist, threads of light stitched together the account balance. His pursuers hadn't seized his assets yet, but as soon as the additional charges hit, they would. The homeless woman sat up, her eyes aglow with his one thousand forty-eight Terminus coin balance.

"I want five hundred T's," she said, her words croaking from a throat better suited for swallowing liquor than speaking.

"Five hundred? Lady," he said, "you smell rotten and have garbage juice all over you."

"You asked fer it," she said, pulling a wet garbage bag under her head. "Five hundred, or you can piss off."

Benny was about to take the ridiculous offer when a man with a torn wool cap across the alley sat up. "If you want a jacket," he said, "you can have mine for three hundred."

Benny and the lady both swiveled in the man's direction.

"Gerald, you ass clown—it's not yer deal," the woman said, an ugly scowl on her face.

"It is if you can't close it," Gerald said and sucked his blackened teeth.

"Two fifty for mine," the woman blurted out.

"Two hundred," Gerald said.

"Gerald, you asshole," the woman said. She smacked toothless gums together. "One fifty, here," she said, shrugging out of the grease-stained jacket. "Take it or leave it."

"One hundred," Gerald said, removing his jacket and extending it toward Benny.

Above, the surveillance drone appeared to circle for another pass.

"Sold," Benny pointed to Gerald.

"Gerald!" The woman sent an empty can of BoBo beans bouncing off the wall next to Gerald.

Gerald hocked a laugh and stuck his tongue out through a sizable gap in his teeth.

Benny rose with a grunt and crossed to the man, whose watery yellow eyes spread wide with anticipation. Gerald opened his palm, the flickering image of his Glom account bearing all zeros. Benny transferred one hundred T's, and Gerald laughed again, standing and handing over his grubby jacket. The collar wasn't as high as the woman's, but it would do.

Benny pulled it on, easing his left arm in with a groan. The interior was warm and smelled of stale body odor and sour, mildewed cloth. Benny jammed the blood-soaked shirt against his neck and pulled the jacket's collar, a size too small, tight around it. He looked at his bare feet, covered in grime, then at the ragged shoes of the two. Shook his head. They weren't worth bargaining for, and he could tell at a glance they wouldn't fit his size thirteens anyway.

"I'm going to the bar," Gerald said, sticking his tongue out at the woman again, "to eat actual food and get ree-al drunk.

"Screw the both of ya. Get off my street!" The woman rolled in the opposite direction, blending back in with the piles of garbage.

Benny took stock of his surroundings. The PD would find him, eventually. And when they did, it would be because of his wrist chip. He had to find a way to neutralize it. He picked up speed, heading for the street.

As the alley opened onto Cordoban Avenue, he realized his arm and upper torso were completely numb. He'd heard stories of suspects shot with noxies. Some of them regained full function, some of them didn't. He needed medical treatment in a bad way.

Beyond the flashing lights and stories-tall holo-projections, he could barely make out the faintest glow of light on the horizon far beyond the haze of the Volkan Heights sector. Almost six a.m. If he could make it a few more blocks, there was a pay clinic down from Cordoban and Rigney. It wouldn't open for a few hours, but the clinic techs always arrived early to prep for the day. Maybe he could catch one at the back entrance and offer them a nice bribe for some meds.

I'll either get lucky or get reported, he thought.

Benny grunted and shoved forward. With no other options, he'd have to take his chances.

Head down, he placed one foot in front of the other, holding the compress tight to his neck. At his side, his left arm hung numb and useless, leaving dots of blood on the concrete as he walked. Above, guided cameras mounted to every building followed his movements, one picking up where the other left off.

Crossing the rain-lashed street, he strolled with what he hoped was a relaxed, purposeful stride. Down Rigney, he turned off into a side alley behind a flashing projection banner that read, *Feels, Boosts, Heals, and Surgery.* Below, a secondary scrolling projection read in flashing red script, *Pay up front or get lost. NO Exceptions.* Above the word *surgery*, someone had spray painted the word *dodgy* in dripping purple.

Benny made his way to the back and found the blast door sealed. The protective measures clinics took to keep creative junkies from robbing them blind were insane but necessary. This place had a pressure-sensitive, four-inch steel blast door at both the front and rear entrances. Benny's eyes flicked up, taking in the scores of shabby apartments rising toward a sea of dark clouds, backlit by the glow of the city. There was no way into the building for anyone without the right chip or a high-tech plasma torch.

As much as he didn't want to, Benny elected to wait in a nearby alcove.

A quarter of an hour had passed when he heard footsteps approaching. Up the alley from the front of the clinic came a cloaked, dwarfish figure walking fast. It paused at the intersection, observing the rear of the building and the alley, one end to the other. Satisfied, the short character approached the blast door.

A buzzer sounded. Red lights flashed in a blinding sequence. Long-barreled muzzles unfolded from two turrets in the wall, swiveling in the child-like figure's direction.

"*Caution, you are trespassing,*" a mechanical voice said. "*If you do not remove yourself, you will be terminated.*"

The little person raised his arms wide, stumpy fingers spread in a power pose.

The numbness across Benny's skin and muscles deepened. *Not much time,* he thought.

"*You have to the count of three. One, two, thruggh…*" The turrets drooped, the long rifles pointing down. A bell chimed, and the red lights around the door turned green.

"*Welcome, Doctor Suchoy,*" the monotone voice said.

"Much better. Ideal, in fact." The little man rubbed gloved hands together.

The heavy blast door slid back. Benny made his move. He pushed from the alcove of the adjoining building and stumbled forward. He stopped short when the small man spun on him, his arms wide, a toothy snarl visible beneath the hood. In response to Benny, the turrets jumped to life, the long barrels locking on Benny.

"*Caution—you are trespassing,*" the monotone voice said again. "*If you do not remove—*"

"Yes, yes, we know. Be quiet," the little person said. The turrets relaxed with a wheeze. His lips stretched wide, the little man flashed something between a smile and a grimace of irritation. "Can't you see I'm preoccupied?"

"Please, Doctor..." Benny gasped.

The little man stood still, squat and hunched, stumpy fingers splayed.

"Do I look like a doctor to you?" he asked. "With a flick of my fingers, these auto turrets will pulp you into a pile of oozing meat." His voice held a thin, childlike quality.

Benny wanted to scream, to dash forward, seize this ornery little turd and give him a good choking. Maybe he could get them both shot to pieces. *Maybe not.* He mastered himself, pressing the confusion, misery, and rage he'd accumulated over the past twenty-four hours deep inside. He took a small step forward. The toe of his limp left foot dragged on a torn plastic bag.

"I said that's close enough," the little man said, the smile-grimace still stretched across plump lips. "I'm on the clock here. Your affliction is not my concern."

Benny stopped, closer now. He saw the little man clear for the first time in the orange glow of a flashing sign advertising dancing nudes. He stood to Benny's waist, draped in a heavy hooded cloak that swallowed most of his features. Beneath the trench coat, he wore a strange, tight-fitting suit that made it hard to tell where the shirt ended and the pants began. A series of brass buckles secured glowing electronics, digital displays, monitors, and controllers to the suit's chest. From beneath the hood, long stringy hair flowed like a dark and icy river across his shoulders. A flashing silver visor shielded his eyes from atop a bulbous nose. A pointy gray goatee angled down from his chin in twisting braids adorned with brass rings and colored beads.

"You're not the doctor here?" Benny managed.

"That's what I said, wasn't it?" The little man's fingers flexed, and the turrets jolted to adjust their laser lock on Benny.

"You're robbing this place?"

"Any other stupid questions?" the little man said.

Benny raised his hands. "I need help."

The little man's bushy eyebrows raised. "And why should I help you? What good are you to me?" He reached into the open slots in the self-service medical vending kiosk. He grabbed syringes, sloshing packets of yellow and green liquid labeled in Japanese, and a few medical instruments Benny couldn't identify. He turned back to Benny. "No answer? Then I bid you good day."

Benny watched as the little man swiped his fingers across one of the pads on his chest and started a T transfer from the clinic's account into his own. The tinkling sound of coins followed in what sounded like an endless jackpot shower. Stepping free of the pressure pad, the little man, cloak swishing behind him, darted away into the night.

The green light around the door turned red with a buzz and the auto turrets relaxed. With the sound of steel sliding upward on greased rails, the blast door *shunked* back into place.

Benny's confusion and bewilderment deepened. If he stayed to speak with someone when the clinic opened, they'd accuse him of the theft. Down the alley, Benny hobbled after the little man, his left leg causing him to stumble.

"Hey, wait," Benny called after the strange little fellow, now nowhere to be seen. "Wait a second."

Turning the corner, Benny stopped at the intersection of two alleyways. He bent and, with a curse, plucked a fragment of glass from his big toe. No wonder the guy didn't stop. Benny must look like a crazy person, wearing nothing but undershorts and a homeless person's jacket, a blood-stained rag pressed to his neck.

A sudden whooshing filled his ears, the sound of rotors buzzing in the air. Hovering above the alley, the light of an NTPD surveillance drone snapped on. A sun's worth of brilliance streamed forth, the night turning to day.

Sputz, Benny thought. *End of the line.*

He squinted and held his hands in the air.

"*Chip scan. Guillermo Benitez,*" a synthetic voice said. "*Wanted in association with felony crimes. Transferring data to... Neo... Terrbrrggg—*"

The light snapped off. The drone elevated above the alley.

"*Thank you for your compliance, citizen. Be well,*" it said and cruised away above the city.

Benny opened his hands, his relief only eclipsed by his total confusion. "Uh, okay?"

It took a moment for his eyes to adjust to the dimness of the alley. In front of him, the strange little man tucked a module inside his cloak and straightened his jacket.

"You're wanted by the police, and you smell like a urinal," the little man said in his dry, squeaky voice. "Why should I help you?"

"How did you do that?" Benny searched the sky.

"Magic," the little man grunted. "Answer my question."

"Look at me." Benny sighed and pointed to his arm, dripping blood. "Doesn't it seem like I need help?" He waved open his coin wallet, now wiped clean, all the zeros like little open mouths. "I can't offer you any T's."

"Why would I want your money? I pulled thirteen grand from the medical kiosk back there, and it was my fourth one tonight," the little man said, wiping his jacket. "No, no, I'm interested in something money can't buy."

"Like what?" Benny said, desperate.

"Favors."

"Favors?" Benny repeated.

"That's right. I do something for you, and you do something for me." The little man cocked his head. "Sound like a deal?"

"Look, I'm not into weird sexual stuff…" He motioned to the little man's one-piece leather body suit.

The little man scowled at him. "I'm talking about a job, you nasty slag-grabber. Do you want my help or not?"

Benny paused, some rational part of his brain trying to question what he'd gotten himself into. But he needed the help. He pressed it away. "Yeah."

"Good, excellent indeed," the little man said. "Try to keep up. You have little time."

The little man opened a manhole cover in the street and disappeared inside.

"What's that mean?" Benny said, eyes probing the stinking dark of the sewer but seeing nothing. "Hello?"

Benny grit his teeth at the pain. He chanced a look up at the brightening sky, then down at his ruined arm, dripping splashes of crimson onto the wet concrete.

"This is great, man," he said, sitting on the edge of the sewer. He squeezed his bulk through the hole and into the festering black of the tunnel below. "Just great."

CHAPTER TWENTY-ONE

"ill that be all, Mrs. Griffin?" the girlish voice said from the front hall.

Hannah shook awake, her new top-of-the-line iVisor hanging precariously from the end of her nose. Across the lenses scrolled a ticking news feed on the left side, a talk show with bright costumed celebrities on the right. She pulled it free and powered it off, setting it on the wireless charger beside the couch. Swiping a strand of golden hair from her face, she took a step toward the entrance and peeked around the opening.

"Yes, Clarissa, thank you."

The young, fit bottle-blonde gave a curt nod and a plastic smile. "He's finished eating. A happy and sleepy little guy—for the moment, at least."

"Thank you for your help," Hannah said with palpable relief.

"It's my pleasure," Clarissa said. "Will you be needing any assistance tomorrow?"

"No, I don't believe so. Thank you."

"Call us at a moment's notice. That's why we're here." Clarissa seemed to glide to the shaded glass of the front door as it slid back with a quiet swish. "Good night."

Hannah waited for the glass to slide shut. She rubbed her eyes and glanced at the clock. Seven p.m. already. How had she gotten so accustomed to such luxury? The horrors of her former life were now only a distant nightmare she'd somehow had the good fortune to wake from. *What have I done to deserve an escape from that hell?*

"Not healthy, Hannah."

She poured from a chilled bottle of Moscato, then pinched the narrow glass by the icy rim and sauntered out toward the open balcony. She passed the strange cocoon-shaped device that had arrived earlier in the day. A note from the building told her to enjoy her new complimentary "base model recovery chamber," whatever that was. Stepping out onto the covered terrace, Hannah leaned against the railing and watched the rain fall from bloated clouds, covering the cityscape in a hazy, dream-like glow.

Her loneliness drew close. The knowledge that she shouldn't be alone made the sting of it all the more powerful. *Chance should be available in some capacity, shouldn't he? Why is he not allowed to see us?* She knew it wasn't Chance's fault. He'd be there if he could.

Even with their every need taken care of, she was still alone, the same as when she'd lived in the slums of Water Town.

Try as she might, Hannah struggled to get her head around what this new position meant for Chance. She'd pushed him into this, forced him to abandon Benny and his brothers and sisters in blue at the police department. *Should I feel guilty about that?*

On the surface, she knew about The Zone, about the show, and in essence, what Enforcers did. But in practice? She had to admit she had no real concept of what that involved or the danger. *Are there safeguards?* she wondered. *Can Enforcers actually die in there, or is that just a metaphor for early retirement? It's only a show,* Hannah thought. *They wouldn't kill their Enforcers off. Would they?*

Hannah took a long sip of her Moscato, the glass chilled and glistening with perspiration in the humid night. She narrowed her eyes and peered past the super structures of Silver City, past the black splinter twisting into the sky, The Glom's headquarters where Chance lived and worked. Her eyes roved across the dark void at the heart of the city, searching for something, any sign of light.

Propulsion jets fired and drew her attention off to the left. A dirigible cruised past her balcony and floated toward the taller buildings. It projected a brilliant, multicolored curtain of light beneath it, lighting up the sky with a projection advertisement for a fizzing caramel-colored soft drink called *Neo Coke*. An Asian woman in a schoolgirl uniform and knee-high white socks took a drink and closed her eyes.

"Mmmm. Wouldn't a refreshing Neo Coke hit the spot right now?" an advertiser's voice said.

Hannah took another sip of her Moscato.

The advertisement changed, and the image of the girl was replaced with a dark wasteland of crumbling buildings and septic fog. Flames licked the hollow windows of ancient auto-junkers, and a series of action shots, Enforcers competing in The Zone, danced across the display.

"Are you ready for this week's contest in The Zone?" The floating billboard said. "New trials, new dangers… and a new hero will emerge. Tomorrow, 8 PM. Don't miss the biggest event since the shocking death of Enforcer Vigilance!" The image strobed and magnified, a gruesome shot of an Enforcer being decapitated.

"Oh!" Hannah whirled her back to the flickering advertisement. She pinched her eyes for a second, then slugged back the last of her wine. "It's just an ad," she said. The breeze ruffled her thin dress as she made her way back into the apartment. Andrew whimpered, a sound made small by the size of the place. Feeling warm and a little fuzzy, Hannah made for the bar and a second glass of wine. She stopped.

The front door of the apartment shut with a distinct *click*.

Hannah strained her ears.

"Hello?" she said.

With a few more cautious steps, Hannah rounded the corner into the entryway. For a single instant, a shadow darkened the frosted glass of her apartment door from the hallway beyond.

Hannah froze. A breath hitched in her lungs as the shadow disappeared from the glass.

"Hey, what are you doing?" Hannah called out, moving to the front door.

As the glass slid back, a sudden fear prickled her neck. *What are you going to do? Physically confront someone while unarmed and a little tipsy?* She scanned the place, desperate for something she could use as a weapon. She grabbed the voice-to-action synthesizer from its charging pad by the front door. Roughly the size and weight of a brick, she could smack it against someone's face. If she had to.

Hannah swallowed and stepped into the hallway. The soft, silent, lamplit glow of empty corridors stretched in either direction. Her shoulders slumped. A shadow had been outside the door, she was sure of it.

Hannah returned to her apartment, now feeling rather foolish with the synthesizer clutched in her sweat-slick palm. She clunked it down on the charging pad. She knew she'd heard the door shut. A prickle of anxiety raced across her scalp.

Andrew. He wasn't whining anymore.

"No," Hannah cried, running for the baby's room. She rounded the corner and flew against the crib, a muffled gasp on her lips. Beneath his blankets, Andrew slept, his face serene and undisturbed.

Hannah covered her mouth, and her shoulders shook with a little sob. She wiped her eyes and took a shaky breath. *Chill out, Hannah.*

She picked up the baby and cradled him against her chest, swaying. "I've got you, sweetie."

She exited the baby's room and made her way back into the main living area. *Ridiculous, letting your imagination run wild like that. Chance isn't here. You have to be the strong one.*

"It's okay, sweet boy," Hannah said, swishing her hips and

cherishing Andrew's little grunts and groans as he nuzzled close.

Across the room, an oil painting of a brilliant blue seascape hung in its gilded frame. There, unnoticed by the apartment's new tenants, a wireless micro-camera recorded every word and logged every move of the young mother and her son.

The knock on the dark glass of Chance's door wasn't really a knock at all. Soft and rhythmic, the steady *tap-tap-tap* reached out to him across the empty apartment. Fresh out of his suite's luxurious bathing chamber, Chance made his way toward the door. Wrapped in a black soft-pile robe, moisture still clung in droplets to the tops of his feet and around his neck and hair.

Working out the kinks with Sam and RITA on the training grid had done a number on him. Now well-cleansed, he needed a good long rest in the recovery chamber to get ready for his first trial in The Zone tomorrow. Maybe a stiff drink first.

A glance through the well-furnished apartment set his mind at ease. The yellow glow of the interior contrasted with the midnight blue of the horizon, the lights of the city at night flung against God's inky canvas like a sea of stars. He touched the St. Michael medallion hanging around his neck. A stroke of anguish filled his chest. How he wished Hannah could be here with him.

He walked to the bar and appraised the crystal decanters filled with a hand-selected assortment of fine Irish whiskeys and oak cask single barrel bourbons.

Chance put his hands on the counter and dropped his head. Everything that mattered to him seemed so far away—his wife, his son, his old life at the PD, Benny. *Will that feeling pass?* He wasn't sure he wanted it to. It was a signpost for him, a directional marker pointing him back to what was important.

He let out a sigh, knowing he should try to call his partner again before he hit the hay.

The knocking started again, steady and unrelenting. He peered at the frosted glass of the front door and the shadow that lingered there. Holding a towel in his hand, Chance patted his face and rubbed at his hair as he walked to the door and hit the release.

"Sam," he said. "I know you love spending all day with me, but this is getting ridic—" Chance stopped.

There, in the clean, modernist hallway, outside his door, were two women. They weren't staff of the building or couriers bringing him a delivery. They were incredible, a hypnotic, make-a-fella's-skin-tingle sort of stunning. Chance stood there, robe tied at the waist, towel pressed against his neck, his mouth forming soundless words.

"Ooh, he *is* cute."

"Told ya."

"Hi, uh… was in the shower, sorry. Can I help you?" Chance said, dabbing the towel against his face.

"Hi."

"Hey there."

The women searched his frame as if appraising his value. The one who'd knocked, a slender, natural red head with porcelain skin and curvaceous features, leaned forward.

"Chance Griffin?"

He caught a whiff of her perfume, the smell sweet and clean and exotic. She wore a tight black dress, more ornament than cover-up.

"Uhm…" He stopped.

The other young woman's scarlet dress sported a slit that revealed smooth, golden-brown skin all the way up to her hip. She pushed a ringlet of chestnut hair back from her forehead and tucked it behind her ear with a playful wink.

"You didn't forget your name, did ya?"

"Yeah, no, I..." Chance chuckled, rubbing the towel through his hair with nervous vigor. "Good grief. Yeah, I'm Chance. Do you need something?" he said with a boyish smile.

"Everyone *needs* something, hero." The red head smirked and took a step closer. "I think *you* might need to blow off some steam." She cast a sly glance at her friend. "What do ya think, Brandy?"

"I think so, Angel," the brunette said, slinking forward. "Mr. Kess wants this guy well rested for his big day tomorrow."

The red head took another step, crossing the threshold into his apartment. "That's right."

Chance took a step back. The backs of his legs carelessly jostled a hardwood and glass side table, and it squeaked across the floor. "About that—"

Angel pushed forward, the fullness of her breasts swelling tight against the dress. She placed a styled nail against his lips. "Shhhh," she said, pulling a pin from her hair. Chance watched, mesmerized, as her gorgeous red locks scattered about her shoulders like a spreading blaze.

Brandy pushed closer to his left, her arms snaking around his torso.

"I'm dreaming. This is a dream," Chance muttered. He cast a nervous look around his immaculate apartment, aglow with warm light.

He heard the sliding of a door farther down the hallway.

"Hey, hey. Look who it is," Sam's voice echoed.

"Sam," Chance said, leaning toward the door, his neck craning. "Sam? What the hell?" He caught his mentor's eyes and motioned to the women still clinging to him. Sam scooped up a voluptuous, raven-haired Asian woman in his arm and raised a chinking crystal glass of bourbon on the rocks to his protégé.

"Cheers, kid." He winked as the woman ran her hands beneath his shirt, pulling it up. He pulled her back, and the frosted glass door to his apartment slid shut with a quiet hiss.

"So what's it gonna be, fella?" Angel said, her voice a saccharine sweet whisper in his ear.

Brandy touched the door release, and it slid shut, sealing the three of them off from the hall.

"Okay, look... I'm married," Chance said, his voice failing to carry the conviction he intended. "I mean," he cleared his throat, "what I meant to say was, I love my wife."

"Aww, that's sweet," Angel winked at Brandy, "he's loyal, too." She turned back to Chance, her fingers grazing the muscles of his forearm. "Where have ya been all my life?"

"Don't worry," Brandy said, sliding up beside Chance, "we don't want to take you from your lady." She made a pouty face. "But she's not here, and you need a little TLC."

"Think of it as one of the many benefits of being an Enforcer," Angel said.

"She'll never know," Brandy said, "it'll be our secret."

"Yeah, but..." Chance could feel their hands running over his skin, his body responding in kind. *The point of no return.* Chance raised his chin and took a step back, gently pushing the two women away. "But I'll know," he said, letting the weight of the words hang in the air, "and I'm not going to disrespect my wife like that."

The seductive auras faded from the faces of his lovely guests.

Angel raised her eyebrows, the spell broken. "Are you for real?"

"I think we just got shut down," Brandy said flatly.

Silence enveloped the three, none of them sure how to proceed.

"Please, don't take offense," Chance said. "You two are amazing. That's just not me."

Angel looked at Brandy and said, "Justice. That's what they're calling him, ya know. Now, this? Can you believe it?"

"No." Brandy put her hands on her hips. She let the tension build. "The company pays us to visit. If we don't visit, we don't get paid. You get what I'm saying, Mr.... Justice?"

Chance rubbed his chin. "Yeah, I got it," he said, stepping

toward the bar. "How about a drink and a little conversation instead?"

"Will we get our fee for having a drink?" Angel said to Brandy, who offered a sculpted shrug.

"Look, you had it right," Chance said, re-tucking his robe and pouring Jack Hammer Irish whiskey into three glasses from a crystal decanter. "I'm a little lonely and could use some company—just not the sort you came here to provide.

"Yeah," Brandy said, clearly miffed, "we can see that."

"I'll tell you what," Chance said. He slid the glasses across the bar. "If the company won't pay you for your time, I will. Out of my own pocket."

His lovely guests eyed the glasses on the bar between them.

Angel glanced at Brandy and gave a little sigh. "What the hell," she said, taking one, the corners of her mouth twitching upward, "first time for everything, right?"

CHAPTER TWENTY-TWO

Exhausted, hunted, and losing control of his body, Benny stumbled down the curving path of the odorous sewer tunnel. Along the ancient brick wall, bulbous lights emitted a pale yellow glow. They illuminated the path ahead in small circular pools, spots of bleach in a thriving Petri dish.

"Keep up, now," the little man said. "I told you. It can't wait." His little bobbing shoulders disappeared into the dark, only to reappear again as he crossed each baleful cone of light.

Benny fought to keep up. His shuffled steps swept piles of refuse from the path. He stumbled and fell against the brick with his shoulder, a wince of pain on his face. He pulled the soiled shirt-rag from his neck, the wound's edges crusted over with dark flakes of dried blood.

The smell of the sewers filled his nose, a putrid, rotten funk that stuck in the back of his throat. Benny gagged and spat in the meandering channel of gray-green liquid teeming with maggots.

"How much farther?" Benny groaned, his vision hazy and dreamlike. He'd never taken a stifle round before, and after this, he hoped to God he wouldn't again. Actual death might be less pain and hassle than getting hit with a noxie.

"Stop your complaining," the little voice echoed back to him.

"I'm... I'm not," Benny said. "I just don't know how much more I can take." His voice took on a wounded quality that went much deeper than the physical.

The little man seemed not to notice, or worse, not care. "You can make it—or you can't." His stumpy legs carried him forward in a shaking waddle far too fast for a person his size. "The universe is unimpressed either way."

Benny stumbled, gripping a rusted section of guide railing with trembling fingers. He was about to protest again when his guide stopped just ahead, where a blanket of green-black fungus draped the bricks and glistened wet in the urine-colored light.

Stretching his arms wide in the same power pose he'd struck at the clinic, the strange little man splayed his fingers open. "Honey," he said, "I'm home."

A section of the wall flickered. The lamp above went dark. Fungus-covered bricks faded to black, revealing a sliding blast door behind it, not unlike the one the clinic used. The door chimed, a series of green lights illuminating the top of the frame. The door slid down into the base plate with the pressurized sound of air releasing.

"Quick, now," the little man said. "I'd rather not welcome *all* of the sewer gasses into my domain." He vanished through the entrance.

With a supreme force of will, Benny raised himself off the railing and shambled through the opening, the holographic brick wall flickering back on behind him. The blast door shot upward into the locking mechanism. A sequence of bolts fired home.

"Hurry now," the little man said, gesturing. "Drop your garments and bandages in the chute there and step into the chamber on your left."

Benny shuffled across the threshold and stopped. A cavern, spacious but not massive, took form out of the darkness. Walls hewed out of the rock, the stone marbled and slick with damp. Projection monitors, rows upon rows of them, winked on. A string of white Christmas lights ringed around a few sticks of beaten furniture and a worn couch that looked slept on.

"Where…?" Benny said.

"Less talking, more doing." More lights clicked and clacked on.

The little man pointed to a shower pod.

"Stop rushing me." Benny recognized the cleansing chamber as similar to the ones he used at the PD.

"Rushing you?" The little man pointed to the nasty wound through Benny's biceps. "This one appears to have hit the bone. Not good. In addition, noxies are supposed to only cause temporary paralysis, but if left to run their course, it has a twenty-eight-point-seven-six percent chance of leaving you crippled for life. Is that what you want?"

Benny grunted a *no*. Too miserable to care for modesty, he stripped naked and balled up his clothes, together with the sodden rag of a shirt he'd been holding to his neck. With a sucking sound, the garments snapped from his fingers into the trash chute. Benny stutter-stepped and grabbed the lip of the vertical cleansing chamber, and the door sealed behind him as he pulled himself inside.

The jets fired hot and fast. Benny ground his teeth with a swear as the jets blasted his wounds clean. A wave of nausea poured over him at the amount of blood swirling down the drain. In seconds the cycle ended. Wincing in pain, Benny held fast as the auto-dryer kicked in, blasting him with warm air that only carried a hint of the sewer gasses outside. The door slid open, but Benny didn't move.

"Quick now, into the recovery chamber with you," the little man said, even more odd having shed his overcoat. "Chop chop, the clock is ticking."

Benny held the outer lip of the cleansing chamber and clenched his teeth as he focused all his effort on raising his left foot off the drain.

"If you're going to be such a big baby," his host said, "you may not be any use to me after all."

Drowning in his own pain, Benny couldn't find the words to argue. The little man took notice. He stepped over, reached up, and released the hatch on the glowing recovery chamber, the lid swinging back wide. A mist rose from the glowing cocoon.

"In you go." The little man gave a sweep of his hand.

Benny's hard eyes betrayed the horrors of the past two days. He'd never seen one of these before. Couldn't manage to ask what this device might do to him and didn't care.

Sensing the question, the little man narrowed his eyes. "If I wanted you dead or crippled, I would have left you to your fate in that alley."

With a grunt, Benny took two shaking steps and fell into the edge of the luminescent recovery chamber. Swinging his lower half inside, he lay back with a sigh of pain. Small mechanical arms wrapped a clean linen cloth around his hips and between his legs, covering him.

"Excellent, excellent," the little man said. He walked to the control panel next to Benny and punched in a few commands. "Now, you said you wanted my help. Is this still true?"

Benny managed a nod, his body flinching when the little man pushed a pistol-shaped injector against his thigh. A *snap-hiss* followed, the sound of fluid injected into his tissues.

"What is it?" Benny said, his voice frail.

"This?" The little man smirked. "A little something to help you relax." When Benny didn't reply, the little man continued. "If you survive the process, you will owe me the life I have given. A favor for a favor."

"If I survive…" Benny watched as the lid to the clear tube shut with mechanical precision. The vapors swirled around his face. He inhaled, the smell sharp and medicinal. Sleep descended on him, too injured and exhausted to care what happened next.

"My name is Magellan," the little man said with a bow. "You may call me Mage."

"Benny."

"Are you ready, Benny?"

"Ready?" Benny repeated, his consciousness fading as the vapors drifted across him.

Mage pulled at his brass-beaded goatee and bared a toothy grin, from which one pointy canine gleamed silver. "Everything you know is about to change."

Ash Stroud entered the Enforcers' lounge in the upper spire of the Conglomerate's headquarters with a confident swagger that made his large, muscular torso sway. Wearing the black flight suit typical of Enforcers, he eased past the others seated around the room and went straight to the open bar. After pulling a frosted mug from the cache, he filled it with golden lager from the tap. Foam spilled over the lip and ran down the outside of the glass, freezing mid-way down. Ash took a long pull and turned to his co-workers.

"What'd I miss? New guy up yet?" He leaned against the bar, clicked his visor down, and cycled through the entertainment feeds.

"Not yet." Jessie leaned back into the plush leather seat, eyes flicking back and forth across streams of net chatter. "Hey, have you guys heard anything about New West City lately?"

Ash meandered over and took a seat near the back. "Who cares?"

"Why do you ask?" Karissa asked from the next seat over. The lenses of her visor reflected the faded pages of a book, an old story from the digital archives by the name of *Treasure Island*.

"Dunno," Jessie said, "there's a lot of chatter out there about something bad going down. No way to verify any of it because, you know." He looked around and whispered, "The Glom."

Karissa smirked, the powerful muscles of her legs printing through her stretchy flight suit. She clicked her visor up. "Yeah? So?"

"It's just weird there hasn't even been a mention of New West

City on the feed." Jessie clicked his visor up. "Don't you think? I mean, we're always hearing something, even if it's a mayoral election, or bandit attacks, or the mutant rat infestation in the sewers, stupid stuff like that."

"You think, what?" Karissa asked. "Something is happening, but they're not reporting it?"

"Maybe," Jessie said. "That's what the net is saying. Who knows?"

"Why would they keep a lid on it?" Karissa asked. "Why wouldn't they want Neo Terminus to know?"

"Maybe it's really bad," Jessie said, glancing at Ash.

"Maybe an overdose of protein powder has diminished your already tiny brain capacity," Ash said.

"Sure," Jessie said, "make jokes. That's how conspiracies thrive."

"Who cares, anyway?" Ash mumbled into his beer. "New West City is a place we've never seen two thousand miles away."

"Yeah," Jessie said, waving over a synthetic attendant in a three-piece suit and selecting a vegan coco protein wedge from the tray, "you're right. We should forget about it. New West City is the only other surviving city, maybe in the world, for all we know. Screw 'em."

Ash watched the dour-faced attendant return to its docking station. He gave a grunt and took another slug of his beer.

Beyond the large projection screen at the fore of the room, lights strobed low across The Zone, casting lancing beams across the dark wasteland. Above, holo-projections of the Enforcers hovered, and arcs of colored lights flashed.

"How was your trial?" Karissa said from the pocket of her black leather lounge chair.

"No sweat," Ash said.

"Yeah, of course, it's no sweat," Jessie smirked, jerking his thumb toward Ash. "Nothing ever is, according to soldier boy here."

"Shut up, Jessie," Karissa said with a wry smile.

"Yeah, shut up, Jessie," Ash said, nose in his beer.

Karissa swiveled toward Ash. "I'm serious. How was it?"

"Why, Gaines?" Ash smirked. "Itching to get back in The Zone?"

"You know it." Karissa held up her fist with a gleam in her eye.

Ash shrugged. "It was easy." He looked at Jessie. "And I'm not just saying that, pretty boy." He took another pull of his beer. "Standard bad-guy detain and extract. Nothing to it—but I'm also not the main event tonight. My trial was filler."

"The main event tonight is just the new guy? Anyone else on deck?" Jessie said.

"Sam is on standby," Karissa said, "but he's only activated if the odds double."

"Doubled odds are awesome," Jessie said.

"Not when you're the one who has to face them," Karissa muttered.

"What's up, d-bags." Rip LaRue slapped the back of the couch as he entered. "Main event on yet?"

"Why, Rip?" Jessie winked at Karissa. "You want to study up on some real action?"

Rip groaned in disgust and took a seat, one apart from Ash. "I'm here to witness the bloodbath. Watch this dumb rookie get straight murdered on live Glom feed." He rubbed his hands together, then draped his arms over the back of the couch. "That'd make my night."

"What's wrong with you?" Karissa said, casting a disgusted look at Rip. "You don't have to like the new guy, but wishing a brutal death on him? Really?"

"If I want your opinion, Gaines, I'll ask you for it," Rip said. "Right, Sam?"

Sam, sitting quiet in his chair off to the side, didn't respond. He watched the pre-game show, an announcer talking with animated gestures about the upcoming rescue trial and how this new Enforcer had a lot to prove.

"He can't hear me. He's not wearing his aides." Rip pointed, wide-eyed, to his own ears. "Hear me, old Sam? I said, are you gonna cry when your little buddy bites it?"

Sam rose and walked to the cooler, retrieving a bottle of sparkling water. He turned and stopped beside Rip, popped the non-twist cap off with a calloused thumb and bent it between his fingers.

"Ooohh, what's that supposed to mean?" Rip said with mock astonishment.

"It means," Sam tossed the twice-folded bottle cap on the table in front of Rip, "stop trying so hard to convince everyone you don't have a little pecker."

Ash coughed and spat beer back into his glass.

Karissa and Jessie broke out into howls of laughter.

"Kiss my ass, you crusty old sputz," Rip scowled.

The group chuckled as Sam found his seat and took a sip of his sparkling water. He needed to stay sober until this one was done. Leaning forward. He placed his elbows on his knees. On the projection screen, the night's main event was getting underway. He chewed the inside of his cheek.

"Come on, Rook," Sam muttered, "you can do this."

Chance huffed out a breath and stepped naked onto the deployment station platform inside the now-empty war room. The cold metal platform caused the bare muscles of his legs to tense. Chance imagined his fellow Enforcers relaxing in the lounge and preparing to laugh their asses off at him. It might look like a game, but the stakes were life and death.

"Okay," Chance said, his heart pounding. He touched the

console and started the process. With a reverberating hum, a sheathe of light wrapped around Chance's body, and his feet hovered inches from the base plate.

There was a whirr as beams of light whipped over him, and the nano skin formed across the surface of his body. In seconds, it covered him from the tips of his toes to the base of his neck, the sleek black body suit feeling like an extension of his own flesh.

"RITA, are you up?" Chance said.

"*I'm here, Chance. I sense elevated anxiety levels. Are you feeling well?*"

"Pre-game jitters, I guess." Chance gave a nervous laugh. "Can you review my load out, please, darlin'?"

"*Darlin'? That's a new one on me.*"

"Yeah, darling. Like a sweetheart." Chance smiled and jabbed a few keys on the digital holo-screen set into the console.

"*You know just how to make a girl blush. Reviewing your load out now.*"

Chance watched as the suit of armor, abilities, weapons, and defensive options scrolled in a stream of text before his face.

"Yeah, we're good to go. Let's do this," Chance said.

"*Ready to deploy to the launch bay?*"

"I'm ready."

In a matter of seconds, the platform clunked apart, the spider-like arms rising, coiling, and retracting as they knit the pieces of Chance's Inteli-suit together. The last two arms clamped together around his neck, the helmet forming across the back of his skull as the faceless black visor plate clamped into place with a *clunk*.

Next came the gear, shoved at him from every direction—slings, holsters, and fast-access pouches stuffed with various ammunition types. Everything found its place, from a bandolier of impact grenades and a retractable blast baton on his left thigh to a twelve-millimeter caseless magnetic battle rifle slung across his back. Rounding it all out was the fabled Peacemaker, secure in a titanium retention holster on his hip.

"*Armor and equipment loaded out,*" RITA said. "*Launching in four, three, two, one.*"

With a sucking sound, the open tube pulled Chance upward with a jerk. He gave a whoop as he rocketed straight up. Increasing in speed through the shaft, he kept his teeth together, his heart fluttering with anticipation.

He flew upward, his jet-black armor adorned with a dark blue streak and a bright white star in the center of the breastplate. An instant later, the G-forces lessened, and Chance slowed to a stop at the flight deck atop Conglomerate corporate headquarters. Beyond the launch pad, the city glittered neon and black.

A series of blinding flashes erupted with a staccato of strobing light. A collective swell like the sound of a giant gasp thrummed the air, then a deafening mass eruption of cheers captured from the strained vocal cords of millions of live stream viewers.

"*Justice, the last hope of the innocent!*" an announcer's voice boomed across the city.

Straight ahead, toward the edge of the platform, a glossy, raven-black Krytech VTOL waited, its blue-flamed thrusters whining in preparation to carry Chance into The Zone. Beyond, the entire city churned with anticipation.

"*You're up, Chance,*" RITA said. "*Do something. Everyone's watching.*"

Chance stood stunned, enormous screens across the rooftops of every structure in sight, reflecting his own image back at him. He couldn't move, couldn't breathe. A feeling of absolute intoxication rolled across him. Inside the helmet, a huge smile stretched wide across his face.

Chance stepped forward from the lift and thrust his fist into the air, and the city erupted with screams of excitement... screams for *Justice*.

CHAPTER TWENTY-THREE

Kimmie ran. She did not know where they were going or what they'd do when they got there. They'd have to figure that out later.

If there is a later ... she thought.

She scrambled on all fours up the slope, the dirty, broken skin of her fingers grabbing for purchase. The uneven debris beneath her gave way, sliding, taking her back.

A howl in the distant night. A wild animal, or worse, a man trying to sound like one.

"No," Kimmie cried out. Her feet stabbed into the shifting slope of broken brick and scattered trash. Her ankle rolled on the loose debris, and the crunch caused her to cry out again.

"Come on, Kimmie, hurry. They're almost on us."

Joshua waited inside the entrance of a ruined office building, below a crumbling façade that still read *Mavin and Associates* in faded white block letters. Cradled against Joshua's chest was their wide-eyed daughter, May, her cheeks streaked with tears.

"I'm coming," Kimmie shouted, her legs burning with exhaustion. *How long can this go on?* It couldn't have been more than a few hours, but perpetual fear had a way of making it an eternity.

Joshua spun, little May's legs dangling as he dashed into the shadows of the old structure. Kimmie let out a groan and powered to the top of the slope. Screams rang out behind her, the sort of sounds men made when they'd become alienated from their humanity. It was the sound of her family's doom. She'd just reached the landing when the groan of dirt bikes grated through the air, and a blinding white search light probed the dark urban wastes.

Kimmie tucked herself into the shadows, her lungs heaving. The light swung across the gray brick wall, filling in the gaps and illuminating the dust particles that danced in the air.

"They came this way," a shrill voice called from out of the void. "Fan out. Find them. I want my bounty."

Staying low, Kimmie slunk away from the safety of the wall and through a smaller deformed doorway covered in vegetation. She searched the dark, the sound of revving dirt bikes echoing across the bleak landscape. A hiss caught her attention. Squinting, she searched the gloom, and her eyes fell on the form of Joshua, huddled with May. He waved her over.

Pain radiated up Kimmie's shin. If they had to flee again, she wouldn't be able to keep up. She limped over to where Joshua cooed softly to their daughter.

She crouched with a wince of pain.

"You okay?" he asked.

Kimmie swallowed. "I think I hurt my ankle."

Joshua was a good man, a capable man, but at this moment, she saw fear in his eyes.

"Can you run?" he asked.

Kimmie's mouth felt like a desert. She wiped the dust from her face and tried to hold back the tears.

Joshua squeezed her arm, and she glimpsed his sad, knowing eyes. "It's okay, honey. We'll be okay."

It was a good lie, at least. She looked down at May, whose shell-shocked expression hadn't changed since the Glom troopers dropped them into The Zone. *How long has it been? Six hours?* she wondered. *It was daylight then.*

Kimmie struggled to get her head around why they were in this hell, surrounded by such terror and madness. A week ago, Joshua had a good job at one of the robotics factories. She'd taken care of little May and sold handmade glass sculptures on the side. They were poor, but they had each other. Life wasn't too bad. Then the late notices arrived. Statements showing all of their Glom accounts long overdue. She'd tried to cancel their services, but they'd already accrued thousands of T's worth of late-fee interest. Money, The Glom threatened, would be paid back one way or another.

One evening while they'd settled down for the night in their small apartment in Havana Straits, men in dark suits came banging on the door. When Kimmie answered, they'd forced their way in and pulled a screaming May from Joshua's arms. He'd tried to fight back and taken a beating. Next thing Kimmie knew, the Glom agents restrained and hooded them and shoved them into a waiting VTOL outside. Hours later, they were thrown into The Zone, each with a bounty of five thousand T's loaded onto their wrist chips. The Skulls, one of the worst gangs in The Zone, found them in no time.

What will happen if... Kimmie felt a void in her chest. *When they catch us?*

They'd murder Joshua and take his head as a trophy. She would be raped and murdered. And only God knew what they'd do to her little May. All of it broadcast in high definition for the world to see. Kimmie stifled a sob.

"What are you thinking?" Joshua said.

"I don't know. Can we cut our chips out? If we did, we wouldn't be worth anything to them, right?"

"Kimmie, they fuse chips to the bone." He pressed the tiny scar on his wrist. "You can't dig it out."

"We have to do something," Kimmie said, trying to keep her voice low. "Do you think an Enforcer will come?"

Joshua jerked his head toward a broken window. Held up a

hand. Kimmie and May fell silent. Outside, the sound of dirt bikes drew near, tires grinding rubble, the wild shouts of men.

"We can't count on any Enforcer to help us," Joshua whispered, his eyes searching the dark landscape.

"Momma?" May said, staring up with large hazel eyes.

"I'm here," Kimmie said, wiping her face. She squeezed May close to her chest.

"Are those bad men going to catch us?"

Kimmie and Joshua exchanged a glance.

"It's not safe here, sweetheart. We need to keep moving." Kimmie tried to stay positive. "Go with Papa."

May's eyes glazed over with terror. She clung to Joshua's neck as he stood.

Kimmie gasped again as she put full weight on her throbbing ankle, testing it.

Joshua sized her up, his eyes questioning.

"Go. I'm right behind you," she said.

Shuffling through the dusty, dark corridors, Kimmie fought back the shockwaves of pain firing up from her ankle into her hip. She ducked beneath the dirty glass of a window as a searchlight swept past. A bike ground across the debris, flinging it in the air as it sped past. Kimmie settled onto the cracked tile floor.

"Kimmie, come on," Joshua said from the end of the hall.

She waved him on but watched in horror as he turned and came back. "Go!" she hissed.

"I'm not leaving you, Kim. Don't ask me to. Get up," he said, his hands clutched tight around the child.

"Don't leave Mommy," May whimpered.

Joshua ducked as a dune buggy and two more dirt bikes sped past outside. "We have to go. Right now," he said, his eyes wild and white.

Kimmie could feel herself breaking inside. "Leave me. You can make it without me."

"We're not leaving you. Get up."

"Where are we going to go? We're surrounded." Tears carved paths down Kimmie's dusty cheeks.

A yelp like that of a wild slag dog echoed from down the hall.

"They're in the building. Get up." Joshua grabbed Kimmie's arm and yanked her to her feet, pushing her forward. "Go. I'm right behind you."

"Josh," Kimmie sobbed.

"Just go."

Kimmie stumbled forward, her ankle ablaze with pain. She fell against the wall, righted herself, and fell again. Joshua's fingers snaked around her biceps, lifting her.

The three of them shambled toward the far end of the structure, an opening that fed into an area between two buildings, decayed and covered in creepers. Joshua pushed his head out of the door, scanning left and right.

A scream echoed from the far end of the hall, a sound of absolute madness. There, from the gloom, emerged a man in black rags. Across the fabric on his chest, a painted symbol of crossed bones. The man let loose another hoot, his face painted white in the image of a skull. Behind him, others in similar garb carried barbaric weapons and various rusted firearms. With howls of death, the men rushed down the hallway toward Kimmie, Joshua, and May.

Joshua shoved Kimmie through the opening, and the three of them rolled down a short slope of rubble. May burst into tears.

A cacophony filled the air, old engines and rusted chassis squealing. Light washed across a fractured parking lot choked with weeds. Kimmie raised a hand to shield her eyes.

"They have us," she cried.

Joshua pushed the child into Kimmie's arms. "Take May. Run!"

"No… no, Joshua." She could hardly utter the words. "They'll…"

"Go now, or we're all dead," Joshua said, his voice hoarse. He grabbed a dusty brick and ran back up, feet slipping on the slope to the opening. "Run!"

Kimmie clutched May against her heaving breasts, legs stabbing at the uneven ground beneath her blistered feet. Adrenaline surged within her, and for a moment, the lancing pain in her ankle seemed to abate. As she ran, the lights swept across her, and she chanced a look over her shoulder.

The first marauder exited the building and shrieked in shock as Joshua slammed the brick against his skull-painted face. The ambient screams of millions of viewers echoed in the air. Together the men tumbled into a ditch, where a wild-eyed Joshua slammed the blood-smattered brick home a second time. Joshua stood, desperate eyes searching for the bandit's weapon. A rifle cracked. Joshua looked down, a crimson stain spreading across his chest.

A squad of dirt bikes and rusted dune buggies lurched forward, gaining ground on Kimmie as she ran with her child, her vision blurred with tears.

Joshua flung another brick at an approaching Skull, who dodged the flying debris and, with a yelp, struck Joshua in the face with a spiked bat. Joshua flailed, blood pouring down his face as the Skulls converged. He tried to push to all fours, his body pressed back to the ground by the savage Skulls. One of them jerked on his hair to expose his neck.

"Run, Kimmie, run!" Joshua's gurgled scream echoed behind her as the savage thugs, whooping with glee, pulled a rusted blade across his throat.

"No!" Kimmie cried. Her body shuddered with violent tremors, her legs churning, driving her forward. The wild men on Joshua laughed, a blood-drunk sound of glee, but she couldn't bring herself to look.

Kimmie slowed as the flaming rod of pain in her ankle returned. She stopped. Clutching a whimpering May close, her eyes roved across the twelve-foot concrete wall ahead, adorned with moss and kudzu. *Nowhere to run.* She turned as dune buggies with white skulls painted on the hoods slid to a stop in front of her. Dirt bikes and men on foot ran up to encircle them against the wall. Blinded by the lights, Kimmie pinched her eyes closed and whispered to May.

"Close your eyes, MayMay."

A bare-chested man wearing a painted half-skull mask that covered his forehead over his nose stood from the back of the nearest dune buggy. A twentieth-century fifty-caliber machine gun hung anchored to a swiveling mount beside him.

"Collect the bounties and assign them to me," the Skull leader said.

The Skulls approached, surrounding them. A dark-skinned man, his exposed flesh painted bone white, yanked a squalling May from the arms of her mother. Another man, a large white pentagram painted across his chest, extended the child's wrist. He produced a chip scanner, held together with fraying black electrical tape, and zapped the child's chip. The claimed bounty chimed.

The stench of their body odor, sour like death, filled her nose. The hands of the Skulls held Kimmie fast, extending her arm. She pulled back. "No!"

The pentagram man with the scanner turned Kimmie's palm up and scanned her chip.

"Bounty collected," the device chimed.

"We got both scans, boss," the pentagram said. "Bounty money is ours."

"Do what you want with the woman, the child is mine," the Skull leader said.

"No, not my May!" Kimmie screamed, clawing at the arms of the thugs who held her. A punch glanced hard off her chin, her vision reeling with the whirling light of a thousand stars. The air filled with the depraved laughter of her captors. Stunned, detached from the peril of the moment, she watched, dazed, as the savage men carried a shrieking May toward the Skull leader in his buggy.

A camera drone dropped from overhead to live stream every terrible moment for the legions of insatiable viewers across the length and breadth of the city.

Kimmie gasped. The swelling mass of men pulled at her clothes and groped at her body, the buttons of her shirt popping, the fabric tearing at the collar. A whimper escaped her. She pushed back in vain, struggling against the sweat-lathered, stinking crew of painted men.

A screech of jet engines fired overhead.

The Skulls groping at her searched the sky, a sudden fear in their eyes.

"Get back, you fools," the masked leader shouted. "It's a—"

An incredible impact struck the ground. A blinding flash of blue light rippled out in waves, blasting everyone off their feet and sending the Skull leader tumbling from the back of the dune buggy.

Across the length and breadth of The Zone, the collective roar of millions of viewers amplified, echoing off the broken ruins of the old world.

Thrown against the ground, Kimmie sat up stunned, the dust swirling about her. She coughed, blinking, "May!"

Rising from a small crater in the rubble, a form stood, jet black armor adorned with a navy blue stripe and a bright white star in the center of its chest.

Curses spilled from the lips of the maddened Skulls.

"Enforcer!" one shouted.

"Kill him!"

The Skulls converged, their battle cries rising, wild and undisciplined.

The newcomer pivoted, driving headlong into the closest bunch. His left arm rose to intercept a machete, and the blade chinked off the obsidian gauntlet. The Enforcer's fist landed with the power of a sledgehammer, the bones of the wild man's face giving way. An uppercut shattered another's jaw.

The screams of fans, delirious with excitement, swelled in the air.

The Enforcer surged forward; a retractable blast baton extended open. A blinding flash and a thunderous electrical crack split the air as the baton discharged on impact and sent a third Skull sprawling. Two more Skulls went down amidst brilliant white flashes and a double crack of the baton that split the air like rolling thunder. With a grunt, the Enforcer delivered a stamp kick, launching a fifth man through the air. He struck one of the dune buggies with a hollow *clang*, his body pinwheeling like a boneless thing across the hood.

The sound of the Skull leader's fifty-caliber machine gun snapping a round into the chamber brought the melee to a standstill.

"Twitch, and I'll blast you apart, Enforcer," the masked Skull leader said from behind the massive weapon. "Even your armor can't hold against this old-fashioned lead slinger."

The wild men sucked at the air, afraid to approach the dark vigilante.

The chanting of the crowd continued to rise and fall, the shouted name of *Jus-tice* cresting the air like an anthem.

"Let the child go." Justice turned to face the bandit leader. "Let her go, and I'll let you live."

The masked man hocked a dry laugh and leveled the fifty bravo at the Enforcer. "Live? For what?" the Skull leader asked. "We already *live* in The Zone, and in this place, you only keep what you scratch and claw for."

"Is that a no?"

The Skull leader shifted. "The child goes to Rico. The rest is mine."

"Not anymore," Justice said.

A humid wind pushed across them, clinging to the skin like imitation sweat. Not a soul stirred amidst the dark and decay of the urban wasteland.

"You don't seem to understand. I already claimed the bounty." The masked leader's voice was little more than a growl. "They're of no value to you now."

"I don't care about the money," Justice said. "Let the child go."

The Skull leader scowled. "No one goes back on a deal with Rico. We'll add your bones to our collection before we do that, Enforcer."

Around the Skull leader, his bandits retrieved janky old-world firearms of questionable reliability. Some grabbed axes, machetes, and clubs and pulled them from the rear of the dune buggies.

"Momma!" May's voice cried from somewhere in the dark.

"My baby," Kimmie whimpered.

"Stay behind me," Justice said, standing between her and the skull-painted men.

"But my daughter," Kimmie begged, "please!"

The Enforcer's smooth, black faceplate surveyed the enemy force before him. His fingers twitched, hovering over the Peacemaker holstered at his side. The weapon's retention bar slid back.

"You're a fool and a dead man," the Skull leader said, taking aim with the fifty-cal.

"Make your move then," the Enforcer said, staring down the horde of well-armed sociopaths, "because I'm not leaving The Zone without that child."

The Skull leader sneered, jangled yellow teeth like a row of broken tombstones in his mouth.

CHAPTER TWENTY-FOUR

Gabriel Kess sat at his desk, a titanic slab of smooth black granite, his eyes roving over the projected surveillance feeds: the Enforcers gathered in the lounge, views of each of their private living spaces, and the apartments of their loved ones. He watched with little interest as the new Enforcer's wife walked across her apartment and retrieved their son, rocking the swaddled form.

Kess yawned.

In Enforcer Escalation's apartment, the glistening nude form of a woman, wearing only her visor, poured herself a glass of champagne before re-entering a balcony hot tub.

Turning his attention back to the ongoing trial, he sat back in his chair with a grunt and rubbed at his face. The genuine leather of the chair creaked as it adjusted to his weight. At this time of night, and considering the event going on right now, the executive suite offices carried an eerie silence. Even those who worked at Conglomerate headquarters enjoyed their vices, and everyone watched The Zone. Everyone.

Kess reached over and plucked up his glass. As he raised it to his lips, the two large cubes of ice chinked together. He took a long sip of the cool amber liquid and savored the burn that followed.

Five minutes in The Zone, and he's already doomed. Damn kid had said he was ready. Warrant even confirmed that he could handle himself. And right here, right now, Kess was about to watch the whole thing collapse.

The muscles of Kess's jaw tightened as he pressed his teeth together.

"Open the security feeds from New West City." He waved the standoff in The Zone to the left side of the wall of projected video before him to create some space. "Director authorization nine five four seven two six kilo."

"Good evening, Director Kess," an AI assistant said. "Opening available security feeds from New West City."

A series of twenty-seven more screens popped to life on the right side of the projection that now engulfed most of his office. Kess scanned the screens, loosened his tie, and swore.

"Remove screens seven through thirteen, twenty-one, twenty-four through twenty-seven."

"Fifteen screens remaining, Director."

"Enlarge," Kess said, picking over the madness of their distant sister city. His eyes flicked from one screen to the next as fires burned out of control, washing screens in a gray haze. Masked marauders dressed in sun-bleached rags smashed through the front of a barricaded general store, emerging moments later with goods in their arms. A malnourished man, trying to escape the madness with two young children, was pushed to the ground and shot in the face as the children screamed. A young woman, terrified and alone, backed into an alley, cornered by a group of thugs, laughing and passing a bottle of shine. On every feed, more of the same. A glance at the perimeter video connected to the Conglomerate headquarters revealed the strewn bodies of New West City's finest. They'd been overrun, protecting the damn slag-eaters who let it all happen. It was as Kess feared all along: New West City had fallen.

"Dear God," Kess muttered. "Get me a direct link with Logan."

"Confirmed. Attempting contact via long-range transfer," the AI said.

The comm-link trilled. Kess raised his glass halfway to his lips then set it back down with a curse. The empty buzz of an unanswered line continued. Seconds dragged into a minute. Kess lifted his hand, about to close the link, when the small screen flickered to life.

"Gabriel." The image of a deeply scarred man filled the screen. Behind him, columns of smoke rose and dissipated into a smog-blackened sky. "I trust this is important."

Kess bristled at the man's use of his first name. "I don't contact you across thousands of miles unless it's important. What's the status on the ground?"

The man flinched at the rattle-pop of gunfire in the background and uttered a coarse laugh. "How do you think it's going, Gabriel?"

Kess bit his cheek. "You're paid to feed me live information. I suggest you remember your place. I can make your life hell." He let that sink in. "What do you know?"

"Your reach only extends so far, Director." Logan leaned in closer to the camera, a smirk on his face. "Look at your security feeds. I'm in Hell."

"Expand on that," Kess said, struggling to hold back the building fury. Logan was a top-notch mercenary. The best in New West City by far. But, hellfire, he could be a pain in the ass. Kess watched Logan duck at another volley of gunfire.

"Neutralize that slag-eater," Logan shouted to one of his men from behind a barricade of sandbags. He turned his attention back to Kess. "What's happening here isn't what we agreed on. You said to expect a small bout of civil unrest."

"Not everything goes according to plan, Logan." Kess waved him away. "Are you going to deliver what I paid you for, or do I have to get my hands dirty?"

"Double my fee."

Kess's face soured. "Talk first."

The merc glanced up, then back to the video feed. "New West

City is dying. We might have just days. Then it's anyone's guess what happens. The street gangs are vying for control, fighting with the Outliers and what's left of the military faction at Firestorm Base. Senterian has taken refuge in the Sand Needle and deployed the Steel Brigade to defend it. The rest of us? We're just trying to make it another day."

"Director Senterian is a coward. He never had the stones to hold that position," Kess said, disgusted.

Logan ducked the zip of a passing round. "Now, double my pay."

Kess jabbed his finger at the image. "Answer me when I *jakking* call you next time."

A slash of his hand rendered the video feed dark.

If the founders hadn't seen what was happening there already, they would soon. If a public mass hysteria took hold in Neo Terminus, there'd be no stopping it. *Just like New West City.* Kess waved the security feeds closed and took another sip of his scotch.

Unlike calculated strategy and steadfastness, panic held no value for him. There always was a way out. One simply needed to possess the nerve and discipline to find it.

Historically, New West City was a mismanaged wreck, more of a glitzy frontier outpost than a well-oiled machine. Other than the overarching Conglomerate influence, only a corporate alliance and a handful of small resource trade agreements connected it to Neo Terminus. Outside of that, nothing about New West City sinking into the desert wastes affected Neo Terminus. They had their own government, structure, currency, and networks.

All he needed to do was keep total media silence regarding the fate of New West City. It was the one factor that could threaten everything—the public's knowledge of the truth of New West City. Kess knew there were rumors. Before he'd shut them down, some of the more obscure network channels theorized something disastrous was going down in their sister city. The gossip, spreading like wildfire across Neo Terminus, was without any evidence or first-hand accounts. Nothing was verifiable.

Yet.

Kess knew as soon as the truth about New West City leaked, Neo Terminus, already on the brink of a citizen uprising, would tear itself apart. And, like New West City, there weren't enough police or security forces to hold it together. This last vestige of civilized humanity would fall.

But New West City never had The Zone. The very thing that was once a stain on Neo Terminus during the early formative years now held the power to save them from collapse.

He turned his attention back to the standoff and shook his head. The draw of The Zone, the entertainment, no, the *distraction* it provided, had to be so great that it drowned out all else. And now Justice, his newest Enforcer, having already lost three bounties, was about to get himself killed and ruin everything.

"Mr. Kess?"

Kess, shaken from his thoughts, waved his digital feed closed and sat forward. In the sliding doorway to his office stood his assistant, Miss Avery, her visor flickering with games, advertisements, and updates from The Zone.

"Miss Avery, I thought you'd gone for the evening." He noted her tasteful yet seductive casual attire. "Heading out now?"

"Yes, sir. Going out to catch the last part of tonight's trial with some friends." She cocked her head playfully. "You're not staying in the office, are you?"

Kess took in the form of his assistant, the long legs and hourglass figure. He could have her if he wished. *Tempting*, he thought, *but no, such distractions at a time like this are not how one kept an empire from toppling. Maybe one day...*

"I am staying in, Miss Avery," he said. "I have a lot riding on this new Enforcer."

"Justice? I see. He has his hands full right now. Well, good night," she said with a little wave.

"Ah, Miss Avery. One quick question." Kess held up a hand. "Off the top of your head, what single event in The Zone sparked the most viewership? The one moment that brought the most critical acclaim or controversy?"

"One event?" she asked.

Kess nodded.

"The death of Vigilance, of course," she said without hesitation.

Kess's eyes narrowed. "Of course, and why is that?"

She opened her hands. "It was unexpected. Vigilance was a strong Enforcer and a safe bet for gamblers. Seeing her beheaded on live feed shocked the public. Up to that point, Enforcer deaths in The Zone were rare and well telegraphed."

Kess sat back and tented his fingers over his lips. "Unexpected," he murmured.

"Yes, sir," Miss Avery said, "but..." A look of realization deepened over her features.

"Thank you, Miss Avery." Kess waved his fingers in dismissal. "Enjoy your evening."

Miss Avery opened her mouth to speak, closed it again, and smoothed her blouse. "Goodnight, sir." She turned from the doorway to disappear into the hall. The door slid shut behind her.

Kess took the rest of his scotch in one swallow and clacked the glass down on the desktop. He opened a link with the network operations manager, Vandervel Korvel.

"Yes, Director Kess?" Korvel's eyes, magnified comically through his thick-lensed spectacles, filled up the entire screen.

"Korvel, have Warrant suit up."

"You want him to deploy, sir?" Korvel said, pushing the specks higher onto the bridge of his bulbous nose.

"Negative, I want him to suit up and be in a VTOL over The Zone. He only deploys if Justice goes down or is outmatched. If this goes bad, it's your problem. Understand?"

"Yes... of course, Director."

Kess closed the comm link and touched the tip of his finger to the floating image of his daughter's face. The anxiety over the unknown future fluttered in his stomach. His own powerful ambition served him well, but it wasn't the only thing driving him.

His fingers closed around the vial in his pocket. He shook away the thought. It wasn't an addiction. It was a legal prescription for his performance anxiety. He could control it. He just needed a little dose to help him take the edge off.

He removed the small cylinder from his pocket, unscrewed the cap, and held the dropper up. Turning it over, he placed a single drop into each eye. His eyelids fluttered. The effect was immediate. An exotic sensation streamed over him, bathing him in a numbing wave of pleasure. Colors grew brighter, the supple chair against his back more sensual and luxurious than it was before. The tether to his anxiety severed, everything suddenly became more exciting and vibrant and full of potential. Kess placed the small ampule into his pocket and leaned back as the full effect of the Feels crashed into him.

He reached his finger up and stroked the floating desktop projection of his sweet Clarissa's face.

"Whatever happens, it's for you, my darling." His words slurred together. "'S'all for you."

Hannah Griffin pulled her visor from her face and stood up from the plush, cream-colored couch, dropping the expensive lenses onto the tabletop in front of her.

"Oh my God, I can't do this." She walked halfway to the kitchen and stopped, turned back to the flickering visor. She

230

pushed her hands as if shoving the air away from her and touched her fingers to her lips. "I can't watch this."

Two rooms over, the baby cried. A swarm of hysteria threatened to overtake her. She started toward Andrew's room, then turned, and instead, made for the kitchen.

Like the horror films her grandfather used to watch when she was a girl, there came a point where squinting and covering her eyes wasn't enough. She needed it to stop. But this was no movie. Chance was an Enforcer, and right now, he was all alone in The Zone with his life on the line.

Because of me.

"What have I done?" She entered the kitchen and poured herself a glass of water. "Okay, Hannah, it's all right." She pushed the water aside and pulled a bottle of vodka from the back of the bar, raising the bottle straight to her trembling lips. "Chance can handle himself. Right? Of course, he can. That's what he's trained to do—handle difficult situations." The straight vodka burned a flaming path down her throat and into her belly. Hannah wiped her mouth on her arm.

"I can't watch it. I shouldn't. Should I?" She looked again toward the living room and the lit visor, video images dancing on the glass of the table.

A sense of shame hung over her. Her husband could die right now, murdered by some blood thirsty gang in The Zone, and she couldn't even support him by watching his first trial. But who wanted to watch their loved one murdered? *Am I the only one in this damn city without an insatiable lust for violence?*

She took a longer drink from the bottle.

Everything they needed was at her fingertips. This new place, all the luxury, food, and treatments for their son—but was it worth it? Hannah set the bottle down on the counter. At this moment, the answer had to be no. They were poor before, but their life was simple. It had constraints. She never knew half of what Chance had to do out there, the things he'd had to do to survive on the streets. Nor did she want to know. But if Chance had died, he would've died quietly as a hero, a defender of the city he loved. Instead, he would now perish to the joyful screams of millions, a celebrity gladiator in a game show designed to appease the gore-drunk masses.

"Oh, Chance…" Hannah said, anguish etched on her face.

She felt insane with anxiety. Here in this foreign place, day and night, with no friends and no family to support her. She needed to talk to someone.

"Open comm link," Hannah said, the dulling sensation of the vodka sliding over her.

"*Opening comm link.*" The apartment's ever-present AI said. "*Name a contact or give their Network ID.*"

"Benny," Hannah said and pushed the bottle down the counter away from her.

"*Benny,*" the hostess confirmed. "*Attempting to contact subscriber.*"

"Come on, Benny, pick up." Hannah tapped her pearl-colored manicure on the countertop.

"*The subscriber you are trying to reach is not available at this time. Please try again later.*"

"Damn, Benny. Where are you?" Hannah ended the call.

She leaned onto the clean, cool surface of the polished marble slab and rested her face in her hands. Her mind reached for someone she could lean on, someone who would support her in this. She shook her head. After the death of her family, she hadn't taken the time to develop new friends. The ones she had either weren't close, moved to other sectors of the city and disappeared, or got sick and passed away. When the baby came, she hadn't the time to hang out with anyone, anyway. For a while now, it was just her and Chance and the baby. Somewhere in the back of her mind, she'd known it wasn't healthy. She knew she needed a better support system, but it wasn't until the move and now Chance's imminent doom at the hands of marauders in The Zone that her emotional circumstances lay exposed.

Hannah stepped away from the countertop, grabbing the bottle of vodka as she went. She crossed the room to where the visor flickered on the table, the swelling rush of cheers rising from the headset. Something was happening. *Can I bear to watch it?*

Hannah sat back on the plush couch and tucked her legs beneath her, the soft, worn T-shirt and sweatpants she wore, a comfort of sorts. Her eyes roved the dark city skyline outside her opulent apartment, the shadowed buildings and towering super structures lit by a wash of neon light and flashing hover drone advertisements. Another gasp from the crowd caused her eyes to drop back to the visor.

Hannah bit her lip and plucked the visor from the table. She slid the stems over her ears, the widescreen image blocking out everything else.

"*Ladies and gentlemen,*" a brightly dressed announcer with narrow hips and the shoulders of a body builder said, his giant pompadour bobbing. "What a tense moment! What will happen? Will Justice prevail? Make your bets now!"

"Come on, Chance." Hannah clutched the vodka bottle to the center of her chest like a safety blanket. "Don't die on me."

CHAPTER TWENTY-FIVE

"**B**arrier," Chance shouted as the fifty-caliber machine gun opened fire with an ear-splitting sound.

Three rounds struck Chance, staggering him and blowing holes in his armor before the transparent glowing white rectangle shot upward between him and his attackers. The volley of heavy machine gun rounds struck the curtain of light, disintegrating in coppery green flashes of fire. Chance crouched low, and the body of the woman snugged close behind him.

"*Chance,*" RITA's voice spoke inside his helmet, "*your armor can only support the energy barrier for ten more seconds.*"

"I'm working on it," Chance said, pulling two impact grenades from quick-release pouches on his rig.

"Keep firing. He can't hold it forever!" the Skull leader screamed.

Bullets zipped and pinged past Chance and the woman, a storm of projectiles fragmenting into the barrier in splashes of emerald fire.

"Oh my god!" the woman cried, scrunching into a ball amidst the hail of gunfire.

"*Five seconds,*" RITA said.

Chance transferred the two grenades to his left hand and primed their pressure activators with his thumb. Then, he drew the Peacemaker from his holster and selected three-round burst. The white energy shield flickered.

"*Chance,*" RITA said, "*you can't fight from here with a survivor behind you. When the shield goes down, you'll have to draw their fire away from her.*"

"I know."

Chance hurled the impact grenades at the Skulls. The fifty-caliber machine gun fire stopped as the Skull leader dove from the dune buggy. There was a dual flash of fire, the Skulls screaming in response. Chance's barrier faded, and he threw himself to the side. His Peacemaker bucked upward, three rounds fired with the efficiency of a submachine gun. Three of the closest Skulls took headshots, their eyes wide with shock as their brains flew into the air.

Senses aflame with adrenaline, Chance rolled, rose to his feet, and engaged the Skulls with directed fire from his Peacemaker. The dune buggies revved high, fishtailing, a shower of debris thrown into the air from the spinning tires. Struck with two more stray rounds, Chance staggered, the impacts blowing more chunks out of his armor.

"*Armor is at seventy-two percent,*" RITA said.

"I need a pursuit vehicle," Chance said.

"*Copy. Power cycle inbound.*"

Chance took down two more Skulls with well-placed center-mass shots. With the roar of the crowd in his ears, he charged forward, knocking one of the remaining Skulls back and splitting the man's forehead with the heavy barrel of his sidearm.

The last of the dune buggies spun out alongside several dirt bikes. Chance dispatched the remaining Skulls and took up a defensive position, searching for any stragglers. Dust from the disturbed rubble swirled at his feet like mist over a bog.

"Please. Just… just…"

Chance turned to the woman behind him, his heart sinking in his chest.

Her hand reached out, quivering with the effort, pointing to the savages fleeing with her child. Blood pumped in thick red rivulets from a ragged bullet wound high in her midsection.

"I'm sorry," Chance said. "I tried…"

"My May… help my sweet May."

Chance's faceplate opened, his eyes betraying the truth before his lips could form the words. "She's gone."

"No. They don't kill children, they…" She moaned. "Promise me. Promise you'll save her. I know you can," she said, her countenance glassy with shock. "I need to hear you say it."

Chance worked his jaw and surveyed the retreat of the bouncing dune buggies with hard eyes. He rubbed his hands together and still felt the sticky blood of one dead child between his fingers. Chance knelt and placed an armored hand on her shoulder. "I promise."

The woman grit her teeth and a groan of pain escaped her. She lay back on the broken rubble, her body shaking before drawing still with a sudden gasp. "Joshua…"

Chance stood and turned, watching the Skulls taillights recede in the urban gloom. His faceplate dropped into place with a snap, the inteli-suit combination of nano skin and armor already repairing the broken sections.

"*Armor restoration will take a while. I'll call for pick up,*" RITA said.

"I'm not extracting."

"*You're not?*"

"No. Locate and lock on the child's chip," Chance said, opening his gait in pursuit of the Skulls. "Hack into the network feed if you have to and keep the cycle en route to my position. I'll be on the move."

"*Chance, according to the rules of play, the trial is over. The child's bounty has been claimed. You have too much to risk and nothing to gain by going after her—*"

"Do it, RITA," Chance said, his voice strained.

"*Searching for the girl now.*"

The screams of the ravenous crowd drowned out in the huffing of his breath. Chance focused, his body picking up speed. He vaulted over a disabled auto-junker and cut through a trashed alley.

Above, The Glom's drones followed, rotors whirring, their cameras capturing his fevered pursuit in ultra-high definition.

"But what's this, ladies and gentlemen?" the stylish announcer said, his ridiculous image littering the screens above the zone. "The trial should be over, but it would seem Justice isn't finished yet. He's pursuing the Skulls in an attempt to rescue the child. How heroic!"

Chance tried to ignore the ridiculous show surrounding his own life and death stakes. He dove through the open rear window of a dilapidated apartment, rolled, and rose to his feet. In a few strides, he slammed through the opposite front door, the wood splintering as the frail door shattered off its hinges.

"Such dogged determination. Such courage! But will he prevail?" the announcer said, his pompadour hair jiggling. "What do you think, my dear?" he said, pushing the microphone toward an excited young woman in a high-collared pink leather jacket and a glowing neon visor.

"He's amazing! I think he can do it!" She clasped her hands and squealed with glee. The high-pitched sound echoed across the length and breadth of The Zone.

"Dammit, RITA, get this out of my face. I've got enough distractions," Chance said, catching a last glimpse of the Skulls' caravan receding. "What's the ETA on that cycle?"

"*Inbound. Five minutes.*"

"I don't have five minutes." Chance cut through another dark alley, rats and slag dogs scurrying at the sight of the pursuing Enforcer. He burst from the alley, dropped to a knee, and slid to a stop. The battle rifle pulled from his back in one fluid sweep.

Crouched in a stable position, Chance initiated the four-power magnification, tracking the taillights of the dune buggies. The rifle cracked three times in repetition. The Skull caravan swerved, and several tires shot out. Three of the Skulls riding dirt bikes broke formation and turned on him.

Chance stood and slung the rifle across his back. He opened his stance, and the retention bar on his Peacemaker slid back. *That's right,* he thought, *come get some.*

The Skulls came for him. Screams of war howled from their open mouths. Steadying their dirt bikes, they drew barbaric melee weapons, two spiked bats, and a large, serrated knife stained with blood. Throttles wide, they zipped across the uneven terrain, the bikes' shocks jumping beneath them.

Chance's hand hovered over his sidearm. In a movement hardwired into muscle memory, he drew the Peacemaker and fired. The bulky handgun recoiled hard with each pull of the trigger, gleaming brass cases flung into the air. The Skulls howled, each clutching at mortal wounds—they toppled from their bikes in a wash of dust and debris.

Chance grabbed one of the wobbling dirt bikes before it fell and cranked the throttle wide open. The engine screamed. The rear wheel flung debris into the air, and the back end swung around in a cloud of dust. Mounting the bike, Chance took off, and the cheers of hysterical fans echoed across The Zone.

As Chance gained ground on the fleeing Skulls, muzzle flashes erupted from the rear of the dune buggies. He flinched as a round snapped past his head. A second struck him in the chest. Safe inside the armor, Chance winced from the blow.

"*Sixty-six percent,*" RITA said.

Another round struck him in the thigh. Chance swore, opened the throttle wide, and black smoke chugged from the exhaust.

"*Sixty percent.*"

"Silence all warnings until it's critical," Chance said through gnashed teeth.

He came alongside the fleeing vehicles as they passed between crumbling brick buildings and dilapidated high-rise apartments into an open area interspersed with trees and overgrown with weeds.

"Chance, the child is in the second buggy. She appears unharmed."

Chance kicked the magazine free with a flick of his wrist and jammed the Peacemaker down into its holster. Drawing a magazine marked with a white star, he slid it into the mag well and snapped it home. The Peacemaker in hand once again, he racked the slide off his armor and aimed across his chest. The hand cannon jolted upward. The rearmost dune buggy burst into licking flames, the shrieking Skulls inside bathed in the incandescent glow of white phosphorous. The vehicle swerved, crested a rise, and rolled as the fuel reserve caught in a volcanic plume of fire.

Crossing the ancient park, choked with weeds, Chance fired a second WP round and watched as it arced into the forward vehicle, the savage occupants igniting in a fiery blast.

Chance maintained pressure on the throttle and performed a tactical reload, this time jamming one of the laser red emblem magazines into the magazine well.

Another two rounds struck Chance, one in the shoulder and the other across the top of his helmet. His internal display flickered.

"Get a signature lock on the driver," Chance said. "I'm not taking any chances hitting the kid."

"I've got it. You're clear," RITA said.

Chance raised the Peacemaker and kept a lock on the fleeing buggy, the Skull leader and his goons dumping the last of their rounds in Chance's direction. He depressed the trigger and heard the weapon whine as the projectile charged and fired. The self-adjusting round jerked to the right at the last moment. It bypassed the vehicle's roll bar and lanced through the driver, punching a jagged hole in his chest.

The buggy wasn't at a full stop before the Skulls jumped from it, weapons trained on the dogged Enforcer.

"Kill that slag-eater!" the Skull leader screamed and pulled the bawling child close.

At speed, Chance holstered and dismounted to the side. As his feet struck the ground, he let loose a scream and, gripping the handlebars, spun, flinging the bike at two bandits. The tumbling dirt bike struck them at full force, smashing them into bloody pulp against the side of their buggy.

But the movement left Chance open. A war hammer struck him in the head, dropping him to his knees. Another blow from a spiked bat spun him in the opposite direction. Chance went for his Peacemaker as a downward swing from the hammer struck his arm and knocked it away.

"*Chance, you've got to get clear,*" RITA called out, a tinge of emotion in her voice. "*Your armor just dropped below fifteen percent.*"

The war hammer came again, but Chance caught the shaft in his fist and wrenched it from the hands of the sweat-lathered, skull-faced man. With the hammer, Chance pummeled the last of the thugs against the turf and turned to see the Skull leader holding the child, a knife to her throat. Tears cut fresh paths down the girl's dusty cheeks. Her throat moved against the edge of the blade.

"Twitch, and she's dead Enforcer!" the Skull leader shouted, his voice frail and falsetto.

"RITA, I need a signature lock right now." Chance dropped the war hammer. "Headshot."

"*I'm ahead of you,*" RITA said.

"I mean it, Enforcer! I'll—"

In a lightning fast move, Chance drew his Peacemaker and fired from the hip like an old-fashioned gunslinger. A slashing sound cut the air. The Skull leader dropped the knife, a gaping red hole in the center of his bone mask. He stumbled, touching his blood-drenched face, and fell flat.

With a strangled sob, the child ran toward Chance, her little arms extended. Chance's faceplate opened to reveal his bruised face, a thin trickle of blood running from his left nostril. He holstered his weapon and bent to scoop the weeping child in his arms.

A wild rush of applause followed, and chants for *Jus-tice* thundered in the night.

Above, the drones circled, focused on the image of him holding the girl.

A growing rumble stopped the cheers short, and a collective gasp swelled from the crowd.

On the horizon to his right, at the crest of the hilltop, headlights aimed down at him. Trucks, dune buggies, and old rusted sedans adorned with shattered skulls lined up one beside the next. Surrounding a dozen of the armored vehicles, scores of men in purple garb spread out shoulder to shoulder.

The air trembled with the growled cough of more engines, and Chance turned to see a second group along a hill of trash and debris to his left. These, he recognized—they wore the signature green of the Hoodie Boys. Two gangs in alliance. As the dust settled and the rattle of the engines ceased, an awful tension took root in the stillness that followed.

"Well, well, look at what we have here. A sweet, sweet child," a dusty voice squawked over a megaphone. "How I love children."

Chance stood his ground, the trembling child secure in his arms.

"Ahh, but what's more valuable than a child, you say?" the megaphone voice scratched. "How about the blood of a broken Enforcer?"

Both hillsides erupted in wild screams, the gangs thrusting their weapons into the air.

"*Chance, your armor is at twelve percent,*" RITA said. "*You cannot survive another fight, not while defending a child."*

"I gotta put you down, sweetheart," Chance said.

"No," the child cried.

"I have to." He sat her on the ground and stepped in front of her. The child moaned, groped at his legs, and stayed close.

Chance took a breath and steadied himself. He unslung the battle rifle and held it across the chest of his scarred and fractured armor, as ready as he was going to be for what came next.

A screech of engines fired overhead. Then the brief *whoosh* of something heavy falling, and an impact slammed into the dirt just feet away. The child cried out and clinched against Chance's leg, eyes pinched.

Inside the crater, a second figure in carbon gray armor rose from the dust. The suit, worn and battle-tested, had a shining gold sheriff's star emblazoned over the left breast.

"*Warrant has entered The Zone,*" the announcer's voice boomed to a barrage of fanfare.

"If you want the blood of a dead Enforcer," Warrant called out, "you can have the blood of two—but you'll have to earn it."

"We'll pull you both apart, Enforcer." The sound of the megaphone scratched the air, echoing across the open space.

Warrant hefted a massive quad-rocket launcher over his shoulder. "Guess we'll see, won't we?"

A stillness descended on the small valley. Even the ravenous crowds watching from across the length and breadth of Neo Terminus seemed to hold their breath. Chance stood firm, the child's arms coiled around his leg.

"Another day, we will see, tough guy," the megaphone voice said. "Rico, doesn't forget." The vehicles rumbled to life and disappeared one by one, followed by their foot soldiers.

The crowd broke into cheers for the victorious Enforcers.

The newcomer turned, lowering the rocket launcher. The featureless mask separated, revealing Sam's smirking face.

"You old patrol dog." Chance sighed with relief. "Am I glad to see you."

Sam shrugged. "Looked like you could use a hand."

Chance patted May's back. "I like to think I had it under control."

"Until just now. And in the process, you broke every rule in the book going after this girl," Sam said, taking a step forward.

"I wasn't aware of any rules." Chance smirked.

"Of course, you weren't. You did good today, partner," Sam said, sticking out his fist.

Chance knocked his own fist against Sam's and feigned shock. "Partner? Not *Rook* this time?"

Sam shook his head. "Not anymore."

Sam grabbed Chance's wrist and raised his arm high like a winning prizefighter, and the air thrummed with the delirious screams of thirty million satisfied viewers.

CHAPTER TWENTY-SIX

Benny groaned, and the bulk of his shoulders shifted against the narrow confines of the recovery chamber. His eyes fluttered. The few sources of light emanating from lamps, screens, and control panels nearby were too much to take. He pinched his eyes shut again and focused on the sounds: the *hiss-peep* of a machine measuring his vitals, the soft whirring warmth of banks of computer servos, an announcer talking with great enthusiasm about a Zone trial that defied all expectation.

"Ugh," Benny said, straining to sit up, "my head. Where am I?"

"Easy now." The small voice reached out to him from across the room. "Your mind and body have been under considerable strain. Don't rush your emergence."

"Can't see," Benny squinted. "And my head is killin' me."

"Yes, I imagine you'll have some unpleasant side effects."

Benny tried to sit up again, his pinched eyes unable to let in even the smallest measure of light. A stinging burn seemed to ebb and flow from his ribcage through his armpit, across the top of his left shoulder, and around the back of his neck.

The cushioned interior of the hyperbaric chamber encased his shoulders, and the machine beneath hummed, a velvety mist draping across his face. He blinked a few times to clear them better.

"Benny." Mage's calm and clinical voice came from off to his right. "I need to tell you something about your condition."

"What condition?" Benny struggled to clear the fog that hovered over his mind. He angled his face toward the small voice, total control of his faculties still beyond his grasp.

"What do you remember?" Mage said, his words soothing. "It's important."

"They were after me… shot me with noxies."

"They?" Mage prodded.

Benny swallowed. "The police."

"And why are the cops after you?"

Benny let out a withered sigh and straightened in the chamber. "I didn't do it—what they said I did—but I guess it doesn't matter at this point. My life is over."

"On the contrary, my friend." Mage's voice took an upward turn. "Your life is just beginning. An opportunity to see the world, unshackled from your perspective."

"What are you saying?" Benny said, his eyes clenched.

"What I'm saying, Corporal Benitez, is your world must change if you want to continue living in it."

"You know about me?" Benny said.

"Everything there is to know," Mage said. "Do you remember who I am?"

"Some sort of tech hacker."

Mage gasped a disgusted sound. "Hacking is for amateurs. What I create is art. It's digital magic. No one can do what I do."

"You said you'd help me." Benny shifted onto his side in the direction of Mage's voice. "So why does everything hurt, and why can't I see?"

A long silence filled the space between each electronic hiss and wheeze. Mage interlaced his fingers. "I dilated your eyes on the off chance you woke up, and I wasn't around to speak with you."

"Why?"

"Benny, you were badly injured," Mage said, his voice softening, "worse than you realized, I believe. The poison from the stifle rounds stayed in your system too long, and the bones of your left arm were shattered. It wasn't salvageable."

"What do you mean it wasn't salvage—?" Benny gasped as the fingers of his right hand touched down on the cold metallic rods that composed his left forearm.

"The hell did you do to me?" Benny screamed.

Jerking forward, he grabbed blindly for the lip of the recovery chamber. Heaving himself up, he stumbled out, his legs shaking beneath him.

"No, please," Mage said, "you're still weak. You need to give the chamber more time to complete the healing process."

Benny took a series of steps and crashed against a wall. Sliding to the floor, his metallic fingers clutched open, the pistoned arm swiping across a table top and sending odd trinkets and electrical components clattering to the floor. He fell to his knees and rolled his back to the wall, lungs filling with irregular breaths. A toppled cup of coffee drained from the table top, splattering a brown stream onto the cluttered concrete floor beside him. Benny clutched at the foreign bionic appendage with the fingers of his good hand. As his breathing slowed, his eyes still clamped shut, he felt the thing over.

It was solid, the rods and pistons in the forearm narrowing at the wrist. The fully articulated fingers clicked open and closed.

"I know it must come as a shock," Mage said, "but you could do worse. It's the best money can buy. Japanese craftmanship. One of the few Toyota-Sony collaborations, made of hardened dimenium alloy. Virtually indestructible. Plus, I've added my own touches."

Having composed himself a little, Benny's mouth pressed into a line. He blinked, his vision blurry. "Let me see it."

"Of course," Mage said. Taking little steps, he grabbed a dropper off the metal tray next to the open healing chamber. He crossed to Benny and unscrewed the bulbous rubber cap. "Tilt your head back."

Benny leaned back. Mage squeezed two drops into each eye where the lids pinched closed.

"Now blink a few times. The drops should neutralize the effects of the dilation," Mage said.

Benny sat against the wall, head tilted back, his eyelids fluttering. He sniffed. Raising the arm up, he peered at it through blurred eyes. The whole of the appendage was titanium gray, with sleek, rounded edges and solid, well-made components.

"My God. I can't believe this…" Benny shook his head. "I mean, bionics are everywhere. I just never thought—"

"You'd have one?" Mage said.

Benny nodded. "Why does everything hurt, though? Is that from this?" He motioned with the arm.

"Unfortunately, no. That's the other bad news," Mage said.

"More bad news?" Benny asked.

"The long exposure to the Noxilam in the stifle rounds caused damage to your somatosensory nervous system," Mage said. "The result appears to be some significant neuropathic pain. Your body will heal, but the nerve damage will remain."

Seeing Benny at a loss, Mage continued, "Which was why I installed this." He tapped a spot on Benny's cybernetic limb.

Still blinking, Benny stared at a small rectangle set parallel to the long pistons of the forearm. A series of small vials hid behind the rectangle, shielded by the rods and metal bracers.

"What am I supposed to see here?" Benny winced with a fresh wave of pain. "This pain is killing me."

Mage leaned closer. Even standing at full height and with Benny sitting, he still was only looking Benny in the face. "Stop your fussing." When no further protest came, Mage continued. "Raise your arm as though you plan to inspect it."

Benny did, squinting as the small dark rectangle on his inner forearm illuminated a screen showing three touch icons. Benny read the names aloud. "Pain, Frenzy, Velocity. What are they?"

"Hold your finger to the pain icon for a moment. It's biometric."

Benny touched the glowing icon, shaped like a miniature syringe. An audible hiss followed. Benny's mouth opened.

"I… I feel it."

"What do you feel?" Mage asked.

"Better." Benny waited as the cooling sensation passed from his shoulder down his torso and up toward his face, smothering the pain. "I feel better." He reached with his good hand to trace the scar where the stifle round hit him in the neck. "What is that stuff?"

"Loaded in your arm are several hard-to-come-by substances. Some are experimental. They should last you a while, but when they're gone, they're gone. What you just delivered into your bloodstream is a low dose, pure grade, medicinal version of the Feels. Only use a dose when you can't stand the nerve pain anymore. Over-use will make you an addict the same way the street version will."

Benny, already feeling much improved, made his way to his feet, his eyes still on the small control panel. "What about the others, Frenzy and Velocity?"

Mage's silver canine gleamed in the artificial light. "Those are something a little more, ah, primal. Not quite ready for human testing." He waved Benny off.

"So why put them in me?"

"Because I felt like it," Mage snapped. "Satisfied?"

Benny's face darkened. "So I'm what to you? Some guinea pig?"

Mage scowled, staring up. "Don't be stupid. I saved your life. Gave you a cybernetic arm that cost hundreds of thousands of T's, and I took the time to add my own special touches. I've done nothing but help you. I only took advantage of an opportunity to see my work in action."

Benny glared at Mage.

"Maybe I should've let you bleed out—or worse, survive as a criminal cripple, cowering on the streets and sleeping in your own sputz." Mage turned away, busying himself on one of his many digital terminals.

Benny beheld at the arm again. A true marvel of modern technology. He'd have to learn to live with it. Mage's little addition had already helped him with his pain. Benny released a sigh.

"You've done a lot for me," he said.

Mage kept his back to Benny, his little fat fingers jabbing at a holo-projection keyboard. Benny sighed. Aching exhaustion seemed to sink to the level of his bones.

"I'm gonna lay back down in this thing now," Benny said, helping himself back into the recovery chamber.

"You should, as I told you to from the beginning," Mage grunted without turning.

Benny lay back with a bloated sigh. "Do you need to turn it back on?"

Mage made his way over, a scowl on his weathered face. "Are you ready to stop crying about it?"

"Yeah," Benny said.

Mage appraised him for a moment. "Hold it up."

From where he lay, Benny raised his cybernetic arm. Picking up two halves of a smooth, titanium gray gauntlet from the table, Mage snapped them into place over the forearm and biceps, concealing the pistons and rods beneath. Only the control panel remained visible, poking through a small cut-out. With a mechanical zipping sound, the two pieces nudged closer, knitting together almost seamlessly.

"I thought you'd want to see it naked first," Mage said.

Benny surveyed the little man's severe, grizzled face. "What is it you want from me, man?"

Mage pulled on the rings and beads adorning the braided strands of his wiry salt and pepper goatee. "A favor for a favor," he said as he restarted the recovery unit, the calming vapors descending over Benny as the hatch closed. "The life I saved is owed to me."

The lift pinged the fiftieth floor, and the clear glass doors slid open to reveal the immaculate, obsidian marble entranceway to the United Conglomerate Headquarters executive offices. A thorn-like spire ringed in stars, The Glom's signature logo, had been set into the floor in gold. The pristine floors, the walls, and especially the gilding sparkled so clean that if one entered at a moment when it wasn't filled with assistants and aides striding past with anxious faces, one might believe the level was not used at all.

Chance exited the gravity lift and crossed the polished marble floor to the front desk, straightening the lapels of his tailored suit jacket. The young man behind the counter—wearing dark eyeliner, his white blond hair swept up and frozen like a knob over his forehead—greeted him with wide-eyed excitement.

"Enforcer Justice," he said, winking and stroking his tongue over his glistening pink lipstick. "What a pleasure to see you in the flesh."

Chance bit the inside of his cheek hard.

"Thanks," he said, "here to see Director Kess. I'm expected."

"Of course," the young man said, tabbing the direct intercom.

"*What is it?*" Kess barked over the intercom.

"Director Kess," the young man said. "Justice is here to see you."

"*Send him in.*"

The young man batted his eyelashes. "All the way to the end of the hallway."

"Thanks."

"You were amazing last night," the young man blurted out, his already blushed cheeks deepening red. "I mean… oh my god, that came out wrong. I… I meant the trial and saving the child." He clasped his hands to his chest. "It was perfect."

"Thank you," Chance said.

"Okay, sorry." The young man fanned his face. "I'll stop harassing you like some hormonal schoolboy now."

"No worries," Chance said, heading into the corridor.

"You keep doing you, Justice," the young man said, adding under his breath, "I know I would."

Chance allowed himself a little chuckle as he made his way down the hallway. He passed plaques mounted beside sliding doors. *Director of Technology, Director of Business, Director of Marketing*: the list went on.

Chance stopped at the end of the hall, unsure if he should knock, when the door slid open to reveal a pristine corner office, bigger than the rest.

Chance took a tentative step in, craning his neck. "Director Kess?"

Like the rest of the floor, the office was meticulous. Black leather chairs with gold accents, marble and glass tables, and furnishings of the finest make framed a breathtaking view of the city through floor-to-ceiling windows. Chance thought he caught the slightest hint of wood smoke and amber in the air.

"Justice," Kess said, standing from behind his desk. "Truly the last hope of the innocent."

Kess approached, his hand outstretched. Chance noted the director's impeccable style, firm physique, perfect teeth, and unblemished face. The man knew how to sell himself and inspire loyalty. It was his job to be this way. But as Chance took the offered hand and gave a firm shake, he wondered if, for this man, there was a difference.

"Have a seat." Kess motioned to one of the black chairs before the desk. "Can I get you something to drink? Neo Coke? Something stronger?"

"No, I'm fine. Thank you," Chance said, sitting.

Kess took his chair. "I trust your accommodations are suitable?"

"They are."

"And your training regimen? All is well there?" Kess paused. "I have to ask—what do you think of the Peacemaker? My idea, you know."

"Oh?" Chance sat back.

"Well, mostly. I got the idea from old-world comics about super cops. Can you believe that?" Kess laughed. "Damn comic book stories. They're what made me want to put on a badge when I was a kid." He shook his head. "So, I put my own spin on those old stories and made the Peacemaker the official sidearm of the Enforcers," Kess winked, "and the toy line sells like hot cakes."

Chance put on a smile.

"So, enough about *my* accomplishments. I'm talking to the hero of The Zone," Kess said. "Have you recovered from your ordeal yet?"

Chance nodded. "Still sore, but those recovery chambers are magic."

"They most certainly are," Kess said. "And wow, what a showing for you last night."

"Intense, to say the least," Chance said.

"You had us all worried there for a second. I wasn't sure how you'd fare, overwhelmed as you were." Kess clasped his hands. "But alas, you prevailed."

Chance waited, unsure of the direction of the conversation.

"Some of your methods are unorthodox." Kess's brow creased. "Never had an Enforcer continue to pursue an innocent after the bounty had been claimed. All risk and no reward, as they say." Kess's expression lightened. "But that's what makes you special, isn't it? Driven by such principle, such moral conviction." He balled his fist.

Chance cleared his throat. "I only did what I thought was right, sir," he said, rubbing the palms of his hands on his pants.

"Of course you did," Kess said with a flick of his wrist, "and the people love you for it." Off to the side, the holo-projector stitched an image in the air, wispy tentacles of blue light forming bands of figures, graphs, and viewership data.

"That's good, right?" Chance asked.

"Good?" Kess said, rising. "It's fantastic. You sparked the highest viewership ratings in months. Everyone is talking about the Enforcer who defied the rules to do *what was right*. Just what we needed around here—a little dose of conscience. Something fresh to shock the desensitized masses."

Chance fiddled with his tie.

"You know," Kess continued, rounding the desk, "I even got a direct call from the founders this morning. They wanted me to pass on their endorsement of you. To have me tell you to keep doing what you're doing."

"The founders? Whoa." Chance struggled with the avalanche of compliments.

"Yes. That's what I wanted to impress upon you—to keep doing what you're doing. Do the right thing. Stand for what is just." Kess took a seat on the edge of his marble desk.

Chance sensed a change, like a shift in the air around them. He waited, expectant.

"Which is why I have a proposition for you," Kess added.

"Sir?" Chance said.

"For a while now, I've heard whispers. They're rumors at this point, though that doesn't make them any more pleasant." Kess exhaled, tapping a finger against his lips. "How to put it? See, I'm afraid, if these rumors are true, one of my Enforcers may have turned against us."

Chance's mouth opened, but he stopped himself.

"I know. That was my reaction. After all the Conglomerate and its affiliates have done for the Enforcers. The money, the power, and all the amenities anyone could ever want. And still, someone wants to bring us down… one of *our own* wants to bring us down."

"What does that mean?" Chance sat forward, his eyes questioning. "What information do you have?"

"I don't want to spin fantasies, but I'll tell you the little I know to be true," Kess said. He cocked his head, eyes narrowing. "Have you heard of Rico? Leader of a gang called the Death Squad, one of the most notorious warlords in The Zone?"

Chance thought back, remembering the name from somewhere. "While conducting this last trial. One of the thugs who showed up at the end said something about Rico…"

"Yes?"

"Yeah. *Doesn't forget.* That was what the guy with the megaphone said. *Rico doesn't forget.*"

"That's him," Kess said. "Former cop, a dirty one, too. Got tossed in The Zone a few years back after he murdered his partner, who caught him taking a little extra on the side. Can you believe that? He's always been a troublemaker, but as other warlords in The Zone got captured or killed, Rico stayed smart, played it safe, and survived."

"What's he doing?" Chance asked.

"No one knows. But my sources tell me he's paid a lot of money for an outside source to develop and smuggle a dangerous weapon into The Zone."

"What sort of weapon?" Chance scooted forward in his seat.

"Something that could ruin us, I'm told. A weapon with the potential to decimate the Enforcers. The details are sketchy at best."

"Even if he was dirty, he was a cop once. He'd know the Conglomerate pulls its Enforcers from the ranks of the NTPD.

Why would he do something like that?"

Kess shrugged. "Maybe he was never stable to begin with, and being a warlord has gone to his head. Who knows?"

"What does this have to do with one of our people?"

"Your guess is as good as mine. My information indicates one of them is collaborating with him. The *why* is what we don't know," Kess said, standing. "I need you to keep your ear to the ground. Report direct to me with anything concerning this. I can trust you, can't I?"

"You want me to be a snitch?" Chance said. "Doing the right thing and talking about your people behind their backs are two different things."

"But if someone has truly gone bad, and something catastrophic is in the works, we have to know before it's too late." Kess opened his hands. "But don't do it for me. Do it for your fellow Enforcers. Do it for yourself, your wife, for the system that will get Andrew the care he needs. A system that keeps Neo Terminus and its people alive."

Chance got to his feet, his discomfort growing. He worked it over in his mind. A bad gig, no matter how he sliced it.

"Just this one thing." Chance eyed Kess. "I'm not going to indiscriminately spy on everyone. This one thing I'll do—Rico's Enforcer-killing device and the Enforcer collaborating with him. But that's it."

"That's all I needed," Kess said. He handed Chance a thin, clear card with data scrolling across its length. "My card. Scan it into your chip. You can send me a private message or shoot me a call anytime."

"Okay," Chance said.

"What can I do for you?" Kess said.

Chance paused, unsure what would overstep his position.

Kess shrugged. "You're helping me out. How can I help you?"

"I'd like to see my wife and son."

Kess's face went slack. "You haven't been able to see them yet? My God, yes. Of course, you can see your family. I'll set up an escort right away. Childcare and dinner on the company for you and your lady tonight. How's that sound?"

A wave of relief washed over Chance. "Sounds great. Thank you." He paused. "And… there's one other thing."

"Oh?"

"Yes, sir. The little girl I rescued in The Zone. What will happen to her now that her family is dead?"

Kess rubbed the bottom of his jaw. "Typically, salvaged kids with no family get turned over to orphanages such as Eulayla's Home in the Heights. Wonderful organization. I'm sure she'll be fine."

"I'd like to pay to have her placed with a good family. This side of town, if that's possible. I'll cover her education and any expenses or needs. Can you make a connection for me?"

Kess, stunned, took a moment to recover. He barked a laugh. "That's why I like you, kid. Uncompromising in your defense of the innocent." Kess reached out a manicured hand.

Chance shook it one last time. "Thank you, sir," he said. "It means a lot, knowing my effort won't be in vain—that the girl will be okay."

"You know," Kess said, putting his arm over Chance's shoulder, "I'm glad to know you're out there, looking out for us all. I know I never have to doubt you'll do the right thing. Keep holding that thin blue line, Justice," Kess said as he ushered Chance from his office with a pat on his back.

The director's office door slid shut, leaving Chance standing in the hallway. Good had come from the meeting. The child would be okay, and he'd get to see Hannah after the craziest few weeks of his life.

He rubbed his neck, still a touch sore. *But something capable of killing all the Enforcers? A rogue Enforcer making it happen? Talk about a bombshell.* Chance made his way back toward the elevators, his heart and mind caught in the emotional tempest whirling inside him.

Gabriel Kess stood at the shaded glass door to his office as his new informant's shadow disappeared down the hall. A sense of confidence welled in him. He'd put the pieces in place, the framework set for the greatest spectacle the network had ever seen. He only had to sit back, be patient, and let the drama unfold in its own time.

His initial assessment had been wrong. A new Enforcer, like the one he'd created in Justice, possessed the ability to drive the numbers up for a time, but projections now showed such a bump in viewership would fade fast, once again leaving a void in the viewers' interest. If Neo Terminus were to survive the fallout of New West City, if Kess himself were going to survive, he needed a distraction capable of buoying the network until New West City's demise faded into obscurity. By then, The Conglomerate would have had enough time to fabricate plenty of believable reports from their sister city to ensure no shred of public mass hysteria ever took hold. Maintaining absolute control of the narrative and protecting his dear Clarissa was all that mattered. Everyone and everything else was expendable.

He reached over and opened a comm link with Miss Avery.

"What can I do for you, Director?" His assistant's face materialized, projected in the air before him.

"You have the new list of candidates ready?" Kess said.

"Yes, sir, but it will take time to vet them."

"So get on that," Kess said, arranging the already well-ordered items on his desk.

"I just don't think—"

"You're not paid to think, Miss Avery. You're paid to *do*," Kess snapped. "If I have to think *and* do, then what the hell do I need *you* for?"

The line went silent. Miss Avery let out a little cough. "It will be done, Director Kess."

"See that it is." He paused. "And, Miss Avery?"

"Yes, Director."

"Everything happens off-site. My oversight alone." Kess leaned back in his chair, tenting his fingers against his chin. A malicious grin formed. "I can't have word getting out that all of our beloved Enforcers are doomed."

CHAPTER TWENTY-SEVEN

Chance rapped three times on the frosted glass sliding door to the upscale apartment. He double-checked the address, then chided himself. Of course, it was the right place. He'd only confirmed it ten times already. Tapping his foot, he willed the swirling butterflies in his stomach to settle.

Butterflies. Imagine that.

A shadow darkened the interior of the glass. Chance brimmed with excitement. He held up the real bouquet he'd paid way too much for at the little boutique in the lobby.

"Hi," he said as the door opened. "I'm your date—"

Hannah flew across the threshold and crashed into him with a squeal. Chance staggered back, almost dropping the fresh-cut flowers. Her arms encircled his neck in a death grip. She kissed his face, his neck, his face again. Chance closed his eyes and squeezed her against him with his free arm. The sweet smell of his girl enveloped him, filling his nose, a secret garden meant only for him.

"Get in here, Mister," she said, stepping back and pulling him into the apartment by his jacket. "Where have you been all my life?"

Lips locked, noses mashed together, Hannah and Chance stumbled against the edge of a coffee table. The flowers flopped onto the end table, knocking a smart lamp onto the marble floor, where it rolled away. The door slid shut behind the couple, the heat between them flaring, reckless like a sudden wind on open flame.

Their foreheads touching, cheeks flushed, Hannah gasped as Chance grabbed the back of her thigh and hoisted her against him. She fumbled one-handed with his belt, the other hand raking across his chest, pulling his shirt open. He kissed her long and deep.

At a soft, distant sound, they froze. Chests heaving, clutched against one another, listening. Another whimper echoed from the baby's room.

"Oh, come on, man," Chance closed his eyes and kissed Hannah's forehead.

"*Your* son has expert timing, as usual," Hannah said with a little laugh.

"*My* son?" Chance leaned his chin down onto Hannah's shoulder, listening to Andrew's groans from down the hall. He closed his eyes, relishing the embrace and scent of his wife.

"He's okay, right?" Hannah smirked, her face flush. She cupped her hands around Chance's face, adjusting so she could gaze into the depths of his eyes. "Right?"

Chance pulled Hannah closer.

"Yeah," he said, lost in her gaze, "the baby's just fine."

Chance pushed back from the white linen tablecloth and wiped his mouth with an embroidered napkin. "That's it. That's all I got," he said, arching his back and patting his stomach.

"No room for dessert?" Hannah said, her new diamond earrings sparkling. She tipped a glass of red wine to her lips.

"Oh, no, I don't think I can." Chance glanced sideways at the elegant dessert menu. "But maybe I'll just have a look."

"Uh-huh," Hannah said, a wry smile pulling at the corners of her mouth.

Chance picked up the small menu with gold lettering offering a choice of a sorbet trio, peanut butter chocolate mousse, or key lime tart with raspberry glaze.

"Did you like what you got?" His eyes flicked up long enough to catch Hannah's quick scowl.

"Did I like what I got?" Hannah said, incredulous. "Chance, a week ago we were surviving on sus-packets—and I didn't even know what a lobster linguini was." She nodded to her bowl, wiped clean. "Yeah, it's safe to say I liked it."

"I mean, surely it's not *real* lobster." Chance smirked. "We're landlocked."

"Ask me if I care," Hannah said, wiping her mouth with a little laugh. "You like yours?"

"Oh yeah, the filet was amazing," Chance said, still eyeing the words *key lime tart*.

Hannah gazed around the elegant dining area. Other couples sat encased in the warm romantic light of the upscale restaurant, some speaking in hushed tones, while others chewed their food with robotic slowness, their expensive visors flickering with endless entertainment. Hannah turned and surveyed the skyline, the entirety of Neo Terminus spread out before them in a neon sprawl under a sea of darkness.

"This place is amazing, I mean," she pointed upward, "that chandelier is flying."

Chance chuckled, watching one of the beautiful crystal sculptures cruise past overhead, thrusters firing as it slowly spun.

"It's a simple trick," Chance said. "The micro-thrusters keep it hovering and in sync with the others as they rotate around the room."

"Okay, whatever. They're flying," Hannah said and took another sip of her wine. "This place is magical." She leaned closer and added with a whisper, "Though I think we might be the only ones talking instead of watching their visors."

"Looks like it." Chance's dimples showed. "I'm glad you like the place. I asked Sam for a recommendation. He said *Elevation is the only place to go.*"

"Well, Sam knocked it out of the park," Hannah said as Chance set the dessert menu down. "How's everything going? With your new partner, I mean? He's a good guy?"

"Sam? Yeah. Old-school lawman. He's a little rough around the edges but solid as a rock."

"I know nothing about the man, but I could have kissed him after he dropped in to help you last night."

"You watched?" Chance set the menu down.

Hannah narrowed her eyes. "Didn't want to. Thought I might have a heart attack."

"I'm sorry."

"Don't apologize, Chance." Hannah reached across the table to touch his hand. "You took this job for Andrew and me. We had to know it came with risks. I just can't have my hubby leaving me widowed so young." A smirk formed on her face. "I mean, then I'd have to use all the money you've made to go shop for another man, and that would be… awkward."

"Stop it," Chance said.

"I'm serious," Hannah teased.

"I am, too. I don't want to imagine you with someone else."

"Then don't die as some psycho's trophy in The Zone."

Chance nodded. "That's fair, I suppose."

Hannah leaned in. "What's it like? In The Zone, I mean."

Chance let out a little whistle as he sat back. "It's fast. Much faster than you think watching it. The whole experience is raw and powerful. It's like all my police pursuits, fist fights and gunfights, all the emotion, terror, and excitement rolled into one extended moment."

"Excuse me, Enforcer Justice?" A full-figured woman approached, waiting off Chance's left shoulder. "I'm super embarrassed to ask this, but can I take a picture with you?"

Chance winked at Hannah.

"Sure." He turned in his chair.

The woman snapped open a small purse to release a micro-drone, which floated a few feet away and swiveled to capture their photograph as she stepped beside him. A small flash followed. The woman swiped open her visor image, so Chance could see it. He watched the picture auto-upload to her social space with the caption, *I met Enforcer Justice tonight!!!! Soooo Hot!*

"Thank you, oh-my-gawd. I was in awe of you last night!" she said, her breasts billowing from the top of a dress far too small.

"Thank you, have a nice evening," Chance said, trying to turn away.

"You were incredible," she went on. "I'm just—"

"I'm sorry, madam." The manager approached. "This sort of behavior is highly irregular in this establishment. Please do not harass our guests."

"She's fine," Chance said, his words unheard as the manager ushered the insistent woman away.

"I love you, Justice!" she called out over the manager's shoulder.

Chance suppressed a chuckle at Hannah's open-mouthed expression. *I love you*, she mouthed playfully.

"Yeah," Chance said. "She's the fourth one today."

"You have women throwing themselves at you now?"

"Stop."

"That's fine," Hannah said, mischievously. "Just be careful. Not sure you want to live the rest of your life as a eunuch."

Chance's eyes flared. "Damn, that's cold."

"Not as cold as the knife will be," Hannah whispered.

"Hannah, stop."

They laughed, trying to keep their voices hushed in the quiet of the restaurant.

Hannah finished her wine, wiped her mouth, and set her napkin on the table. "I guess people like that lady are the reason they sent a security detail with us?"

"Yeah," Chance jerked his head at a couple of men in dark suits nearby, "for fans and everyone else who wants me dead."

"Wants you dead?"

Chance shrugged. "If you bet on the Skulls last night, you lost your shirt."

"Oh." Hannah touched her lower lip. "This world is still so foreign to me. I can't imagine how you feel."

"I feel like I'm getting the hang of it." He eyed Hannah. "What about you? How are you getting settled in?"

"Good," Hannah said, her face dropping ever so slightly.

Chance raised an eyebrow. "I'm not convinced."

Hannah waved him off. "No, everything is wonderful. We have more than enough. It's just empty without you there, and…"

"And what?"

Hannah shifted, embarrassed. "I don't know." She leaned forward. "Just a strange feeling, like intuition."

A silence hung between them until their waiter stopped to ask if everything were to their liking. When Chance only nodded, the man assured them he'd check again soon. Chance leaned across the table. "What sort of strange feeling?"

Hannah let out a sigh. "Like I'm being watched or something. I know, it sounds stupid."

"It's not stupid," Chance said. "Cameras are everywhere. There's nowhere you can go that isn't recorded."

"I'm talking about inside the apartment. Private areas." Hannah bit the edge of her lip. "Am I paranoid?"

"Well," Chance rubbed his chin, "what makes you think someone's watching you?"

Hannah opened her mouth to respond and stopped herself. "I guess I don't have a good reason. Forget I said anything."

"Hannah, you sure?" Chance lowered his eyes. "I can look into it."

"No." She patted his outstretched hand. "I think I'm just not used to being in the new place, that's all."

A soft chime pulled Chance's attention to his visor, folded on the edge of the table.

"Hey, I don't know what made me think about this, but tell me about Andrew's treatment plan," Chance said, ignoring his visor. "You met with the specialist?"

"The technology is incredible." Hannah's face lit up. "It's outpatient surgery performed by a bot. Can you believe it? I mean, he may never walk completely unassisted, but the procedure will give him much higher chances of increased mobility." She put her hands to her face, her new diamond tennis bracelet and wedding ring combination catching the light, tears welling in her eyes. "Chance, I have more hope for him than I ever thought possible."

Chance clasped his wife's hands. He breathed a sigh of relief. "Wonderful news, honey. What's the time frame?"

"Soon. We still have one more preparatory meeting. But it shouldn't be long. I'd love you to be there if you can."

Chance squeezed her hands, then his visor chimed again.

"I'm sorry. Do you mind? It could be work."

Hannah waved for him to go ahead.

Chance woke his visor from sleep and slipped it on, accessing the new message. It was from Sam.

10 PM at Kersey's down the street from HQ. Be there. No excuses.

"Oh, man." Chance checked the time before pulling his visor and putting it back to sleep. *Nine fifteen.*

"What?" Hannah said, fixing him with those smokey eyes.

He leaned forward, drinking in her natural beauty, her dirty blond hair laying in perfect curls over her shoulder. "Dude, I love you."

"Dude?" She leaned forward. "How about we bust this joint

and go straight back to my place?"

"Yes…" Chance looked at the visor.

"But?" Hannah's playfulness dimmed.

"The message was from Sam," Chance said.

"And?"

"He said to meet him at a place down from headquarters at ten. No excuses." Chance gave a sheepish shrug.

Hannah scoffed. "Tell him no. This is *our night*."

"I know, babe. I'm just in a strange position as the new guy," Chance said. "Lots of expectations. It's hard to explain."

"Chance." She gave him a withering look.

"I know. I'll go have one drink and see what he wants."

"You are staying with us tonight, though, right?" Hannah asked.

"I'm on approved leave for twenty-four hours. I'm all yours."

"Not *all* mine, apparently." Hannah sucked her teeth.

"One drink, I promise," Chance added. "New job. I gotta jump through the hoops."

"One drink," she repeated.

There is no way it'll only be one drink. Chance put on his most charming smile. *She's going to kill me.*

Kersey's place, considered a hole in the wall by many locals, was the closest thing to a dive bar that existed in a place like Silver City. Tired, slump-shouldered executives and dark polished hardwood packed the narrow, dimly lit space, a refurbished relic from a time before the collapse when this place was still called Midtown, Atlanta.

After dinner, Chance had walked Hannah to the car, a Biljang VTOL driven by one of The Glom's security escorts. The jowl-faced man had insisted on dropping Chance off at Kersey's on the way, which Chance refused. He'd assured the man that as a veteran cop and an Enforcer, he could walk the short distance just fine. With a kiss and a reassurance he wouldn't be too late, he saw Hannah off and got on his way to meet Sam.

Now, standing across the street from Kersey's, Chance watched the bar teeming with servers and elbow-to-elbow patrons who laughed and toasted each other. He side-stepped a woman in a pantsuit, walking a cat on a leash, her visor casting a ring of light around her face.

"Stand in everyone's way, why don't you?" said another woman in a tinted visor and a see-through plastic dress, her chin tilted up at him. Images of runway models streamed across her face.

Chance smirked and stepped into the street. He still couldn't believe this place, a far cry from the desperate squalor he'd known his whole life. Most of these entitled asses had no concept of how the rest of the inhabitants on the other side of this city fought tooth and nail just to stay alive.

Expensive electric vehicles with elevated spoilers, flashing neon, and thumping music cruised past in the street. Passing between them, Chance crossed beneath a bright blue sign that read *Kersey's Public House.* The bar's door slid back as he approached, the noise of the place quadrupling in his ears. He stood at the entrance, surveying the crowded bar. Near the back, a hand shot up, waving him over. *Jessie.*

Chance made his way through the crowd and, to his surprise, saw all the other Enforcers seated around a circular slab of mahogany, a motley crew of knights at the round table. It took him a moment to shake the strangeness of seeing them all in street clothes.

"The man of the hour," Sam said, holding up a pint of beer.

"What's up, guys?" Chance said.

"Hey there, Enforcer," Karissa said.

Jessie fist-bumped Chance. "There's a new sheriff in town."

"He's done one trial," Ash said. "and it's arguable if he completed it or not, so let's not get carried away." He took another slug of his beer.

Rip, as usual, sat with his arms crossed, looking like someone had pissed in his drink. The only one at the table with his visor engaged.

"Have a seat, partner," Sam said and pushed an empty chair away from the table with his foot.

"All right, I've been trying to figure this out," Chance said. "Let me take a stab at what divisions of the PD you guys each came out of."

"Oh, this should be rich." Karissa folded her arms with a smirk.

"Sam's easy," Chance said. "I met him back in the day, so I already knew he was SWAT."

Sam toasted Chance with his glass. "One percent."

"Karissa, I'm going to say you came out of patrol."

"Impact patrol, but yeah, easy guess," she said.

Chance stroked his chin. "Jessie? Investigations?" He shrugged.

"Motor division. Hover patrol."

"Ahh, the fly boys. Makes sense," Chance said. "And Rip was narcotics. No question."

"Yeah." Rip's eyebrows shot up. "I was, actually. In the play-your-stupid-guessing-games-with-someone-else squad."

"Okay." Chance waved him off. "And Ash? I'm not too sure."

"Mobile Field Force and Riot Control," Ash said around a cheek full of beer nuts.

"And you?" Karissa said.

"The slagging nursery," Rip said.

Karissa cut her eyes at him and turned back to Chance. "I'm going to say gang suppression."

"Close," Chance said, taking his chair, "high crime saturation, but we handled a lot of gangs. Me and my partner Benny."

"Benitez? I remember him," Karissa said. "Good dude."

"The best," Chance said.

Their server, a tall, smartly dressed woman with a fire-red crew cut, approached and set a frosty pint of dark beer in front of Chance.

"Porter. I guessed." Sam shrugged.

"I'll take it." Chance held up the frozen mug, foam dripping and freezing down the side.

"Well, good," Rip said, "now that we're all besties, can I go?"

Sam turned in his chair. "How come you always have to be such an insufferable asshole? Can't you sit and have a drink with your team?"

"No," Rip said as he stood up, "because you're not my team. The only one on my team is that guy." He pointed to Ash. "I came to hang with him. The rest of you are just…"

"Say it," Karissa said, pushing to her feet. She locked Rip down with a stare meant to kill.

"Here we go again," Jessie muttered.

Rip, undaunted, returned Karissa's steely gaze. "You people are nothing like me."

"You people? What's that supposed to mean?" Karissa said, her fists balled.

"It means I'm a predator." He leaned across the table. "And you're sheep."

"Hey, relax, bro," Ash said. "If you want to go, then go. It's no problem."

"Yeah, go," Karissa said, "or this *sheep* is going to kick your ass in front of all these nice people."

"Okay, partner, have a seat," Jessie said, setting his drink down with an air of calm, his hand on the back of Karissa's chair.

The patrons at the closest tables fell quiet, having taken notice of the squabble.

"Come on, Karissa," Jessie said.

With deliberate slowness, the former decathlete took her seat, her golden eyes fixed on Rip.

"This is why I don't come to these things," Rip said. "Everyone wants to measure dicks." He leered at Karissa. "Even when they don't have one."

The muscles of Karissa's jaw flexed.

"Besides," Rip continued, "I've got things to do, like prep for tomorrow's team event." He turned to Ash. "You coming?"

"In a minute," Ash said.

"Suit yourself," Rip said, waving open his coin wallet and settling his bill. "I'm outta here." He pushed past the table on his way out.

As the remaining Enforcers sipped their drinks in silence, the tables around them returned to their own conversations, and laughter filled the bar again.

"Why's he gotta be such a prick?" Sam said. "I mean all the time. I'm surprised he came at all." He turned to Karissa. "You good?"

She took a sip from a dirty martini. "Much better, now."

Ash sat forward, setting down his empty glass. "I'll go check on him. Busy day for us tomorrow anyway, and it's going to start early."

"You're good to go, Ash," Sam said. "I've covered yours already. Thanks for coming."

Ash gave a two-fingered salute and took a step, then paused. He turned to Karissa. "Take Rip with a grain of salt. You may not know this, but…" He rubbed his mouth. "This week marks the tenth anniversary of his family's death. All of them."

The table nodded and nursed their drinks.

"Give my condolences," Karissa said.

"Yeah," Ash said, rapping on the wooden table with his knuckles. "G'night."

The other Enforcers mumbled their goodnights as Ash made

his way out of the bustling bar. Chance checked his watch, drinking a long sip of his heady porter, the foam tickling his upper lip. As the minutes ticked past, the tension bled from the air, and before long, the remaining Enforcers were laughing, telling stories, and enjoying Sam's open tab.

"This is them." Karissa beamed, projecting an image of three children, the youngest of which was about six.

"Oh yeah, those eyes." Chance chuckled. "Can't deny those three."

Karissa dismissed the picture with a wave. "Those girls are my entire world. When I'm trapped or injured or alone in The Zone, it's the thought of my kids that always brings me back. Been that way even since my days policing at NTPD. Gives me true purpose, you know?"

"No doubt." Chance scooted his chair forward as a man in a red leather jacket and a popped collar squeezed past to embrace a woman.

"What about you?" Karissa asked. "What drives you? What do you fight for?"

"My wife and son, of course. But this first trial, I don't know. I had to save that little girl." Chance shook his head and picked up his drink. "One too many dead kids on my watch, I guess."

Sam raised his glass and clinked it off Chance's.

"What about you, Sam?" Chance asked. "What brings you back home when the chips are down?"

"Well," Sam stroked his gray-stubbled chin with a sage nod, "there *is* this Asian girl…"

"Okay, stop right there." Karissa laughed. "I've heard enough."

"What?" Sam pretended to be offended. "Old guys need lovin' too."

"Jessie?" Chance said.

"What do I work to come home for every day?" Jessie said. The others waited expectantly as he set his drink down and pulled up

271

his sleeve, veins popping as he flexed a bulging biceps. "To get that next great gym pump, baby!"

The Enforcers all broke out into laughter, followed by groans and rolled eyes from Karissa. Their laughter died down as each slipped into their own thoughts.

"You guys are like family, I can see that," Chance said, breaking the silence. "A family I've busted in on."

"No," Karissa said, "you're one of us now."

"She's right," Jessie added. "Change is tough, especially when you lose someone, but we do our best to embrace it. It's the life we've chosen."

Chance looked at Karissa and Jessie, then turned to Sam. "Tell me about Valarie."

Karissa and Jessie exchanged a glance. Sam pressed his teeth together and sat back.

"You know what," Chance said, "I'm sorry." He held up his hands. "I overstepped."

"No," Sam said, "you should know about her." He nodded to Karissa.

Karissa's face brightened. "She was a firecracker, that one. Valarie came out of the NTPD's riot unit."

"Five foot nothing," Jessie said. "You wouldn't look at this woman and think Enforcer, but man, was she tough. Could fight like the devil."

"Best person I ever knew," Sam said. "She'd do anything for anybody, and did, all the time. A real guardian angel."

"So, what happened?" Chance asked, unsure if he wanted to know.

"Sam…" Karissa said and touched his arm.

"It's fine." Sam sighed and ran a hand through his close-cropped hair. "Val was on a remove-and-exclude mission in The Zone. We separated, and she got trapped by two allied groups. Her armor was toast by the time the third gang showed up. There was no way out, and I couldn't get to her in time."

"She was all in, committed to the fight despite the odds," Karissa said. "Total warrior."

"Yeah, but it was a perfect storm she got trapped in," Jessie said, "an' a lot of people thought they set it up. Like The Glom meant for her to go down."

"What makes you say that?" Chance asked.

Karissa leaned forward. "Near the end, she was holding her own when something happened, and she stopped fighting. She froze." A flicker of pain crossed Karissa's face. "Almost like she let those savages kill her."

"And laying down wasn't like her, man," Jessie said. "I mean at all. Valarie wouldn't have ever quit. Something happened to her."

With a nervous glance, Sam looked around the room. He rubbed his eyes. "All right, change the subject, dammit."

Chance eyed his partner, a real fury simmering in Sam just below the surface. "I'm sorry to bring it up, guys," Chance said. "She sounds like an amazing person."

"Yeah." Sam raised his glass. "I'll drink to that. To Valarie—may she find peace in the halls of Valhalla."

"To Valarie." The rest of the group repeated, clinking their glasses together.

"Well." Sam drained the last of his beer and slammed the mug down. "Guess it's about that time." He fingered his breast pocket.

"Oh, here comes the old man watch." Jessie smirked.

Sam froze and met Jessie's eyes. "I'll have you all know," he said, feigning dire seriousness, "that this *old man's watch* is a priceless family heirloom." He held the tarnished silver time piece up for the group to see.

"We know, Sam," Karissa said with great dramatic flair. "It originally belonged to a US Marshal by the name of Slade Shepherd. It's been in your family for generations, and you keep it on you to remember the noble lawmen of old."

"And," Sam said, in a playful and mocking tone, "the time is never wrong." He snapped the watch shut and dropped it back in his pocket. "Jackasses."

The Enforcers chuckled.

"I gotta go, too, or my wife will kill me," Chance said. "This was supposed to be our night together."

"Get out of here." Karissa nudged his arm. "What are you doing with us?"

"That's on me. I guilted him into coming," Sam said with a shrug.

"Sam, seriously?" Karissa said, aghast. "Chance, tell your lady we're sorry for interrupting."

"Forget about it." Chance waved her off. "Sam and I needed to talk strategy for tomorrow, anyway."

Sam stood and waved open his account, settling the enormous bar tab without complaint. Everyone shifted, standing and clearing the table.

"Hey." Chance paused, unsure if he should say anything. "So you guys are going to think I'm crazy."

"What?" Jessie said.

"This is random, but… you guys ever hear of an Enforcer going rogue? I mean, does that happen?"

Sam ran his wrist under his chin, cleared his throat, and looked at Karissa and Jessie.

"Probably a stupid question." Chance rubbed the back of his head.

"Rogue, how?" Karissa frowned.

"I don't know," Chance said, "like allying with gangs for personal profit?"

"For personal profit? No way," Jessie said. "Even the most self-absorbed Enforcers wouldn't stoop to that. We were all cops once, remember?"

"Why do you ask?" Sam said.

Chance stood. "I don't know, man. Just rumors. You know how it is."

"Don't let it get to you," Sam said, clapping Chance on the shoulder, "go spend some time with the missus."

Jessie winked. "Quality time."

Karissa nudged him hard with her elbow. "Such a juvenile."

"What?" Jessie said.

"See you guys tomorrow." Chance waved at Karissa and Jessie.

"Later," they said.

Chance exited Kersey's with Sam in tow, the neon-lit streets far less crowded than before.

Chance took a deep lung full of the humid night air. "Sorry about bringing up Valarie."

"Forget about it. You had a right to know." Sam shrugged it off. "You headed to your wife's place?"

"Yep," Chance said. "We're all set for tomorrow?"

"Ready to rock and roll," Sam said, "but it's not until after lunch. All the non-prime time events are less pressure. Not as many viewers."

"Right," Chance said.

"But don't let your guard down," Sam chided. "It's still The Zone. Anything goes, even on a routine detain and extract mission."

"I got ya. I'll see you first thing."

"Be safe partner," Sam said.

Chance summoned his driver from his visor's menu. He turned up the street, sticking to the sidewalk. Cleaning bots buffed the pavement with their whirring brooms, and he flicked his visor down, avoiding them. After all the talk of losing friends, he needed to talk to Benny—if for nothing else, at least to catch up. He selected Benny's name from his list of contacts as his private car descended and came to a stop beside the curb. The door to the expensive Biljang VTOL opened upward, revealing the jowled driver.

"To your apartment?" he asked. "Or heading back to your wife's place tonight?"

"I'll stay the night at my wife's, thanks." Chance climbed into the back seat.

"Of course, sir," the driver said, the VTOL thrusters whining as it lifted away from the curb.

Chance closed the privacy screen between him and the driver and placed the call to Benny. It didn't even ring.

Subscriber account canceled.

CHAPTER TWENTY-EIGHT

Inside an active recovery chamber, time had a way of losing step, skipping, and jumping ahead in unmeasured gaps. Two weeks might feel like ten disjointed minutes, and for Benny, it did. Benny ducked under the half-open lid of the recovery chamber, teeming with glowing particles of light, and placed his bare feet flat on the floor. He lifted his arms over his head to stretch, still a little surprised at the mechanical wheezes that greeted him from his left side. He lowered the cybernetic arm. Staring at it, he flexed the clicking fingers open one at a time.

"It's tied into your cerebral cortex," Mage said from the far side of the room. "You think. It does."

Benny stood there in his briefs, looking dumb.

"That's what you're thinking, was it not?" Mage hopped down from a projection console littered with scrolling blue data and waddled across the cave-like space.

Benny touched his head with his good hand, the stubbled prickle scratching the skin of his palm. "Did you shave my head?"

"We must alter your appearance as best we can."

Benny shook his head. "Do I get clothes, or do I work for you dressed like an Egyptian slave?"

"Egyptians," Mage chuckled. "You think you're clever because you learned some ancient history? You know nothing."

"Clothes." Benny scowled.

Mage pointed to a short metallic cart on wheels. "There."

"How long have I been down here in this stinking sewer?" Benny sauntered over to the cart.

"Two weeks. Long enough for me to be tired of you already," Mage said.

"Two weeks." Benny stopped. "Really?"

"Better to leave you in for a spell," Mage said.

"For losing an arm, I feel all right."

"You have my repurposed recovery chamber to thank for that."

Benny grabbed the worn garments off the cart. The synthetic utility pants were a little tight in the thighs and seat, and the dated T-shirt, with crossed katanas over a neon rising sun, was a size too small, but they would do.

"Best I could come up with on short notice," Mage said, touching the auto close button on the recovery chamber. "I don't typically shop at the big and fat store."

"No." Benny stepped into a pair of boots. He motioned to Mage's one-piece body suit adorned with brass buckles and electronics. "You shop at the BDSM for Nerds store."

Mage thrust a stubby middle finger in Benny's direction.

Benny's side and neck felt raw, hot, and uncomfortable. He winced and held up his metallic arm, waiting for the screen to initialize before pressing and holding the pain management button. A hiss followed, and Benny breathed a sigh of relief. "So this place is what? Some sort of creepy sex dungeon?"

"It's a command center, and I'll have you know," he waved at the vast array of computer technology littering the space, "from here, I can pull the entire city's strings. Like an ingenious puppet master, or," an inspired look spread across his pockmarked face, "a god."

"Sure thing." Benny let out an exasperated sigh. "Why am I here?"

"Well, for starters, if you're done being cute, it's time for you to get out there and fulfill your end of our bargain." The little man took a few steps and stopped before a bank of floating digital displays.

"Give me a straight answer." Benny started to cross his arms, stopped himself, and eyed the cybernetic appendage again.

Mage eyed Benny with curiosity. "A favor, Benny. All this information at my fingertips, and you still think our meeting was coincidence? If so, you are dumber than I thought."

"You meant to run into me?" Benny asked.

"I watched the news, the NTPD chatter on the net, and monitored your whereabouts. In your wounded condition, I knew you'd have to get help eventually. I analyzed your route, made an educated guess at the clinic you'd use, and timed it so we arrived at that kiosk at the same time."

"Then why the games, acting like you didn't expect to see me?"

Mage's eyebrows raised. "Deception is the ultimate power play, is it not? Besides, one can never be too careful."

"Why?" Benny asked. "I mean, why go to all the effort? I'm sure there are a lot of goons you could pay to work for you. Why me?"

"Why, why, why—why so many questions?"

"I'm serious," Benny replied.

"I am too." Mage appeared to consider his words. "I don't want to pay some hood rat. Payment is a lousy form of contract, easily broken, and those that would take such a job can rarely be trusted. You, on the other hand?"

Benny just stared at the little man. "What?"

"Well, you're a wanted man, and your life is on the line." Mage shrugged. "You have much to lose if you default on me. You're also a former cop. Maybe a bit more backbone than some street moob. You need help, and I need some muscle. A favor for a favor, like I said."

For a moment, the cavern's rock walls hummed with vibration at the passing of a light rail train somewhere above.

"And you want me to do what?" Benny shrugged. "You said it yourself, I'm a wanted man. NTPD will hammer my ass as soon as I hit the street."

"Ahh, that *would be* the case if it weren't for my genius," Mage said with a clap of his hands. The screens flicked to new images. Personal data, Glom account information, and employment history streamed alongside photographs of Benny's face from the front and side.

Except the info was all wrong.

"Who the hell is Enrique Galvatorez?" Benny asked.

"He's you." Mage smirked. "Or should I say, he's who you are *now*. Memorize all this." Mage clasped his hands behind his back and popped up on his tiptoes for an instant, studying his own handiwork.

Benny laughed. "The PD will see right through this. It'll take their analysts five minutes to connect this photograph to my real identity."

"Yes." Mage raked a few stubby fingers through his beaded goatee. "You do still look like you, and, unfortunately for me, I don't have a cure for ugliness."

Benny crossed his arms this time.

"But I can make Guillermo Benitez disappear." Mage gestured at the bank of fabricated personal data. "Your work history, your life, your accounts, even your active warrants. It will be as though you never existed—technologically speaking."

"You act like it's no big deal. You're erasing everything that makes me who I am. I have a sister. What about her?"

"She's not your sister anymore. Forget you ever knew her."

The nerve of this damn guy. Benny's eyes narrowed. "You're joking."

"Life is hard," Mage said, his voice taking on a bitter edge. "You can either become harder or let yourself be destroyed by its cruelties. Adapt or die."

"Real sentimental speech there, Mage, thanks." Benny clapped. "But why ruin my life? If you can erase my warrants, why not do that?"

"Your life was already ruined—by your own people, I might add." He tapped his wrist. "It's your chip that is the problem. As long as you have it, you are Guillermo, and your wanted status is tied to your person."

"You're going to, what? Try to cut it off the bone? It doesn't work without mutilating the host. I've seen it."

"Do you think me a barbarian?" Mage gasped his hands to his chest.

"You're telling me there's no other way to do this?"

"Not unless you want to spend the rest of your life in these sewers," Mage said.

Benny sighed, his chin dropping to his chest. "Do what you're going to do, man."

Mage waved Benny over, pointing to a horizontal cylindrical tube adorned with twisting hoses jutting from it in all directions. "Stick your arm in there. The meat arm."

"No warning at what this damn thing is?" Benny peered down the length of the glowing two-foot-long cylinder, just large enough to accommodate the bulk of his forearm.

"Stop being a big baby and do it." Mage grunted, flipping a handful of switches.

"You are something else," Benny said, sticking his arm up to the elbow into the cylinder.

Mage flipped a few more switches. "Now, don't move," he said, shuffling to the other side of the device and checking the calibration. A hum vibrated from the thing, small rings within the device rotating faster and faster until it was all a blur of light. Benny's arm heated in the tube—not just the skin, but through to the bone.

"Hey man, this thing is getting mega hot."

"Hold still, I'm warning you." Mage adjusted a few levers. The sound of the thing changed.

"You little slag-happy runt, if you ruin my one good arm." Benny gnashed his teeth, the heat almost unbearable.

"Hold…" Mage's hand hovered over the master power switch. Benny felt and heard a sharp *pop* in his wrist.

"Ow—damn!" He jerked his arm from the tube as Mage slapped the power switch down.

The hum subsided, the glowing tube drawing dark. Benny waved his arm in dramatic arcs as if trying to fly.

"There," Mage said, pleased with himself.

"It burns like a sonofabitch," Benny said, still waving his arm. "What was that?"

"Focused microwave stimulation," Mage said. "Your old chip is now fried."

"Great, man," Benny said. "That's great. Now I'll have arm cancer and no access to anything in the city. Looking forward to it."

"All you do is complain." Mage wagged a stubby finger at him. "You should bask in my benevolence."

"Oh yes, allow me to worship you, *your greatness*." Benny bowed.

"Would you shut up for once and let me finish?"

The bizarre little man hefted a thick brown leather jacket from the nearby table. Faded Japanese script ran vertically down the back. Checking the size, Mage gave a grunt and handed it to Benny.

"By all means." Benny took the jacket. "Please finish."

"I imbedded your cybernetic arm with your new chip and identity." When Benny remained silent, Mage continued. "Now it's time for you to do something for me."

"And if I refuse?" Benny said.

Mage's eyes narrowed. "That which I've given can also be taken away."

Benny noted the fierceness in the little man's tone, a solemn guarantee he meant to make good on his words. "What is it you expect me to do?" Benny asked.

Mage stepped over to his workstation and shoved a computer tower to the side, revealing a hidden strong box attached to the station's underside. He waved his palm over a scanner inset in the door. A soft chime followed, and the rapid clunks of bolts released. Mage opened the lid wide. Reaching his hand into space, he removed a single item and slapped the hatch shut.

Benny felt the tingle of irritation across his face as Mage approached with a narrow rectangular box no wider than two fingers.

He held the small black box out to Benny. "You will transport this to a buyer—"

"What is it?" Benny interrupted.

"Don't interrupt me," Mage snapped.

"Relax, it's my job to ask questions," Benny said.

"You don't have that job. You don't exist. Understand?" Mage frowned.

An air vent in the ceiling whistled, pushing garbage-scented air into the cramped stone space, warmed by too many electronics. Benny, unamused, cleared his throat.

Mage let the silence build for a moment before continuing. "I'm sure this will come as an enormous shock to you, but while I am everyone's intellectual superior, other more physical engagements are not my specialty. I avoid brute force and physical intimidation—if I can help it. That's where you come in."

"This is a joke, right?" Benny said. "You want me to be your muscle?"

"Why do you think I rescued you in the first place?" Mage extended the small black box. "You will negotiate my product deliveries and act as my avatar."

"And I shouldn't ask what this is?"

"No, you should not. Stop thinking like a cop. You will go where I send you, collect my price, and deliver the item."

Benny squinted. "I have a feeling it's not that simple."

Mage pointed to a black folded garment on the table. "Put this on under your shirt."

Benny set the jacket aside, then picked up the shimmering, paper-thin shirt.

"It's a nano skin vest like the Enforcers wear. Older model, but still," Mage said.

Benny took off his sword-and-sun T-shirt, flexing the muscles of his hairy arms and chest. He pulled on the black vest, which sparkled like a sheet of ground gems. He eyed it for a moment before slipping back into his T-shirt and putting on the brown leather jacket.

"The skin is a concealable body armor. The nano platelets can attenuate the potency of high-velocity projectiles. Outdated, but better than nothing."

"I'm going to get shot at?" Benny pulled the jacket back on. "Do I get a gun?"

"No."

"You're sending me to God knows where to deal with God knows who, and I don't get a piece?"

"I already gave you a weapon." Mage gestured to Benny's arm.

"Right," Benny said, "and when I'm done with this errand, you'll help me straighten out my sputz life?"

"Your old life doesn't exist anymore. The faster you accept this truth, the better off you'll be."

"This… this is incredible."

"In fact," Mage said, ignoring Benny's grumbles, "I think we should give you a code name. We don't want you to slip up and refer to yourself as the old you." Mage pulled on his braided goatee. "What to call the man who doesn't exist?"

"Oh, this should be good," Benny said, his face deadpan.

Mage's face lit up. "How about Specter?" He spread his little hands open.

Benny rolled his eyes. Stuffing the black box into his jacket, he headed for the door. "Specter? Sounds like a D-list noir superhero."

"I like it," Mage said, digging through a drawer. "Specter it is."

"You can call me Mary Poppins for all I care, guy, as long as we can get this nonsense over with." He grabbed a silver-lensed visor from Mage's outstretched hand and stopped at the exit. "Let me out of this stinking sex dungeon."

"It's a command center," Mage shouted.

Benny popped the collar of his jacket. "Whatever." The bolts clunked free and the blast door shot downward into the floor. The potent stench of sewage set upon him like a physical presence. Benny raised his cybernetic appendage and delivered Mage a one-fingered salute as he disappeared into the steaming black warmth of the sewers.

Mage couldn't help but laugh.

Hazy afternoon sunlight jabbed in irregular intervals through a heavy ceiling of ashen cloud cover. The streaming ribbons of light caught the moisture in the air and radiated like apocalyptic pixie dust. A dusty wind laced with the smell of decay sent little cyclones of trash and debris tumbling, adding a dramatic intensity to the Mexican standoff occurring in The Zone.

Chance and Sam, back to back, a high-value target pinched between them, leveled their Peacemakers at the criminals surrounding them—a small but enthusiastic gang in burnt orange calling themselves The Wasted.

"Make your move, boys," Sam said, adjusting the selector on

his Peacemaker to a three-round burst. Above, two raven-black Glom drones circled, picking up the action.

Chance pulled the target, a man in orange with a bruised face and one eye swollen shut, closer. Behind his back, cable restraints secured his arms. The devices covered the hands, connected to each other at the wrist, and continued halfway up the prisoner's forearms like medieval gauntlets of hammered steel.

"*Chance, their heart rates and cortisol levels are elevated,*" RITA said. "*Keep up the pressure, and there's a high likelihood their resolve may break.*"

"You don't have to like it," Chance shouted, "but we're leaving. We can go around you, or we can go through you. Your choice."

"What about our captain?" shouted a dirty man with a gaunt face and fractured brown teeth.

"Reggie comes with us," Sam said. "His ticket is punched. Yours doesn't have to be. Not today, at least."

The motley group squirmed, some clenching melee weapons while others, terrified these could be their last moments, extended firearms of questionable reliability.

"Well?" the Wasted's captain said to his men. He jerked his arm, caught in Chance's grip. "What are you waiting for? Kill them and set me free. You have the numbers."

"But they're Enforcers—they'll kill us," said a malnourished man with a heavy scar across his face.

"I'll kill you all if you don't," the captain shouted.

"You're scheduled for summary execution," the one with the broken teeth called out. "You ain't gonna do nothin' to us, Reggie."

"Yeah," another nervous man shouted, not so sure.

"You boys made a good go of it, and I salute you," Sam said, motioning to the fresh pockmarks in his armor, "but we don't have all day."

The gang members glanced back and forth. After a moment,

the man with brown teeth stepped forward. "Take him and go, but we won't forget this insult."

Sam waved him off. "You're still here?"

The remaining Wasted mounted their dirt bikes, spray painted orange and covered in splattered mud, and took off down the desolate, cracked street.

"You are not fit to call yourselves The Wasted!" the captain screamed, his voice disappearing into the unified growl of the two-stroke engines. "I'll have my revenge. I'll—"

Sam gave the prisoner a vicious shove from behind, causing him to stumble. "Enough of that."

"RITA, what's the status of our extraction?" Chance asked.

"*Incoming,*" RITA said, "*thirty seconds.*"

"Copy," Chance said, scanning for threats. He popped a red smoke and tossed it forward of their position.

"You Enforcers with your fancy toys and highbrow attitudes," Reggie said. "You murder us and call it law enforcement, but it's all done for sport. You're not better than me."

"Maybe not," Sam said, "but in twenty-four hours, we'll be a lot more alive than you."

Reggie hung his head and muttered obscenities. The screech of thrusters filled the sky. A glossy black Krytech VTOL dropped down from above. As it lowered to within feet of the ground, the thrusters whipped smoke and grit in a shower of fine particles tinkling across the armor of the Enforcers. Reggie pinched his eyes shut and kept his head down.

Closing the distance, Sam popped the door on the VTOL's cage and shoved Reggie in, slamming the wing door down.

"Look out for rocket-propelled grenades," Sam said. "They're still watching us. Wouldn't be the first time a gang tried to drop us during extraction."

"I got it," Chance said. Scanning, battle rifle at the high ready, he backed up toward his partner and the waiting VTOL.

Loading up, Sam and Chance took their seats in the open cab, knocking their fists together.

"We're in," Sam called to the driver.

With a whine, the thrusters fired, and the VTOL rose into the sky. Chance continued to scan until they rose out of the range of small-arms fire. The two drones, which had followed their every move since they dropped in, broke formation and zipped away toward headquarters.

"*Bounty collected in full,*" RITA said. "*You're off the air.*"

Sam and Chance's faceplates separated, their helmets receding back into their armor.

"Piece of cake," Chance said.

Sam shook his head with a little guffaw. "Don't get cocky, kid. Just like patrolling the street. Cocky gets you dead."

"Don't steal the joy out of everything. We killed it today, even if this wasn't a major trial."

"In The Zone, the only easy day was yesterday, partner," Sam said. "Don't ever forget it."

"You got it, Dad." Chance elbowed his partner.

Sam shook his head and chuckled.

Two weeks and seventeen trials in The Zone already, Chance thought. *How did I get accustomed to this world so fast?*

A transmission broke across their radios in a wash of static. Chance flinched and turned the volume down as a garbled voice reached out in severed bits. Chance looked at Sam.

"Can you make it out?" he asked.

"No," Sam said, "local transmission. It's not hitting the repeater."

Brows furrowed, they waited, listening as the VTOL soared over the ruins of The Zone.

"*Pard... copy?*" the voice said. "*... on... to suit... south... copy?*"

Chance shook his head again. "I got nothing, Sam."

"*Chance, it sounds like some sort of distress signal,*" RITA said.

Sam motioned to the driver. "You getting that?"

"Getting what, sir?" the driver said.

"Forget about it," Sam said. "Head south and take us lower."

"South, sir?"

"Yeah." Sam smacked the back of the driver's seat. "Just do it."

Chance and Sam held on as the VTOL banked hard and dropped low over The Zone.

The static transmission gained little clarity through the garbled distortion. "*Shepherd, do you... down... eed extrac... now...*"

Sam's eyes snapped up to meet Chance's. "Sounds like Ash, and he said my name."

"Weren't he and Rip supposed to be out by now?" Chance asked.

"Yeah, they were."

"Hey," Chance yelled to the driver, "pick it up, we have a situation here."

The thrusters fired full, the VTOL rocketing forward, drifting lower over the crumbling wastes of former downtown Atlanta.

"Hey man, what's going on?" Reggie called from the cage. "Where are we going?"

"Shut up," Sam said, straining to hear the words. With a squawk, the transmission cleared, causing Sam and Chance to catch each other's glance again.

"*Emergency transmission. Shepherd, do you copy this signal—suit to suit? Rip is injured, and we're pinned down. In need of support. Over?*"

"We gotta go," Chance said.

"Yeah," Sam said, "suit up, and man that heavy."

"Roger that," Chance said, his faceplate clunking down into position. He stood and clipped into the safety strap beside the mounted mini gun hanging in the open doorway. With a tilt, the massive cylindrical barrels aimed up as Chance checked the mounted ammo can and belt.

"Ash, I copy," Sam said. "Location?"

"*Sending direct,*" Ash said.

"Got it." Sam tapped his visor. "Griffin and I are one minute out."

"*They're giving us hell. Be ready,*" Ash said.

Though Ash still sounded like his usual ultra-cool self, there was an edge in his voice Chance hadn't heard before. It could only mean bad things.

As they neared Ash's coordinates, the whiz and pop of gunfire cracked across the landscape. Helmet secure, Sam leaned from the doorway to get a better view. Chance could see it, too, the smoke of battle rising into the air ahead.

"South sector. Not good," Sam said, looking back to Chance in the opening of the VTOL.

"What are they doing down here? Their trial was on the West," Chance struggled to get Kess's words about corrupt Enforcers out of his head. "We gotta go—even if it doesn't add up."

Sam didn't reply but turned to the driver. "We're pulling a hot extraction. Stay high and circle 'til we locate our people."

"Got it," the driver said, bringing the VTOL around.

"*Chance, this doesn't look good,*" RITA said.

The battle below came into full relief. Two Enforcers hunkered down, firing at scores of attackers from behind a low, two-foot-thick concrete wall eroded by projectile strikes. Ash and Rip faced an alliance of gangs, a rare and dangerous situation. Chance recognized the signature purple colors of Rico's gang, the Death Squad. Alongside them, Hoodie Boys in dusty green and Night Raiders in dark blue. Mixed into their ranks, repurposed auto turrets stalked forward like giant robotic spiders.

"I see them," Sam called out, pointing, "get us down there."

"Hey, what the hell, man?" Reggie cowered in his cage. "I didn't sign up for this."

Swooping low, the VTOL jerked left to dodge a rocket-propelled grenade, then touched down on rocky, uneven debris.

"I can't stay here long," the driver shouted.

"Hit 'em, Chance!" Sam yelled, pulling the quad launcher from the rack and jumping from the open hatch.

Chance clenched down on the mini gun. A whining surge filled the air as the spinning barrels hurled hundreds of rounds in the bandits' direction. Many of the men fell flat to the ground, scrabbling for what little cover they could find. The massive multi-barreled weapon caught others unaware and tore them in half.

Fifty feet from where the VTOL landed, Ash appeared from behind the low concrete wall, his armor a dingy, scarred olive green, a tattered American flag printed across the right shoulder and pectoral. He struggled toward Sam and Chance, wedged beneath his partner's arm. Rip limped, his jet black armor identifiable by the crimson handprint on his helmet and the red splattered blood graphic across the torso. A nasty wound in his abdomen leaked the real thing. Supported by Ash, his legs struggled to handle his weight.

"Get behind me!" Sam hurled a bundle of distraction devices at the enemy. The multi-bangs exploded, bouncing in puffs of white smoke before each exploding a second and third time in a chain of deafening thunderclaps that stunned the superior force. Raising the quad launcher, Sam sent a homing rocket streaking across the battlefield, where it obliterated one of the Death Squad's walking auto-turrets.

"Get in!" Chance shouted, loosing a blaze of fire from the heavy.

Ash pulled Rip into the waiting VTOL, hovering inches above the ground. Small-arms fire pinged and zipped off the armored shell. Rip screamed out in pain, his body dragging in behind Chance.

"Sam, move your ass!" Chance shouted between bursts from the mini gun.

Sam fired a second rocket and, not waiting to see it strike home, un-shouldered the huge launcher and ran for the waiting VTOL. Bullets glanced off his carbon gray armor in showers of sparks as Sam jumped into the VTOL. An RPG slammed into the nose, dragging the front end across the ground.

"Get us out of here!" Sam yelled.

The driver groaned, pulling hard on the yoke. Bullets clanged as the VTOL lifted away from the ground and shot into the sky in a hazy trail of smoke.

"Whooo!" Ash yelped, his faceplate releasing. "Quality sputz, boys!"

In his cage, Reggie sat, eyes wide, his white-knuckled hands clutching at the brace bar.

Chance stood anchored where he was, fury boiling over inside him at the reckless incursion against terrible odds. He needed answers.

Smoke billowed from one of the main thrusters of the sleek black Krytech VTOL as it touched down against the landing platform. From the edge of the landing pad, a crew of Conglomerate trauma technicians rushed forward, their medical gear in hand. Working together, they off loaded Rip onto a waiting stretcher. The wounded Enforcer, his helmet retracted into his suit, grimaced as the medical techs handled him.

"Hey, hey, go easy," Rip said through gnashed teeth.

Chance assisted as the techs buckled Rip in and carted him away. Ash spoke with animated hand gestures to the stressed-out driver of the cooling VTOL. It looked to Chance like Ash made a fund transfer to the man before slapping him on the shoulder with a word of thanks. Chance strained to hear the conversation but couldn't make anything out over the pop and click of the cooling thrusters.

A security team approached, shackles in hand. Sam exited the VTOL, hopping down onto the platform next to Chance, towing a terrified Reggie by the arm. Amid all the excitement, the poor slag-eater had wet his pants.

"Y-y-you guys were supposed to bring me straight back here," Reggie stammered. "N-n-not take me with you to-to…"

"Put on your big boy pants, Reggie. You're supposed to be a tough-guy gang leader." Sam handed him off to the security team, a pair of stout-shouldered men in shiny black and gold armor. Reggie continued to blubber as the security team escorted him away.

"You good?" Sam knocked the back of his fist against Chance's armor.

"What?"

"Are you good? You're all right?" Sam repeated.

"I'm fine," Chance said, his face betraying the conflict within. "What happens to him now?" He motioned to Reggie.

"Well," Sam let out a little whistle, "for troublesome gang leaders, it's a scheduled execution."

"Why don't we just smoke them down in The Zone?"

"Too fast. They want to make a spectacle of it. You know there's a channel on the network that only live streams the summary execution of criminals." Sam pressed a gloved finger to his bottom eyelid and pulled it down to expose the white of the eye. "Laser, right in the eye socket. Scrambles the guy's brains like a pan of eggs. They scream all the way through."

"Damn," Chance said. "I mean, he deserves it, but damn."

"Yeah," Sam said, grabbing his rocket launcher from the deck of the VTOL. "Let's go drop our gear, partner."

"All right," Chance said, turning toward the deployment tubes as Ash returned.

"Good show, fellas," Ash said. "Thanks for the assist."

"Rip?" Sam asked.

"He'll be fine," Ash said. "Nothing a turn in the recovery chamber can't fix."

"That was a little close, Ash," Sam said. "What were you doing over there?"

"Running a little side op," Ash said. "It's fine."

"A side op?" Chance asked.

"You're lucky we heard you on the suit-to-suit channel," Sam said.

"I saw your VTOL in the distance. I knew you guys were close enough."

"Hang on. Will someone tell me what's going on here?" Chance broke in. "What the hell is a side op? Why wasn't it broadcasted?"

Ash looked at Sam. "He doesn't know about side contracts?"

"Know what?" Chance's face creased into a frown.

"Bro, I'm exhausted." Ash, turned toward the tubes. "I smell like I've been living in my gear for a month, and I just want a beer. Can we do this another time?"

Chance grabbed the edge of Ash's shoulder plate, and Ash spun, knocking Chance's hand away. "Get your needy hands off me, Rookie."

Chance flushed, driving back at him. "You're gonna shove me, you prick?"

Something changed in Ash's scarred face; a wild fury enveloped him. "Come on, then!"

"Whoa," Sam said, stepping between the two men, their armor clacking against his sides. "Hey, relax, both of you."

"This little sputz wants to grab at me," Ash said through clenched teeth, "as he tells me what to do."

"Side ops?" Chance spat. "If you and Rip are dirty, at least have the balls to own it."

"Dirty?" Ash pushed forward into Sam.

"Yeah, I know what you're doing," Chance said.

"You cocky little—"

"Enough!" Sam shoved Ash back, still keeping a flat palm against Chance's breast plate. "Go cool off, Ash. I'll handle him."

"You'll handle me?" Chance pushed Sam's hand away. "What's that supposed to mean?"

"Relax, Chance," Sam said, his hands outstretched toward them both. "Relax."

Ash spat toward the deck and wiped the back of an armored hand across his chin. "Here's what you need to know, Rookie." He pointed at Chance. "What happens on the Enforcers stays on the Enforcers. We don't talk about our own. You can be a team player, or you can have problems."

"Is that a threat?" Chance bristled.

"Yeah, it's a threat," Ash said, walking away. "Time to grow up."

Sam turned toward Chance, placing both hands on his breast plate. "Look at me."

Chance watched Ash go, a fresh adrenaline rush prickling his body with pins and needles. A humid breeze whipped across the landing pad high atop the Conglomerate corporate headquarters. Along the horizon, beyond the smoke and haze of the festering city, a blood-red sunset cast brilliant shades of tangerine and violet across the clouds.

"Chance, look at me," Sam said, his voice calm and reassuring. "Let it go. We'll work it out. I promise."

Chance turned his eyes to meet those of his friend and mentor. He managed to nod, watching with grim resolve as Ash climbed onto the launch tube platform and dropped out of view.

CHAPTER TWENTY-NINE

Ghost pains, strange and persistent, danced the length of his arm, causing fingers he knew he didn't possess anymore to tingle and ache. Benny inspected his cybernetic appendage and flexed the fingers open. Grasping the splayed metal digits with his other hand, Benny stretched them open as far as the pistons would allow. A sigh escaped his lips. Bizarre how the stretching of a mechanical appendage seemed to give him some sense of relief in an arm no longer there. With a grunt, his gaze followed the drainage-slick rungs leading up out of the sewers.

"What are you waiting for?" The sound of Mage's voice grated in his ear and caused Benny to frown.

"I'm sizing it up," Benny said before adding beneath his breath, "pesky little slag-grabber."

"What was that?"

"Nothing, dear." Benny reached out, the dimenium-alloy fingers of his left hand clicking against the first steel rung.

Hoisting himself up, the bulk of his shoulders tight against the slick, molding walls, Benny stopped just beneath the rusted sewer grate, then pressed it up and slid it over. It scraped against the broken asphalt of an ancient street. Poking his head through the hole, Benny took in his immediate surroundings.

Factories and warehouses, long abandoned, lined the narrow lane, their clouded and broken windows like dark unseeing eyes. To the left, the strobing lights of the Volkan Heights sector set the horizon aglow; to the right, only the spectral glow of a few distant fires punctuated the darkness of The Slags.

"*The light rail station is two blocks down on your left inside Volkan Heights,*" Mage said.

"And where am I going?"

"*To the Future Club district.*"

"You're kidding me, right?" Benny said. "That's where I used to walk foot patrol. People know me over there."

"*Keep a low profile. You're a smart guy. Blend in.*" Mage laughed.

"Yeah," Benny grumbled. "I bet it's real funny getting other people to stick their necks out for you."

"*Just do what's expected.*"

"Sure," Benny said, raising himself out of the manhole entrance and sliding the cover back into place with a *thunk*. He scanned the sky for NTPD drones and, satisfied there were none, headed toward the shimmering heart of the Volkan Heights sector.

"*And stop acting so twitchy,*" Mage scolded. "*Remember, you're not you. You're Enrique Galvatorez, a VTOL mechanic with a gambling problem from the south of Volkan Heights. Drones and routine NTPD patrols won't know any different.*" Mage grunted a short laugh as the connection ended with a hiss.

It's not the people I don't know that worries me, Benny thought.

Shoving his hands deep into the pockets of his leather jacket, he crossed the street and walked two blocks to the light rail station. Past a gathering of homeless who tracked him with yellowed, bloodshot eyes, Benny mounted the stairs to the magnetic turnstiles. He eyed the dingy scan-droid with suspicion.

"Scan your chip, please," it said in a sterile, robotic monotone.

"Right." Benny felt a tingle on the back of his neck.

"Pass your chip over the scanner, please."

Benny waved his flesh-and-blood right arm over the scanner out of habit.

A buzz sounded. "Damaged chip. Do not block the lane. I will notify the police."

"*Your cybernetic arm, dumbass,*" Mage said.

Sputz, Benny thought. "My mistake." He held his cybernetic hand over the scanner. A chirp sounded.

But the scan-droid didn't react. The people in line behind Benny peered around him—one barked at him to get the hell out of the way.

Then the stall light turned green.

"Thank you, Enrique Galvatorez," the scan-droid said. "Have a carefree evening."

"Carefree. Right," Benny said, a wave of relief crashing over him. He passed through the stall and onto the platform.

"*I told you,*" Mage said in his ear. "*Relax.*"

The graffiti-tagged eastbound light rail train whistled into the station. Benny boarded and took an empty seat in the corner of the second to last car. He pulled his jacket close and tucked his chin down, the chrome visor covering a large swath of his face.

"News feed," Benny said, watching as the city news live stream flicked across his field of vision.

"*You don't want to do that,*" Mage said.

Benny didn't reply.

As the cascade of reports rolled past, Benny's mind drifted from the present. How had he fallen this far? He'd gone from a sharp, well-respected officer of the NTPD to a one-armed fugitive wanted for the assault of his fellow officers, forced to abandon his true identity and pay back a life debt to the imp-like criminal mastermind who'd saved him.

Benny released an exasperated puff of air.

Can I shed the man I was like a used skin? Is such a thing even possible?

The NTPD didn't have a good reputation regarding the resolution of false accusations. Kip Monaghan and Deyvar Whaley knew this simple truth when they set him up to take the fall for their dirt. He was a wanted man—wrongly accused but wanted, nevertheless. None of the rest mattered.

Benny clenched his fist so hard the blood left his fingertips. He forced himself to breathe.

"*You're watching Neo Terminus News Now,*" said a plastic-faced man with a frozen smile and sculpted hair. "*Neo Terminus Police arrested notorious Death Squad Lieutenant Kybo Marconi today. Marconi, known for his ruthlessness on the street, was taken into custody with other members of his group after a street war broke out between factions of the Death Squad and the Ghouls in the south Straits. Sixteen people were killed in the fighting, including a four-year-old child. The investigation is still underway. Marconi has been sentenced to death in The Zone.*"

"Mister Gold Teeth." Benny huffed. "Can't say I'm surprised."

Benny's eyes focused on the image of his own face filling the space of his visor.

"*In other news, the NTPD has asked for help in determining the whereabouts of this man. Guillermo Benitez, a highly decorated former officer with the department, now gone rogue.*"

"Oh my God," Benny said, his stomach souring. His large frame sunk lower in the plastic bucket seat.

"*Benitez, who resisted arrest and fled when contacted, is wanted on charges surrounding an elaborate drug trafficking scheme inside the NTPD. Charges include multiple counts of aggravated assault on a peace officer, endangering the peace, reckless endangerment, conspiracy, possession with intent to distribute, as well as other weapons and narcotics-related charges.*"

"Go on, stack them up, you sons of—"

"*Citizens are asked to report any information regarding Benitez to their local precinct. Benitez should be considered armed and extremely dangerous...*"

You have no idea, Benny thought.

The image changed to a scroll of video clips of Enforcers

competing in The Zone. One with a dark blue line and a white star on his armor laid waste to throngs of attacking gangs.

Benny rolled his eyes. "Show-boating, celebrity trash—"

The words stuck in his throat as the Enforcer's helmet retracted to reveal a beaming Chance, arms raised to hordes of adoring fans.

"*In other news, the newest Enforcer, Justice, has been making a splash since dropping into The Zone for the first time just weeks ago. With a combination of boyish good looks, genuine heart, and courage under fire, Justice has risen to the top of the rankings as the most beloved Enforcer in The Zone.*"

"I'll be damned. Of course, he did," Benny said. "Justice. Good for you, bro."

Benny pulled the visor from his face and struggled to fight off a crushing wave of self-pity.

"*Specter,*" Mage said. "*Keep the visor on. I need you to—*"

Benny folded the stems and put the device to sleep. He turned to peer out the window of the train at the smog-covered cityscape, glowing with radioactive luminescence in the growing dark of night. He dropped his hands to grip the sides of the hard plastic seat. A coldness filled his heart, icy talons digging into the soft, warm tissues. In the midst of his own turmoil, he'd lost track of his best friend. He missed Chance's support and counsel more than anything. More than his own arm. More than his life. As Chance's fortune improved, Benny's own took a horrible downward turn. To make matters worse, it all stemmed from Chance's request. If he'd said no, that he couldn't get RITA, he'd never have encountered Kip and Deyvar in the evidence locker. And they wouldn't have had a reason to frame him.

There was a crinkling sound beside his leg. Benny glanced down and, with a start, released the buckled plastic of the seat, still caught in the grip of his cybernetic fingers.

"Hey man, chill." A visor-clad man with spiked hair looked back at Benny from the seat in front of him.

"Sorry," Benny said, putting his powered-up visor back on.

The guy regarded him, the network's news feed scrolling on his lenses. "Do I know you from somewhere?" the guy asked.

"No, you don't." Benny stood as the train pulled into the Future Club district station.

"You sure?" the man asked. "I've seen you somewhere…"

"I'd know," Benny said.

"Yeah, but—"

"Mind your own business, sputz-stick." Benny stuck a metal finger in the wide-eyed man's face.

"Okay." He held his hands up.

Benny shoved through the commuters, who cursed at him as he made for the door. He had to keep moving. Pushing free of the train, he trudged away from the outraged shouts of the easily offended.

"*Slick*," Mage said.

"What do you want from me?" Benny asked, blood pounding in his ears.

"*How about trust me and keep your visor on so I can help steer you away from screwing the pooch?*"

Benny descended the stairs and exited onto the damp, steaming street amidst the hustle and bustle of the Future Club district. Here he could blend in. He inhaled the smells of the city; a strange mixture of sweat, spiced perfumes, and tropical-scented nape vapors issued from a nearby parlor. The oily aroma of a food stand selling noodles and steamed buns reached out to him, the delicious smells of meat and warm dough tainted by a hint of wet garbage stacked in towering piles in the adjacent alley.

Scores of signs flashed and strobed in endless advertisements for nudes, nape vapes, Feel-boosted vid sex, and booze. A fresh track of electronic synthwave filled the air with the sound of smooth sax-infused synthesizers, the crowd shifting in tune with the beat. Benny popped his collar and settled into the mass of club goers gyrating through the streets. Something about this place calmed him, a beat he'd walked a thousand times, sultry familiarity in an otherwise lost existence. He trudged on with lengthening strides into the shifting, intoxicated crowds of the neon-lit Future Club district.

Deep within the concrete bowels of the Conglomerate's headquarters, Chance loaded another gold-labeled magazine of standard rounds into his Peacemaker. He straightened his arms to ninety percent lockout and picked up the combat optic. All the fundamentals of shooting came together like a harmony of the senses: grip, stance, sight picture, trigger control. Chance squeezed off a round, the impact landing dead center of the silhouette's forehead at fifty yards.

"Mind if I join?"

Chance glanced sideways to see Sam loading his Peacemaker in the shooting lane next to him. Turning his attention forward again, he loosed another round, key-holing the first shot.

"Suit yourself," Chance said.

Sam readied and got off a string of rounds in rapid fire, all striking inside a fist-sized pattern at fifty yards. He set his weapon down on the bench in front of him, slide locked to the rear. Chance fired off a third and fourth round, his face intense with focus.

"Chance," Sam said. "Let's talk, buddy."

"About?" Chance dropped the large magazine and prepared another.

"Come on, man. Don't be like that," Sam said. "You freaked out on Ash up there."

"I freaked out because he almost got us killed. Over what?" Chance set his weapon down. "Some secret personal agenda?"

"It's not like that," Sam said with a sigh.

"What is it, then? Why didn't I know about this?"

"You're just getting settled into this life. I thought I'd give it some time. I didn't realize it would be shoved in your face."

"Sam, tell me straight. What are we talking about here?"

"Look, sometimes, off the clock, Enforcers take on private contracts." Sam holstered his weapon. "It's a way to make a little extra on the side."

"Make a little extra on the side?" Chance scoffed. "Sam, we have more than everyone else in this godforsaken city."

"Yeah, I know, but there's more to it."

"Answer me this. Are these missions restricted to The Zone?" Chance asked.

Sam pursed his lips.

The color drained from Chance's face. "You're saying the Enforcers take private contracts in the city, too?"

"Rarely," Sam said.

"What kind of private contracts are we talking about?"

"Asset forfeitures, warrant service, and personnel seizures, maybe the occasional elimination contract on someone a rival gang wants out of the picture."

"Sam," Chance swallowed, "that's theft, kidnapping, and murder. You're talking about our people being used as tools for organized crime."

"Don't look at it like that," Sam said.

Chance pushed away from the stall and holstered his Peacemaker. "It *is* that." He stormed from the range, through the exit, and into the armory with Sam on his heels. "Just the other night, I asked about rogue Enforcers, and you all looked at me like I was crazy. Now I find out you're all taking shady contract jobs in the city."

"Chance, come on." Sam looked around to make sure no one overheard. "It's not as big a deal as what you're making it out to be. It's the same thing we always do, just paid for in a private contract. What's the difference?"

"Have you ever committed murder for hire?" Chance turned on him, his eyes hard.

"Chance—"

"Tell me," Chance pressed.

Sam leveled his gaze. "What do you think it is when we go after a gang leader in The Zone? We go in there to kill them."

"We're forced to kill them when they try to kill us first. It's not an assassination."

"You sure there's a difference?" Sam said.

"Yes," Chance said.

"Okay, let me ask you this." Sam crossed his arms. "The child you rescued on your first trial—where did she and her family come from?"

"What does that mean?"

"The innocents we rescue in The Zone," Sam said. "Where do they come from? They're not already in The Zone."

Chance's shoulders slumped, his aggressive attitude falling. "They don't live there." It had never occurred to him.

"Chance, those people are in debt to The Glom. They're kidnapped from the other sectors, dropped into The Zone for you to rescue."

"No," Chance said.

"Yes. Don't you see? Citizens in debt are dropped into The Zone. The Glom supplies the gangs with tech and resources." Sam rapped a knuckle against the Peacemaker. "It's all a game," Sam said. "The Glom controls everything. Kess pulls everyone's strings, and it's all for the show."

"Stop," Chance said, turning away.

"This is what you signed up for." Sam held up his hands. "It's part of the culture. We're not cops anymore."

"Yeah," Chance said, loading his Peacemaker into the auto-clean chamber. "I can see that." He locked the unit closed, then turned and headed for the archway scanner.

"Chance, if you refuse this," Sam said, still following, "the others won't trust you. They're going to think you're with *them*," he pointed up, "and not *us*."

"I'm done talking," Chance said, crossing beneath flickering orange blades of light. All he could think was how badly he missed Benny and the clear-cut, black-and-white nature of his old life. Sure, they'd been poor and hungry, but he never once worried about where he stood. Now, for the first time, a genuine fear filled his chest, a fear that he might have allied with something terrible. He leaned hard into the vault door, pressing it open. At the end of the concrete corridor, Jessie appeared, stepping from the lift.

"What's up, dude?" Jessie said, holding up his fist. "You and Sam killed it today."

Chance shouldered past the well-styled Enforcer without reply and made for the open lift.

"Whoa, okay," Jessie said, lowering his hand. He turned as Sam emerged from the armory door.

Chance mashed the button, calling the lift back.

"What's his deal?" He heard Jessie say.

"He knows," Sam said.

"Everything?"

The lift dinged, and Chance stepped in. Sam shook his head, and for a moment, he and Chance made eye contact.

"No," Sam said.

Chance rode the lift to his apartment high above. He felt restless, his skin crawling with unease. Sam had tried to downplay everything, but it was criminal activity, plain and simple. Chance felt he'd done his best to buy in, to be one of the gang, but this was worse than his worst fears about the Enforcers.

With nowhere to go, Chance paced around the small space of the elevator like a caged predator. He pressed his teeth together, a hiss of frustration whistling through them.

They can't all be dirty, he thought. *Can they?*

At best, the Enforcers were nothing more than celebrity gladiators; at worst, assassins for criminal entities. He'd spent his entire police career standing against injustice and corruption, and now, in this place, his team expected participation in such ugliness.

"Damn, Benny," he whispered. "Where are you when I need you?"

Before he could second guess himself, he scrolled through his visor and pulled up the direct link number for Gabriel Kess. The voice-to-text function transcribed his words as he spoke. The prickle of perspiration dotted his forehead and neck. He read the message over five times, his finger hovering over the *send* icon.

> Director Kess, I have reliable information that the Enforcers are involved in criminal enterprise. Unsure which one is dealing directly with Rico, but I do know one thing: All of them are guilty.

CHAPTER THIRTY

abriel Kess stood still as a statue, shoulders back, posture ramrod straight. Though at attention, he had a relaxed air of confidence as he waited to address the founders inside their remote chamber atop the Conglomerate's headquarters.

Kess allowed his eyes to rove around the room. Jet black stone and sheets of glistening obsidian marble framed in gold accents encircled the high-ceilinged octagonal council chamber. Golden sconces burning with soft light lined the dark walls. A twisting black thorn ringed in gold and crowned with eight stars shimmered on the floor at Kess's feet. Above the crystal glass ceiling, out of the reach of even the founders, ageless stars glittered against the expanse of the heavens.

One by one, the shadowed forms materialized as the founders logged on and joined the meeting, projected silhouettes vivid against the room's black walls. Kess had met not one of them in person. If they were the original founders of the Conglomerate, they'd each be over a hundred years old by now. Had some manner of high-tech sorcery prolonged their lives? Whatever the case, they conducted every meeting by hologram. Though Kess didn't like this system, he respected the founders for rescuing human civilization from the brink of collapse and was willing to entertain their eccentricities. Regardless of their lack of physical presence, there was no doubt of the influence the founders held over him—

over everyone everywhere. He knew without question if he did not work to justify his existence, they possessed the power to make him nothing. Considering this, it had always been his policy to remain respectful yet firm and confident.

If he was to survive, he had to stay one step ahead.

"Director Kess." A strange, synthetic voice echoed across the open chamber. "I assume in requesting this meeting, you have something of value for us?"

"I do, Founder Delta." Kess gave a slight bow toward the shadow and paused for dramatic effect.

"Well, what is it?" another voice said, distorted and ageless.

A thin smirk formed across Kess's lips. "I've been hard at work designing a plan that is sure to see us through the coming storm—"

"Might I remind you," the scratchy, digital voice of Founder Beta broke in, "the storm is not coming. It is here. New West City has fallen. Much of the Conglomerate's leadership there have met their grisly end, carried through the streets by angry mobs. Only the coward Marko Senterian remains, reduced to a life in hiding. Such a thing will not happen in Neo Terminus."

"Of course, Founder. I misspoke," Kess said with another dip of his head. "As I was saying, I've been hard at work on a plan that will see Neo Terminus through these unfortunate events."

"The numbers are already beginning to decline," a founder said. Above the shadowed head, the outline of the Greek symbol for Eta flickered with static. "Right now, the rebellion in New West City is at its height. Underground sources there seek to reach out to Neo Terminus to broadcast the rebellion to our citizens. We cannot allow this propaganda to reach the public."

"Founders." Kess opened his hands. "I would submit the news has already reached the public. Rumors are spreading. What we can't allow is any real validation of this news. If there's no evidence, no video or eyewitness reports to confirm it, who could say it even happened? This is how my plan will work—and I assure you, it's much more elaborate than the addition of a new Enforcer."

The digitized gray images hovered, floating, lost spirits on their way to the underworld.

"Well, out with it," Founder Iota said.

"The plan is threefold," Kess said. "First, we restrict network usage to the primary channels and funnel the attention of the public where we want it—on The Zone."

"And the second stage?"

"I will shut down all independent attempts to cast signals onto the net. Security teams will dispatch to each site of origin to dissuade future attempts. Top brass at the NTPD assure me they will allocate specialty units to this task." Kess spoke with panache. "I have already implemented the first and second stages."

"Go on," the eighth founder said.

"The third element is a bit of a surprise," Kess continued. "I plan to pull the most daring, thrilling, and, ultimately, distracting event The Zone has ever seen. The tech-addicted public will have no choice but to stay glued to their visors, bet on the games, and forget they care about anything regarding New West City."

A series of indiscernible whispers passed between the shadows. The floating images drew silent, waiting until one voice spoke. "We will assist you in this regard."

"Assist me?" Kess frowned. "I guarantee my plan will succeed."

"Your guarantees are worthless, Kess," Founder Beta said. "We will deliver some tech we've been saving for this very moment."

"What sort of tech?" Kess fought back his irritation.

"A little something we developed to ensure we kept the public's attention. A cerebral link of sorts. Install and activate the signal during your grand trial while viewership is at its peak. We'll handle the rest."

Kess crossed his arms. "Are you saying people won't be able to disconnect once the signal is sent from your device?"

"Don't be such a simpleton," Founder Theta snapped. "Mind control is for comic books. They can disengage the effects of the device when the threat of rebellion has passed. Until then, everyone will be happily immersed in the network."

Kess said nothing. A strange and sudden turmoil brewed inside him.

"We are graciously offering to help you do your job, Director Kess," Founder Epsilon barked. "Do you want to accept our help? Or do we need to find someone who will?"

"Of course." Kess swallowed and gave a little bow. "I will take care of everything."

"Good," Founder Kappa said. "We will conduct this operation the way we see fit. Failure on your part is not an option."

"Failure is not something I tolerate. I assure you."

"Then we agree on this point. Should you fail and Neo Terminus falls into chaos, we will watch with great interest as the city pulls you apart."

The threat struck a chord in Kess. The truth slipped beneath his flesh like the cold steel of a sharpened blade: It was true. He had much to lose, but so did they. Kess folded one hand atop the other at his waist and stood relaxed. He held up an index finger.

"But should my distraction succeed," he allowed his implication to sink in, "a distraction you need to spike viewership so your device can work—"

"You want us to, what? Reward you?" The digital shadows laughed in unison, the air crackling with digital disdain.

"It's only logical," Kess continued. "You could appoint someone else, but I'm the only one who can pull off the spectacle you need in time. I will save this city, and the savior of the city should be rewarded."

"Calling yourself the savior of the city seems premature, don't you think, Gabriel?" Founder Zeta chuckled icily. The Greek symbol above his head flickered out and returned. "Especially when we are providing you with the tools to do it?"

"I don't think so," Kess said with an air of finality. "My plan will work, and when it does, I want a stake in the Conglomerate."

Sharp, inhaled gasps and murmurs filled the room. The spectral images wavered. Kess stood firm, his head up and shoulders back.

"Outrageous," Founder Delta called out.

"Impossible," another said.

The wraiths seemed to pop and shudder with menace. "Only the founders have stakes in the company. You know this," Founder Beta said.

"That is why I want to be inducted as a founder," Kess said, his demeanor stoic.

"You can't!" the gray digital shadows screeched. "You are not fit to be one of us. One does not simply ascend!"

Kess flushed, his chin thrust forward in defiance. "Neo Terminus is on the brink of oblivion! When the city falls—and it will fall without my intervention—I'll watch as they tear you from your crystal palaces! I didn't grow up with a silver spoon in my mouth! I can survive the fallout! Can you?"

Kess words rang out, hurled into the air like the daggers of an assassin. The sound of his shouts echoed across the walls of the room and slipped into silence. The shadowy gray forms hovered silent and still. For an instant, Kess wondered if he'd overplayed his hand. He imagined his own death sentence: Strapped to a gurney, crying out as a hundred tiny mechanical arms sliced and cut, peeling back the layers of flesh, dissecting him piece by piece. But as the silence dragged on, he knew this would not be the case. They needed him. If Neo Terminus had any chance of weathering this storm, it lay with him and his distraction, and the founders knew it.

His case well made, Kess stood relaxed, one hand clasping the opposite wrist at his waist. Not a word was uttered until a sound like a small, irritated sigh greeted his ears.

"Implement the plan in full," Founder Iota said. "If it is successful, and you do as we've told you, we will discuss your situation at a later date once the founders have had time to confer in private. Does this satisfy your ambition?" The Founder spat.

"It does, Founder." Kess gave another dramatic bow. "Thank you for your consideration. And now I must take my leave. I have much work to do."

Kess turned on his heel and marched from the room, the hard soles of his real leather shoes clopping against the polished black marble. He passed beneath the entrance arch and stepped into the gravity lift. As the lift descended, a little three-note chime alerted him of an incoming message. Kess opened the direct message from Chance, a devious grin stretching over bleached white teeth.

Benny stepped from the meandering hustle and bustle of the steamy neon-lit main drag, stopping on the littered sidewalk before the black, sliding glass doors. Club goers, entranced in their visors, formed a line that snaked around the corner and into the street. He remembered the place from his early days, walking a beat, and paused to eye the curving electric blue signage above the door that read *Crave*.

"What do you want?" said a hairy-armed bouncer with shoulders as wide as the doorframe.

Benny held up an index finger for the burly man.

"Is this it?" Benny tried to be discreet. "Club Crave?"

"What'd you say?" the bouncer said.

Benny shook his head and re-emphasized the index finger. "I'm on a call, pal. Just a sec."

The Cro-Magnon bouncer scowled and crossed his python-thick forearms. The next in line, a wild-haired woman with her scrawny man on a spiked leash, moaned about people cutting in.

"Yo," Benny said.

"*Yes. Yes. Don't rush me,*" Mage said.

"This is a known Death Squad hangout," Benny said. "That's Rico's gang. As in, the warlord who runs the entire Zone these days."

"*So?*"

"So?" Benny chuckled, incredulous. "Are you serious?"

"Hey, you're taking up space in front of my club, and the line is over there," the bouncer said, pointing to the ranks of style-savvy clubgoers wrapping around the block.

"*Tell him you're on the VIP list,*" Mage said.

Benny cleared his throat. "Sorry about the delay. I'm on the VIP list."

The bouncer scowled again, eyeing Benny's cybernetic arm. He held up the back of his tablet. "Scan your chip, please."

Benny passed the metal wrist beneath the scanner and waited for the blip. The man waved open a vibrant green digital projection of names that floated in the air between them.

"Name?"

"I just scanned—"

"I'm checking your name to the list, and I wanna hear you say it," the bouncer growled. "Got a problem?"

"It's Guill-ahhmm—" Benny stammered and let loose a cough.

"*Dumbass,*" Mage groaned.

Benny felt his skin flush. He coughed into his hand a second time. "Excuse me. Damn, chest cold. It's Galvatorez. Enrique Galvatorez."

The bouncer stared him down, making no attempt to conceal his growing suspicion of the large, augmented stranger. The man turned his attention to the list, his eyes scrolling. He gave a grunt.

"Here it is. Galvatorez," he said. His posture relaxing, he

stepped aside. "Have a nice time."

The little spike-leashed man stepped out of line. "Da slag, cupcake! You believe dis?" He raised two bony fists, and his scowling companion gave the leash a little jerk. The man coughed, cut his eyes at his girl, and stepped back in line.

With a nod to the bouncer, Benny stepped up the stairs, the tinted glass sliding back before him. An electronic beat rushed over him, buoyed by the energy of the crowd. Benny stepped inside and waited for the dark glass to whisper shut behind him.

"Make your way past the dance floor to the staircase in the back. It's to the left of the bar."

"Mage, you want to tell me what the hell I'm doing in a Death Squad club?" Benny asked as he navigated his way through the twerking masses of entranced dancing club goers.

"I think you know. You have the item?"

A sick feeling of unease pushed over Benny as his fingers pinched the box in his right front jacket pocket. He was about to do some sort of shady back alley business transaction in one of the most notoriously violent, gang-run clubs in the city. An activity over which, less than a few weeks ago, he would have busted everybody involved and thrown them in the Blocks.

"Yeah. I got it," he said.

"Good. Now, remember, I didn't tell you anything about this for a reason. The less you know, the safer you are, understand? If they have any sense, they'll make you power down and go dark on your visor. Make the exchange and get out of there. I'll be watching."

Benny kept his pace relaxed and his eyes forward as he pushed past the long neon purple bar, where the purple-clad bartenders bobbed to the electronic synthwave beat and poured watered-down shots. Rows of tough, scarred men in plum-colored jackets eyed him as he passed, their countenance dark and knowing, the singular visage of predators observing their prey. One of them, while staring holes in Benny, pulled open his own jacket to reveal a police-issue MVX pistol, likely taken off the corpse of a downed cop.

Benny averted his eyes in what he hoped was a submissive gesture, suppressing his hardwired instincts to feed the man his teeth. He was almost at the stairs when a square-jawed man, every bit Benny's equal in height and weight, stepped in front of him. His visor flashed with a stream of naked children.

"What do you want, moob?"

"*You're here to see Big Roach. Rico's second in command.*"

"I'm here to see Big Roach. I'm expected." Benny pressed his teeth together. The big man's visor content was enough to set him off. *Sicko slag-eater.*

The big man narrowed his eyes. "What's the color of death?"

A prickle of heat danced across Benny's neck and shoulders as he waited for Mage to tell him. He cleared his throat.

"*Ahhm… hold on…*" Mage said.

"Answer the question, moob." The tough ganger leaned forward, his eyes cold and humorless. "Now."

Benny glanced to the right and, seeing some men at the bar stand from their stools, knew he'd be dead in about seven seconds. His survival instincts kicked into gear. He did the only thing he knew how to do—handle these tough guys the same way he would have if he were on the job.

"Listen, kiddie play." Benny leaned closer to the big man. "Call me moob again, and I'm going to slap that expensive visor off your ugly face and stick it so far up your ass you'll be chewing synthetics for a week."

The square-jawed man cocked his head in shock. "Tha jakk you say to me, moo—?"

Benny's right hand shot forward, slapping the man across the cheek and sending his visor flying into the air. A hidden knife flashed in the thug's hand. Benny intercepted the upward stab, the fingers of his cybernetic hand closing around the big man's wrist.

Bone cracked, the unmistakable pop and splinter that accompanies human deformation. Square Jaw's eyes grew large and white, a shrill howl of pain erupting from his throat as his knife clattered to the floor.

"My arm!" he shrieked, dropping to his knees. "My slagging arm!"

Benny squeezed harder. More bones popped and crinkled. Square Jaw cried out, fingers digging uselessly at Benny's vice grip.

"Get a new hobby and leave the kids alone, slag-eater." Benny hissed.

The barrel of a pistol pressed against Benny's ear. "Let him go," one of the thugs from the bar said.

"*Tell them you'll shut this joint down. Say it with some gusto,*" Mage said.

Benny held tight to the man's broken arm, his jaw set. "You think you can big-boy me because you don't know who I am and who I work for. What you simple-minded punks don't understand is I have the power to shut this slag-pit *down!*"

The entire club went dark. The music stopped, the crowds drawing silent. Every visor and every holo-screen flickered and turned black. All except Benny's, casting a pale blue glow over his face and the outline of his now whimpering victim.

In an instant, the crowds gasped as the lights returned and the music re-engaged. The patrons of the club looked around bewildered, whispering and pointing at Benny. His hand still clamped onto Square Jaw's wrist, he stood amidst a semi-circle of shocked Death Squad goons, a pistol still aimed at his head.

Mage gave a low chuckle in Benny's ear. "*Works every time.*"

Benny released the injured man and reached up to press the other goon's muzzle away. "Take me to Big Roach, now."

"All right, dog. Chill," one man said, while others helped the broken man up on quivering legs.

Benny took a step forward, stopped by the barrel of another

pistol in his chest.

"But check this out," said another gang member, a short, angry little man. "Touch any of my boys again, and I'll burn you, big man. I don't give two slags who you are. Ya, feel me?"

Benny held the man's gaze. "Do you mind?"

The short man held out his hand. "Your visor. It stays."

"*Give it to him. Verify the data packet before you make the exchange. And for god's sake—stick to the plan,*" Mage said.

Benny pulled the visor and powered it down, handing it to the man.

The thug stepped to the side. He lowered the pistol, eyeing Benny with pure hate.

Escorted by the angry but cautious entourage, Benny ascended the stair to a private loft overlooking the dance floor. There, the fattest man Benny had ever laid eyes on leaned back on a gaudy, dark purple couch. The massive, walrus-like creature seemed to be a permanent fixture in the room, as much as the lamp beside him or the low granite table scattered with white powder, inhalers, and eyedroppers. The obese form, rolls upon rolls of fat pressing through stretched garments, melted across the couch, and left a fixed depression in the cushions where he sat. With a flick of his wrist, he shooed away a handful of topless dancers with tasseled nipples who lounged on the couch beside him.

Benny took inventory of the pair of stoic bodyguards flanking the fat man, each holding a chopped-down rifle strapped to their chests.

"Let me guess," Benny said. "Big Roach."

Big Roach brought his hands together, clapping with an irritating slowness. Cybernetic implants carved into the flesh of his broad face pulsed with a soft light.

"Nice trick, with the power," he said, his voice gurgling out of his throat like volcanic mud.

"Those punks that work for you liked it," Benny said.

"You can spook my boys, but you'll find me a touch harder to scare, Mister…"

"Galvatorez."

"Uh-huh," Big Roach said, eyeing Benny's arm. "Expensive hardware you got there. How much for it?"

"Not for sale," Benny said.

"Everything is for sale if enough money goes on the table. Name a price."

"Maybe you didn't hear me, Mr. Roach," Benny said, taking note as the bodyguards tilted their weapons up. "It's mine, and it's not for sale."

Big Roach shifted, subdued confidence plastered across his jowled mug. "And what's going to stop me from cutting it off you?"

A nearby goon in all purple tapped the flat side of a honed machete into his palm.

"The rest of me." Benny clenched his cybernetic fist. "Are we done with the games already?"

Big Roach laughed, a wet, bubbling sound. "I like this guy. He's got balls." He waved open a visual of Enrique Galvatorez's information. "Let's see, former dark-net VTOL mechanic with a gambling problem," he grunted. "Game of choice?"

"Roulette."

A gurgled laugh escaped the fat man. "Naturally." He eyed Benny with suspicion. "I'm a bit of a VTOL enthusiast myself. Do you prefer the solid-state drives or the latest and greatest liquid jobs?"

Benny felt a prickle of anxiety tingle over him. "Solid state. Can't beat a classic."

"Hrmph." Big Roach rubbed his chins, flicking away a crumb of food. "Plagued with problems, though. How do you deal with the sticking elevation module?"

Benny licked his lips.

A chime sounded, and Big Roach touched his ear. "What is it?"

With a wave, he dispatched a few of his men down to the lower level and touched his ear again.

"Everything all right?" Benny said.

"You let me worry about that, Mr. Galvatorez."

"Okay, well, I'm here on behalf of—"

"I know who you're here representing. The Imp," Roach said. "He's a crafty little runt. Can't trust him, though. You'd do well to remember that."

Benny shifted his weight. "Do you want to continue with the small talk, or shall we get down to business?"

"Business..." Big Roach sampled the word.

"That's right," Benny said. "The data packet. You have it?"

"You have the item we requested?"

"Yeah, but I'm going to see the data first."

"Down to business it is," Roach said. With a dull snap of his meaty fingers, All Purple approached and held out a metal tray with a micro card storage drive. Benny glanced at Roach and picked up the drive.

"You'll need that," Roach said. A moment later, his man handed Benny his visor. "The recording and communication features have been temporarily disabled."

Benny popped on his visor. With a wave, he scanned the data drive into the chip in his arm.

In an instant, Benny's visor sprang to life with images of death and destruction. Benny felt his shock deepen as scores of Glom troopers fired upon terrified unarmed civilians caught between the madness of the burning outpost and their dark oppressors. Men, women, and children were cut down by rifle fire as they clamored and clawed, their bodies falling in heaps before the Conglomerate's private sectors loaded with food and security.

"You didn't know?" Roach laughed. "The Glom committing mass genocide in New West City? Now, that's news. News your imp wants to use to set the world on fire. Once he releases this onto the net, it's only a matter of time before the people of Neo Terminus revolt against their masters."

"And you're not worried about this?" Benny said.

Big Roach chuckled. "I'm the criminal element, my friend. A roach always survives."

Benny dismissed the image, double-checked the secure upload to Mage, and discarded the wafer. He took a slow breath in. *No way out but through. I'll deal with Mage later.*

"Now the box," Roach said.

"May I?" Benny reined in his shock and motioned to his pocket.

Roach gave a sluggish nod.

Extracting the box, Benny leaned down to place it with two fingers on the granite table. All Purple picked up the box and handed it to Roach, who popped the top and examined the finger-sized device inside.

"Bet you know nothing about what you're delivering," Roach said. "Correct?"

"Safer that way."

"You ever bet on The Zone, Mr. Galvatorez?" Big Roach said.

"Here and there," Benny lied.

"Always so much risk, the fear of losing your shirt." Big Roach smirked as one of his men powered on a mini courier drone and handed it to him. "But what if you could eliminate the risk?" the fat man asked.

Big Roach loaded the device into the courier drone and released it. With a light whirring, the drone zipped away, disappearing through an open window.

"Think of it," Roach clapped his hands together, "what if you could drop all your money on a sure bet like the Death Squad? And what if they, at just the right moment, neutralized all the Enforcer's nanobots? Think how much jakkin' money we'd make by betting on our own and killing *all* of the Enforcers in one fell swoop. It's brilliant!"

A wave of terror smashed over Benny. Chance was walking into a trap. Benny swallowed a lump.

Big Roach smirked. "See, Rico runs things inside The Zone, and I run the business outside. We like money, and we enjoy making it however we can."

Benny felt Roach's men close in on him from all sides.

"Once in a while, I'll even tip off the cops if there's a reward involved," Roach said. "Isn't that right?" The fat man gurgled. "*Officer Benitez.*"

"That's not me. You've got the wrong guy," Benny said, desperation in his voice. "I'm not a cop."

"But you were, before you went on the run," Roach said. "I have little birds everywhere. I know about your friend who made the Enforcers, and I know about you. You think I wouldn't recognize a pig who used to walk this beat? You even had my club shut down once, cost me a boatload of cash. Payback's a bitch, ain't it?"

Benny sobered, the muscles of his body tightening, an electrical fight-or-flight response banging into overdrive.

"This concludes our business, Officer Benitez. As much as I'd like to burn a dirty cop myself, I think I'll keep my hands clean this time and let your brothers in blue do it for me." Big Roach leaned back into the deep purple couch, absolute pleasure dripping from his sagging features. "In fact, I estimate the NTPD will have the building surrounded in about thirty seconds."

Benny shoved backward, drove into the goon in all purple and blasted him into the wall. He vaulted over the railing and landed with a *thud* on the dance floor below, the dancing club goers screaming and running out of the way.

"Run, Benny, Run," Big Roach shouted from above with a final gurgled laugh.

Blind with fear and panic, Benny threw himself toward the rear emergency exit. His legs pumping, he crashed into a bouncer, bowled him over, and sent a waitress's tray of drinks shattering against the wall.

He couldn't stop. He had one chance to get out alive, and it was slim.

Chance leaned against the bar and drained the last of his whiskey. After messaging Kess, a choice he half regretted, he'd decided it was best to stay in his place for the evening. He glanced again to the shadow darkening the frosted glass of his apartment door.

"What do you want?" Chance called out. The alcohol wasn't doing anything for his current state of agitation.

The shadow shifted with a sigh, leaning against the door frame.

"I just want to talk, partner," Sam said.

"Nothing to talk about." Chance set the empty glass down. Poured another.

"Chance, it's important. I need to clear the air about something I said."

"No you don't. Goodnight."

Sam's shadow stood unmoving, the silence lengthening to the point of becoming awkward.

"Yeah," Sam muttered. "Okay. G'night, buddy."

The silhouette shrank and receded into the floor, the footsteps of his mentor fading down the hall. A moment later, Chance heard the faint whoosh of Sam's door.

Chance suppressed the anxiety bubbling up like a toxic pool inside him. *Who the hell can I trust? Are the Enforcers dirty, or am I twisting things out of proportion?*

Kess was of little help, offering only a generic *Keep up the good work* response to his earlier message. Was Kess using him, too? Was he caught in the middle of some organized power play, a pawn manipulated by all sides?

A bloom of heat rose inside him. Grabbing his drink from the counter, Chance flung it across the room, his shoulders heaving as it shattered against the far wall in a splash of whisky and glass. A faint peep sounded, and a small hatch opened near the baseboard and a cleaning bot emerged.

"*Spill detected. Possible sharp objects present,*" a soft, robotic voice said from the in-ceiling speakers overhead. "*Please stand by while the scene is contained.*"

The anger in him subsided, evolving into the worst sort of looming sadness. His face and head tingled with a warmth brought on by the whiskey.

His visor trilled from across the room on the small table beside the recovery chamber. With a grunt, Chance leaned away from the bar and walked toward the sound, wincing at the pain of a strained knee. He couldn't say when it happened, only that it had at some point during the day's trial or rescue.

The idea that he'd torn something in his knee while sticking his neck out for Ash and Rip on their little side contract only caused the anger within him to grow. He pressed it away, and bent to pick up the ringing visor.

Hannah. Unfolding the stems, he slipped the device on and answered the vid call.

"I need you, baby," Chance said.

"Hey, love." Hannah's face seemed to glow. "How's my guy holding up?"

Chance pursed his lips, unsure what exactly to say, or if he should say anything at all.

"Are you okay?" Her light faded. "What's wrong?"

Don't worry her. She doesn't need that right now.

"I'm all right," he lied. "Just stressed out from work. I've got a lot going on."

She bounced a whimpering Andrew, swaddling against her chest. "Like what?"

"Just, ah…" Chance rubbed his head, "stuff I gotta figure out, you know?" He smiled for her. "I'll be okay. I'm missing you guys already."

"This place is too big and lonely without you," Hannah said, lifting Andrew so Chance could see his sleepy face. "We had a pretty good day, though."

Chance sat on the rim of the recovery chamber. "You saw the surgeon?"

"We did," Hannah said, smiling. "He said Andrew's case is a tough one, but with the right treatments, he has a good chance of being able to walk unassisted… someday."

Chance watched his lovely wife, choked with emotion, wiping the tears of joy from her eyes. Chance's lip quivered and he clenched his teeth to try and stop it.

"That's great, baby."

"We're going to be okay," she said, and burst into a tearful smile.

"Yeah, I hope so," Chance said, swallowing the emotion back. *A little longer. We'll get Andrew the help he needs, then find a way out of this madness.* He looked at the little swaddled form of his son. "I knew you'd be okay, buddy. Momma and I will make sure you get what you need. All right?"

Hannah rocked the little bundle and kissed him gently on the forehead. "Okay, I'm going to go lay him down. I love you," she said.

"I love you, too, sweetheart."

"Okay. Night." She blew him a kiss, and the image winked out.

Chance pulled off his shirt and pants, wincing. He supported his injured knee and raised his leg into the recovery chamber. Scooting down, he powered the chamber on. A soft night-light glow illuminated the space as Chance lay back on the soft bedding, and the lid shut over him. Whirring with soft pulsating sounds, faint ribbons of light crisscrossed over his body, a fine soothing mist drifting over his face. He inhaled deep, the calming influence of the chamber taking effect.

"Home screen," Chance murmured.

In the lid's underside, the soft blue light of a network home screen faded in.

"Where would you like to navigate on the network?" the sterile AI said.

"Directory," Chance said, his voice drowsy.

He knew it wouldn't show him anything different from what he'd already seen, but he couldn't bring himself to accept it. It wasn't possible for a person to disappear, was it?

"Guillermo Benitez," Chance said.

The screen flickered and displayed a row of subscribers, none of whom were Benny.

"Back out. Search NTPD officer database for Guillermo Benitez," Chance said.

No results flashed on the screen.

Chance let out a sigh, his limbs laden with exhaustion, his eyes only half open. "I dunno. Scan the entire net for that name," he murmured.

The word *Scanning...* hung on the screen for a moment, then *Four matching items found in news.*

"Open," Chance said, rousing a little, an icy fear sinking in his chest. He swallowed as the first article unfolded across the screen.

Search continues for rogue NTPD officer wanted on multiple felony crimes, including assault on a peace officer. Authorities say former officer Guillermo Benitez should be considered armed and extremely dangerous.

"Oh my God." Chance tried to reach for the emergency chamber release, his stomach sour, his fingers fumbling with the pull lever. "Benny... I gotta... find you..." He strained, his strength leaving him. With a moan of resignation, Chance lay back, unable to keep his fear and confusion at bay.

The chamber hummed, the vapors falling from the lid like misty golden rays of a false heaven, as Chance's mind and body drifted into the bottomless chasm of restless, drug-induced sleep.

CHAPTER THIRTY-ONE

Benny hit the emergency break bar on the alley door of Club Crave, flung it wide, and found himself face to face with a young NTPD patrolman.

"Hey!" the officer screamed, keying his mic. "Dispatch!"

Benny slammed into the smaller man with his shoulder, knocking him backwards over the low rail and interrupting his transmission. Carried forward by too much momentum, Benny hit the rail and toppled as well, flipping and falling the short distance. He smacked flat on his back in an oily puddle next to the dazed officer and rolled to his side on the wet concrete.

"*What did I miss?*" Mage asked.

"Dammit, Mage," Benny said through clenched teeth, rising to a knee. "Damn you."

The patrol officer, gaining his bearings, rolled onto his back and made it to a knee, his chest heaving. He drew his MVX pistol and leveled it at Benny.

"Stop! I'll shoot—"

Benny snatched the gun from the young officer's shaking hands and brought it back across the bridge of his nose with a crack. Body locked stiff, the fresh-faced rookie fell back. Benny grabbed him by the vest and lowered him down.

"Damn, kid," Benny said, scanning the alley for the young patrolman's backup. "Why'd you make me do that? Had to be a hero and get here first, didn't you?"

"Four zero five six two. Did you have traffic?" dispatch squawked from the radio hooked to the patrolman's vest.

"*I know you're pissed at me right now,*" Mage said, "*but you need to listen. More officers will enter the far side of the alley in about fifteen seconds. Get the kid and get out.*"

Benny checked the rookie's face. Satisfied that the poor guy would only suffer a broken nose and a ribbing from his fellow officers for letting the perp slip, Benny grabbed him under the arms and dragged him into a trash-littered alcove.

Seconds later, Benny watched as more NTPD officers, members of the warrant squad, rounded the corner and set up a perimeter on the club.

Droplets of mist hung in the air, falling in a tickling curtain of lace, giving the garishly lit Future Club district a soft and hazy glow. Benny looked from one end of the alley to the other. The warrant squad faced the club, eyeing the windows. If he moved from where he crouched alongside the unconscious patrolman, they would see him.

"Mage, I'm stuck," he whispered.

"*Hang on a second. I'm working on a diversion.*"

"Make it quick." Benny scanned the searching officers.

"*Can't rush genius.*"

The muscles of Benny's jaw flexed. He clutched the MVX pistol to his chest and waited, damaged nerves burning with pins and needles, eyes scanning the alley. Beneath him, the patrolman stirred with a groan.

"Come on, dammit," Benny grunted.

"*All right. I've put out a report of a mass casualty incident two blocks over. Active shooter at Club Dreadnought.*"

Benny heard echoes of gunfire. He shifted. "Is there an active shooter?"

"*Hell, no.*" Mage sounded pleased with himself. "*But they don't know that.*"

"I hear gunfire."

"*Isn't technology amazing?*" Mage chuckled.

The warrant squad exchanged glances with each other.

"That call was for all available units," one guy said. "We gotta go. It's two blocks over."

Another shook his head. "We're supposed to keep containment. This Benitez guy is a priority target."

A barrage of gunfire, followed by the screams of club goers filled the air.

One waved his arms. "Screw the warrant! People are dying! C'mon!"

The warrant squad dropped their perimeter, running toward the sound of gunfire, their feet slipping and splashing through neon-lit puddles.

In the alcove, the young patrolman stirred and moaned again. Benny dropped his head and released a breath. The rookie officer's eyes fluttered, a trickle of blood running from his nostril.

"*You should kill him,*" Mage said in Benny's ear. "*He'll report you.*"

"You're a cold son of a bitch, Mage," Benny said. "Poor kid's just doing his job—a damn desperate, thankless one at that." Benny patted the rookie patrolman's chest and pulled an extra MVX magazine off his carrier, which he shoved in a cargo pocket. "Take care, kid. Sorry about the nose."

"*You've gotta move,*" Mage said. "*Get your ass out of there.*"

Benny rose and took one last look to ensure the coast was clear, then ran down the alley, the MVX pistol clenched in his fist, his boots splashing in the colored puddles of the darkened alley.

"*Left at the next intersection, then straight, then left again. That'll be the fastest way out of the search grid.*"

Benny shook his head as he ran. "You and I have a lot to discuss, Mage. Like why the hell you want all the Enforcers dead and why you plan to release footage of NWC that'll tear Neo

Terminus apart?"

"It's all about principle, my friend," Mage said. "Nothing is more important than freedom of information. Nothing. When authority restricts information, people become slaves. The truth must come to light."

"You're going to get a friend of mine killed over principle." Benny labored to fill his lungs as he ran.

"You're worried about your old partner, the Enforcer? Have a little faith in me," Mage said. "Looks can be deceiving."

"You slippery little—"

Benny stopped dead in his tracks, a snap of blinding white light causing him to flinch and cover his eyes. He raised his hands, paralyzed by the brilliant glare.

"Benny, Benny, Benny," the familiar voice reached out from beyond the lights.

Benny wheeled in the opposite direction, only to stop again as a shadow stepped around the corner, blocking his exit.

"Look who it is, Kip," Deyvar Whaley said, his MVX trained on Benny, a menacing scowl beneath the curtain of dreads that hung down over his face. "This little bitch thought he'd just squirt out the back."

"No doubt," Kip Monaghan said, stepping forward of the blinding white lights of his unmarked VTOL. He raised the MVX in his hands. "I have to say, I like the new cyber look. But you should've stayed underground, Benny."

Benny half turned to hold both men in his peripheral. His eyes darted to his surroundings, adjusting to the light. Mist dangled in the air, thick as fog. Sullied brick walls on either side. No real cover. No way out.

"Drop the weapon," Kip said, raising his MVX, "we've got you dead to rights."

Benny clenched the patrolman's MVX in a white-knuckled grip, fury boiling within. "You dirty slag-eaters took everything from me. You ruined my life."

"*Benny, you fool, you're about to get yourself killed,*" Mage said. "*Surrender. I'll work something out.*"

"Drop the weapon. Now," Kip said.

"*Benny,*" Mage said. "*All of this will be for nothing if you—*"

Benny pulled his visor from his face, and crushed it in the grip of his cybernetic hand. He dropped the mangled frame, sparking against the sodden concrete.

"Don't do anything stupid," Deyvar said from off to the side.

Benny took a step to his right and watched as Kip registered the move. Neither of the men now had a shot without endangering the other.

"Tricky son of a bitch. Don't think it makes you safe," Kip said, flicking his head at Deyvar, now flanking out of the line of fire.

"We're going to put an end to this, right now," Benny said. A drop of water huffed from the end of his nose.

Distant sirens echoed off the rain-soaked streets. A fine mist continued to fall. It gathered and dripped from every surface, its smothering, gray-tinged haze causing the neon lights of the Future Club district to bleed color into the night. A lone rat scurried into a burrow of sodden trash. The air grew chill.

Flinging himself toward Deyvar, Benny hit the ground, sliding, the MVX bucking in his hands as he and Kip fired on each other.

"Kip, no!" Deyvar screamed as he tried to duck. One of Kip's rounds struck him in the side and sent him spinning into a row of trash bins.

Laying in a stable side position, Benny loosed a hail of gunfire on Kip, causing the narc to dive behind the cover of his matte black VTOL. Benny ejected the spent magazine and went for the reload in his cargo pocket as Deyvar, behind him, struggled to his feet. Benny fired two more rounds in Kip's direction, forcing the man to keep his head down.

"Jakk," Deyvar wheezed. He stumbled, clenching his side, blood seeping through pinched fingers. His eyes, lost in a sea of pain, searched the trash at his feet for the pistol he'd dropped.

Benny pointed his own MVX at Deyvar, who raised his free hand.

"I'm unarmed, man," he gasped, blood dripping from his lips.

"I know," Benny said.

The blast of the MVX slung the traitor narc's gray matter against the moldering brick wall.

A jolt of pain struck Benny in the back, knocking him into the trash pile. He pushed himself up with a groan, but another volley of rounds zinged off the brick overhead. Amidst the stinking piles of alley trash, Benny's free hand closed on Deyvar's MVX.

Rising again, he turned on Kip and a second round staggered him, high in the chest. With a scream, Benny charged forward, both pistols extended, their muzzles barking flames. Flanking the front of the VTOL, Benny took a third shot, center mass. He emptied his magazines at Kip, hiding behind the bumper of the vehicle. The narc screamed and fell, clutching at his wounded legs and torso.

Gasping, Benny leaned against the rear of the VTOL, the slides of both MVX pistols locked back, empty.

Kip rolled onto his back with a pained groan. His empty MVX shook in his hand as he retrieved a spare magazine and fumbled with it, finally inserting it into the mag well and dropping the slide.

Benny dropped his empty pistols to the ground. He bent forward as Kip extended the shaking pistol in his direction. In Benny's cybernetic fingers, the bones of Kip's gun hand crackled like brittle plastic. Kip gave a cry of anguish as Benny plucked the loaded MVX from the broken hand.

"Why don't you just die?" Kip quivered, mist soaking his face.

Benny winced and raised his soiled katana T-shirt ringed with bullet holes to show the pock-marked nano vest beneath.

"You... You..." Kip mumbled through blood-stained teeth, "you'll be marked for this. They'll never let you stop running."

Benny stepped over the wounded narc and pointed the MVX at Kip's face.

"This is for Muck," Benny said, his voice almost gentle.

The flash of the muzzle licked across the rain-slick walls of the alley, the report echoing and fading away in the high-pitched wail of approaching sirens.

No time to deliberate the path he'd chosen. His brothers were coming for him.

A chime signaled the recovery chamber's timer, and the lid separated with a hiss and hinged open. Chance sat up and tried to shake the fog from his mind, rubbing his face. He glanced out the long row of floor-to-ceiling windows at the early morning sky, which cast a murky gray half-light across the room. The drab scene did nothing for the sense of despair in his heart.

He quickly dressed in street clothes and headed for the door, stopping only to see that the morning coffee the auto-steward had poured for him was not coffee at all, but steaming hot water. No beans. He'd have to grab some on the way down, and put in an order for more Arabica. Exiting his apartment, he went straight to the elevators and selected the level for the Enforcer lounge.

Now that Chance knew Benny was in trouble, he had to find him. He had to do something. Damn the Conglomerate and their rules. He was a free man and if he wanted to go somewhere, he would go. *They can kiss my ass*, he thought.

The elevator came to a stop, and as the door slid back, Chance stood listening. Someone was already in the lounge. Rounding the corner, he saw Sam and Karissa. The conversation stopped as they both looked in his direction.

"Morning," Karissa said.

"Morning." Chance made straight for the coffee bar. "Sorry to interrupt."

"Oh, you're not interrupting anything," Karissa said. She glanced at Sam.

"I'll get my coffee and go," Chance said, pouring from the pot into a paper cup.

"Actually, we were hoping you'd talk with us," Sam said. "It's important."

"I don't think so," Chance said. "I've got a problem I need to resolve."

"Chance," Karissa said, approaching with Sam in tow, "we've got a problem, too. Talk with us for a sec."

"I'm not in the mood for drama," Chance said.

Karissa sized him up. "You okay? What's going on with you?"

"What's with the interview?" Chance cut his eyes at her.

Karissa raised her hands. "Just asking, Chance."

"Bro," Sam said, "you've got us all wrong. We're not doing anything unethical by taking these side jobs. We're trying..." He motioned for Karissa to start the coffee grinder.

She reached over and with a turn of the knob, the high-pitched whirr of grinding beans filled the room.

Sam leaned in toward Chance. "We're trying to locate something."

"Like what?" Chance said, not trying to keep his voice down.

"Look." Sam crossed his arms, leaning close to talk over the whine of the coffee grinder. "Something that could protect us. Call it insurance. Sometimes it means dealing with the criminal element in a way that allows us to find out what we want to know and get access to what we need."

Chance shook his head in frustration. "Insurance? For what, Sam?"

"It means we've got to look out for our own." Sam glanced up. "They're always listening. You'll have to trust me."

"Hey guys," Jessie called from the doorway, breathless.

Karissa turned off the grinder. "We're in the middle of something *important* here, Jessie." She flared her eyes at her partner.

"Yeah, well, everyone's just going to have to deal. We're being deployed," Jessie said, anticipation in his face.

Karissa shrugged. "You and I have our trial this afternoon."

"No," Jessie shook his head, "they've upgraded it. They're activating *all of us* this afternoon."

"At the same time?" Sam asked.

"That's right," Jessie said, still breathing as though he'd run here to tell everyone. "They're boosting it all over the net as a live special event, calling it the biggest thing to ever hit The Zone."

Chance, Sam, and Karissa looked at each other.

"I'm not sure I like the sound of that," Karissa said. "They never deploy everyone."

Sam nudged Chance. "Hey, I need you, man. You're my partner and I need to know we can put this misunderstanding behind us, that you've got my back when we get in there."

Chance only wanted to find Benny and make sure his friend was okay, but activating wasn't a request. Who knew what would happen if he refused, what they'd do to him—or his family? He'd have to play their game. Once he got through this, he'd try to find Benny and maybe together they'd find a way through this nightmare.

He swallowed and gave a resolute nod. "You know I've got your back, Sam, but you have to be straight with me from here on out."

Sam gave Chance a firm handshake. "You got it, partner."

CHAPTER THIRTY-TWO

Benny jerked awake, a sudden rush of panic: *They've found me.* His eyes searched back and forth, taking in the interior of Kip's unmarked Aeron VTOL. A gray tarp still covered the vehicle as it sat hidden amidst a fleet of broken down VTOLs in one of Volkan Heights' many junk yards. Kip and Deyvar's bodies had likely been found by now, dumped in that back alley with the rest of the trash. *Slag-eaters. It's everything they deserve.*

He glanced at the dashboard clock: 10:00 a.m. Benny hadn't meant to fall asleep, but the parasympathetic backlash of his nervous system following the adrenaline dump didn't give him much choice. A breath whistled across his lips as he lay back with a grimace of pain. He'd broken something. Felt like a rib. The pungent funk in the vehicle reminded him he direly needed a full body cleansing.

"Two Forty to Zero Six Nine—any sign of that stolen unmarked in your sector?" the radio squawked. Benny lowered the volume.

"That's a big negative, Two Forty. No sign yet."

"Two Forty to Dispatch, did we get a lock on the vehicle?"

"Negative. He appears to have disabled the GPS," dispatch responded. "All units be advised, both officers have been pronounced DOS with a third assaulted. Suspect is a Guillermo Benitez, former NTPD officer. He may have shaved his head, has a cybernetic appendage, and is now using the alias Enrique Galvatorez. Per Chief Langulen, all other non-priority duties are suspended until the perpetrator is contained and subdued."

Benny turned the volume to an almost inaudible low. He leaned back against the headrest, breathing through the rising feeling of nausea at killing his own—no, not killing—executing.

What does that make me? A murderer? Was it murder if they'd persecuted him, if he'd only done it to stay alive?

Benny grit his teeth. The pain in his ribs mixed with the burn of the nerve damage up his opposite side. He needed some relief so he could think. On the inside of his cybernetic forearm, the display of the small screen lit up with three icons. *Pain, Velocity, Frenzy.* Benny pressed the pad of his index finger down on the icon labeled *Pain* and held it. *But what in the hell are those other two?* The arm hissed, and a cooling wash descended from his scalp to the soles of his feet. Benny's eyes rolled back, a gasp escaping his lips.

He gazed down at the arm. A touch more wouldn't hurt. The pain was serious. His finger hovered over the button, but he clenched his fist. *No*, he thought, *I've got to be clearheaded for what comes next.*

Mage wouldn't be happy that his walking investment had gone dark. Maybe he'd shut Benny's arm down, or kill him with some reserve of poison hidden in the appendage. Try as he might, though, Benny couldn't reason Mage would kill him. The guy had done a lot for him, even if Benny remained unsure where the man's true motives lay.

Mage had kept vital information from Benny about New West City, as well as the plot to wipe out the Enforcers. Benny would never have gone to Big Roach if he'd known—the exact reason Mage hadn't told him.

Chance was walking into a trap. He and the other Enforcers were about to get murdered with something Mage created and Benny delivered. *How damn ironic.*

Benny sat forward, an idea forming in his mind. He'd created this mess, but maybe he could fix it. Maybe he could get a message to Chance and warn him of the trap. That, at least, would be something.

Benny pulled up the Neo Terminus directory database on the VTOL's holo-screen. Searching the listings, he found no sign of Chance's name—but of course there wouldn't be. He was an Enforcer. They couldn't have fans harassing him.

Benny cleared the search bar and input the name Hannah Griffin. An address in Sky Rise popped up with no direct contact number. Hope rose inside him like a flame.

"That's it. If I go to Hannah, I can tell her Chance is in trouble. She'll know how to get in touch with him," Benny said, rubbing his chin. "The issue is getting there."

NTPD had no jurisdiction in Sky Rise or Silver City. The Glom security barrier at the northern wall between Water Town and Sky Rise would lock onto and disable any vehicles, police or otherwise, that tried to cross without clearance. He needed to ditch the narc's unmarked for something with barrier clearance. If he could get over there, he could lie low in Sky Rise for a spell. The NTPD couldn't touch him, and as long as he stayed off The Glom security troopers' radar, he'd have time to figure out what to do next.

A low whine interrupted his thoughts. Thrusters fired above. Benny swiveled in the seat, peeking out from beneath the tarp: an NTPD patrol, checking cars in the junkyard.

"If only you guys weren't so damn good at your job," Benny said.

A zipping sound filled the air as two armored patrol officers cabled down from their VTOL, MVX pistols sweeping left and right. Covering down, they navigated through the junk yard as one unit, each protecting the other's six. Benny recognized them as Marks and Holder, two hard-chargers from the street crime suppression unit.

"The tarp." Marks pointed. "Check that one."

"I got it," Holder said.

"Here we go," Benny grunted, his hands poised at ten and two on the VTOL's ridged steering wheel. "Good luck, boys."

Engaging the thrusters, Benny pulled back hard on the wheel, and the bullet-riddled vehicle lurched to life, blasting Marks and Holder with a storm of swirling dust. They fell in different directions as the unmarked VTOL rose into the sky above the run-down factories of Volkan Heights. The old gray tarp fluttered like a winged beast too old to soar; it spun, catching the wind in awkward circles as it fell. Two rounds pinged off the undercarriage of the VTOL.

"Too little too late, fellas—" Benny laughed, the words dying in his throat as several NTPD beat cars shot in his direction, emergency lights strobing—a fast response to Marks and Holder's inevitable call for assistance.

"Damn." Benny shoved the wheel forward.

The nose of the unmarked VTOL dove, dropping through the air like a stone. Leveling the thrusters out, Benny swerved between the housing structures and elevated platforms with reckless fervor, swooping low over one of the pedestrian walkways. The patrol vehicles dropped in behind him, thrusters shrieking in pursuit. Clothing wires stretched between tenant buildings, adorned with garments, snapped across Benny's windshield, and a frilly pink brazier clung to the side mirror. Below, people on the street screamed and shielded their heads as the chase rocketed past, just feet overhead.

Benny pulled up on the air brakes, the flaps flicking opening as expected. The back end of the unmarked swung around ninety degrees as he hit the next street. He dropped the flaps and fired the thrusters again. Right on his six, the NTPD officers weren't playing games. Benny knew all too well the advanced VTOL training the men and women of the hover division received, and it wasn't to Benny's advantage.

One of the sleek gray pursuit VTOLs, with NTPD stenciled in large black letters down the side, made its move. Accelerating, it hit his bumper with a pit maneuver, jolting his back end to the outside. Benny swore, over corrected, and struggled to regain control. Another bumped him from the opposite side. They'd boxed him in.

Benny pulled back, and a string of warning lights flashed across the display. He screamed as he raced up toward the underside of a crowded high-speed hover lane. Blasting straight through the center of the lane, Benny jerked the wheel left and right in a desperate attempt not to kill any civilian flyers. He grimaced as the unmarked glanced off the side of a passing van, wide-eyed children plastered to the windows. Behind him, a patrol vehicle hit its air brakes and slammed sideways into a series of morning commuters.

"One down," Benny said as he leveled out and watched the other two fall in behind him, sirens blaring.

A band of morning sunlight cut through the oppressive cloud cover, filling the cab of Benny's VTOL with warm light. Rain peppered his windshield in fat drops that beaded and streaked past, catching the golden rays as they went, the strange collision of sun and rain a mirror of the opposing forces at war within him.

High enough to see clear across the city, Benny looked to the horizon. There, the hover station, referred to as the Carrier, chugged in his direction from above the Havana Straits sector. A floating precinct, the hover division's units deployed directly from this massive station. Once it arrived, they'd overtake him, and the longer this went on, the higher the likelihood that someone innocent got hurt. He had to end this *now*.

Benny dropped the nose again, angling the unmarked VTOL, now gushing black smoke, toward Water Town and the northern barrier. As he kept the throttle pegged open, two rounds zinged off the rear bumper as muzzle flashes erupted from the pursuit vehicles behind him.

Benny dropped into one of the lanes of traffic—nestled among the other commuters, he sped toward the barrier. The gunfire stopped, the officers trained to avoid hitting civilians with stray fire. Horns blared as Benny's VTOL picked up speed, muscling the other vehicles out of the lane. The pursuit held steady, weaving through traffic behind him.

"You want to shut me down, but you can't." Benny hocked a coarse laugh, knowing full well NTPD patrol vehicles didn't possess the ability to drive-stop their own the way they could all the other vehicles out there. But he knew who did.

Rising out of the lane, Benny flew higher than regulation permitted, soaring upward, another row of lights flickering across the dash. The most prominent read *Maximum VTOL Altitude Exceeded.*

The drive core stuttered, the thrusters faltering.

"Come on," Benny shouted, shaking the wheel.

Ahead, the northern barrier loomed. He was well above the wall, but the invisible energy field extended far higher than he could fly. Violation of the barrier without proper Conglomerate-issued clearance resulted in immediate VTOL failure.

Benny sent the unmarked VTOL screaming forward, the remaining two NTPD units in hot pursuit. Waiting until the last possible second, Benny jerked the wheel hard to the left and locked his air brakes open. The unmarked VTOL swung around with violent centripetal force, causing Benny to groan as he clung to the steering wheel. The rear end of his vehicle arced through the field, and the lights across the dash winked out.

"That's it, baby," Benny said as the auto emergency land function took over, the vehicle now out of his control. "Set me down."

Swiveling in his seat, he watched as the NTPD units, following too close to react, hit their brakes too late and slid sideways through the energy barrier over the far side of the wall, their strobing emergency lights going dark.

His VTOL lowered on the far east end of Water Town, alone, but the frustrated officers in the pursuit vehicles would be detained and interrogated by Glom security troopers on the other side of the barrier.

Benny breathed in through his nose and took his hands off the wheel, allowing the auto land function to complete. With a whine, the VTOL touched down on a low open roof. Benny threw the wing door up and exited, searching the sky for other units. He coughed, waving away the black smoke billowing from the unmarked unit's damaged drive core. It wouldn't be long until the Carrier, and other pursuit units located him.

Shutting the wing door, Benny hit the rickety, rust-covered fire escape and headed for the street. He needed another ride, one that could get him through the barrier into Sky Rise.

Chance didn't have much time.

The expensive Fiducci Express bag, stuffed with a purified water bottle and a fresh change of clothes, hit the floor of the apartment's entranceway and piled into a heap. Hannah's feet rooted to the spot. She watched in stunned silence as the newsfeed ticker scrolled across the bottom lip of her visor.

Rogue cop, Benitez, kills two police and injures a third in wild south city manhunt. Suspect still at large, considered armed and extremely dangerous.

A small, strangled sound emerged from Hannah's throat. "Oh, Benny, no..." She placed a hand on her chest. "Enlarge news."

Hannah searched for Benny's name, but it was gone in a sea of revolving reports. She watched as images of thousands of people fighting in the streets filled the screen.

"In other news, food riots broke out across the south of the city this morning due to shortages. Four rioters were killed in the ensuing clash with police. As tensions grow, Chief Langulen of the NTPD expressed a no-tolerance policy today and vowed to crack down on the anarchist elements perpetrating these uprisings..."

"Hi, Mrs. Griffin," the peppy, doe-eyed babysitter said, emerging from the back room with a swaddled Andrew in her arms. "How was your voltage cycle class?"

Hannah blinked and shook her head. "Uhm, it was fine, Dorine, thanks."

"Is everything okay, Mrs. Griffin?" Dorine asked with a syrupy whine, a frozen look of happiness plastered on her doll-like face.

"Ah." Hannah removed the visor from her face. "No, I mean, yes." She composed herself, extending her arms. "Everything's fine, Dorine. Andrew okay for you?"

Dorine handed over Andrew. "A little fussy, but I guess that's to be expected considering his issues—" Dorine stopped short beneath Hannah's withering gaze. "I meant, I'm sorry, I didn't mean to..."

"Forget about it," Hannah said. When Dorine didn't move, she added, "I transferred your fee. You can go now."

"Of course. Thank you, ma'am." Dorine ducked her head as she exited with all haste through the open apartment door. The frosted glass slid shut with a whisper behind her.

"The nerve..." Hannah said, giving Andrew a kiss and laying him down in his bassinet by the sofa.

She eyed the visor sitting on the countertop. "Project news feed."

The image on her visor flickered. An overhead projector dropped from the ceiling and cast the image into the air in ultra-high definition. The news feed reloaded. Hannah searched the headlines but couldn't find the article she'd just seen. Something bad was going on with Benny, the reason they hadn't been able to reach him.

"Search news for..." Her voice trailed off as an advertisement took over the big screen.

"Are you ready, Neo Terminus?" the pompadour announcer said, images of all the Enforcers fighting in The Zone filling the screen. "Don't miss tonight's exclusive special event. A show so unbelievable it can only be described as the most daring and dangerous trial ever devised in the history of The Zone. A trial in which Enforcer is pitted against Enforcer in a battle royale!"

Hannah folded her arms, squinting past a ray of afternoon sun to see the projected images of gladiatorial combat.

"Who could prevail against such odds?" the announcer said with a flourish, ridiculous hair jiggling. "Will it be the ruthless duo of Sanction and Escalation?"

Hannah eyed the tough, scarred Enforcers in full battle armor standing back to back.

"Or maybe you favor the combination of style and strength only found in Pursuit and Takedown?"

A powerful, dark-skinned woman gave a high five to a dark-haired man with chiseled good looks.

"Or maybe your money will ride on the undeniably tough Zone veteran, Warrant, and his new partner, the heroic fan-favorite—Justice?"

Hannah touched her fingers to her mouth as Sam offered the crowd a thumbs up and Chance, gushing his adorable boyish charm, held his fist in the air.

"Which of these incredible warriors has what it takes to survive and to prove themselves the undisputed champion of The Zone?"

"Wait, what's going on?" Hannah whispered. "They're going to fight each other?" She felt a stab of anxiety. "Why? For money?"

The sharp, blinding beam of direct sunlight felt like a laser directed at the corner of her eye. Her annoyance spilled over as she squinted to see the details on the screen.

"Rotate the projection ninety degrees to the right," Hannah said with a swear.

A quick zipping sound followed, the projector swiveling at a right angle away from the sunlit windows. She never watched projections in this direction because of the distracting golden framed painting on the far wall, but the damn sun…

A different glint of light caught her eye. Only a momentary flash, the reflection of a beam cast on glass. Her eyes narrowed, the spectacle of the Enforcers ad now lost on her. She took a step forward, straining to see beyond the projected image.

"Stop all media," she said.

The projector flicked off. Hannah blinked again. With slow, deliberate steps, she walked toward the painting, her eyes roving across the canvas's impressionistic surface.

You're being stupid, Hannah.

Following the edge of the frame with her eyes, she stopped. A tiny black chip poked out of the edge of the frame's ornate knurling, smooth and ovular, the size of a trimmed fingernail. Hannah took another step closer, reaching up to the frame, her fingers closed on the wafer-thin oval disk, the back sticky with adhesive, the front smooth and clear, like a little black mirror… or a camera lens.

Dread descended on her, her heart free-falling through the floor of her stomach.

"What the hell is this?" she said, but she knew the answer. Her index finger touched the long side of the wafer to a tiny, raised ridge that seemed to flex. She clicked it. Nothing. Hannah pressed and held the button down. After a few seconds, it made a soft *ding*, and an internal light flashed three times, then dimmed. In response, a series of identical *dings* sounded throughout the spacious apartment. Hannah felt her terror deepen as a handful of other lights scattered around the apartment blinked three times and dimmed.

"What the *hell!*" Hannah screamed, her eyes wild. The *huff huff* of the startled baby's cries filled her ears as Hannah ran into the kitchen and climbed onto the counter, where she'd seen the light flash. As she stood, she saw another tiny black wafer hidden in the overhead lighting fixture. She pulled it free, the adhesive sticking to her thumb. Clutching the devices in her clammy hands, she powered the first one on again. The soft chime followed as it synched with the other hidden cameras, all of them chiming throughout the apartment. Her skin burned hot, flush with panic.

They're everywhere, and they're watching me.

CHAPTER THIRTY-THREE

In the concrete bowels of the Unified Conglomerate Headquarters, the war room was bloated with silence and anticipation as each Enforcer worked at their station, prepping their load outs and murmuring with their partners. Typically unfazed by anything, Rip and Ash had an unusually solemn air about them as they double-checked their gear.

Chance glanced up from the digital holo-display listing his current load out, specs, and an exhaustive list of tactical options to select from. For a moment, his and Sam's eyes connected. His mentor offered a smirk, but it wasn't enough to conceal the concern etched across his weathered face. Chance swiveled in his seat to see the same seriousness worn by both Karissa and Jessie. None of them had said anything about tonight's event, but they'd seen the ads like everyone else. By all appearances, Kess and the Founders planned to pit the Enforcers against one other—a proposition once considered unconscionable.

Rip closed his screen out and leaned back, the attitude returning. "I know why you guys are nervous. Don't worry, we won't kill *all* of you."

"Nobody's killing anyone," Sam said. "If The Glom wants a friendly competition, we can do that and make a show of it. That's all."

"Not what it looked like to me," Rip said.

Chance was about to reply when a projection of Gabriel Kess

filled the front of the room.

"Enforcers. Are we ready?"

All the Enforcers, including Rip, stood to accept their mission brief.

"As I'm sure you've all seen, today's trial isn't just another trip into The Zone. The founders have requested a special display from all of you: a contest of champions. You will work in your assigned teams for this trial."

Unmoving, the Enforcers stood listening to the director's words.

"The mission parameters are as follows. Your primary aim will be to seek out and capture The Zone's most notorious gang leader, Rico, for a bounty of two million T's."

The Karissa gasped and shot a glance at Jessie. Ash and Rip whispered to one another.

"If you can't take him alive, a smaller bounty of five hundred thousand T's will be paid for claiming his head. As you well know, Rico and his Death Squad have killed more people, including Enforcers, than any other single gang in The Zone's history. Our intel suggests Rico may be in possession of an Enforcer-killing weapon. We have not verified this or determined what it might mean, so stay frosty."

Chance eyed the other Enforcers, searching for any tell, any break in composure that might show involvement with Rico. Their faces betrayed nothing.

"Two million." Sam whistled and looked sideways at Chance.

"As usual, you will pick up extra T's for any scalps you collect. There's just one catch, one I'm sure you all are aware of by now." Kess paused for effect. "It's a race. We will drop you ten miles out. Once you hit the ground, the race is on. Whoever reaches Rico first and extracts him clear from his gang will be crowned the champions of The Zone."

Chance rubbed his head, sobered by the realization. *This is it:*

The trial to best all trials.

Kess clasped his hands, the practiced delivery as much a part of the show as everything else. "Lethal force against your fellow Enforcers is not suggested."

"See." Sam crossed his arms.

"That doesn't mean it's off the table," Kess added.

"Are you kidding me?" Sam turned, outraged.

Rip covered a sinister laugh.

"You want us to kill each other?" Karissa asked.

"Of course not. That would represent a significant loss for the Conglomerate, but the spectacle takes precedent over all else. The stakes have to be real, and," Kess paused, "well, I guess it depends on how much you want to win."

"This sputz just got serious," Jessie said.

"There's more," Kess continued.

"What more could you possibly add?" Sam said.

"An unfortunate caveat. The losing teams will have their assets repossessed, medical coverage dropped, and Sky Rise apartments reclaimed. Assuming you survive your loss, your tenure as an Enforcer will be over. You will be indentured to the Conglomerate for your debts, and your family members will be relocated to the other side of town with you."

Chance couldn't process the director's words. *My family back in the slums. No more medical coverage for Andrew*, he thought. *That can't happen.*

"Kess, this is outrageous," Sam shouted. "It's... It's completely unethical."

"This is bullshit," Karissa said.

"You can't do this to us. Not after all we've invested here." Jessie jabbed a finger into his palm.

Kess, unblinking and unfazed, displayed no emotion.

"A little steep, isn't it, Kess?" Ash narrowed his eyes, a furious scowl on his scarred face.

"Director Kess." Chance tried to keep his tone soft. "I don't understand this—"

Kess clasped his hands. "I'm sorry, everyone, but we all have our orders."

"And if we don't play your game? If we refuse to compete?" Sam said.

"Your forfeiture will be summarily counted as a loss," Kess said. "Don't you all at least want to try your luck?"

Rip knocked Ash's shoulder with his knuckles. "You got that right."

The rest of the Enforcers remained shocked, anger following on the heels of their surprise.

"Stage your load outs. You'll deploy from the flight deck in fifteen minutes. That is all. May the best team prevail." The image winked out.

"That devious son of a bitch!" Sam grabbed an image stabilizer off his desk and threw it across the room.

The device clattered across the concrete floor. A numbing silence descended on the group. Chance rubbed his jaw. Karissa and Jessie looked at each other, stunned. Ash and Rip turned and continued working, a smugness crossing Rip's face.

"What are you so pleased about?" Sam jabbed a finger in Rip's direction.

Rip leered. "It's simple. I don't plan on losing, old man."

A coldness, pale like death, covered Sam's features. He turned to Chance. "We're on our own, Chance. Get your load out right and your game face on."

"Roger that," Chance said, breathing through the growing tightness in his chest. Jessie's face dropped. Karissa forced a smile for Chance and gave him a thumbs up, mouthing the words *good luck.*

Chance turned his holo-display, hovering, showing his gear set up. Had his reporting to Kess caused this? The vice-like clamp on his chest doubled.

His visor trilled, *Hannah*. Chance opened the call.

"I can't talk right now, baby," he said, listening to her quiet sobs through a wash of static. He realized with dismay that the concrete was affecting the signal.

"Hannah?"

"Can't stay here… Chance," she whimpered through the static.

"What's going on?"

"They're watching us… Cameras in the apartment… I told you."

Sam made the motion for him to hurry up. Chance cleared his throat.

"Hannah, I don't know what you're talking about."

"Yes, you do. They're everywhere… Someone's been watching me… There's one in the slagging shower, Chance!"

"Okay, okay," Chance said, "go somewhere else for a while, and I'll figure it out when I get clear."

"Get clear? You can't go in. This is serious," she sobbed. "I need you."

"I know, honey, but I don't have a choice. I have to go." He realized he might never talk to her again, might never hold his son in his arms one last time, the thought ice cold. "I love you, Hannah. We'll get it figured out, okay? Be strong for me."

"Please, Chance, I have a bad feeling about this one. Don't do it—"

Chance cut the call and removed his visor. He swallowed back his fear and mounting anxiety. Maybe she'd be okay when he was gone. Or maybe there was no way out for any of them.

Benny touched at the dark circles under his eyes, hollow black pits that seemed to swallow the features of his face. The figure in the clouded glass of the dirty public restroom stared back, now only the ghost of a man who'd once held so much promise. Mage called him Specter. He hated to admit the name now fit.

The burn of the nerve damage had intensified over the last few hours, combined with minor injuries and an overload of stress. The last dose of painkiller hadn't delivered the same effect it once did. He needed another. Benny raised his cybernetic arm and checked the display on his inner forearm, the cool blue button marked *Pain*, so appealing it made him ache.

"Deal with it, Benny." He spat and gripped the filthy sink, searching the hollow eyes in the occluded mirror for confidence in his words. "Stop acting like a damn addict. Life is pain. Get used to it."

He waved his cybernetic arm over the sensor at the faucet.

Authorize water distribution for one Terminus coin? The message hovered in the air before him.

"Yes," Benny grunted and caught the questionably filtered water in his palm, splashing it on his face. He rubbed his eyes. They didn't look any better. Another message flashed in red above the sink.

Enrique Galvitorez, AKA Guillermo Benitez. You are wanted by the Neo Terminus Police Department. Your location has been reported.

Benny swore. *Some good that damn fake ID did,* he thought. He hurried from the bathroom, water still dripping from his face. At the entrance, he collided with a visor-clad punker sporting tall, spiked blue hair and dangling chains.

"Watch it, junkie," the punker said, shoving Benny's chest.

Before he knew what happened, Benny grabbed the punker by the face, shoved him back, and thrust him up the dingy tile wall, the pistons in his cybernetic arm wheezing. The punker tried to scream, the muffled cries lost in the dimenium metal joints of the palm. The man's legs thrashed as the metal fingers clutched, digging at his face.

Benny struggled against the tidal wave of rage breaking over him. Maiming this punk would be too easy.

He gasped. The hand opened, and the man fell. Benny swallowed his shame and tried to hide the fear on his face. *I almost killed that stupid punk. Over what? A simple insult?*

The stunned punker slid to the floor, holding his face, his terror worn like a mask.

Benny turned away and ducked from the Water Town public restroom into the stream of meandering pedestrians. "Get a hold of yourself, damn you. You're better than that."

Everywhere, people congregated at bars and food stalls, holo-projections of the upcoming Zone trial on every screen in sight. T's changed from one account to another as bets circulated, and everyone spoke in excited whispers, touting the reasons their favorite Enforcer would win.

They were all wrong. In hours, all the Enforcers would be dead, and it was Benny's doing. He felt his gorge rise, the sour taste of bile in his throat.

He watched as a smiling Chance, decked out in battle armor, waved to the cameras, and loaded into a transport VTOL alongside his new partner. *How easily I've been forgotten*, Benny thought, instantly cursing his own selfishness. *Chance just wanted a better life for his family, and now I've marked him for death. I have to warn him.*

As he walked north, his eyes flicked back and forth, searching the lane. He needed a ride, but not any ride. He needed something with clearance through the barrier, a VTOL taxi or car service—but where would he find one around here? No one had the money or clearance for that in Water Town.

A meat-delivery barge cruised overhead and lowered to dock

on the back side of the market. An idea jumped into Benny's head: the barge came from The Glom-controlled Hayseed agricultural sector—but they weren't going to just give him a ride. Protected by troopers and enclosed within an electrified barrier, the loading dock wasn't open to the public. He'd have to get creative if he wanted in.

He turned into an adjoining alley and walked to the end, his neck and face burning, his ribs and chest still aching from the rounds he'd taken to the nano vest. He approached the corner and peeked around the edge as market workers unloaded the slabs of horse and slag dog under the strict watch of two Glom security troopers, battle rifles at the ready.

Slinking forward as quietly as a man of Benny's size could, he stacked a series of boxes and climbed. Grabbing the top wire, his cybernetic arm crackled as it absorbed the electricity. He dropped over the far side of the electrical fence and into the loading area. Moving quick, he approached the front of the barge, the troopers preoccupied with the unloading process at the rear.

The barge's pilot watched him through the front windshield, stupefied.

"Hey, who are you?" a worker called out, pointing at Benny.

Benny intercepted the closest trooper, grabbing him by the face and twisting him around. His cybernetic hand closed over the battle rifle, raising it at the opposite trooper. For a surreal moment, the men screamed at each other, each trooper telling the other not to shoot. Benny's finger closed over the trigger, and it cracked, blowing a large hole in the armor of the opposite man. As he fell, he fired, finger spasticly jerking against the trigger. Two rounds struck the armor plate of the man pinned in front of Benny as he held him close, a human shield. Others zipped past. The small crowd of gawking dock workers fragmented. Some ran for cover, others clutching at flesh wounds caused by the stray bullets.

Benny felt the man sag in his arms and knew he, like his

counterpart, had taken a mortal hit. For an instant, he acknowledged his mounting shame. *How many people am I willing to kill?* he thought. *How many bodies will I stack to save myself and my own?* He let the man fall and pulled the battle rifle from his hands. Around him, the dock workers cowered, hiding behind pallets and crates, whatever they could find.

Still belted in, the barge's pilot shook with terror as Benny trained the battle rifle on him.

"Draw that pistol you keep under your seat," Benny said, "and I'll shoot your brains out."

The pilot managed a nod.

"Close the rear lift gate."

The pilot hit a few switches, and the gate raised, artificial lights illuminating the stacked coolers. The smell of old meat, sour from over exposure, filled Benny's nose.

"You're going to fly me into the Sky Rise district." Benny pushed the warm muzzle of the rifle beneath the pilot's ear. "Can you do that?"

"I'm n... not allowed t... to—" the man stuttered, turning silent when Benny pressed harder with the muzzle.

"Let me phrase it this way," Benny said. "Do you want to fly me? Or should I shoot you, put you in one of those coolers with the other meat, and fly myself?"

"I'll do it, sir."

"Good man," Benny said, holding one of the supports and resting the rifle muzzle on the pilot's collar bone.

The jittery pilot flicked a few switches, and the barge jolted into the sky. Thrusting forward, cruising at a moderate pace, they sailed with ease over the wall, through The Glom's invisible barrier. The barge rose ever higher, entering the heights of Sky Rise air space. Benny's stoic visage cracked as a sense of relief poured over him.

He was in.

Inside his command center, hidden in the bowels of the decrepit Neo Terminus sewer system, Magellan Dovorov watched the internal camera feed of Hayseed Transport Barge 06274. There onscreen, his investment stood behind the pilot, with a rifle trained on the man as the barge cruised between the towering structures of Sky Rise.

Mage checked the schedule. It would be a while until Hayseed control realized the barge was off course and not en route back to the packing facility. By the time they noticed, Benny would be gone. That wouldn't stop the hammer from falling on him once Glom security realized Sky Rise had an intruder wanted for felony crimes in the south of the city.

"Stupid," Mage said, "ignorant fool. Working this hard to get yourself killed."

He'd underestimated how desperate Benny was; he knew that now. He knew the remarkable power friends and family could hold over a person. Still, Benny hadn't been stupid enough to go straight into The Zone after his Enforcer friend. If Mage had to guess, he'd try and find Chance's wife. Maybe to give her a message or warn her of what he now knew.

Mage shook his head. Part of him knew he shouldn't have kept the truth from Benny. He knew how it would seem to him; Benny's unwitting delivery of a device capable of killing his best friend. Pure treachery. Except that wasn't the true purpose of the nano disruptor. Mage spent far too much time perfecting the thing to be ignorant about what it was for, a purpose linked with his own: disrupting the status quo. It was the whole reason he'd taken Rico's job.

Well, that and the enormous payout.

Mage took one last look at the barge cockpit, analyzing the

projection screen and the look of anxiety on his friend's face. Mage caught himself at the thought, scoffed, and shook his head.

Friends, pah, he thought. He pulled on the beads in his goatee.

The idea was so foreign. He was unaccustomed to the concept of having someone to ally with, even to the point of risking life and limb, as Benny was right now. Mage frowned at the thought. *Friendship is a concept better suited for children.*

Still, he had to admit he'd taken a liking to the cynical former cop, and his gruff sense of humor, if only enough to keep the man from ending up dead. Maybe he could still help, show Benny he wasn't an enemy.

Mage turned from the view of the barge to assess the array of other screens laid out in front of him, a grid of moving pictures from all over the whole of Neo Terminus. Ironic, here in the stinking safety of the sewers, a place no sane person would make their home, Mage had done just that and now had command control of the entire city, watching and manipulating as he saw fit. Like a god.

Only gods don't die.

He frowned, plucked an amber capsule from the small flip-top container on the desk, and examined it before popping it into his mouth and swallowing it down.

Hellfire, he thought. Time was running out. It was time for humanity to sink or swim, unshackled by barriers and social division, and the grotesque spectacle of The Zone. Steeped in addiction, the people, so enamored with the spectacle of it all, never noticed the shackles on their hands and feet. Maybe they didn't care anymore. At the end of the Age of Information, The Glom convinced everyone they'd rescued humanity from the brink. In reality, the survivors of the old world were subjected to a degree of slavery and oppression not seen on the planet in hundreds of years. The Glom was crafty, though, leading the people of Neo Terminus to believe the Conglomerate was a savior instead of a self-serving regime run by the corporate elite, squeezing humanity amidst a global apocalypse.

Mage was about to give them all a wake-up call.

"*Mage.*" The nasal voice in his ear stopped him.

"Signus. Is it done?" Mage asked.

An image flickered and appeared on his screen. The hawk-nosed face of his operative starred back.

"*It's done. The last broadcast tower at the requested coordinates is up and operational. That's twenty-eight, as requested.*"

"I shall reward your diligence."

"*Mage.*" Signus stopped, glanced over his shoulder, and lowered his voice. "*There's a sense of tension out here. Glom security troopers have been hitting hard—anything broadcasting a free signal onto the net. They're killing the signal and leaving bodies in their wake. You know you'll be Public Enemy Number One as soon as the message goes live.*"

"Good thing I transferred your usual fee in full ahead of time," Mage said.

"*You ready for that sort of heat?*"

"They'll have to hack through multiple repeaters and ghost broadcast hubs to find me. By then, it will be too late. Only the freedom of information matters, the ability for us all to choose our own destiny."

"*Will it work? Your plan?*"

"We will all find out soon enough," Mage said. "I have one last task for you if you will humor me."

"*I owe you much for the release of my family, Mage. You know that.*"

"A favor for a favor, then?" Mage asked.

"*Name your task, and it will be done.*"

"Do you still have the unmarked transport with the cloned Sky Rise sector identification?"

"*I do.*"

"Good." Mage rubbed his hands together. "There's a large-framed man, Hispanic, shaved head, sporting a cybernetically enhanced arm. He's currently on the north side of town. I'll send his active track location to you. Take a few men and recover him for me. Provide any assistance you can and tell him I sent you."

"Just getting into Sky Rise is an arduous task, Mage..."

"This man represents a significant investment to me. Can you do it or not, Signus?"

Signus seemed to consider the job for a moment before answering. *"I can. I'll need you to provide interference."*

"I can do that. Anything else?"

"No. That should cover it."

"Good. Do this, and your debt to me is repaid. When you're done, I'd suggest lying low for a while. I'll come to you." With a flick of his wrist, Mage terminated the call.

He checked the secure data stream upload he'd received from Benny and found it rendered and ready to deliver. But having the information was only the first step. He needed to control the access. He needed to break the signal. Hijacking the Conglomerate's network wouldn't be easy, but it could be done, maybe even long-term.

Jabbing at a holographic keyboard, Mage played back the loop that would accompany the footage from New West City. It was the catalyst. A proverbial ice bucket of water in the face. When the people's eyes opened, they would see the chains that held them and know anarchy was the only way forward.

The time for revolution had come.

CHAPTER THIRTY-FOUR

Soaring low over the urban wasteland, the Enforcers' gloss black VTOLs maintained pace with each other as they cruised toward the southern sector of The Zone. Shattered old-world skyscrapers, hollowed out by fire and the constant beating of the elements, stood stark against the horizon. Beyond, the fiery orange blaze of a late afternoon sun cast lengthening shadows across a city of ghosts. Weeds choked the rubble-filled streets and pushed through the craggy concrete, and ivy hung like loose garments from the broken structures, leafy arms tossed in a restless wind. A slag dog, thin as death, scampered into the dark of an occluded lane. The south, home to Rico and his Death Squad, was a gangland stronghold, a deathtrap. Other gangs avoided it like the plague, and Enforcers often conducted their trials elsewhere.

Chance did another check of his armor and gear, the Peacemaker snug on his hip. A bandoleer of grenades clacked lightly against his armor. He leaned from the open side of his VTOL to check the others cruising alongside. Karissa stood in her doorway, suited up in her signature deep purple over black, with a gold Spartan chevron across the upper torso. Jessie crouched beside her, his armor imbued with white gloss and a silver lightning bolt jutting from his right shoulder to his left hip. Ash and Rip's transport nosed ahead on the outside.

"Chance, we're on," Sam said with a nudge of his elbow.

A sleek black Glom drone rose beside them, its ultra-high-definition camera swiveling in their direction. Sam gave a thumbs up, and Chance threw up a *Rock On*, index and pinky fingers extended. After a moment, the drone cruised over to capture Karissa and Jessie's pregame style.

Chance sobered. "I don't like this, Sam. Pitting us against each other for sport."

"It's just an elaborate game," Sam said. "Karissa and Jessie won't kill us. We'll offer them the same courtesy."

"But Rip? Ash?"

Sam shook his head. "Rip is an asshole, and Ash a hard case, but I refuse to believe either of them wants our deaths on their conscience."

"Assuming either has one," Chance said.

"Stay in your lane and focus on the mission," Sam said, extending his fist, "And when we win, we'll remember our friends."

Chance clacked his armored knuckles against Sam's.

The VTOL pivoted, turning in place over the landing zone.

"*Dropping your Grinder on the LZ,*" the pilot said over their radio comms. "*You're good to go on the signal.*"

Their turbo-charged, armored all-terrain buggy, or *Grinder*, disconnected from beneath the VTOL and bounced to a stop amidst the swirling dust of the LZ. In its open-topped hatchback, a massive belt-fed grenade launcher swiveled on its base.

Up ahead, one of the drones hovered thirty feet off the ground, projecting a large holo-board: *Enforcers Ready? Stand By to Deploy.*

In unison, Chance and Sam's helmets formed around the back of their heads, faceplates snapping down over grim expressions.

"RITA, you got me?" Chance said as his field of view blinked on.

"*I'm here, Chance. Ready to get to work,*" RITA responded, her sweet feminine voice clear and calm.

"Good. I think this one is going to require a lot from us."

"*Copy that, Chance. I believe in you.*"

Her words struck a chord deep within him. All the way back to his first days of policing, she'd been there. As real a presence as Benny, her diligence had saved his life more than once.

"Thank you, RITA," Chance said. "For everything."

"*Don't mention it,*" RITA said, a smile in her voice.

With a blast of fanfare, the hollow board counted down. "*The trial begins in five, four, three…*"

The light on the board blinked from red to green. With the roar of the crowd in his ears, Chance jumped from the VTOL's open side door, free falling, the dust rising to meet him from where the Grinder sat below.

"*Buffering the landing,*" RITA said. "*Standby.*"

A brief light flashed from beneath his boots as Chance landed, the weight of his armor crushing the broken stone underfoot. Sam landed with a thud on the other side of the Grinder, his carbon gray armor like a dull reflection of the drab sky above.

The *thunk-thunk* of other Enforcers landing nearby drove Chance to move faster.

"You're driving," Sam said.

Chance grabbed the Grinder's roll bar, swung his feet up, and pulled himself inside. The auto-harness clamped over his shoulders, and the power core hummed to life. On his left, Karissa and Jessie shot forward, their Grinder bouncing over the rough terrain.

"I'm in. Go, go," Sam yelled, vaulting into the rear of the buggy.

Chance's foot jammed down on the pedal, the Grinder's knobby tires flinging dirt in the air. Following the thick dust trail left by the other vehicles, Chance swore as he watched Ash and Rip launch off the crest of a hilltop a hundred yards ahead.

"We're losing ground," Sam called out, anchored behind the massive grenade launcher.

"I'm working on it," Chance said, swerving left and right to avoid rusted heaps of junk.

"*Ash and Rip are on course to get there first,*" RITA said. "*They appear to be aiming to hit Rico's stronghold head-on.*"

Chance checked the target position on his helmet's Heads Up Display.

Against the far south wall of The Zone, the Death Squad barricaded and claimed a jumble of old-world hospital towers as their base of operations, a veritable fortress. Ash and Rip wouldn't have it easy knocking on the front door. A feat such as this had never been attempted by any Enforcer in the history of The Zone—much less all of them at once.

Chance gained on Karissa and Jessie. The Grinder launched off a small rise, its shocks absorbing the impact as it bounced and slid across the ragged terrain.

"Keep it steady, kid. We've got company," Sam said, swiveling the mounted grenade launcher around.

"Which gang?" Chance said, laser-focused on the track ahead.

"Ahh." Sam swiveled the launcher back and forth. "All of 'em?"

"What?" Chance looked over his shoulder. The motley horde of rust-covered vehicles raced behind them, stirring up a massive cloud of dust. "Sputz."

"Yeah," Sam said, "keep it pegged out and head for Rico's. I'll watch our six."

Chance took the Grinder down a narrow lane, the towering, decayed ruins of The Zone rising around them. For a few moments, they lost sight of everyone else until one of their fevered pursuers, a vomit-green truck loaded with Hoodie Boys, swerved into the lane behind them.

"I got em'," Sam said.

Flashes of light emanated from the Hoodies' truck, the rounds zipping by and zinging off the decrepit walls on either side of the Grinder.

"Any time now," Chance said, flinching as a round whined

past.

"Relax, these jokers have nowhere to go." Sam clenched the trigger.

The grenade launcher thumped twice, and a double flash of fire and smoke erupted from the Hoodies' truck. The green-jacketed men screamed, some of them burning and falling from the truck, others frozen like dime-store mannequins set aflame. The truck's hood flapped open, belching smoke into the air. It slowed, idled, and bumped to a stop, wedged between the walls of the lane. Two more pursuit vehicles screeched to a stop behind it, blocked by the burning wreckage. The piped-in sounds of the cheering masses echoed across The Zone.

"Piece of cake," Sam said.

The Grinder shot out of the mouth of the alley. Swerving amongst the ruin and wreckage of the old world, Chance maintained control of the vehicle as the speedometer registered one hundred twenty. Ahead, Karissa and Jessie's Grinder disappeared between two broken towers, their jagged open tops gaping at the sullen sky.

RITA's voice broke in, serene amidst the chaos. "*Chance, the other Enforcers have a significant lead on you. You need to find a way to gain ground.*"

Chance said nothing, his armored hands clenching the steering wheel at nine and three.

"Dammit," Sam said, "hang on."

Chance didn't need to ask. Squads of Night Raiders merged from the streets on their left, The Wasted on their right, and their vehicles veered inward in a pincer movement. Sam pivoted. As he swung the heavy weapon to the driver's side, the grenade launcher thumped with violent repetition. A streak of explosions followed the swinging muzzle of the launcher, sending several Night Raiders tumbling and flipping from their dirt bikes. Chance drew his Peacemaker, leveling it across the passenger seat as the wild-eyed crew of The Wasted approached in an open-topped sedan, toxic orange flags flapping in the wind.

"Boarding," Chance shouted above the whining of the Grinder as The Wasted sedan slammed against the passenger side.

Two men jumped from the sedan onto the Grinder before Chance got the shot off. The thirty-caliber round punched a hole through the driver's cheek, spraying the cab with blood. The goon's eyes lolled back, and the vehicle struck an embankment and flipped in a spray of debris. More screams from the ravenous crowd filled the air.

One of the men vaulted with a wild scream into the rear of the buggy, but Sam was ready. With one hand on the grenade launcher, he jerked a combat knife from the rig on his chest. Parrying a machete swipe, he drove the knife through the neck of the orange-clad man and shoved him tumbling from the Grinder.

"Hold on," Chance said. The last goon let out a short scream as the all-terrain vehicle raked him against the brick of a windowless structure, a streak of crimson left in the wake of the speeding vehicle.

Chance angled left for another cluttered street. The toppled, broken high rises of a long-forgotten age gave way to open sky, the ancient, junk-strewn roadways more hindrance than a help. Ahead, Karissa and Jessie slowed as they fought off a second squad of Hoodie Boys.

"RITA, cut all non-vital vehicle systems. I need all the juice this thing's got," Chance said.

"You're not going to get much more."

Chance gripped the wheel with both hands and held steady.

"You want some of this?" Sam yelled from the bed, the grenade launcher banging. The Night Raiders, their resolve broken, swerved to avoid the explosions as another dusty midnight blue truck burst into flames.

Almost in line with Karissa and Jessie, Chance watched several

Hoodies jump from tattered green vehicles onto the Grinder. From the bed, Jessie kicked one in the chest and sent him sprawling. Karissa neutralized another with a well-timed throat strike and shoved him from the passenger seat, all while maintaining control of her Grinder.

Up ahead, Ash and Rip's Grinder churned up a storm of dust.

Sam shouted at the pursuing gangs as they slowed and veered away. "Aww, you don't want to play anymore?"

"It's not us," Chance said, motioning ahead to the dark fortress looming closer on the horizon. "We just dipped into Squad territory."

Chance checked the power levels of the Grinder. The hard push had worn the power core thin, and they weren't out of the woods yet. Bumping forward, Chance and Sam pulled alongside Karissa and Jessie. Karissa's helmet retracted.

"Let's get 'em," she shouted, jerking her head at Ash and Rip ahead. "Unless you want some?" She flashed an adrenaline-spiked smirk and swerved playfully at Chance.

"Oh, you don't want to do that," Chance said, swerving back.

Ahead, Rip swiveled his launcher to the rear.

"Chance, Chance—" Sam shouted.

The concussive blast wave hit him with an astonishing force. In terrible slow motion, Chance watched as Karissa and Jessie's Grinder burst into flames right beside them. Jumping and flipping, the crushed vehicle, streaking smoke, rolled to a stop. Fire gushed from the wreckage. Another blast hit, the impact so close it rattled Chance's teeth. He blinked, his brain locked in the chaos. He swerved to the right as a third blast struck just behind Sam.

"You slag-eaters!" Sam screamed, swinging his stove-pipe barrel forward.

Rip fired on them again from the bed of his Grinder. Ash swerved to avoid one of Sam's explosive rounds, the Grinder disappearing in a blast of smoke and dust.

"He just killed them…" Chance said. A haze of smoke and dust, pulled by the wind, billowed around them.

"Get us the hell out of here," Sam said.

Veering away to the right, Chance sped out of range of Rip's launcher. He looked back one more time at the burning Grinder receding behind them. No movement, no sign of either Jessie or Karissa.

"*Chance, I've lost all readings on Takedown and Pursuit's vitals,*" RITA said. "*I'm sorry.*"

In the distance, Rip held up a middle finger, and Chance knew he was laughing. A cold rage descended on him.

"I'll kill him," Chance said.

"Lock your feelings down," Sam said, his voice hard and steady. "We can't allow Ash and Rip to get there first. Too much is at stake. Don't check up, you hear me? I have a way in."

Chance slipped beneath the perimeter fence on the easternmost corner along The Zone wall and stopped to scan for threats. Utilizing natural points of concealment provided by the decaying urban landscape, he crouched behind a wall gouged in half by the bullet strikes of another age.

"All right," Sam took a knee, a touch out of breath. "It's just ahead."

Chance didn't respond, his morbid thoughts still with Karissa and Jessie. They'd been good to him from the beginning. A fresh swell of hatred seized him at the thought of Rip's treachery.

Beside Chance, Sam waited until the lone sentry turned his back. Crossing the space with a speed and surefootedness that belied his age, Sam struck the sentry with a solid blow to the jaw. The man toppled against a pile of rubble and lay still, unconscious.

Sam motioned Chance onward.

Approaching the medical complex, Chance could only guess at one time in the distant past it might have been a regional trauma center. Sam activated his glove laser. A white beam projected from Sam's wrist and sliced through four sets of looped chains on an angled set of sub-basement doors. Pulling them wide, he and Chance searched into the musty, cobwebbed depths of Rico's Death Squad stronghold.

The pop and thud of not-too-distant gunfire told them Ash and Rip has engaged Rico's forces head on, a solid distraction for their more covert entry.

"Let's go, we're on the clock." Sam took a step into the cellar. He stopped when Chance didn't move. "Come on, man."

Chance's helmet retracted. He found himself unable to conceal his sorrow. "Sam," he shook his head, "he just killed them like it was nothing."

Sam's helmet retracted to reveal his furrowed brow. "I know, partner. I didn't want to believe Rip would take it this far. But he did. And now he and Ash are enemies."

"We're killing each other for a damn game show."

A Glom drone lowered closer to capture their words. Sam eyed the drone and shook his head at Chance with a look that said, *Shut up.*

"Listen," Sam said, "we've got a mission to accomplish, and that's what we're going to do. The best way to honor Karissa and Jessie is to win. If we're going to do that, we have got to move."

Chance managed a conflicted nod. Their helmets re-formed, the faceplates snapping down.

They stepped into the hospital cellar, and Chance pulled the doors shut behind them. With a flicker, their Inteli-suits auto-activated a series of tactical lights. Wheeled cots and old world medical equipment covered in a sheen of cobwebs and dust, littered the space.

"Strange." Sam swept his lights back and forth. "I'm not picking up any security on this level."

"RITA, release the firefly and get me a scan on this place. Include Sam in the video stream," Chance said.

"*Copy.*"

The stealth drone detached from his armor with a scraping sound, little wings whirring in the dark. An infrared light activated, and the firefly's video feed appeared on both Chance's and Sam's displays. Over their shoulder, The Glom drone whirred, capturing it all in ultra-high definition.

"*Scans indicate armed enemy presence on the floors above,*" RITA said so they could both hear. "*Though I count a significant number of unarmed individuals as well.*"

Chance turned to Sam. "They know they're under attack. That doesn't make sense. They should've all geared up."

"Only one way to find out," Sam said.

After completing a full scan, the firefly returned, and mated back with Chance's armor. As they pushed through the damp dark, the sounds of the battle on the surface grew louder, muffled by layers of concrete. Only the drip of water and the scurrying of rats accompanied their own movement. They climbed several flights of stairs to a landing and stopped before a steel push door.

Sam turned to Chance. "I'm sorry I couldn't be more forthcoming with you before. Can you trust me one more time?"

"What's that supposed to mean?"

"I need you to trust me. No matter what," Sam said. "Can you do that for me?"

"Sam?"

Sam pushed open the door and walked into the yellow light of a spacious room, his helmet retracting. Chance squinted at the sudden light.

"Hey, hey. What the hell—?" Chance said, the words fading in his throat.

He stood there, unable to move as Sam crossed the room and stopped, his hands up. The room drew into focus. Along cinderblock walls, huddled in groups, people muttered and whispered from the dark corners of the large room. A sickly half-light seeped through scum covered windows.

"Our guest has arrived." A shadowy long-haired figure rose from a metal folding chair on the far side of the room, flanked on either side by heavily armed Death Squad goons.

Chance's eyes adjusted to the light. Around the room, men, women, and children hunched together, their faces turning up wide-eyed toward the Enforcers. A few meandered further into the corners, while a couple stepped over and reached out to shake Sam's hand. A young child ran up and Sam stooped to give her a high five. Around the gutted cafeteria, seasoned members of the Death Squad, in their signature plum colors, stood at their posts without so much as aiming their chopped down rifles at Sam or Chance.

Chance turned to The Glom drone hovering behind them. The light that indicated a live broadcast had gone dark.

"Well, well, you did come after all, Enforcer," said the weathered man with long lank hair and brooding eyes.

"How you holding up, old man?" Sam slapped hands with the long haired man, and a brief embrace followed. "You got the supplies I sent?"

"We needed the antibiotics in a bad way. Thank you for being a man of your word, as always."

"A deal is a deal and we've got too much history to ignore," Sam said.

The weathered man offered a quizzical look toward the door. "Is young buck gonna join us?"

Sam turned and motioned to Chance, standing rooted in place, his helmet still engaged.

"Chance," Sam said, "this is Rico."

Chance's helmet retracted. He took a step forward, struggling to move his feet. It was Sam all along, right under his nose.

Before Chance could think, his hand had whipped his Peacemaker from the holster and leveled it at his partner. "Drop your weapons."

The room burst to life as guards lurched forward, pointing chopped-down rifles at Chance, everyone shouting. Children cried. Innocents, families, huddled together with terror in their eyes. The adrenaline jacked gang members jerked their weapons back and forth at the Enforcers, shouting for their surrender. Rico folded his arms.

Sam raised his open hands. "Chance, holster your weapon or you're going to get us killed."

"You... it was you!" Chance shook. "All this time. You lied to me. *Again.*"

"None of this is what you think," Sam said.

"It's exactly what I think, what Kess said—one of us turned. I thought Rip, Ash maybe, but you?"

"Lower the gun," Sam said, an edge to his voice.

"They're gonna blast me as soon as I do." Chance motioned to the trigger-happy gang members.

Sam nodded to Rico.

With a resigned movement, Rico raised a calloused palm. His men, scowls etched on their faces, all stepped back and lowered their weapons.

"Holster up, Chance," Sam said. "Let's talk this out."

"Talk? You've done nothing but lie to me."

"Not true. I told you what I could in the lounge, but The Glom was always listening. They'd sabotage our recovery chambers if they knew what I was doing."

Chance held firm, his Peacemaker trained on his partner. "What *are* you doing, Sam? Dealing with Rico?"

"Is your guy going to cool out, or what?" Rico said, unamused.

"He's fine," Sam said, turning to Chance, "right?"

Chance re-gripped his trembling Peacemaker, the idea of having to shoot his own partner unfathomable.

"Chance, look around you," Sam said. "I told you. It's all a game. It's not just good guys and bad guys. The Glom pulls everyone's strings."

"You're dealing with Rico," Chance said.

"Yeah, he's a warlord. Yeah, we would throw him and his guys in the Blocks if we were still cops. But we're not, and in here, he's the only one doing anything good."

"What's that supposed to mean?"

"It means Rico's name is actually Cristoff. It means he was one of my SWAT guys a long time ago, before he was framed for the murder of another badge and thrown in The Zone. We went to academy together, for god sakes."

Chance looked from the long-haired warlord back to Sam, his eyes blinking.

"Look around you," Sam continued, "look at the children. They haven't been raped or tortured. Cristoff has hidden and protected children dropped into The Zone for years now. Yeah, he collects their bounties, but then his people take care of them and eventually smuggle them back out. These might be rough dudes, but they have a code. That's why he deals with all the other gangs and requires the children they capture unharmed."

Chance turned to see a trio of kids perched like monkeys on the low section of a broken interior wall nearby. They giggled at him.

"But the Death Squad?" Chance said. "They killed Valarie."

"It's a myth, perpetuated by The Glom," Rico said. "When she went down, my boys fought the other gangs off to get to her. We were too late. Your fellow Enforcer wasn't killed by conventional weapons."

"What are you saying?" Chance lowered his weapon.

"Open your eyes, kid," Rico said. "Vigilance was long dead prior to having her head removed."

"I've been trying to tell you, Chance, but I couldn't," Sam said. "The Glom killed Valarie. Kess killed her *internally*—used her nanobots to do it. We're vulnerable with The Glom's nano-machines inside us. That's why Karissa and Jessie and I have been searching for a solution. A way to protect ourselves."

"Why?" Chance said. "Why would Kess kill us?"

"For the show. For the money it generates. We're all expendable. I told you that on your first day."

"But The Glom?" Chance pointed to the drone, still dark. "They're not watching right now?"

"Livestream disruption tech," Sam said, tapping the side of his head, "comes in handy sometimes."

Rico motioned to one of his men, who approached and extended a small black box to Sam.

Sam took it in his hand. "Rico desperately needed medical supplies and food rations for his people. In exchange, he said he could get me this." He showed the box to Chance.

"It cost us all a great deal," Rico said. "You know what we had to trade for it?"

"If I had to guess I'd say it has something to do with the truth about New West City," Sam said.

Rico nodded. "It's bad, Sam. Evidence of The Glom's true nature. When New West fell, they did nothing but protect their interests. When this gets out, it breaks the system."

"Why be willing to trade something like that?" Sam said.

"I live in The Zone, brother." Rico smirked. "How bad can it get for me? Besides, a civil uprising is tomorrow. We needed those antibiotics today."

Sam opened the top of the box and extracted a smooth cylinder the size of a finger. He paused. "After this," Sam said, looking at Chance, "everything we know is going to change. None of us can go back."

"I hope it's worth it." Rico snapped his fingers, his people moving and gathering their things. "Listen, I've been told you have to scan it direct into your chip for the nano virus to be effective."

"Nano virus?" Chance repeated.

"You should go now," Sam said to Rico, "we'll cover for you, say you fled before we got here."

The old friends shook hands.

"Until we meet again, pal," Rico said.

"*Chance, I am confused as to the nature of our mission...*" RITA said.

"Standby," Chance muttered. "Sam?"

The crack of a gunshot echoed across the room, causing the gangsters to flinch and eliciting a scream from the huddled innocents. Rico, wide eyed, tumbled backward, blood spurting from a bullet wound high in his chest. Sam's helmet snapped into place. He caught the gang leader as he fell.

Chance turned, his faceplate dropping over his face. The Glom drone hovered behind him, the smoking barrel of a rifle protruding from the front. A trio of drones crashed in through the scum-covered windows, their broadcast feeds dark, rifle barrels extended.

"RITA!" Chance screamed as the room burst to life with the rippling staccato of gunfire. Chance crouched to shield a group of children as the curtain of white light rose from the ground before him.

Sam had his barrier up, too, but it wasn't enough. The drones swarmed, whirring and pivoting, their mounted weapons blazing. Rico's men dove for cover. Some fell where they stood, riddled with bullets. Others screamed and opened fire. The bodies of parents fell limp across their dead children as the fusillade of gunfire tore through the room. A woman and her toddler fell together, spattered in blood, as she tried to pull the child into the safety of a stairwell. A man raised his hands in surrender and the wave of bullets tore him apart.

Jerking the Peacemaker from his holster, Chance fired as the small targets zipped through the room. With their barriers engaged, Chance and Sam worked to save what lives they could.

"Chance, you have five seconds left on your barrier," RITA said.

"Run." Chance called to the children behind him. "Get away from here."

Chance and Sam worked together, shielding the remaining children long enough for them to run for their lives. Their barriers flickered and went out. Back to back, they fought off the remaining drones, the cameras now live, until the last one spun and crashed into the wall in a shower of sparks.

Sam dropped to the floor and grabbed his old friend's hands. "Cristoff. Hey, Cristoff, talk to me," Sam said. Around them the dead lay in heaps, the voices of the injured crying out. A few blood-stained Death Squad members stepped out from behind positions of cover.

Rico took a ragged breath, the wound in his chest bubbling.

"It's nicked your lung," Sam said, and placed the man's hand over the hole. "Keep firm pressure here. Can you move?"

"I think so," Rico grunted.

"Sam, what the hell?" Chance said.

Sam helped Rico to his feet and met his eyes. "Follow the children and get somewhere safe. They're on to us. This is about to become a war zone."

Rico faltered.

"Hey, you hear me?" Sam asked. "Don't stop until those children are safe. You have a place?"

"Yeah," Rico said.

"Then go," Sam said, ushering him and the others toward the rear of the room, "and be careful, brother." Rico shambled on, clutching at his wound until he disappeared with the other survivors into the shadows of a darkened stairwell.

Sam turned to face Chance. They stood amidst the piles of scattered bodies and drone fragments, lungs heaving.

"Sam, please tell me what the *hell* is going on here," Chance said.

Before the veteran Enforcer could answer, The Glom network feed piped into their helmets and displayed video of Sam and Rico's embrace.

"In a stunning display of treachery, Enforcers Warrant and Justice have gone rogue," the buff announcer with the jiggling pompadour said, eyes wide with feigned shock. "As you can see, they've violated the rules of play and are in league with the warlord Rico. When the deal went south, they murdered an entire group of hostages, unarmed women and children mercilessly gunned down. It appears the Enforcers then turned their weapons on the Conglomerate's security drones in an attempt to hide their treachery."

Chance and Sam watched, aghast, as the video showed them standing amidst piles of dead bodies, the drones shot down one by one.

"My word..." The announcer touched his lips. "And now folks, a word from Director Kess."

Gabriel Kess appeared in the image, his face solemn. "What a terrible day, a day of such tragedy and deception. Never in all my years presiding over this network have I seen anything so vile. My fellow citizens of Neo Terminus, the game has changed—as of right now, the bounty on Rico is transferred to Warrant and Justice. Dead or alive—we will see them held responsible for what they've done. The other surviving Enforcers are our only hope for redemption now. Make your bets. May only the strongest prevail."

"We gotta move if we want to survive this. You good?" Sam said.

"No," Chance said, eyes roving the piled bodies of women and children around them. He stifled the urge to vomit, retracting his helmet in case he did. "No, I'm not good, dammit, Sam."

"I know, buddy." Sam put his hand on Chance's shoulder. "Listen to me, after Valarie, I knew I had to do something. I had to protect the rest of us. It was the only way. Do you understand now?"

"You did this to protect us." Chance shook his head. "But we're still screwed."

"Hey," Sam smirked, "we're going to beat this. Together we'll get through—" His eyes widened. "Watch out!"

Sam shoved Chance to the side. A barrage of bullets raked upward, slinging concrete dust from the walls where Chance had stood just a moment before. Sam stumbled and clutched at his neck, blood running through the fingers of his armored glove. He fell back, his Peacemaker bucking in flashes of fire as he collapsed against the dusty floor.

"Sam!" Chance screamed, his faceplate dropping down. Spinning, he drew his Peacemaker and dove for the low wall as several rounds zipped past. Chance landed hard and rolled to his side, jerking a blue armor-piercing magazine from his carrier.

"Drop your weapon, traitor!" Rip shouted as he advanced into the room. Behind him, two Glom video drones followed, eliciting roars from the crowd.

Chance dared to look at Sam one last time. The veteran Enforcer leaned against the wall, his Peacemaker extended at Rip as blood poured from his neck down the front of his armor. Slowly, the weapon lowered to his lap. He turned his eyes to Chance with a strange, peaceful resignation. The Zone veteran nodded, that same self-assured smirk on his weathered face under the blood and grime.

"Stay the course, brother," Sam rasped. "There's hope for us still…" His blood-soaked glove loosened from the Peacemaker and scraped across his armor as it fell to the floor.

"*Sam just flatlined,*" RITA said.

"Surrender, now!" Rip shouted.

Rounds punched through the broken cinderblock wall above Chance and sent him crawling on his belly, concrete dust showering his armor. Chance racked the slide on his gun and pushed to all fours, his body shaking with adrenaline and rage.

"Drop your weapon or get smoked like the old man!" Rip shouted.

Chance screamed, a terrible and reckless fury erupting from deep inside him.

Rising, heedless of the danger, Chance rounded the edge of the wall and opened fire. Rip charged him with a scream, his Peacemaker barking. They each took opposing angles, firing on one another as they closed the distance. The deafening concussion of traded gunfire lingered only for a moment.

Chance gasped, stumbled, and fell to his knees, clutching a wound to his abdomen.

Rip's faceplate released, a malevolent look of disgust on his face. "I got you... you little..." He coughed, blood splattered from his mouth down his chin. His eyes dropped to the two holes in his chest plate. Rip stepped back, faltered, and fell, the Peacemaker clattering from his hands.

"Drop it!" Ash screamed as he surged into the far end of the room, his aim locked on Chance.

"Ash, stop!" Karissa shouted, her dusty Peacemaker trained on Ash. Jessie followed her through a window, his armor imbued with red clay and fresh scars.

Ash swung his pistol on Karissa and they both shouted for compliance.

"Drop it, Ash, that's enough!" Jessie held Ash in his sights.

"He just killed Rip!" Ash shouted.

"And Rip killed Sam!" Karissa shouted back. "Where does it end? When we're all dead?"

"Come on, man, lower it!" Jessie said.

Ash set his jaw. A moment passed, the drones whirring as they broadcast the standoff. He swiveled to draw down on Chance, then back to Karissa.

"Don't even think about it." Karissa shook her head. "Chance?" She said, her eyes on Ash. "You okay?"

"I don't know," Chance groaned, "but it's damn good to see you guys."

"Power cage saved our asses in the rollover," Karissa said, still holding her weapon on Ash.

"*Chance?*" RITA said, a tinge of worry in her voice.

"I'm here." Chance gritted his teeth as his armor applied auto-compression to the injury. "Give me a status report."

"*The wound appears to be through and through. The armor piercing round missed your kidney by four centimeters. Your nanos are already at work stopping the bleeding and repairing the damaged tissue.*"

"What happened?" Jessie said, staring at the bodies. "There are dead kids in here…"

"You know we didn't do that," Chance said. "The Glom used their security drones to kill these people. They're framing us for it."

"And Sam was trying to protect us by dealing with Rico," Jessie said with a tone of finality.

Chance shifted to see the still form of his friend and mentor, a stroke of agony filling his chest. "Don't you see?" Chance said. "This is what they want—us killing each other. For the spectacle of it. For entertainment. Are we going to be good little slaves and go along with this madness or are we going to show The Glom they don't control us?"

Ash faltered, turning from Chance to Karissa to Jessie. His faceplate popped open, revealing an expression of anger and confusion.

"Go on, Ash, kill me." Chance holstered his Peacemaker and popped his faceplate open. "Make your puppet masters happy."

Not a whispered breath crossed the space. Ash slowly lowered his weapon. Karissa and Jessie followed suit, and their faceplates opened. Chance sighed.

"I'm nobody's puppet," Ash said, his brow furrowed.

"Prove it," Chance said.

Ash holstered his weapon. "The Glom controls everything. How do we go against them?"

Chance shifted to the side and reached into the clenched hand of his dead partner. "We break our chains," he said, holding up the cylinder, "with this. It's what Sam risked everything for. It's what he died for."

"What is it?" Ash said.

"A nano virus," Karissa said with awe, "he got it."

"Valarie wasn't killed by the gangs," Chance said. "It was Gabriel Kess. He had her nanos do the job, and he made it look like the gangs killed her. All for the sake of viewership." Chance pointed to The Glom drone broadcasting live. "We all once took oaths to serve and protect the people, not some faceless corporate monster. We're being used, and I'm done with that."

The group drew silent.

Ash knelt and popped Rip's helmet open. He pushed Rip's eyes closed. "I didn't want this," he said, and let his hand hang limp in front of his partner's face, then fall to his shot-through breastplate. "But I couldn't reason with him. For Rip, it was win, no matter what." Ash locked eyes with Chance. "I know you had to do it. He would have killed you, too."

The other Enforcers looked on, their faces grim.

"I hate it," Chance said. "Despite our differences, he was a great Enforcer." Chance shook his head. "We'll miss his gun and his skill in what comes next."

"Sam too." Ash rose and crossed the space. He lowered his head. "This is all wrong. We can't go out like this. Not like this." He extended his hand to Chance and pulled him groaning to his feet. "What do we need to do?"

Karissa and Jessie approached, all three focused on the rookie Enforcer.

"Scan it into your chip," Chance said.

"You sure about this?" Ash said.

"Hell no," Chance said, "but Sam was."

"Wait," Karissa said, reaching out to cover Chance's hand. "Your nanos are repairing your wound. If you disable them, you could be in trouble."

The blood only oozed now from the hole in his armor, the compression and nano repairs staunching the flow.

"*Chance, it's true,*" RITA said. "*You'll be much more vulnerable to injury and infection if you disable your nanos.*"

"Better than being dead at the snap of some elitist's fingers. I'll take my chances," Chance said.

Chance held the disruptor up as the other Enforcers watched, then scanned the device into his own chip with a *pip*. After a moment, he shrugged. "Guess that's it."

He handed the device to Karissa, and she scanned it in, followed by Jessie, and, after some deliberation, Ash.

"What now?" Ash said.

"*Chance, your connection to headquarters was just severed. We've been cut off. Resources and support are showing unavailable.*"

The Enforcers' helmets formed to cover their faces as each one checked their HUD. But they already knew what came next. Flashing in bright red letters across each of their displays was a single word.

Disavowed.

CHAPTER THIRTY-FIVE

A hazy third season sun drifted low on the horizon. The evening light filtered through the patchwork holes in the oppressive cloud cover, casting glimmering pools across the city. There was a strange silence. Few vehicles crisscrossed the skyways, the sidewalks and open spaces of the Silver City filled only with the slightest foot traffic. There was an electricity in the air, a sense as if the entire city were holding its breath.

"Miss Avery, what's the network status?" Kess said from the head of the conference room table. "Show me the numbers."

Miss Avery composed herself. "As you can tell from the lack of activity out the window, viewership has skyrocketed to an all-time high. But that's expected with the extensive ad campaign we ran, and all the hype surrounding this one." She waved her hand and the department heads turned toward the corner of the room where a holo-screen showed a bullet-ridden Warrant lying in a spreading pool of blood. "Not to mention, this is an unprecedented event," she bounced on the balls of her feet. "We've never had Enforcers killing each other before."

"I don't care about all that." Kess waved her off. "They're all just players on the board. If they go down, they go down. What I need to know is whether the network is secure and that no one is watching anything but what we are showing."

Miss Avery turned to the department heads sitting around the table and gave a slight bow of her head. They fidgeted, looking at one another. Each person in various states of anxiety over how their head might be on the chopping block next if things didn't go Kess's way.

"We definitely seem to have everyone's attention, sir," Miss Avery said.

Kess touched his ear. "Ardmore, you there?"

"Yes, Director," the IT system's lead said.

"What's the status on the founders' addition?"

"It arrived this morning, sir." Ardmore's words carried a certain frailty. The sound of a man who didn't like the direction they'd taken, but was too scared to speak out. "It's installed and ready to activate on your command."

"Good. Do it and report to me on the status," Kess said.

"Yes, sir."

Kess turned to those present at the meeting. "I suggest each of you completely power off your visors until this is over." His eyes narrowed. Turning, he addressed Miss Avery. "How secure is the network at present?"

Something in his voice caused a cascade of nervous glances around the room.

"Well?" The room starred at Kess wide eyed. "How secure is it?"

"Sir." Miss Avery clasped her hands in front of her. "It's as secure as we can make it, sir. I have to tell you, though, even if we jam and disable every pirated signal, there's always a chance—"

"Not acceptable," Kess said. "No rogue signals will worm their way onto this network. Is that clear? If they do, it's your problem." He waved his hand across the room.

A man in an expensive suit and a bloodless white face spoke up. "Sir?"

"What is it, Gibbs?" Kess said with mounting irritation.

"Sir, we have squads of our best troopers smashing rogue

broadcasts as fast as they pop up, but as Miss Avery said, there are a ton of—"

"Don't make excuses, just do your damn job." Kess turned to the holo-projection screen above, the Enforcers now congregating amidst the piles of bodies in Rico's stronghold. Kess let a hiss escape through his teeth. "And what the hell is this? Shouldn't they still be killing each other?"

"I don't know, sir," Miss Avery said.

"What are they saying?" Kess asked.

Miss Avery tapped a few keys, and the audio from the show filled the room.

"Ladies and gentlemen, this is unprecedented, indeed," the big-haired announcer said, excitement in his voice. "Warrant and Sanction are down, and word is their vital signs have gone dark. But just when we thought the Enforcers would all go out guns blazing, they've holstered their weapons and now seem to be calling a truce. Keep in mind, Justice still has the full Rico bounty on his head, and by ignoring this, the other Enforcers are in violation of their contracts. Make your bets! There's no telling how this will—"

Kess waved his arms in exasperation. "Cut that silly garbage off. I want to hear what *they* are saying." He jabbed his finger at the Enforcers on the screen.

"Sir," Miss Avery said, a genuine fear in her face. "They've muted their comms."

"Well unmute them."

"We can't," she said. "Somehow they've disabled their internal nano-systems. They have total control."

"How are they doing that?" Kess shouted.

Miss Avery shrugged. "It must have had something to do with Warrant's deal with Rico. Some sort of tech contingency we weren't prepared for."

Kess rubbed a hand over his mouth and chin. Everyone in the room seemed to shrink back, preparing for the worst.

"You're telling me my Enforcers are openly defying me right now and I can't do anything to stop them? Do I have that right?"

The room fell silent, full of the vacant stares of people with much to lose.

"Switch them off. All of them. If they want to go rogue, we'll handle them as rogue assets." He said to his assistant, his gaze piercing. "Initiate Operation Ground Clear."

"Sir?"

"Do it. We have the replacements on standby?" Kess said.

"Well, sir, they're in development." Miss Avery shrugged again.

"Fine. Wait until the Enforcers are engaged with our troopers and switch them off. Do it one at a time, and in a way the public won't suspect. Just like Vigilance."

"But, sir," Miss Avery said, trembling now, "it won't work. Ground Clear relies on their internal nanos to be active. We can't switch the Enforcers off. We've got nothing."

Kess gawked at her. He'd opened his mouth to speak when the broadcast screen flickered. The image went black, then returned, gray script floating in the static. Interspersed with the words, images of chaos and rebellion. The fall of New West City.

You are a slave to The Glom, the screen read. *New West City has collapsed because of the greed of its masters. Neo Terminus is next. Wake up.*

Kess stared at the screen, his mouth open. "Shut it down."

Gibbs fumbled with his holo-keyboard. "Uh... Um, we're working on it, sir. It's taken over two of the four main channels."

"Shut it down now, for slag's sake!" Kess screamed, spittle flying. "Find the signal source and hit it with everything you've got."

"Yes, sir, but... it just..." Gibbs stuttered.

"Shut. It. Down!" Kess shook with the words.

Kess's personal comm link rang. "It's Ardmore, sir. The

founders, ah, their device isn't functioning. We don't have control of the entire network, and it relies upon our—"

"Fix it!"

"It's not that simple…" Ardmore's voice trailed off.

"Do your damn job, you incompetent ass!" Kess screamed, ending the call.

The direct line from the founders, a line that never rang, trilled softly. Kess wheeled around in wide-eyed desperation. "Fix this or I'll see you and everyone you've ever loved deported to the slums. Now, get out of my sight!" The nervous department heads shoved their chairs back, all too eager to comply. He turned to his assistant. "Wait for me in the hall."

Miss Avery's face was pale. She whispered a "yes, sir," and ducked out.

The founder's line continued to trill.

Kess waited until the door slid shut. He smoothed his shirt, running a hand over his hair, and answered the call. The synthetic voice scratched at his raw nerves.

"You want to tell us what exactly is going on, Kess? We thought you had this under control? We thought you'd devised a master plan? Activate the device. Now."

"Yes, Founders, it's only a momentary lapse. I assure you we are doing everything possible to get things under control."

"Under control?" The founder's words scratched through the static. "The exact thing we wanted to avoid is happening, Kess. You've lost control, as well as the faith of the founders."

"No, wait," Kess said, holding up his hands. "I can fix this. We'll shut the rogue signal down. I'll get the device online."

"Round up the Enforcers' families. We'll need them for insurance."

"Round them up? You want me to kidnap their families? Are you mad?"

"Handle it, or we will." The founder's voice wheezed, vacant as a final breath.

Kess swallowed, pulled at his tie. "I assure you, I'll personally handle our Enforcer problem. I can salvage this, but I'm not kidnapping families."

"Oh, you absolutely will." A scratching laugh. "You have such a beautiful daughter. We'd hate to see some terrible tragedy befall her."

Kess's composure broke; a wave of fury breaking over him. He slammed his balled fists against the hardwood table. "Now hold on just one damn second. You stay the hell away from her. You hear me? Destroy me, but my daughter is off limits!"

"Nothing is off limits for the founders, Kess. You'd do well to remember that."

Click.

Kess shrieked into the air, his fists clenched white with rage. Picking up his chair, he slung it against the giant conference room window, a spider's web of cracks stretching across the glass. He sucked at the air, pulled his tie off, and rolled up his sleeves as he stomped for the door.

"Nothing is off limits, huh?" Kess said. With a hiss, the door slid back and he hit the hallway at full stride, a pale faced Miss Avery falling in behind him as he went.

"Mr. Kess?"

Kess tabbed the call button for the elevator. "It's been too long since Gridlock entered The Zone."

"You're going in?"

"That's right. They want it handled. I'll handle it. Personally. Call down and prep my suit," Kess said, his eyes shining with madness. "I'm going to show these *clowns* what a *real* Enforcer looks like."

Hannah threw together a few changes of clothes and stuffed them into her overnight bag. She sniffed and wiped her face, closed her eyes, and inhaled deep. *I got them all. At least, I think I did.* Her eyes flicked open, and she scanned the room again. The thought she might have missed one sent a fresh wave of panic crawling over her skin. *They've been spying on me. Why?* she thought.

"You got them all, Hannah," she said, mastering her fear. "There are no more cameras."

She surveyed the space. The apartment was a disaster area: furniture toppled, cushions tossed, the fabric sliced with a kitchen knife, the stuffing strewn about the apartment like a whirl of low-lying clouds. *Am I mad? I've done this to my dream apartment.*

Hannah swallowed. She'd wanted to take a shower, let the scalding hot water wash the feeling of exposure and betrayal away, but she couldn't bring herself to get naked in this apartment one more time. Not even knowing she'd hunted down and found every last camera, smashing them all with an ornamental stone paperweight on the quartz kitchen counter.

Need to get the hell out of here. But where? She hadn't thought that far yet; all she knew was she needed another place, one not controlled by the Conglomerate. Hannah froze, stuffing a pair of leggings into her bag as she glimpsed the holo-projection hovering in the living room. Her heart skipped a beat.

Two Enforcers down, the rest disavowed by the Conglomerate, read the ticker at the bottom of the screen.

"Oh no," Hannah said, the rest of the clothes falling from her fingers onto the floor. She walked closer as an image of Sam and an Enforcer called Sanction flashed on the screen, both dead. Around them, the other Enforcers congregated—all facing her husband.

"Volume," Hannah said, feeling guilty for being glad it was Sam and not Chance lying there on the floor. She read the ticker again. *Disavowed.* Hannah touched her lips. *What could that mean?*

She watched as the closeup of a well-groomed, hard-eyed man filled the screen.

"My fellow citizens, this is Director Kess. As you know by now, a rogue signal recently slipped through our security's defenses and broadcast horrific, fabricated images onto the network. Let me take a moment to assuage your fears—New West City is fine. I spoke with Director Senterian this afternoon. While they've had some mild unrest, New West City's public safety has been working to ensure the city's continued safety and security. There is nothing to worry about. Your safety is always our primary concern. In addition, we are working hard to restore your entertainment. To the anarchists who would use this as an opportunity to disrupt our beloved city, shame on you! The consequences of any such criminal uprising will be swift and severe."

In his bassinet, Andrew whimpered, but Hannah couldn't turn away from the projection.

"Due to this crude interruption to your paid services, the Conglomerate will compensate every network subscriber a week's worth of network programming, absolutely free. It's our pledge to you to make this right."

Kess turned, walking, as the camera angle expanded. Hannah realized he wore a gray nano-skin body suit just like the one she'd seen Chance wearing. Hannah swallowed. Stepping onto a glowing platform, his body rose in the air, mechanical arms attaching blizzard gray Enforcer armor to his chest and limbs.

"As for the madness that's just taken place in The Zone." He shook his head. "A sad state of affairs. Our beloved Enforcers have defied you, the consumer, and in doing so, defied the Conglomerate. Their refusal to compete would cause many of you who've placed your hard-earned T's on them to lose money."

Kess's armor knitted together, forming and encapsulating him as the camera zoomed in on his face.

"Let me offer you a way to salvage your investments. By law, the remaining Enforcers must be disavowed–stripped of their titles and assets. If they resist, they must be destroyed."

A helmet formed around the back of Kess's head, his eyes narrowing as the smooth, eyeless faceplate slammed down. "I will be the instrument of that destruction."

Hannah listened as the masses swelled and cheered with wild approval. Her hand hovered over her mouth.

"My friends, cast your winning bets for the Conglomerate, now," Kess said, his body loading into a massive power mech. "Gridlock is entering The Zone."

"Chance…" A lump the size of a boulder lodged in Hannah's throat.

A knock sounded. Hannah turned, appraising the shadows outside the frosted glass of her apartment door. Another course of light, polite rapping caused her to bite her lip.

"Mute all audio," Hannah whispered.

"Muting all audio," the apartment's auto steward said.

Hannah walked toward the door, pausing at Andrew's bassinet long enough to touch his little socked foot. Then up the two stairs to the short landing, Hannah eyed the shifting shadows on the other side of the glass. She wasn't expecting anyone.

"Hello?"

"Mrs. Griffin?" a man outside said. "This is Conglomerate Security Officer Mike Hooper. May I come in? I need to speak with you."

"What's this about?" Hannah said through the door.

"I'd rather not discuss your personal matters out here in the hall. It's about your husband. May I come in?"

Hannah swore. She eyed her apartment, realizing to her horror the smashed surveillance cameras still lay on the countertop. She couldn't let Hooper in, or he'd know. But maybe that's why he'd come. *They already know*, she thought.

Her eyes flicked to the bassinet. The baby was still asleep.

Andrew was her out. After a moment of deliberation that included the stupid idea of climbing out the apartment window with her child in tow, she popped the door latch and let it open a mere four inches.

"Hi, sorry," she whispered. "I'd have you in but the baby is sleeping and man, is he a terror to get down." She forced a little laugh and noted the not one, or three, but five men standing outside her apartment. They weren't desk jockeys either—all five had a hardness about them that stood in stark contrast with their expensive black suits. "Ahh, what did you say this is about?"

"Your husband." Hooper paused and glanced at the men behind him. "Are you sure I can't come in? My counterparts can wait in the hall. Promise I'll be quiet." He smiled a most disarming gesture that almost caused Hannah to relent.

She blinked, looking each of the men over again. For a moment, she thought she saw the heel of a gun stashed beneath the smiling point man's suit coat.

"No," she replied with an air of pleasant indifference, "whatever you need to say, you can say it from where you are. There's a problem with my husband?" she asked, careful not to give too much away by using his name.

"Yes, as a matter of fact. Have you been keeping up with what's going on in The Zone?" Hooper asked.

"Not really," Hannah lied, "can't watch the stuff. I prefer VR Texas Hold 'em."

"Ahh, I see." Hooper exchanged glances with one of his men. "Well, your husband has made some tough decisions during this trial. Decisions which have cost many people a lot of money."

"Oh?" Hannah said.

"Yes. He's made a lot of enemies, and some of these enemies might try to hurt him or his family," Hooper said. "Which is why we've been tasked with escorting the Enforcers' families and loved ones somewhere safe. Just until this all blows over."

"Where?"

"An undisclosed location," Hooper said.

"Where?" Hannah repeated.

"It's undisclosed—for your safety." An edge clung to Hooper's voice.

"No thanks, I'm going to go somewhere else for a few days anyway. I'll find somewhere—" Hannah waved her coin wallet open. *Access Denied* flashed in the air. "What is this...?" she muttered.

"See, Mrs. Griffin. Due to credible threats, we've frozen all your assets to protect your investments. But everything is fine. We'll take good care of you." Hooper flashed his disarming smile. "Trust me."

Hooper's fingers had barely snaked around the edge of the door when Hannah slammed it shut. His scream raked the air, the door flung back hard, its inset glass shattering with a pop. Hannah stumbled backward and turned to run, tripping down the stairs. If she could make it to her bag on the counter, the Street Defender was still inside.

Hannah made it within reach of the counter when she felt the crushing blow to the center of her back. Tackled from behind by one of the agents, a man with shoulders like stacked brick, she fell onto the expensive carpet strewn with cushion stuffing. Hannah grunted as the wind knocked from her lungs. An area lamp toppled from a side table, shattering on the white tile in large tusk-like fragments. In the bassinet, Andrew broke into a shrill scream. Hannah rolled to the side, gasping. Brick Shoulder's heavy hands groped at her hips, fingertips digging.

"No," Hannah grunted from the void in her chest. "Help!"

"Help," the auto steward replied in its sterile monotone, "dialing Conglomerate Corporate Security."

"No, stop," Hannah cried, trying to wriggle free of Brick Shoulder's grasp, "not them, damn you."

"Call canceled."

"Don't be stupid," the broad-shouldered agent grunted, pulling her by the hips, "we don't want to hurt you."

Hannah rolled hard beneath his weight, pushing back, his stale coffee breath warm on her face. Pulling her knees up, she thrust out with her legs. The first kick caught the groping agent under the chin, his teeth clicking. The second hit square in the nose, whipping his head back. His eyes rolled, and he pitched to the side.

Scrambling to her feet, Hannah grabbed for the bag on the counter and jammed a hand inside. Shoved forward from behind by another agent with wire brush red hair, her fingers slipped away from the Street Defender. Gripping her by the shoulder, Red spun her to face him, a slap driving hard across her cheek. Hannah gasped. Her knees buckled, and pinpoints of light blinked across her eyes. As she grabbed and flailed, a second slap struck her across the face, causing her body to sag. She hung, pinned there, Red's sinewy hands encircling her throat.

"Hey, Hoop," said another agent standing beside Red hair. "She was trying to get to this stinger." The agent pulled the Street Defender from the bag. "Those are illegal here."

"Please," Hannah whimpered. "I didn't do anything."

"Didn't do anything?" Hooper approached, clenching his hand. Gone from his voice, any sense of civility. "I think you broke my fingers, you stupid bitch."

"And my damn teef," said Brick Shoulders, now rising and holding his hands to his mouth.

The agent at the counter gestured with the Street Defender at the little smashed pile of surveillance wafers. "She destroyed the cameras too, boss."

"Please," Hannah wheezed, pinned to the countertop by Red.

"Oh, no." Hooper wagged a still intact finger, clenching the other mangled hand to his chest. "You had your chance to cooperate, now you're going to do what we want."

"Yeah, *what we want.*" Red winked at his counterparts. "Feisty little tart's got some fight in her. I like that," Red Hair said, pressing himself against her, hands still on her throat. "Maybe we should have a go at her, boys."

Hooper shook his head. "Later. We're on a tight timeline. Gotta link up with the other teams."

Red laughed. "Hoop, I swear I'll be quick."

The coarse laughter of the men filled Hannah's ears.

"Little dick'd pervert," Hannah spat, eyes wild, body thrashing. "You'll try!"

Red punched her this time. Hard. The force of the blow rocked her head back. Hannah groaned.

"I said later," Hooper snapped. "Grab this bitch up, and let's go. The baby too. We need them unharmed—for now."

"Wait," Hannah protested, digging her heels into the carpet. "I'm not going… anywhere."

One of the men jerked a wailing Andrew from his bassinet. The baby broke into shrieks of pain.

"Stop! He has a condition!" Hannah gritted her teeth, kicking without success at Red's groin. "You're hurting him, you slag-eating son of a—"

The man at the counter pulled a gag tight between her gnashing teeth and snatched a hood over her head. An unexpected punch in the stomach followed, knocking the wind out of her a second time. Hannah wheezed, doubled over, carried with her arms pinned behind her back. She strained against the pinching hands of the men. It was no use. Hannah moaned, twisting, as the hostile Glom agents dragged her, flailing across the plush, expensive carpet to the door.

CHAPTER THIRTY-SIX

From the terminal inside his gloom-shrouded command center, Mage watched thousands of information feeds flicker past. Far more than the average person could take in, his eyes bounced from screen to screen, missing nothing. His eyes flashed with excitement as another attempt by the Conglomerate to jam his independent signal failed, and the source rerouted to another false hub. He could keep this up for hours, maybe even days. All he had to do was outlast The Zone.

The Conglomerate's network leadership, with the self-serving Director Kess at the fore, had done an admirable job making the current Zone trial irresistible. According to pirated viewership stats, upwards of ninety percent of network subscribers now watched. Pitting Enforcer against Enforcer was a nice touch, but without the neural trap device the diabolical founders had tried to implement, their plan was already dead in the water. Before the night was through, Kess's teetering house of cards would collapse.

Mage let the jamming cycle continue. He turned his attention to another series of floating holo-screens showing thousands of cameras across the city.

"Sky Rise," he said.

The scrolling feed flickered and changed, limiting it to several hundred cameras.

"Give me the block and the interior cams at the intersection of Corporate and Raben down to Pope."

The central screen adjusted again, now showing a dozen cameras. Mage scanned the images, his stubby little fingers stroking the beaded braids of his goatee. After a moment of searching, his eyes narrowed, focusing on the meat barge as it circled and landed in an alley.

"There you are, you colossal idiot," Mage said.

Mage isolated the appropriate cameras and watched with great interest as Benny appeared, scanning with caution up and down the street from the safety of the barge's rear lift gate.

Mage released a sigh. "Well, the least I can do is crack it open. The rest is up to you." Mage's fingers fluttered against the holo-keyboard that rotated in a sphere around his gloves. Boxes popped up on the overhead screen, and he dismissed them faster than the eye could view, the hacking process more a form of mental acuity than visual examination.

"There," Mage said. He closed the additional screens out.

He sent the update to Signus regarding Benny's current location. Troubling, the fact he cared to any degree about what happened to this oversized clown. It was a crutch. To consider Benny something of a friend amounted to nothing more than human weakness.

A ding from the other side of the room brought his attention around. His eyes narrowed. He switched to the command center's security overview. Mage waved his hands, cycling through the hidden camera feeds below ground and above. He stopped, watching as Conglomerate Shock Troops exited an armored transport. Wearing their signature black armor with gold accents, they formed up and lifted the manhole cover, disappearing one by one into the sewer.

Mage checked the outgoing signal. The auto jamming program was still up. He shook his head.

"Unfortunate but expected," he said, activating the command center's security protocols. "Though much sooner than I would have liked. No matter. These fools will relish no reward for seeking me out."

Mage transferred the overhead security feed to his personal visor as he made his way back to the center of the room. Mage slipped on two larger gauntlets riddled with bizarre electronic components jutting like pipework in all directions. With a *chink*, he connected them to his haptic gloves.

Down the tunnel, the security forces marched at a rapid pace, single file. Slowing, they stacked on the fake wall, the squad leader initializing a scan that Mage knew would reveal his blast door, hidden behind the holographic image.

"There." The squad leader pointed to the spot. "Cut it."

Two troopers approached, extending the telescoping legs of a large conical device, and placed the needle-like end against the hinges of the door.

"Set," one trooper said.

"Fall in," the squad leader barked.

The two dropped back into the stack, a female trooper holding up the device control. "Stand by to activate," she said. "Stand by for breach."

"Go with it," the squad leader said.

A bright light flashed from the nozzle as the plasma torch began the cutting sequence at the top of the door, slicing the eight-inch steel bolts on its way to the floor.

Inside, Mage stood still, his heart rate picking up speed. He rubbed his tacky gloves together. Bright orange liquid metal oozed through the gap to the right of the massive door and pooled on the stone floor, sending up tendrils of putrid smoke.

"Come on in, you slag-eaters," Mage said, a feral snarl breaking across his face, the pale light of the monitors gleaming on the silver canine.

One of the troopers pointed straight at the hidden camera. The squad leader opened a digital order and waved it in the air.

THE ZONE

"By order of the Unified Conglomerate," the squad leader said, *"you are charged with hosting and facilitating a pirated signal onto a closed network. You are to cease and desist immediately. We have you trapped. Any response other than total surrender will be met with deadly force. Do I make myself clear, citizen?"*

"Perfectly," Mage said, the words whistling through clenched teeth, "and tyrannical oppression will be met with the same."

The bolts holding the blast door in place popped as the plasma torch cut through them with ease. Mage flexed his fingers, the control gauntlets lighting up as they powered on. Out of the ceiling dropped two mechanical arms, unfolding from their resting place. The arms, long and thin with gangly fingerlike clamps, stretched out, coming within inches of the blast door before retracting to a neutral position. With a twitch, they jerked to life as they paired with Mage's gloves. A *shink* sounded in the confined space as an enormous katana sword unfurled from the forearm of the right appendage.

The little man brought his hands together, stacking his fists atop one another. In response, the clamps came together around the handle of the massive blade. He twisted his torso left and right, the robotic arms tracking his movement.

"And for the final touch," Mage said.

Threads of projected light danced across the room, interlacing and combining to form the image of a giant, grim-faced samurai. The image of the warrior mapped over the metallic arms, his holographic sword aligned with the real seven-foot katana blade clasped between the vice of metal fingers.

The last bolt severed, the door protested with a squeal of metal, and fell to the floor. A plume of acrid smoke rose in front of the figure of the samurai.

"Activate security measures, corridor defense protocol Lima," Mage said.

As the troopers stepped into the doorway, a series of explosives detonated down the tunnel in a domino effect. The screams of the shocked Glom troopers disappeared in the deafening blasts. The initial assault force surged into the room. Behind them, the bodies of their comrades came apart in showers of fire and blood.

The five-person squad entered, stunned, their mouths agape at the massive lifelike samurai. Mage raised his arms, and the digital warrior followed suit. He swung down, and the samurai lurched to glorious life. The giant blade found its mark, slicing with ease through the stunned troopers. The first two, severed at the midsection, watched in horror as their lower torsos fell away. Another swing and three more, decapitated, shot geysers of brilliant red into the air, their frames slumping to the blood-painted floor. Mage pivoted and raised his stacked hands again for another cut. He tracked the disoriented troopers, each blow a precision stroke, as more ran blindly in, desperate to escape the exploding tunnel. Shrieks filled the air, accompanied by the raking scratch of the sword as it carved trenches in the blood-splattered brick.

The violence ended in seconds. The sword inverted and stabbed down through the last trooper as he tried to drag himself from the room. After a moment, the stoic samurai gave a nod, his digital eyes searching for other threats. The image of the grim warrior flickered and went dark. The arms returned to a neutral position, and the glistening crimson blade retracted.

Exhaust fans kicked into high gear, sucking smoke from the room. As it cleared, Mage held his position, unfazed at the carnage before him. Severed bodies littered the space, like some otherworldly entrance into Hell, the doors and walls decorated with crumbling gouges and generous splashes of dripping crimson.

Mage waited another moment and, hearing nothing, deactivated his gauntlets. With a hiss, the arms retracted back into the ceiling. The Glom wouldn't stop in their pursuit of him now, but maybe they'd think twice before hitting his next location.

"Such a waste," he said, a hint of sadness in his voice.

THE ZONE

It was not the loss of life that troubled him. Mage removed the gauntlets and placed them on a table. He double-checked his server backup and took a moment to ensure the broadcast signal transferred to the next hub. Satisfied, he located the switch beneath each bank of servers and performed each sequential flick of a switch with care as though laying a loved one to rest.

He started the timer. In three minutes, his beloved command center would be scrubbed clean in a wave of blistering fire. Surveying it all one last time from the corner of the room, Mage sighed with a brief nod of resignation. He lifted a hatch in the floor, then disappeared inside, and the steel lid banged shut behind him.

Benny approached the end of the alley with one last look back at the sealed meat barge. Inside, the terrified pilot lay, hands tied behind his back, in the rear compartment. Benny knew he couldn't let the man leave, not yet anyhow. He had no doubt the guy knew who he was. If let go, he'd waste no time reporting him.

Benny had been so intent on making it to Sky Rise that he hadn't taken the time to think through what he'd do once he got here. He knew how to find Hannah, but getting in her building? Dealing with any security? *How the hell do I do that?* he thought. *Walk up and say, "Hey, I know we lost track of each other over the past few weeks, but can you get Chance a message for me? Oh, and by the way, while you've been living in luxury, I've become a wanted cop killer."*

Benny shook his head. *Should've thought this through.* Just because he found Hannah didn't mean she'd be able to get Chance a message while fighting in The Zone. *Idiot.*

Reaching the end of the alley, he still couldn't believe his eyes. The pure splendor of this place was nothing short of stunning.

Crystal towers of steel and glass stretched into the sky. Expensive electric vehicles buzzed past in a blur. Benny scowled. These people had lived in this place for decades while he and everyone else had it hard on the other side of town. It stirred an old passionate hate deep inside.

After scanning for a moment, he realized the street was strangely empty. The would-be pedestrians packed every café and bar in sight. While citizens could stream the network live on their visors, good competitions still had a way of forcing people together for the social experience of a euphoric crowd.

The Zone trial must be well under way by now. Chance didn't have much time. Benny took advantage of the distraction and rounded the corner onto another empty sidewalk. No chance he fit in here, grubby and unshaven, wearing a T-shirt and jacket peppered with bullet holes and sporting a questionable cybernetic enhancement. He approached the front door to Hannah's apartment building and adjusted the nano-skin armor beneath his shirt. It felt different, looser, compromised after taking direct hits from Kip's service weapon.

Benny reached the door and eyed the façade, trying to determine if he could climb the exterior. He took a tentative step forward. The door chirped and slid open. He stood there staring at it. Felt the wash of the cooler air inside as it pushed over him. *How does a building a world away from where I'm from recognize my chip? Is Mage still looking out for me?*

Benny stepped inside. At a glance, the comfortable, air-conditioned lobby appeared empty. He crossed the area at an easy pace as the lift doors opened ahead. A man exited the lift, his visor strobing in his eyes as he walked, mouth ajar, zombified. Benny heard the surge of the crowd from his HD surround audio. He pushed past Benny, oblivious to his surroundings.

Benny let out a nervous chuckle and entered the lift. Hailing the lift's AI, Benny waited as it started its long climb toward the upper floors. It rose with aggravating slowness, and Benny forced his eyes away from the endless upward ticking. If he knew Hannah at all, she would be worried about him. He needed some answers for her.

Benny huffed out a breath and put his anxiety in check. He'd tell her straight and get right to the point. *She'll understand. Chance's safety is what matters most.*

With a *bing*, the lift doors opened, and Benny stepped into the hall. Checking the digital directory, he saw her place was just a few doors down on the right. As he approached, he heard the muffled sounds of a struggle. He stopped, feeling a distant sting of regret at having left his weapons in the meat barge.

One of the apartment doors ahead whooshed open. Two men in black suits entered the hallway, one with heavy shoulders rubbing his mouth and chin, the other with a shock of red hair. A third followed, dragging a moaning figure with a bag over the head.

"You there," Heavy Shoulders called. "Get back in the elevator."

"Mind your own business, citizen," the red-haired man snapped.

"What's going on here?" Benny asked, more out of habit than anything.

With renewed vigor, the hooded figure thrashed and kicked. "Bemmy! Bemmy!"

Benny knew the sound of a gagged person. But not just any person. Hannah. Icy dread descended across his shoulders as a fourth and fifth man entered the hall. The last agent, awkwardly tall with long spindly arms and legs, carried a wailing Andrew.

"Hey, get your hands off them—" Benny stopped dead in his tracks as the two men in front raised stubby black sub-machine guns from beneath their jackets.

"Get back in the elevator. This citizen is wanted for crimes against the Conglomerate. It's not your business," Red Hair said.

"But it *is* my business." Benny clenched his teeth.

"Do it," the grim-faced man, arm around Hannah's torso, said from behind them.

"No—" Benny raised his hands as the sub guns blazed to life. The bullets pinged off his enhanced arm, striking him in the thighs and raking up across his chest cavity. He staggered back, gasping, and fell against the wall, his vision blurring with catastrophic pain.

Sliding to the floor, his gaze dropped to see his ruined legs gushing blood. He felt weak, light as a feather, his breath drawing shallow. Hannah's muffled screams for help and the pained wail of Andrew's cries grew distant.

"He's down," Heavy Shoulders said.

"Finish him. Do it quick."

Hannah sobbed with uncontrollable gasps now. She jerked free, stumbled, and fell. The kidnappers shouted, struggling to contain her as she fought.

Benny took a shuddering breath and looked down, rolling his cybernetic arm to see the inside panel. The display lit up as he moved. With a monumental effort, he reached over to press a finger to the pain icon. A small hiss followed. The overwhelming agony cleared a little. Benny swallowed the taste of clotting blood from his throat and pressed the button again, listening to the sensual hiss of a second dose of powerful painkillers entering his bloodstream.

The pain ebbed and slipped away in a euphoric glow. And with it gone, an all-consuming rage descended upon him.

He swallowed another mouthful of blood, and the world took on a slow, dreamlike effect. The only thing standing between Hannah and Andrew and some terrible unknown fate was Benny the Unwanted. The fugitive. The outcast. But even after all his personal failure and misery, after his whole life imploded on him, Benny knew—even if it meant the end of him, he'd do whatever he had to do to protect Chance's family.

Because that's what brothers do.

Benny peered down at the illuminated screen on his arm and, with only a moment's deliberation, extended two fingers to press and hold the pulsating red and orange icons labeled *Frenzy* and *Velocity*.

CHAPTER THIRTY-SEVEN

I n the abandoned hospital cafeteria amidst the ruins of The Zone, flies gathered on the strewn dead, the air stronger with the sour stench of death with every passing moment. A waning half-light sliced through the murky windows in orange-gray blades that stretched across the long-neglected space and speared up the walls. Chance knelt on the concrete next to the shrouded body of Sam, his eyes turned down. He'd tried to say a few last words to his friend, to tell him he should have trusted him all along, but he'd felt foolish talking to a corpse. The Sam he knew was long gone. Though Chance hadn't pulled the trigger, the guilt over his mentor's death pressed down on his shoulders, a physical burden.

With the utmost care, he reached into Sam's utility pouch and removed the antique silver pocket watch. Scarred and battered, it ticked along, still keeping perfect time after decades of service. *A reminder of the noble lawmen of old*, Chance thought.

Chance slipped the watch into his own pouch and dropped his head. "Dammit, Sam," he whispered.

The abandoned cafeteria took on a somber aesthetic as the sun dipped lower into the western horizon and purple shadows grew long across the war-torn landscape. The old hospital, decrepit and in a state of ruin, only added to the growing feeling that everything had gone bad and fast.

Only occasionally now, a Glom drone cruised past outside the broken-out windows of the hospital, keeping its distance, its broadcast light blinking. The Glom and its founders wouldn't miss an opportunity to profit from the fallout of such an event, even as everything went up in flames around them.

"Chance," Jessie said, leaning into the doorway, "sorry to interrupt."

"It's fine." Chance looked up from Sam's body. "What you got?"

"Another group of Death Squad guys just showed up," Jessie said. "Karissa is negotiating with them downstairs, but it's... a little tense. Thought maybe you could explain what happened with Rico since you were there. They're not happy about it."

"Yeah, I'm coming," Chance said, putting his hand on Sam's shoulder. "Sorry, partner. Gotta go handle business." He stood and took one last look at Rip, stoic even in death. "RITA, geo-tag Sam and Rip. We need to locate and give them a proper burial when this is all over."

"*Already done, Chance.*"

He followed Jessie down the steps toward the front of the building, crossing a large open lobby covered with a dusty gray sheen and the shattered medical remnants of a time long ago. Exiting the front through antiquated double doors, Chance stopped. Ahead, Karissa and Ash stood at forty-five-degree angles to the door, weapons drawn down on a large group of Death Squad goons who had recently returned from a raid. Chance estimated fifty of them, every single one pointing a firearm of some sort in his direction. No one spoke a word.

Chance cut his eyes at Jessie. "A *little* tense?"

Jessie shrugged, a smirk cresting his dust-and-grime-smeared features. "Yeah?"

Chance raised his hands. "I just want to talk, guys."

"We're done talkin'," the man up front said, sporting a chopped-down AK-47, facial tattoos, and a mouth full of gold teeth.

Chance looked closer. A laugh escaped him. "Kybo?"

"You don't know me, Enforcer," the man said, pointing his AK at Chance's face.

Chance took another step forward, his hands still raised. "I do, though. You don't remember? The Boy Scout? I cut you a break in the southern Straits. Looks like you still got your ass thrown in The Zone."

The man squinted a moment, astonishment forming on his face.

"Ho-lee shee-it," Kybo said to his comrades, all staring in dull confusion.

"What is it, Ky?" one man said.

"Officer Griffin—excuse me, Enforcer Justice—used to work my neighborhood in the Straits. He's a fair dude. Cut me and our boys a break once when we needed it." His face hardened. "But this ain't that. You and your friends here have now occupied our headquarters and killed our people. That's an act of war." He spat the words and pointed at Karissa and Ash.

"Kybo, look at me," Chance said, holding the gang lieutenant's gaze, "that wasn't us, man. We didn't do that."

"Is Rico dead?" Kybo said, keeping the AK-47 trained on Chance.

"No," Chance said, "but a lot of people are. Good people."

"And you didn't come here to wipe us out, *Enforcer*?" Kybo narrowed his eyes.

Karissa and Ash stood tense, their weapons raised. Jessie stood close to a stationary machine gun, ready to jump behind it if need be. Chance waved for them all to lower their weapons. Reluctantly, the Enforcers complied.

"I can't lie to you, Kybo," Chance said. "You know the name of the game. It's The Zone, right? Yeah, we came here for the Rico bounty, but things have changed."

Kybo shifted and gave a grunt. "Doesn't look that way to me.

406

Looks like you killed my people. The only reason we still talkin' is you once did me a solid." He took a step closer to Chance and lowered the rifle just a little.

"I know, and I appreciate it, but you've got to hear me out. The Glom did this. They set us up to take the fall live on the net. It's all part of the show. They're going to burn the Enforcers."

"Man, shut up. You expect me to believe this sputz?"

"Yes, I do," Chance said, "because, in a minute, The Glom is going to send everything they've got in here to wipe us out."

"How do you know?" Karissa said, a subdued fear behind her golden eyes.

"Call it a hunch. We've been disavowed," Chance said, his countenance cold and hard. "That means they're going to make us disappear. Our families, too, if I had to guess."

"They can't—" Karissa said.

"They can," Chance said. "Everything we have, they gave us. Everything else, our families, they'll take just to spite us."

"Well, what are we going to do about it?" Jessie said from behind them.

"We fight them tooth and nail," Ash said, his expression resolute, "to the death."

Chance nodded. "That's right. The only thing they can't take from us is our will to resist. We've got to survive this before we worry about anything else." He turned to Kybo. "That's all of us, brother. The Glom will not draw any distinction here when they come. Are we going to kill each other first and let them come mop up for an easy win? Or are we going to give them hell together?"

"I don't know, Kybo," said a tattooed man beside the gang leader. "The Glom might spare us if we take these Enforcers."

"We will not surrender to you, or to them, or to anyone," Chance said. "It's going to be a fight one way or another. You've just got to decide who it's going to be with."

"You sure we can trust them, Kybo?" said the tattooed man.

Kybo regarded Chance long and hard, searching his eyes. "I don't trust The Glom, and I don't know the rest of these Enforcers, but I do trust this loco Boy Scout. He's a man of his word." He reached out and knocked his fist against Chance's. "The Squad will get your back this time. But after this? All bets are off."

A rumble grew in the distance, the sound of a mechanized army on the move. Pouring in from the streets and lanes of the ruins ahead, Grinders loaded with Glom security troopers, transport trucks carrying soldiers and weapons, and walking AI-controlled auto-turrets formed into lines.

"I'll be damned. Right on cue," Ash said.

Chance looked to Kybo. "No egos here. I respect what you and your boys bring to the table, but my people have more tactical experience. We're going to head this up. You good?"

Kybo nodded. "What chu need?"

"Get your people marshaled up. Gather any ammo you can and get these defensive turrets online."

"You got it," Kybo said, already moving and waving to his men.

Chance looked at Karissa, Jessie, and Ash. "We're about to have a major fight on our hands, and we're cut off. Are we good to go on deployed gear that's still usable?"

"Yeah. It's all right there, gathered from the Grinders we came in on," Ash said, pointing to what remained of their ammo and equipment.

They all took a few moments to resupply and re-arm, testing their suit's functionality and armor ratings. Chance laid a hand on Sam's formidable quad launcher, then hefted it into his arms.

The sound of engines firing grew loud as several VTOLs, door gunners at the ready, slowed to hover over the vast number of Glom Security Troops amassed before the fortified structure. Two of the VTOLs carried a blizzard gray object the size of a tank, dangling low on braided chains between them.

"God a'Mighty," Chance said. "What is that?"

With a popping sound, the gargantuan thing fell, slamming into the ground in a cloud of dust. Steam shot from vents along its sides as it rose on two thick piston-powered legs.

"Oh, hell no…" Jessie said.

"It's a slagging mech," Karissa said.

"No," Ash said. "It's not just a mech. It's Gridlock."

The thing hissed again, rising two stories tall. Big-bore cannons and rocket launchers unfolded along its arms and snapped into place over its shoulders. Its mechanical fingers flexed, curling into fists the size of wrecking balls.

"Attention rogue Enforcers." The amplified voice of Gabriel Kess rose into the night air. "This is the sound of your doom."

The whooshing rush of multiple unknown substances firing into his bloodstream filled Benny's ears like a torrential current of water. His lungs ached with an arctic cold, his heart fluttering like a mad bird caged deep in his chest. He gagged and coughed. His mouth stretched open, eyes wild and blind. Blood ran from his nose and pooled in the shallows of his ears.

A strangled cry clawed from Benny's throat. A wave of fire, like the inside of a blast furnace, ripped through his veins and swarmed his brain, drowning his senses in a lake of molten flame. He clawed at his face, his fingers digging and dragging. He screamed again— a horror-laced sound of absolute madness.

The Glom agents stopped, staring, unnerved by the bizarre display. The man with heavy shoulders turned to the guy with red hair, then cast a glance at the squad leader.

"Hey, Hooper, something is wrong with this guy."

"Yeah, it's called sputz'd," Hooper called out, holding up a weeping Hannah.

"Yeah, but... something's wrong..." the heavy-shouldered man said, wincing at Benny's deranged screams.

"Do him. We gotta go," Hooper called.

Red Hair smirked. "Poor slag-eater." He raised his weapon.

Benny exploded up from the floor with a scream. A clipped burst of two rounds loosed from Red's submachine gun. The rounds stitched the wall beside Benny, whose cybernetic hand jammed beneath Red's chin, and thrust him toward the ceiling. With a metallic *snap*, the dimenium hand clenched shut. The lower half of Red's face burst like an over-filled balloon. A shower of blood and bone sprayed across the width of the hall.

The heavy-shouldered man shrieked, raising his own submachine gun. Benny caught him with a brutal downward blow of the metal fist, caving his forehead in with a pressurized spray of gore.

Another wild scream flew from Benny's throat. The blood of his foes drenched his face, hands, and body. Moving faster than should be humanly possible, he threw himself down the length of the hallway.

Terror plastered on their faces, Hooper and the other two opened fire. The bullets streaked down the hallway leaving powdery splashes that hung in the air and drifted in the light as Benny charged. Time seemed to alternate from so slow Benny could see each individual bullet to so fast he couldn't comprehend his own movements. He rocketed forward, a howl of rage on his lips.

Benny slammed into the closest man, delivering a blow that sent him crashing against the wall. With a savage stomp, he dashed the stunned man's head to pieces against the floor. Another breaking rattle of sub-machine gun fire. Benny raised the cybernetic arm to protect his face. The rounds found their mark, riddling Benny's body as Hooper and the tall, lanky agent holding

Andrew bounded back, covering each other's movements in retreat.

Hooper shoved Hannah to the ground. The lanky man holding Andrew turned and fled, his coat streaming behind him, legs wobbling in long, loping strides.

Benny coughed, choked on his own blood. He lurched across the hall and grabbed the squad leader, who fumbled with another magazine. The impact rocked Hooper back, knocking the stubby pistol-gripped SMG from his hands. Holding the squad leader by the jacket, Benny struck him with his cybernetic fist, pulping the guy's face. Hooper moaned, clawing in desperation at the enraged mountain of a man.

Lifting him high overhead, Benny groaned, took three stumbled steps, and pitched the disfigured squad leader headfirst against the window. It shattered, breaking in a spray of diamond-like glass. Hooper cried out as his body went into free fall, tumbling in a crystalline shower from the high-rise apartment.

Andrew's lanky captor opened his gait, his free arm pumping as he sprinted the length of the hallway. Benny tried to pursue, took a series of stumbled steps, and fell against the wall. He rolled to his back and slid down, a crimson streak in his wake. There he lay, irregular, wheezed breaths gurgling from ruptured lungs.

Hannah struggled to jerk the hood from her head, bound hands groping against the cloth. She groaned, jerked the hood free, and yanked the gag down from her open mouth. "Motherslaggers!" Hannah shouted at the top of her lungs. She made it to her knees and drove to her feet, pulling one hand free from her bonds. Her body surged with reckless energy, a lioness furious with the primal instinct to protect her young.

At the far end of the hallway, the awkwardly tall Glom agent slammed through the door and into the stairwell, the jolting movements eliciting another hysterical scream from Andrew, clenched in his arms.

Absolute horror swelled inside Hannah at the sight of Andrew's little shoulders clutched in the man's spider-like fingers—the sight of his little face, beet red, eyes pinched, mouth wide as he screamed for her.

"Benny!" she cried. "They're taking Andrew!" She started for the stairs, stumbling over a dead agent, when her eyes fell on Benny's ruined form for the first time. She crouched in shards of glass under a shattered window, paralyzed with anguish, half-turned after her child again. She shook, one hand outstretched toward her son, the other reaching for Benny on the floor.

Little Andrew's cries faded and disappeared.

Hannah had less than no chance of catching the fleeing man. *And if I do? What then? Fight with him? Take a bullet to the brain?* She needed Benny, but he lay on the floor, eyes glazed and far away. She groaned, an anguished sound, clutched at her shirt, her face. "No..."

Gunshots echoed from the roof, through the broken window, the erratic staccato signaling another gunfight.

A gunfight... God save us. Hannah's body shook, the stunning loss of her boy echoing across the void inside her.

She sank to her knees, and her arms stretched out to her mortally wounded friend. Her eyes welled. "Benny. Get up, I need you. Get up, please..."

"I'm..." Benny gurgled, struggling to fill punctured lungs, his eyes distant. "I'm sorry, Hannah."

"Oh, Benny. Oh my God." She grabbed him and cradled his blood-soaked form against her, as tears poured down her face. "Those filthy slag-eaters. Look what they've done."

A whooshing shriek sounded from above as a jet-black Glom

VTOL lifted off from the roof and fell over the side of the building, whipping the wind through the broken out window as it thundered past. Hannah watched it go, screaming into the sky as the main thrusters engaged. She wept, tears of sadness and fury dripping from her chin and nose. She pulled a wheezing Benny close, applying pressure to his wounds.

Little Andrew was on that VTOL. She knew it.

Time dragged past, stuck in a terrible feedback loop of Hannah's whimpering and Benny's sucking attempts to draw breath. Wind, cold and brisk, whipped in through the shattered window and left the hall chilled and barren.

"I've got him right here, boss," a baritone voice shouted from the end of the hallway.

Three men in dusty cyber-tactical equipment emerged from the stairwell, swinging their weapons left and right as they navigated the hall.

"Are you injured, lady?" a thin-faced man with a nasal voice called to Hannah.

"They took my baby. Why would they take my baby?" Hannah whimpered.

"Are you hurt?" thin face repeated.

She shook her head and shrugged her shoulder against her cheek to catch a running tear. "No, but my friend is…" she said, tears falling on Benny's face.

The thin-faced man took a knee and pulled a hypo-injector from his cloak. "He's in bad shape, but this will help stabilize him. It's a medical booster."

Hannah watched as he pressed the loaded syringe to Benny's thigh with a hiss.

"Who was that guy with the child?" The thin-faced man didn't look up. "He exchanged gunfire with us and fled."

Hannah could only shake her head. "The Glom. They stole my baby."

"That's some cold slag," the thin-faced man said.

"Ice cold," the deep-voiced man said, wedging a tablet device back into his assault vest. "Scan's positive. This is definitely our guy, boss."

The thin-faced man tilted his head and caught Hannah's eye. "I'm Signus. This guy doesn't have much time. If he's going to live, he's got to come with me. Now."

"No," Hannah shook her head, "where are you taking him?"

"To see a friend who can help." Signus leaned close to Benny's face. "Mage sent me."

Though glazed and distant, Benny's eyes showed a spark of recognition. His hand reached up to squeeze Hannah's fingers. She swallowed and looked once again at the strange men.

"I'm coming with you," she said. "Maybe your friend can help me, too."

"We don't have orders to fetch you too, lady," Signus said.

"I don't give two sputz what your orders are," Hannah said, "I'm not leaving Benny alone." Hannah stood, an iron look of defiance on her face. "Understand?"

After a moment, Signus gave a single nod. "Yes, ma'am." He jerked his narrow chin up at his two men. "Let's go, the clock's ticking on this guy."

The two men dragged an unconscious Benny toward the stairs. Signus pushed ahead of them, clearing the stairwell of threats before motioning them on. Hannah wiped the last of the drying tears from her chin and bent to pick up one of the stubby black sub-machine guns left scattered in the hallway. She checked the chamber and, seeing the gleam of brass, let the bolt snap back into place. She stepped into the stairwell after Signus and his men, her face cold and hard, like a thing of stone.

CHAPTER THIRTY-EIGHT

"Chance." RITA's voice emanated from his suit. "*It's Kess. He's got a few hundred nano-jacked troops with him. That's not counting the AI-controlled turrets, the VTOL support, and Kess's Combat Power Mech, Gridlock.*"

"Okay," Chance said, wincing as he placed a hand over the oozing wound in his abdomen.

"*I estimate our chances of survival are—*"

"No, RITA," Chance said. "We're not going there right now. Just get us ready."

"*Copy.*"

Chance watched as a host of Glom drones revolved around the massive white and gray suit of armored pistons and stove-pipe cannons. Far overhead, hovering lights popped on one at a time, illuminating the space before them like the sports arenas of old. The sound of the cheering crowds amplified as audio piped in from homes and bars and public venues all over the city.

"You have defied your orders, as well as the law, and are hereby in violation of your contracts with the Unified Conglomerate." Kess's voice boomed across the makeshift arena. "You have betrayed us all. Surrender now, and I may still spare your lives."

The roar of the crowd thrummed in the air. Chance stood his ground as Karissa, Jessie, and Ash fell in alongside him. From the ruined hospital, Kybo and his remaining foot soldiers emerged.

415

Armed to the teeth, they took up defensive positions.

Kybo gave a nod to Chance. "Turrets are online. We ready, Boy Scout."

Chance returned the nod and looked back to Kess in his intimidating suit of power armor.

"How low you sink when faced with total annihilation," Kess mused. "I expected more from you, Justice—seeking the help of those you swore to dispatch. Give me your answer now. I won't wait forever."

"You're the traitor, Kess. This," Chance motioned in the air, "all of this is to keep the people distracted, isn't it? You can't have them knowing The Glom butchered its citizens in New West City, can you?"

"You'd say anything to save yourself," Kess said. "It's a lie."

"You and The Glom may have played us, but you don't own us," Chance called out, hefting Sam's quad rocket launcher to his shoulder, "and you don't own the people of Neo Terminus. If you want a fight, you've got one."

The shrieks of the remote audience grew deafening, the ground trembling with the sounds of millions of viewers.

"So be it!" Gridlock pointed his massive arm, a salvo of rockets launching from his back as the Conglomerate's security forces opened fire.

"Come on!" Chance screamed, his faceplate slamming down.

Fists balled, ready for action, the faceplates of the other Enforcers slammed down one by one. Kybo and the Death Squad hoisted their weapons, calling into the air in unison.

"*I've got a quad lock on priority targets,*" RITA said.

"First blood is for you, Sam." Chance held the quad launcher steady. Proper eye relief gained, each of the four rockets loosed in sequence. They screamed and twisted, the sound like tearing cloth as each streaked across the desolate landscape to find its mark, crippling one of the two walking auto-turrets and smashing into the three hovering VTOLs. The auto turret stumbled and collapsed on its side. The flaming VTOLs twisted, falling to the earth in streaks of fire. Chance dropped the launcher and surged forward, gritting his teeth at the pain in his abdomen.

The first of Gridlock's rockets slammed home, obliterating a swath of Kybo's men and a large section of the Zone's outer wall. A chain of explosions followed as the other rockets struck, dotting the battlefield with flashes of fire. The Death Squad's members dove for cover as vast rolling balls of flame immolated friends and comrades.

Karissa leaped over a concrete barricade, blasting a security trooper into the air with a vicious uppercut, then falling back to decimate three more with a kinetic shockwave.

Jessie advanced with the skill and grace of a figure skater, weaving between the junk and debris. He dropped Glom troopers with precision shots from his Peacemaker. When the mag went empty, he snagged three combat knives from his rig and flung them into the chests of the enemy troopers with deadly accuracy.

From his position of overwatch, Ash worked the bolt on his fabled Lance Systems precision rifle, each blistering crack signaling the death of another prized Conglomerate asset.

"I want you," Kess said, stomping forward. The Gridlock power mech extended a massive steel hand to point at Chance.

"You won't have to wait long, you son of a bitch," Chance said and sprinted at the massive white and gray figure.

Even though running at full stride, at a speed of thirty miles an hour, Chance dispatched six more Glom troopers. Their armored shells burst in showers of obsidian glass beneath the force of the Peacemaker's armor-piercing rounds. The jets in Chance's suit fired, thrusting him left and right as RITA identified threats.

"Three more on your left, ten o'clock."

Chance's Peacemaker blazed three more times. He slid across the hood of an ancient auto junker, a relic half-dissolved into the cracked concrete beneath it. Chance extracted a loaded magazine from his carrier, ejected the spent mag with a flick of his wrist, and jammed the fresh one home. A round struck him in the side, followed by another in the side of the helmet.

"Armor's down to seventy-two percent. You're taking fire from a Grinder squad behind you. Four o'clock," RITA said.

"A little help?" Chance said.

"I got you." Jessie slammed headlong into the Grinder, grabbing the undercarriage and upending it with a yell. The troopers inside fell, their bodies crushed beneath it as it rolled.

Ahead, the last of the auto turrets stalked forward on spidery legs. The AI brain, connected to a single red eye, swiveled back and forth. It locked on Karissa, who ran right at it.

"All right, boys, time to watch how it's done," she said between breaths.

The auto turret's twenty-millimeter rail gun swung in her direction and fired. Karissa's directional thrusters launched her to the left to avoid the shot. The turret's cannon tracked her, too slow to gain a lock on the former decathlete.

Karissa drew her Peacemaker from its holster and fired a handful of well-placed shots, disabling the hydraulic pistons in the thing's legs. She threw herself forward and crashed through one of the extended legs, breaking it in two. Driving up, she slammed her fist through the steel plate protecting the brain box and jerked free a handful of sparking wires and shattered components. The auto turret faltered and fell, sending up plumes of dust.

Kybo and the last of the Death Squad let loose howls of victory as the thing fell. They surged with their weapons blazing into the fray.

Ash loosed another round and raised his eye from the scope, a smirk on his face. "And that's why you don't mess with that one, fellas."

"I've known it for a long time," Jessie said, pulling a sixteen-inch laser wakizashi from the small of his back. Ducking, spinning, and deflecting, he cut down a dozen Glom troopers who couldn't get a shot off on him in close quarters.

With The Glom's lines broken and the unstoppable Enforcers carving their way through them, the troopers panicked. Dropping their weapons, they turned and ran, the pay of a mercenary not enough to justify imminent death at the hands of trained killers.

"Cowards!" Kess screamed. Stomping forward, a titan awakened from its age-old slumber, Gridlock advanced. Another salvo of rockets fired from his back, looping in an arc across the night sky.

Ash raised up from the scope. "Ahh, sputz," he said, leaving the cumbersome rifle where it was. In two steps, he dove from the ledge, the rockets slamming in behind him and obliterating his position of overwatch. Tumbling and bouncing, Ash rolled to a stop with a curse.

"Ash?" Chance shouted, hurling an impact grenade toward a squad of troopers.

"Not dead… yet," Ash grumbled.

"Enforcers, form up. When we move on Gridlock, it's got to be as a team." Chance took cover as his grenade exploded, blasting troopers in all directions.

"Roger that," Ash grunted, standing.

"On my way," Karissa said.

"Right behind you," Jessie said.

The sound of the crowd swelled at the approaching conflict, throngs of ravenous fans who'd bet life and limb on this moment.

Kess brought Gridlock's hands together as the Enforcers rushed him. "You think you're ready? As far as you're concerned, I might as well be God."

A rumble of thunder above heralded a blast of lightning. It struck the field meters from Chance, and his display flickered with the surge.

"*Chance, he's harnessing some sort of massive electrical discharge,*" RITA said. "*If it hits any of us, we're done for. Keep moving.*"

"Great," Chance said as another rumble rolled across the sky.

Jessie fired two white phosphorus rounds in succession. An explosive blast of pearl-colored fire engulfed Gridlock.

With a hiss, extinguishers all over the massive suit smothered the flames.

Another deep rumble of thunder followed.

"You really think that's going to stop me?" Kess said. "You think you can escape the wrath of the Conglomerate?"

Jessie screamed as a blast of lightning struck him. His armor jolted with bands of twisting electricity. Locked stiff, streaming smoke from the vents of his armor, from his helmet, he collapsed to the ground.

"Jessie!" Karissa screamed, sprinting onward.

"RITA, status?" Chance said.

"*His armor is down. Vitals are failing.*"

"Damn you, Kess." Chance fired a barrage of armor-piercing rounds at the giant mech. Each shot pinged without effect off the outer shell.

"Dimenium hard plate." Kess's amplified voice gave a grim laugh. "Good luck breaking through."

Chance ducked behind a crumbling concrete barricade. "RITA, analyze his suit and find me a weakness."

"*Chance, they designed the Gridlock armor to be indestructible.*"

"Find me something," Chance said, holstering his Peacemaker.

Another rumble of thunder from above—Chance gave a worried glance at the sky and checked his remaining ammo.

Gridlock's particle disruption cannon charged, a glowing green light growing brighter at the muzzle. With a zapping sound, it tore a hole in the barricade Chance hid behind. He slid belly down in the debris.

"Our weapons aren't effective," Chance said, "he's got us

outgunned."

"Then we go hands-on," Karissa said, driving in.

Chance vaulted over the ruined barricade after her.

"And to think I liked you, Takedown," Kess said as Gridlock took a fighting stance.

"You're about to find out how I got the name." Karissa vaulted into the air.

She landed a stunning double kick, and the massive suit staggered back. Karissa dodged a grab of one of Gridlock's hands, heavy metal fingers that raked the broken concrete.

"Thrust!" Karissa shouted, the vents in her suit flaring with fire. Rocketing upward, her fist slammed under the armor's command module and rocked it back.

Chance gave a victory shout, but his excitement turned to horror as one of Gridlock's hands snagged Karissa out of the air.

"This is what happens to those who defy me!" Kess said. With two massive hands clenched around Karissa's torso and legs, he brought her down in a brutal motion across the knee of the giant mech. There was the horrible sound of metal distorting, followed by a short, anguished cry.

Chance screamed and launched himself at the monstrous suit of armor.

Gridlock flung Karissa's limp form off to the side and caught Chance with a backward swing of the giant arm, slamming him against the ground.

"*Your armor just dropped to fifty-three percent,*" RITA said, a tremor in her voice.

Gridlock raised a giant foot to crush Chance.

"*Chance!*" RITA cried out.

"Nuke fist!" Ash crashed into Gridlock with a thunderous flash of light. The strike staggered Gridlock to the side, and a miniature mushroom cloud rose from the impact. Kess bellowed, and the mech flailed, slamming its balled fists into everything in sight. Ash ducked and rolled, attacking the piston-powered legs, as Chance jumped up and threw an impact grenade against the titan's upper axis.

"RITA, a little help here." Chance rolled out of the way of a trio of blasts from Gridlock's particle disruption cannon.

Another rumble of thunder above. Ash swore, throwing himself sideways as a blast of lightning snapped against the ground.

"*I have an idea,*" RITA said.

"Go with it." Chance sucked at the air.

"*Gridlock is dated. Its electrical defense systems were created over a decade ago. Wait for the next rumble of thunder, then jump on Gridlock's back and hold tight. You'll take the blast, but so will he, and the Gridlock armor won't fare as well.*"

"Can I survive that?"

"*According to my calculations, if your armor is still above fifty percent and the charge disperses between the two of you, there's a good likelihood...*"

"But?"

"*Chance.*" A pause, emotional, human, clung to the soft static of the speaker. "*I evolve in real-time. I can't survive an overload of that magnitude.*"

"Then it's not viable." Chance prepped his last grenade.

Gridlock tracked a sprinting Ash, the rounds from its chain gun chewing up the turf behind the special forces veteran.

"Chance, what are we doing?" Ash called.

"I'm working on it."

"Work faster," Ash shouted.

"*Chance. Please, it's the only way. The longer this plays out, the worse your odds. If you or Ash falls, the remaining Enforcer is doomed.*"

"RITA, I'm not having this conversation. Find me another way."

Sadness trembled in the voice of his AI companion. "*It's okay, Chance. You need to survive. I'm not real. I don't matter.*"

"RITA, damn it—"

A massive hand pinned Chance against the broken stone.

"I've got you now," Kess said, the Gridlock armor leaning its weight on top of him. "You've burned everything I've built, boy. Now you'll get what you deserve." The particle cannon charged, hovering over Chance's face as he struggled against the titan's grip.

A crushing blow from Gridlock's free hand knocked Ash from the air and whipped his body against the earth.

"'Ay, Kess. Incoming!" An odd cockney accent gurgled over Chance's radio.

The screeching sound of jets seared across the sky, a VTOL racing into the battle. Swooping down, the engine at full throttle, the VTOL cut through the air like a missile. It smashed into the side of the Gridlock armor and exploded into the debris. Gridlock toppled, then righted itself. The titan swung its massive fist down and tore the VTOL's cab open. But the pilot chair was empty. On the console, the vehicle's remote pilot beacon blinked.

The sound of Grendel's voice twittered in a laugh over their comms.

"You!" Kess screamed. "Did you remote this in? You disgusting troll. I should have killed you years ago!"

A rumble of thunder rolled across the sky and into the distance.

"*Now, Chance. It's the only way. Go now,*" RITA said.

A stroke of agony filled his chest. He drove to his feet. "Thrust."

A flash of fire surged beneath his boots, and Chance sailed into the air.

"Power Slam," Chance shouted. Fists raised high overhead, they glimmered with charged energy.

He struck the back of the Gridlock armor, dropping his balled fists with a flash of light. The brute rolled on its side, twisted, and reached its limbs beneath it to rise again. Clinging to the rear hard plate, Chance clamored to stay on the mech's back.

"*Hold tight, Chance.*" RITA's voice wavered in his ears. "*Here it comes. I'm happy to have—*" The targeted lightning blast struck Chance with a blistering electrical surge. He screamed, his body frozen in space, his entire heads-up display flickered and faded to black.

A sustained scream of pain resounded from inside the Gridlock armor. The armor jerked and writhed, sparks flying into the air alongside curling bands of smoke. Its mechanical arms reached up toward the heavens, then collapsed.

The crowd's stunned silence descended on the wreckage of the battlefield. An age seemed to pass as smoke and dust rose in swirling pillars that dissipated into the sky.

"Chance." Ash sat up, pushing aside a broken chunk of concrete. "Chance, respond, damn you."

Chance's helmet popped loose and slid back. "RITA, disengage my..." Chance stopped and listened to the bitter silence. He swallowed, then pulled the emergency release himself. The rest of the damaged armor pieces, no longer tethered to each other, slid free. Chance blinked his eyes. Everything ached with a tingling numbness. He touched his damaged earpiece.

"Grendel?"

A moment passed, soft digital static playing in his ears.

"I 'eard... what you said about not bein' controlled, and choosing my own path, an'... I thought to myself—what the 'ell." The giant's voice was little more than a wet gurgle, amplified by the static-shrouded radio.

Chance slowly stood free of the pieces of shattered armor, the black skin suit still clinging to his body. "And you chose to help us?"

"Well, I jakkin' hate Kess, and... you were fair to me once," Grendel said, his voice fading in the distorted digital static. "Cheers, mate."

"Yeah." Chance sighed. He turned to search the urban wastes. "Ash?"

"I'm here, you crazy son of a bitch," Ash groaned and sat up.

"You good?" Chance asked.

"I'm still breathing," Ash said.

"Check on Karissa and Jessie?"

"I'm on it." Ash watched Chance take a step toward the Gridlock armor, flames curling around the edges of its massive bulk. "Don't... Let him burn. It's what he deserves."

Chance stepped up to the body of the massive suit. "Yeah... it is."

The crowd's pensive silence rang in his ears. Chance pressed his teeth together and gave a brief shake of his head. He found Gridlock's emergency release and popped the hatch. Smoke billowed out. Kess, bleeding, his face burned, coughed weakly. Chance released the director's harness and dragged him from the ruins of the hulking mech. Stopping a few feet away, he dropped Kess to the ground as flames engulfed the rest of the great machine.

A Glom drone lowered to capture the moment in full.

Chance hefted his Peacemaker from where it lay in the holster and leveled it, arm straining without the support of his armor.

"Do it," Kess rasped.

The muscles of Chance's jaw flexed, the massive weapon shaking in his hand. *It is what he deserves.*

"The founders..." Kess coughed.

"What are they planning? Our families?"

Kess laughed dryly and shook his head. "You. Me. Nobody is safe."

Fury, pure and unrestrained, boiled within him. Chance let his finger cover the trigger. "Tell me what you know if you want to live."

"You don't get it, do you, kid?" Kess sat up weakly and spat a stream of blood. "For this insult, they're going to take everything from you. *Everything.*"

Chance's eyes narrowed. "I'll stop them."

Kess huffed. "No, you won't." He leaned forward and touched his forehead to the muzzle of Chance's weapon. "Do it. You've already ruined me. Why spare my life?"

Chance swallowed and lowered the weapon. "Because I'm not an executioner," he said, his penetrating gaze locked on the ruined director. "But what you've done is unforgivable, Kess. If I ever see your face again, I *will* kill you."

"Big words—"

Chance whipped the slide of the Peacemaker across Kess's face, rocking his head back. A stream of blood ran from a long gash beneath his eye. With a wheeze, Kess slumped back against the rubble. The crowd cheered.

Chance exhaled, fury turning to dismay as he watched Ash carry Karissa's armored form past Jessie, who lay immobile, streaming smoke.

"They okay?" Chance asked, stumbling across the rubble.

"Readings are dark on Jessie," Ash said. "Karissa's rig says her vitals are elevated. She's not responding. We need an emergency evac and a few recovery chambers."

Chance bent and put his hand on Jessie's shoulder. He released the downed Enforcer's faceplate. A gasp caught in Chance's throat, and he shrank back, his forearm covering his mouth. Smoke wafted out from the shell, accompanied by the smell of charred meat and burnt hair. Jessie's blackened, skeletal jaw hinged open. A swell of gasps echoed from the crowd.

Chance swore.

"Is he…?" Ash called out.

"Yeah." Chance coughed and stood, shaking his head.

Ash bristled with anger. He pointed in Kess's direction. "You should go back over there and kill that slag-eater."

Chance turned away and shook his head. "It won't change anything."

Ash swore again, struggling to support Karissa in her armor.

"Come here and give me a hand with her."

Chance crouched by Karissa's side where Ash held her. He popped the release on her helmet. She blinked, swallowing hard.

"Did we win?"

"Yeah, Karissa, we won," Chance said. He offered his friend a ghost of a smile and watched as Ash injected her with a medical booster.

"Jessie?" she asked. "Is Jessie…?"

Chance lowered his head and nodded.

A tear streamed from the outside edge of Karissa's golden eyes. "Right."

"He died a hero. Drew Gridlock's fire so we could make our move." Chance surveyed his friend's face. "You okay?"

Karissa shook her head, her eyes welling with more tears. "Can't move my legs."

Chance grabbed her hand. "We're going to get you some help."

"Chance," she said, squeezing his hand, "my girls. What if The Glom retaliates?"

He squeezed her hand back. "We'll stop them. Again."

She sniffed.

"You got her?" Chance asked.

"I got her," Ash said.

Chance stood. He thought of Hannah and Andrew and the rest of their families and knew the next most important step was to find and secure them.

An ear-scraping screech of static brought Chance around. He turned to face a lone Glom drone hovering behind him. The sizzling white noise filled the air as the drone projected an ethereal humanoid image. The phantom watched him without eyes or features.

Chance squinted, taking in the flickering form. "What do you want?"

"You know what we want," the shade whispered in a death-like

427

sigh. "And you know what we're capable of, yet still, you rise against us."

"The Glom, the founders, whoever you are—you don't own us, and you can't threaten us anymore."

A laugh wheezed through the static. "Your precious loved ones might disagree. A price must be paid for your treachery, Enforcer, and it will be paid in blood."

Chance raised his Peacemaker and pointed it at the drone. "Show's over."

The single crack of gunfire echoed across the landscape. The spectral image flashed away. The last Glom drone whirled down and came apart against the turf, a smoldering pile of junk.

The roars for *Jus-tice* sung by millions filled the air.

The obsidian gleam of his shattered armor caught his attention. He crouched. Reaching out, Chance touched the faceplate of his helmet, now dark amidst the swirling dust and crackling fire.

"It was all you, RITA," he murmured. "You saved us."

Chance sat for a moment, listening as the roars of the crowd died away, replaced by the sounds of a restless city.

A chill fear at the unknown fate of his family clutched at the edges of his heart.

He turned to see the destroyed section of The Zone's wall, pulverized by one of Gridlock's rockets. His eyes roved out over the city beyond. In the distance, an explosion ignited with a pop. Fires flickered with intermittent billowing flares amidst the dark and neon glow of Havana Straits and Volkan Heights.

A soot-covered Kybo stopped short of the gap in the wall and ushered a hobbling Rico, the children, and the last of the Death Squad through to their freedom. He raised two fingers and gave Chance a salute. Chance responded in kind and watched as the gang leader-turned-ally disappeared over the far side.

The illusion was broken. The people awakened, a fragile shred of freedom within their grasp—but at what cost? They may have fractured the Glom's organization, but the founders were still out there. Chance looked to the horizon and found the promise of the unknown now terrifying and exhilarating all at once. He winced and applied pressure to his gunshot wound.

He had to cling to the hope that his wife and son were safe. But in the depths of his heart, he knew his defiance had stirred a terrible foe from its dark slumber.

Chance nodded to Ash and Karissa, taking strength from comrades courageous enough to hold the line with him. He straightened with a grimace of pain and gazed out through the crumbling Zone wall as the fires of revolution spread throughout the city—the old and decrepit giving way to a dark new fate, like the arcane birthing of a phoenix.

EPILOGUE

The lone figure in drab street clothes neared the end of the trash-strewn alley. Gloomy and wet and smelling of rotten garbage. It was the sort of place most people wouldn't be caught dead at this hour—and others had been. Stock still, the figure cocked his head and listened, eyeing the feet of a stinking corpse hastily stashed amidst the garbage. The rustle of rodents under piles of soggy refuse blended with the din of a somber, restless city. A string of gunfire peppered the air. The yelp-howl of police sirens echoed in response.

Neo Terminus had fallen, and no amount of police intervention would save her now.

The figure accessed his visor's global positioning map and rechecked the address. He scanned the building and found the dingy numeral markings on the southwest corner of the moldering brick façade.

This is the place.

At the opposite end of the alley, a trash bin toppled, empty tin cans scattering from torn bags of rubbish. The lone figure spun, an MVX pistol jerked from the holster in the small of his back. The weapon locked on the toppled bins as a slag dog ran, paws splashing in neon-tinged puddles until it disappeared into the musty dark of an adjoining alley.

"Damn." Chance lowered the pistol. He winced and clutched at the wound in his abdomen, bandaged and stitched but still weeping. With a snap, the MVX locked back into the concealment holster beneath his jacket.

He paused at the door as the skyline jumped with the dancing flash of neon lights. Mercifully, after the collapse, not everything tech-related had gone down. The Conglomerate's network was still up and running, along with a majority of the failed city's systems, such as the power grid, the waterworks, and sanitization. The automated infrastructure chugged along as if it were just another day in paradise.

But it wasn't another day in paradise. It was a neon-infused hell, and he was the damned. Ten days of fruitless searching. Ten days that felt like an eternity. *Don't let it be for nothing.*

Sizing up the door to the ancient packing facility, he inhaled the dank musk scent of the city at night, turned the knob, and entered.

The door squawked on rusted hinges. Chance took a step inside, his silhouette in stark relief to the neon glow of the city beyond. He scanned the darkened shipping warehouse. In the stale gloom, nothing stirred. Moving quickly now, a sense of urgency filled his chest. This tip was good, he was sure of it, but for how long was anybody's guess. *I have to know...*

Ascending a rickety metal staircase as quietly as he could, Chance found the door, touched the cold of the handle, and gave it a slow quarter twist. Secure, but not at the knob—latched from the other side. He placed his ear to the wood frame. The slightest rustle of noise scratched inside.

Chance pulled back with a sharp intake of breath and lurched forward, slamming his boot against the single latch. The door rocked open with a splintering of wood, tiny fragments of the frame thrown into the room. The latch hit the cheap, cracked linoleum floor with a tinkling sound.

Gunfire raked across the disheveled efficiency apartment, stitching a jagged line of holes up the wall beside Chance. With a grunt, he dove behind a worn couch, the cushions stained and damp with sweat. Bullets zipped off the wall and punched through the wood and foam of the old sofa, showering Chance with little bits of cream-colored stuffing.

He wanted to return fire. Wanted it with everything in his being. But deadly force wasn't an option, not when he was *so close*.

Chance grabbed for the thrift store lamp within reach, his fingers closing on the base. He flung it across the room at the shooter and watched as a tall man, partially concealed in shadow, ducked into a roach-infested kitchenette to avoid it.

Now.

Chance vaulted the couch, which stunk of hair grease and cat piss, and crossed the space in two strides. The man rose again, a well-used Castor revolver aimed at Chance, who sidestepped as it flashed with fire. He slapped down at the tall man's narrow wrist, knocking the weapon free and driving him backward. With a grunt, Chance smashed his assailant's head through one cabinet, pulled him back, then drove him into a second, breaking the door off its rusted hinges.

"Where are they?" Chance shouted, stretching on his toes.

The lanky man scrabbled in desperation, grabbed at Chance's fingers sunk deep into his soiled jacket. His eyes grew frenzied, spittle frothing on thin lips. "I... I don't know what you're talking about!"

Chance caught the man beneath the chin, rocking his head back with a furious uppercut. Teeth clacked. Something fractured. The man let loose a shriek of terror and pain. Chance pivoted hard, slammed the lanky man's face down against the plastic countertop, and stepped on the back of his spindly leg, enough to break his posture. Chance's free hand closed on a worn butcher knife. Not too sharp. *Sharp enough.* He drove it into the counter, burying it inches from the trembling man's gawking expression.

"Talk," Chance said. "Or I cut things off you might want."

"I… I… don't know… anything." The lanky man panted, spit flecking the countertop. "They don't trust us enough to tell…"

"What *do* you know?"

The lanky man gave a muffled whinny.

A message notification trilled on Chance's visor, a small red exclamation indicating its urgency. Pain, deep and throbbing, radiated from the half-healed gunshot wound in his side.

Chance jerked the knife from the counter and drove it deep through the man's shoulder. The screams of agony wavered like a falsetto note, high and sustained. Chance wondered, even in this hell-hole of a dive, when someone might notice. Not that the police had the resources to respond, even if they got the call.

Chance leaned in close, his nose almost touching the man's gaunt, stubbled cheek. "You want to kidnap women and children? Huh? You like the thrill of it? The power it gives you?"

"No."

"No?" Chance pulled back. "This is the last time I'm going to ask. You've already tried to kill me. I'll end you and leave you here in this rat-infested dump. It won't bother me at all." Chance adjusted his grip on the knife. The lanky Glom agent cringed in anticipation.

"Where did you take my wife and son?"

The agent seemed withered, shrunken, and scared from too much hiding and a steady diet of fear. He groaned, mastered himself, trembling. "I just got the boy. We had orders to get them both, but this big Hispanic jakker intervened. Like he was waiting for us. Killed my whole jakkin' team."

Chance's eyes widened. *Benny?* "What happened?"

The lanky Glom agent winced as the knife sunk deeper through his shoulder. "We shot him up. Tried to get away but couldn't get the lady, so I took the kid and fled."

Benny. Shock descended over Chance. *Hannah's not kidnapped. She's out there somewhere. Alone.* "He's not *some kid*, he's *my son*."

Chance twisted the knife to a new chorus of screams. "Where did you take him?"

The ghastly pale agent, lathered in sweat, faltered. "I don't know... I just handed him off..."

"Where was he headed?" Chance shouted.

"I. Don't. Know!" The agent's legs buckled, consciousness fading.

With a snarl, Chance grabbed the agent by his hair and slammed his face against the counter. The lanky Glom agent's eyes flashed wide, fluttered, and rolled back in his head. Chance stood there, lungs laboring in the dark. He turned, leaving the beaten man hanging by his knife-pinned shoulder.

A rod of pain spiked through Chance's abdomen. With a grunt, he lifted his jacket to see the blood-soaked bandage had bled through his shirt. *Stitches ruptured. Again.*

The urgent trill of a second message chimed. With a sigh of resignation, Chance opened the newer of the two. It was from Karissa.

Vid call me. Now.

Chance selected her name ID from the dropdown menu on his visor and clicked it with a tap of his index finger. It rang once.

"Chance." Karissa's face appeared. She grimaced as she sat up from her cot, then grabbed her legs to let them dangle off the side of the small bed. Almost two weeks, and she still couldn't feel them, stand, or walk. *Not a good sign.* "Can you hear me?"

"I hear you," Chance said.

"Did you check your messages? I forwarded something that bounced from your spam deflector and hit my message stack. It's burn encrypted, so I couldn't see the contents. Your eyes only. Something's up."

Chance glanced at the unconscious Glom agent pinned to the counter. "I've been a little busy."

"Anything new?" Karissa asked.

"Something… Maybe." Chance pictured his wife navigating the fallen city alone. His son at the mercy of the founders.

"Check the other message, dummy," Karissa said. "It looks important."

Chance scoffed. "I'll let you know when I head back that way."

"Be careful, it's the wild west out there right now. With the North-South barrier down and The Zone cracked open, anything goes," Karissa said.

"Yeah."

"All right, we'll talk when you get here," Karissa said.

"Sure." Chance closed the call with a swipe.

He lowered his chin to his chest. So much had gone wrong so fast. He stood in the gloom of the dirty one-room apartment, struggling to hold back the black tide of helplessness that surged within him. He raised his hand, lethargic with despair, and clicked open the message.

The muscles of his body locked rigid. A tingling bud of hope bloomed in his chest. He read the message over, then read it again.

To the hero of The Zone,

The footsteps of the great are lonely, though their impressions sink deep. And you, sir, are on the path to greatness. Meet me at lot 17567 in the abandoned Bothar market district. Volkan Heights. Midnight. Come alone.

Your family is alive, and I have the information you seek.

—Mage

Chance closed the message and strode for the door, renewed purpose swelling in his heart. Who this Mage was, he'd know soon enough. Could be a trap, but he didn't care. It was the best lead he had, and knowing the truth was all that mattered.

The groan of The Glom agent stopped him short of the doorway. He half-turned.

"Wait," the lanky agent said, struggling to get his feet under him. "What happens to me?"

Chance's face was a mask of cold indifference. Blood pooled beneath the agent's shoulder and pattered onto the grimy floor. "The blade has severed your brachial artery at the shoulder junction. Remove it, and you'll bleed out in less than two minutes. Or you can wait and hope good Samaritans still live in this God-forsaken city."

"What do I do?" the agent said, desperation enveloping his features.

Chance turned away and cleared the door on his way to the stairs. "Choose."

"Wait! You can't leave me like this!" The lanky agent's scream echoed in the shadowed place, a place well-suited for hiding and poorly suited for being found.

Chance hit the street at full stride, his steps turning to a run. *My family is alive.*

Heedless of the stinging ache in his abdomen, he made for the gloss-black VTOL stashed beneath a tarp at the far end of the cluttered lane. As he ran, hope radiated inside him, a ray of pure sunlight illuminating the shadow-cast walls of his heart. And there, Sam's last words whispered—a promise to him if he stayed the course.

There's hope for us still.

ABOUT THE AUTHOR

A veteran law enforcement officer, Stu has worked in patrol, narcotics, criminal investigations, as an instructor of firearms and police defensive tactics and as a team leader of a multi-jurisdictional SWAT team. He is trained and qualified as a law enforcement SWAT sniper, as well as in hostage rescue and high-risk entry tactics. Recently, Stu served for three years with a U.S. Marshal's Regional Fugitive Task Force - hunting the worst of the worst.

He is the author of multiple sci-fi/action/thriller novels, including the multi-award-winning *It Takes Death To Reach A Star* duology and *Condition Black*, written with co-author Gareth Worthington (*Children of the Fifth Sun*).

Known for his character-driven stories and blistering action sequences, Stu strives to create thought-provoking reading experiences that challenge the status quo. When he's not chasing bad guys or writing epic stories, he can be found planning his next adventure to some remote or exotic place.

Stu is represented by Italia Gandolfo of Gandolfo-Helin-Fountain literary.

For more information check out stujonesfiction.com and follow on social @stujonesfiction

CPSIA information can be obtained
at www.ICGtesting.com
Printed in the USA
BVHW042042200623
666167BV00002B/26